ALONE
AND ON MY
KNEES

John DeCoste

authorHOUSE®

AuthorHouse™
1663 Liberty Drive
Bloomington, IN 47403
www.authorhouse.com
Phone: 1 (800) 839-8640

Published by AuthorHouse   01/28/2016

ISBN: 978-1-5049-7504-9 (sc)
ISBN: 978-1-5049-7471-4 (e)

Print information available on the last page.

Acknowledgment

The writing of the manuscript Alone And On My Knees was a refreshing experience and a number of people need to be thanked for their support and encouragement at the time of its composition. A special thank you to Muriel Cornwall, my very dear friend who bought me the journaling book while in Lourdes, France; I used this journaling book to begin the writing of the manuscript. A big thank you to my sister Claire DeCoste who was able to decipher my hen scratching and put it into more readable form while she either cried her eyes out or laughed her head off as she read through some of the unknown episodes of my life. This deciphering was later continued by my friend Teresa Keogh who panicked at times when the text appeared sideways on the computer; she seemed intent on pressing the wrong key as she attempted to breeze through the typing of the text. Once the text was completed, it was passed on to Anne Louise Mahoney, a dear friend and a former parishioner of St. Margaret Mary Parish and to my niece Stephanie Martell who is an English, Math and History teacher in the Halifax school system to be read by both of them. These women are very dear to me and both gave me an excellent critique of the text. Last but not least is a thank you to Jennie Lee who took the time to edit the entire manuscript, editing it quickly and with care and concern. A heartfelt thank you also goes to Loretta McCarthy, Sr. Jenita Methot and Fred Miller who read the manuscript and gave me very valuable feedback on it.

Circled Areas: Where Fr. John worked.

AFRICA

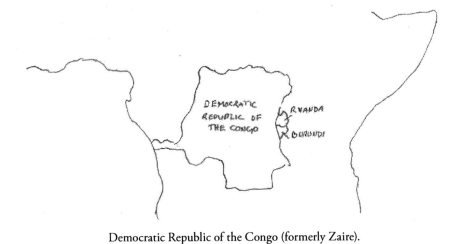

Democratic Republic of the Congo (formerly Zaire).

Prologue

It was bedlam. A helicopter circulated overhead — noise, gunfire, shouts, people running, fleeing, bundles on their heads, fear written all over their faces. Fr. John stood close to a small building at the Bukavu Airport. His four students, Francois, Jean-Paul, Serge, and Edmond huddled close to him, clutching their passports. Fr. John, however, was very distressed and worried. He could not forget his two other students, Roger and Claude. He had had to leave them behind since they did not have the proper documents to board whatever aircraft would take them out of the country. Their voices still echoed in his mind as they pleaded with him as they watched them get into the vehicle headed for the Kavumu airport. "Please take us with you. Don't leave us behind." These words ripped at his heart. He had tried to explain to them that they would be safer there at the seminary since they had no papers. At the airport they could be stopped by the soldiers, arrested and even worst still, simply killed. Since they were Rwandese and from the Tutsi tribe, they could be seen as spies for the rebel faction. Fr. John could still see their horrified faces as they stood there watching them pull out of the compound of the Murhesa Major Seminary. A sick feeling came over him and he had the urge to vomit. He knew, however, that he had to keep his wits about him if he wanted to get the four students with him to safety.

The small makeshift airport was a simple cluster of small buildings in the village of Kavumu, just thirty kilometres outside the town of Bukavu in the eastern region of Zaire, formerly known as the Belgian Congo. These buildings, arranged in a semi-circle, were part earth, part wood and thatch, and opened onto a braided rafia enclosure attached to two large wooden gates that gave access to the planes. It was a far cry from the big airports of Kigali, Kampala and Brussels. There was only one runway and it could only be used during the day since there was no lighting for night flights.

It was early morning when they arrived at the airport and, although the sun was shining brightly, it was cool and pleasant. It would eventually get warmer but not overly so since the dry season was approaching its end and the rains would soon be upon them. Fr. John shivered in the pleasant air, more from fear and worry than from the cold.

The airplane taking them to Kampala, Uganda, had not arrived yet. Would it ever arrive? What was the delay? He was so very concerned. The students talked in their native tongue, laughing nervously. Fr. John wondered what could be so funny! He just wanted to get them to safety. Of the four students, three were Burundian and one Rwandese. Two of the Burundians were Hutu and one was of mixed blood, part Tutsi-part Hutu, therefore in much danger, not accepted by either group. The one Rwandese was also of mixed blood, part Hutu part Tutsi, so also in grave danger. Here in Zaire, they were all in danger because of their Hutu connections. The killers at that moment in Rwanda were mainly from the Hutu tribe so Hutus were suspect in the surrounding countries. Fr. John knew that he had to get them boarding passes for the flight coming from Kampala or the soldiers would not let them board. He was fearful of the reaction he would get from the soldiers manning the desks. Nonetheless, he took courage, collected all the passports along with his own and slowly walked to the first small building to request the boarding passes.

Through a community of Italian priests known as the Xaverian Fathers, who worked with Fr. John at the training center of the Missionaries of Africa in Bukavu, he had learned that the Italian Consulate in Kampala would be sending a plane to bring out any Italian nationals and personnel working with them for as long as it would take to get people to safety. The reason for the rescue flights was the genocide that was taking place in Rwanda. The killing had begun following the tragic downing of the plane carrying Juvenal Habyarimana, the President of Rwanda and his personnel, as it approached the capital, Kigali. The plane was returning from an important meeting in Arusha, Tanzania, that would seriously affect Rwanda's political situation. The violence that had erupted between the Hutus and Tutsis after this tragedy had spread into Zaire and the danger, especially to Rwandese and Burundians living or studying in Zaire, had become very real.

The first blow that had created a strong possibility of war had come from a group of Tutsi rebels who had infiltrated the northern region of Rwanda from Uganda in 1990. They were attempting to protect their people who were in danger of being massacred; that was the reason given for this first attack. The Tutsi tribe, however, was strongly opposed by the Zairean government and its president Mobutu. All persons of Rwandese extraction were being stopped for questioning by the Zairean soldiers or police. That was why the boarding passes for the students were absolutely necessary. Fr. John did not want to think of what would happen if he failed.

The soldier at the first desk took one look at the passports and became furious. These students were the enemy, and he, a priest, was harbouring them.

"You are a traitor Father! Why are you protecting the enemy?" he asked vehemently.

"But they are not the enemy," he responded. "They are simply students and have nothing to do with the war. For the last three years they have been with me at the school in Bukavu. They have not been home to Burundi or Rwanda, except to visit their families. If they do not leave, then I do not leave either. They are my responsibility, my children!"

Suddenly Fr. John realized that the soldier wanted money. He discretely passed him a few American bills. As he snatched up the bills, the soldier glared at him and sent him to another desk with the passports. It was the same scenario – more money! The last desk, however, was that of the Civil Guard, President Mobutu's henchmen. They took the passports and shoved them into a desk drawer and Fr. John knew he would not get them back. They threatened to jail the students since they were the enemy. Fr. John's heart was filled with fear! Without another thought, he fell to his knees in front of the soldiers and implored them not to harm the students.

With tears streaming down his cheeks he told the soldiers that they were his children, his responsibility. The soldiers were furious that a priest had fallen to his knees in front of them. They screamed at him to get up! He wondered if some kind of superstition was not at play here with the soldiers. Many were Catholic, and may have felt treating a priest in this way was against God. Whatever it was, it seemed to have worked in his favour.

"But you have the power, you have the guns, we have nothing, so what else am I to do?" cried Fr. John.

"Get up! Get up!" The soldiers screamed. "You'll get the passports back, you'll be able to go but you will have to bring us more money! Otherwise.........!!"

Fr. John had never dreamed that he would find himself in such a situation. Would they get out of this alive? Would his students see their families again? Would he see his home again? Would he see the ocean, the small boats moored at the marina, smell the salt sea air again? His childhood flashed in memory and for the first time he realized how happy he had been in that small village by the sea, in spite of all the difficulties he had experienced growing up. At that moment Fr. John felt very much alone with his thoughts of home and his life in the small village of Arichat.

Isle Madame, where
Father John grew up

Nova Scotia

Isle Madame

Arichat

Chapter One

John was the third of five children of a poor fisherman's family, living in the village of Arichat on a small island off Cape Breton Island called Isle Madame in the province of Nova Scotia. It had been named so by one of the kings of France in honour of his wife Madame de Maintenon. This small island had four villages on it of which Arichat was one. Isle Madame was linked to Cape Breton Island by two green iron bridges spanning the waterway called Lennox Passage. The green bridges had been installed before electricity was available on the island. This meant that the bridges had to be opened manually if a sail boat needed to come through the passage.

The bridge operator, Joe LeLacheur, would be contacted when the need arose and he would come with his horse. He would fit a triangular apparatus in place in the middle of the bridge. The horse would then be attached to it and made to go round and round. As the horse wound round, the bridge would swing open to allow the sail boats to pass. This manual method took up to an hour. If someone was in a hurry, it would not be a good thing to arrive when the bridge was being opened. It was, however, quite the attraction for both the residents and any tourists who happened to be visiting the area. This bridge was replaced in the 1970s by a faster, automatic draw bridge, in part to accommodate those people being transported to the hospital for emergency purposes.

Arichat was small and picturesque as it nestled on the ocean shore. It was inhabited by French Acadian, Irish and Scottish families, with the Acadians making up the major portion of the population. In by-gone days, Arichat had been a very fine ship-building seaport and history relates that it had been attacked by John Paul Jones during the American Revolution, precisely because of its importance for ship-building. It was feared that war frigates would be in the making there! It had a beautiful open harbour called Chedebucto Bay and on a clear, sunny day one could see for miles out to sea, in spite of Jerseymen's Island at the mouth of the harbour. This small island was situated in such a way that it split the water into two entrances to the harbour. That was how Arichat got its name; it was a Mik'maq name which meant "split waters". One of the entrances to the harbour was narrower than the other. A lighthouse stood on that side of Jerseymen's Island to alert the ships coming into that section of the harbour so they wouldn't run aground. During foggy days and nights, a loud fog horn blared out its mournful sound to warn the vessels of the possible danger upon entering the harbour. The villagers were so used to the fog horn that they hardly heard it.

On a sunny summer's day John loved to sit on the grassy hill overlooking that part of the harbour. John loved his little island home and he loved the sea. He loved to play along the shore in both summer and winter; in summer he found many interesting and beautiful seashells and pieces of driftwood on the shore while in winter he would hop along on the small ice floes, that were also called "clampers", coming from the open sea that gradually settled along the shore, glistening in the winter sunshine.

Many of the homes along the main street of the village were beautiful Victorian-style homes. Many had neat white-washed picket fences in front of them. One that John found particularly enchanting was the beautiful, stately-looking American House only three doors down from John's own little bungalow. Many of the business people and tourists who came to Arichat stayed at the American House, since it was the only hotel in the village. John would have loved to explore all that there was to discover in that beautiful building. But he was never invited in by Clarey, the son of Stan Robins, the owner. He sometimes caught a glimpse of the polished floor and gleaming woodwork when he delivered a newspaper there.

The American House, courtesy of Isle Madame Historical Society

John would have loved to live in such a big house. He often wondered what it would have been like to live in a house that had lots of rooms and spaces to explore. Of course it was only a dream. His house was just a small bungalow at the center of the village. It was white with green trim and a small dormer on the roof. The dormer added to the charm of the house and provided more light to the interior before there was electricity.

John's house had a fine homey kitchen. Off the kitchen was a pantry where his mother baked and prepared food that she cooked on the coal and wood stove in the kitchen. From the kitchen, one entered a fair sized parlour divided into two parts by an arched doorway which made it possible for one part to be used as a sleeping area. Off this parlour there were two bedrooms, one large and one small. When the children were young John's parents used the big bedroom for themselves. The small bedroom was originally used by John and his older sisters. This arrangement changed when they got older. Then John and his brother slept on the sofa-bed in the parlour and the girls were given the large bedroom. As John got older there were times when he came home late from a friend's house and his brother had fallen asleep without opening the sofa, so John, not having room enough to lie down next to his brother, would climb into the large metal crib in his parents room to sleep. Of course, once he started to get taller, he became longer than the crib and would have to stick his feet through the bars at the foot. This was a funny sight to see each morning.

There was no bathroom since they had no running water in the house. John's job was to make sure that the water buckets were filled each day and the chamber pails emptied and cleaned both morning and evenings. All the same, John loved their little house. It was very clean, thanks to his mother, Rose, and very cozy. He did sometimes envy his friends who lived in bigger homes and had the luxury of a bathroom and running water.

Of course, many beautiful homes were situated along the main street of the village and John eventually got a good look in some of them when he began to do chores and run errands for some of the elderly residents of the village. John enjoyed running errands for the elderly. They needed the help. There were times, however, when the chores were rather disgusting especially when it involved emptying their garbage pails and chamber pots. It could turn out to be disgusting enough for John to be forced to refuse. At times he would be totally repulsed by the odour and contents of the chamber pots and garbage cans.

John still remembered so vividly the situation of Mrs. Mary Letourneau who had become so upset with him when he had refused to empty her commode. It had been so disgusting that he had not been able to make up his mind to remove the chamber pot from the commode. He had come into their house as he usually did in the early afternoon and first greeted Eadie, Mrs. LeTourneau's daughter who was preparing food in the kitchen. He had then gone to Mrs. LeTourneau's bedroom to greet her and found her already sitting in her rocking chair next to the bed having an enjoyable catnap. When John greeted her she woke up startled saying, "Oh my dear child you caught me dozing, didn't you? Did you empty the garbage pails yet?"

"No, not yet Mrs. Letourneau, I've only just arrived," said John.

"I've more work for you after the garbage is done," she responded with some difficulty since she would often lose her dentures as she spoke.

"What is it that you want me to do extra?" asked John.

"Well, I will need you to clean and empty my commode that's on the other side of my bed. Do you see it there?" She asked John. She indicated the commode with her cane.

John went over to the side of the bed to inspect the commode and chamber pot. He could not believe his eyes. First of all there were newspapers soaking wet with urine covering the commode. They must have been there for days because the stench was overwhelming. The chamber pot itself was another nightmare. It was smeared with feces and part of it had spilled over into the corner and around the bottom part of the commode. John could not bring himself to touch any of it; he was gagging so badly. John looked over at Mrs. Letourneau saying, "I can't do that, I can't clean up that awful mess, it is making me sick. You will have to get Eadie to do it. I don't understand why she let it go so long! How have you been using your commode in such an awful state? I'm sorry but I just can't clean that up!"

Mrs. Letourneau became furious at John. "You impudent little pup," she retorted furiously. "You finish what you have to do today and don't you come back here again, do you hear me?"

"I certainly do hear you," said John. "If that is how you want it, that's fine with me, but you did not hire me to clean your commode Mrs. Letourneau, you hired me to empty your garbage; that's what you pay me to do. You take care of yourself and let me know if ever you want me to come back." John was not too disappointed about this outcome in a way. They were only giving him a quarter for doing the garbage. It was worth twice that. He had to drag the garbage pails down to the shore, empty them in the ocean and then rinse them with salt sea water. It was difficult enough to do.

He said "good-bye" to Eadie on the way out and at the same time explained to her what had happened. Eadie was very upset and said to John, "Don't you listen to her. You come back again next week. She will have forgotten that by then and I cannot lift the garbage pails to empty them; they are just too heavy for me. Don't you let me down now, okay?"

Arichat Church: Our Lady of the Assumption
(Courtesy of the Isle Madame Historical Society)

"Okay, I won't," replied John. He also knew that they would not get anyone else to do the garbage for only a quarter, even if that was a lot in those days. He collected his quarter and once home put it in the small Angel bank that he kept hidden behind the hide-a-bed in the living-room. He had got that Angel bank when he began his training to be an altar server.

Once John became a fully trained altar server, he loved to explore the huge wooden Church that stood as a sentinel at the entrance to the village. He never tired of admiring the big, beautiful painting behind the main altar of the Virgin Mary rising on a cloud into heaven. This painting had come from Rome years previously, brought from Rome by one of the priests of the Parish, the parish known as Our Lady of the Assumption.

The lovely pipe organ up in the choir loft gave out the most beautiful musical sounds. He remembered that when he was just a young boy the organ had to be pumped by hand. It wasn't until years later that it was electrified. The church had formerly been a cathedral since Arichat had originally been the seat of the Church diocese. This meant that the Bishop of the diocese had resided in Arichat. The people were all very proud of this part of the village's history. Next to the left side entrance of the big church stood a monument in the shape of an open book. Engraved on this monument was an inscription indicating that the first classes of the well-known St. Francis Xavier University had begun in Arichat, another historical fact of which the villagers were very proud. This university had later been transferred to the town of Antigonish along with the Bishop's residence and main diocesan office.

Arichat Court House
(Courtesy of the Isle Madame Historical Society)

Just below the church, on the same street, was the little outpost hospital, dedicated to St. Ann, the mother of the Blessed Virgin Mary. There were eighteen regular beds in St. Ann's hospital as well as four nursery beds and four maternity beds. It was all efficiently managed by the Sisters, Les Filles de Jesus. The hospital had formerly been the Bishop's palace. John had heard many stories about that building since his aunt Laura, his Mom's sister, had grown up there. John's Aunt Eliza was the parish priest's housekeeper and would take little Laura to work with her.

Old Canons overlooking Arichat Harbour
(Courtesy of the Isle Madame Historical Society)

Fr. Bourque, the parish priest at that time, eventually became so attached to the child that she stayed with him, was educated by him and became like his own daughter. In his old age he would be cared for by Aunt Laura who was one of John's favourite aunts. John would often go and stay at Aunt Laura's to do chores for her. He remembered Fr. Bourque so well, especially when he would speak very loudly when he knew that someone had come into the house. From his comfortable chair in the living-room he would cry out, "Who is there? What do you want?" John always found this somewhat frightening, but he would answer in as loud a voice as the old priest's, "It is just one of the altar servers, Father!" That answer always seemed to satisfy him.

Not far from the church and on the same grounds was the big convent where the Sisters lived. When John went to Eucharist in the Chapel of the convent, he loved the smell of fresh wax and polish that the Sisters used on the floors and furniture; everything was always so neat and clean, and the smell of soup coming from the big kitchen always made his mouth water.

Old Canons overlooking Arichat Harbour
(Courtesy of the Isle Madame Historical Society)

The Sisters who taught John lived in this old, heritage convent building and were the same Sisters who were at the hospital. The first two Sisters had come to Paul's island home from Brittany in France over one hundred years before. They had brought education and health care to the people. Many young women from the region had become Sisters. They always looked beautiful, fresh and crisp in their black and white nun's robes. John eventually learned that the covering and veil that they wore on their heads were similar to what was called a "coiffe Bretonne" since they had first come from Britanny where the "coiffe" was worn by the women. The "coiffe" was a cap of varying shapes and sizes that covered the head; the Sisters had attached a long, black veil to a plain version of the "coiffe" that resulted in quite a pleasing ensemble. The Sisters maintained a fine school and made sure that their students had proper education, religious training and spoke correctly in both French and English. It was in this big house that Sister Gemma and Sister Madeline and all the other Sisters that John had as teachers lived.

Our Lady of Assumption Convent, courtesy of Isle Madame Historical Society

The first five years of John's childhood were relatively happy, and the fact that the family was poor, and that he was not able to have a lot of things other children had, did not seem to bother him much. He loved to play outdoors, no matter what season of the year. In fact, he loved it so much that even in the cold of winter he did not want to come in at night and had to be carried in bodily, as he shouted, cried, kicked and screamed to stay outside. He wanted to play outside forever. His two older sisters, Martine and Della, often had to be the ones to battle with him to get him to come in at night.

One battle that had taken place, however, had been with John's father, Batist, when the time had come for John to have his first haircut. Being still just a young child at the time, John had been terrified of this experience. It had proven to be a real ordeal for John. He just simply did not want the barber, Mr. Clarence Pond, to cut his hair. He became terrified when he saw the hair clippers and the scissors. It seemed to John that the barber would cut his head and his ears off.

"You be a good boy now and come sit on the board here so I can cut your hair," said Mr. Pond gently. He had placed a shiny varnished board across the arms of the barber's chair so John could sit there comfortably and high enough for the barber to reach his head without too much difficulty. John's father lifted him gently onto the board.

As Batist sat John on the board, John started to kick and scream. "No, no, no, I don't want you to cut my hair! Daddy, daddy, daddy, stop him, I don't want to do this! Pleeeease, pleeeeease, don't do this! I don't want to, I don't want to, no, no, no!" He cried. His father and the barber continued to try to calm him while holding him on the board. The barber, with much difficulty, cut and snipped and the long, silky blond hair fell to the floor. After fifteen minutes it was over and what a battle it had been. Little John sat there with tears streaming down his cheeks and with his head down refusing to respond in any way.

"Why did you do this to me?" John cried.

The barber at that moment turned the barber's chair to face the huge wall mirror so that John could see himself in it. "Look, look, you look great," said Mr. Pond.

"Now you look like a real little man," said John's father. John did look up but was not at all convinced by their comments. It would take time for him to get used to his new look.

Once they got home, Batist made sure that the whole family told John how great he looked. Of course, his mother made a big fuss over his appearance. "You are so handsome, a real young man," commented his mother.

Martine, who loved her little brother very much, ruffled his hair with her hand and exclaimed, "Hey there, little man, you are the cutest of all the boys in this village!" And they all laughed together, John included. Martine's approval meant very much to John. However, he would never forget this first haircut and he would wonder years later if that was why he hated to have his hair cut so much. However, if Martine found that he looked great, then that must be so.

Martine, the oldest of the children, was a tall, slender, intelligent girl, quite even tempered and poised. She was filled with challenging, creative ideas and would later become a skilled interior decorator. Martine had an eye for what was different and popular in clothing, furniture, ornaments and anything to do with decorating. John felt totally at ease with his sister Martine and always enjoyed her presence. In later years he would enjoy visiting with her and her family. John could not remember Martine ever saying one unkind word to him in his whole life. She had always been good to him and there for him.

Della, the second oldest of the children, was of medium height and had a freckled complexion that she did not like very much. She resembled John's mother, Rose, in many ways, especially in her way of working and keeping her home. All had to be well-placed, tidy and squeaky clean. She and John had argued a lot when they were growing up, but that had changed when they became adults. They had become very good friends and Della became very much of a mother figure for John. She would always be in his thoughts. When John eventually left home, Della was the one he contacted the most to relay messages to the family and find out news about everyone. Della had finished high school but had not been interested in further education. She had left school early to help her mother who had health problems at the time. She had soon gone to work after high school, working at the same fish factory as their father. Being a hard worker and quite frugal with her money, Della had made certain that her house was built and ready to be occupied the very day of her marriage.

John had only one brother, Timmy, who was next in line after him. Timmy had blondish, curly hair but was somewhat dark in complexion. He was very determined to learn all that was of practical use in life, such as working with wood, painting and drawing. He did not like studies much, especially if it involved history, English grammar and composition. He was in his element when working with mathematics, science and drawing. Timmy was also quite athletic and very interested in sports such as baseball and hockey. He made friends easily and they admired him greatly. He and John argued at times but John felt it was caused by jealousy on his part. He thought their father preferred Timmy as a son.

The youngest child was Clarisse, Paul's little sister. As a child she was quite fair in complexion with a cute, round face. Rose always dressed her up in pretty, stylish outfits that she sewed for her. All the children doted on her. John enjoyed teasing her, something she hated with a passion. He would tease her about the little boys in her class and most of the time about the ones who would be the most unlikely to be her friends. This would infuriate Clarisse and she would scream to their mother, "Ma, he's at it again! Make him stop!" Rose would implore John to stop teasing or else he would be punished. But John enjoyed hearing Clarisse yell this way. He also enjoyed her giggle when things were funny and pleased her. John had to admit that he always feared that something would happen to

Clarisse. He watched out for her at school, especially when a snow storm would threaten in winter.

There would have been a sixth child, another little sister, but she died at birth. Linda was born late in the night at the small village hospital. John and his siblings were all aware that their mother was expecting a new baby. They were filled with anticipation and joy! What would this new child look like and what kind of character would the child have? But all their hopes were dashed when John's father came home from the hospital with the terrible news. She had been an eleven pound baby, but a diabetic one. John's mother was diabetic at the time and did not know it. All was spoken in hushed tones, as if speaking about it too loudly would bring the heavens crashing in upon them. Their first question to their father, of course, was, "How is Mom; is she alright?"

"Your mother has had a very difficult time with hours of labour," said their father. "The doctor thought at one point that he would not be able to save her!" They were all simply terrified in hearing this. They could not lose their mother! What would they do with her gone?

"When will she come home?" John asked.

"In a few days," answered Batist. "She needs to get some rest and get her strength back.

That frightened them even more! They needed their Mom to come back home; she was such a stabilizing factor for the family. John had difficulty understanding why there was such difficulty for his mother to get this baby and bring it home. Was the baby not brought to the parents by the doctor in his famous black doctor's bag? John could not figure this out. There was definitely something fishy in the whole affair. John, however, listened intently and observed everything. He did not ask too many questions but he hoped that with time he would get answers to his many questions.

Rose finally did come home. She was devastated at losing the baby. She cried often. John knew why her sadness was so great. Linda had come into the world, that was true, but she had left as quickly as she had come; and there had been no proper baptism! The belief at that time in the theory of limbo was still strongly entrenched in the minds of the people in the French Catholic Community. Rose was devastated by the thought that her little girl would never see the face of God. Limbo was a theory in some quarters of the Church community that had come about because of St. Augustine's theological interpretation regarding baptism and salvation. The theory of limbo stated that babies who died without baptism would go to a place called limbo, where they would never see the face of God, although they would not know suffering. Just the thought of such a thing made John sick. It had a worse effect on his mother. It took months for Rose to recover from the ordeal of the birth, but more so to recover from its spiritual consequences. Rose would die before the teaching would be thrown out of catechetical instruction by the authorities in Rome.

John grieved for his mother. He hated this doctrine of limbo. For John it did not even make sense. He wanted to be able to take away his mother's sadness. In those days, however, John did not have the training in theology and spirituality to give his mother a better interpretation for the salvation of unbaptized children. He was also convinced that doctrine as stated by the Church was the only valid one. He knew, however, that his mother would get through this horrendous grieving; she was a very strong and determined woman. She also had a very deep and strong faith. It was because of Rose that the family remained so connected to the Church.

Rose did eventually get over her grief. She knew that she had to for the sake of the rest of her family. They truly needed her. John always enjoyed the warm company of this short, somewhat plump mother who was always there when he arrived from school in the late afternoons. She would always be either baking homemade bread or some delicious meal for the evening supper. Rose was an excellent cook and knew how to create a homey, comfortable house. She was scrupulously clean not just on her own person but also in her home; you could have eaten off the floor! She knew how to take charge and also how to train her children to take their share of responsibilities. They each had their chores to do each day. Rose, however, was a worrier. She worried about having enough money to provide for her family. She worried over the welfare of her children, about their being brought up properly, about their growing up to be good, responsible adults. She would never sleep at night until she heard the last one come in, no matter what the time. John remembered well the many times that she had called out to him when he had come in well after midnight from studying with a friend, "Did you lock the porch door properly, John?" He knew that she needed to hear his voice, so he always responded, "It's solidly bolted, Mom!"

Rose had been born into a family of ten children and her own mother, Elizabeth, had gone to an early death in childbirth. Little Rose had to leave school after fourth grade and learn how to run the household. Since her oldest sister, Elizabeth, worked as the housekeeper for the parish priest and her oldest brother was running the farm for the Sisters at their convent, Rose had to pull her weight in the house as the next in line. When Rose spoke to her children about her childhood, she would tell them things that totally amazed them.

"You know when my mother died," she would say, "I had to learn to do everything in the house, even if I was only eleven years old. I was so short that I had to stand on a chair by the kitchen stove to stir my soup as it cooked, making sure it did not burn. Of course, we were happy to have soup, some of our neighbours were not so fortunate. Our father worked at the canning factory far from the village and so brought in a bit more money than most. He was very strict and wouldn't buy many things he thought were luxuries and a waste of money."

Rose would shake her head when thinking of it. Then she would add, "If any of my sisters worked in the village doing chores or servant's work for the more well-to-do in the village, they would have to bring the money home to father. He would give them a penny for the Sunday collection from their own earnings and place the rest in the housekeeping budget. He was so very strict! He even forbade us to play cards, listen to music or dance, especially on Sunday. For our father, that was sinful and irreverent!" Again she would shake her head, and then add, "What was so hard was that we just loved to dance, listen to music and play cards. Those were the few pastimes that we had. In those days there simply was no television and we needed a license or permit to own a radio; would you believe that the government authorities had inspectors going around to see who had radios and if anyone had a permit! Those who had radios were constantly hiding them when any stranger appeared in the village. People would be fined a hefty sum of money if they were caught. The radio permit was ten dollars at least which we could not afford. I was so pleased when I met your father; he could play several musical instruments and was a superb dancer. I just loved that so much about him! He would sweep me off my feet!! I loved it!"

One story that never ceased to amaze John was his mother's account of the haunted house experience. "It was terrible and frightening to live in that big, old house," she told them. "Every night we heard strange noises when we would wake up to go to the bathroom. There was also a boxed in staircase to go to the second floor; there were times when we would hear someone walk down the stairs, but never come up again, and this was when everyone should have been sleeping. John would listen to his mother with eyes wide open, riveted to the spot. It was deliciously frightening! Rose would continue, saying, "The worst thing of all was the evening that we were returning from visiting relatives in the next village. As we approached the house, around nine thirty at night, we noticed that there were lights on in the house. We thought that maybe father had come home earlier than usual from the canning factory. But as we got closer to the house, we could see an old woman sitting in the rocking chair in the kitchen holding a baby. Frightened, we stopped in our tracks and looked at one another, bewildered. Who could that be? When we got to the gate of the yard surrounding the house, the house was once again in total darkness. This was the last straw for us; we had to do something about our haunted house."

"That is really creepy, Mom," said John. "What did you all finally do about the haunted house?" asked John, excitedly.

"Would you believe, we burnt it to the ground?" said Rose.

They all looked at their mother flabbergasted. They were speechless, incredulous.

Rose, seeing their reaction, repeated what she had just said, "We burnt it to the ground!"

John was the one who finally spoke. "Oh my goodness, how did you manage that," said John. "That is truly unbelievable! You guys were truly brave. That is just too much!"

"Well, this is what we did. First of all, we had to all be in on this. There could not be any of us who would not be part of the plot. Once we had all agreed, our brother Joseph got some kerosene and I found a bunch of old cleaning rags that were good and dry and we all went up to the attic. Our haunted house had a fair sized attic with a small staircase going up to it, so it was easy for all of us to get up there. We placed the rags in a corner well away from us, doused the rags with the kerosene and set a match to it. The rags burst into flames and we ran out of there. We went outside onto the veranda immediately and waited. In a short time the smoke was billowing out from under the eaves. That is when we started shouting, 'Fire! Fire!' We yelled for someone to come and help us. We started to drag some of the furniture out of the house as well as what we could get of our clothing. Of course, many of the neighbours came to help us. We were all so grateful for this. At least we had to pretend to be!"

One of our neighbours, Mr. Vincent, asked, "What happened? How did the house catch fire?"

"We don't know," we answered. "Suddenly we could smell smoke and when we went upstairs, the smoke was already coming through the attic door. We were so frightened that we panicked and ran from the house."

"Oh, that is terrible, terrible," Mr. Vincent had gasped. "Your father will be devastated when he arrives home from work."

"We managed to get a fair amount of the furniture from the house and all of our clothing, so we were pleased about that," said Rose.

"Old Philomena, our next door neighbour, was sitting on her veranda throughout this whole ordeal, just watching. She did not utter one word. She did speak up, however, when our father arrived home from work that day. It was a Friday in summer and he always came home for the week-end. Of course, when he saw the charred remains of the house, he just stood there dumbfounded. For once he was speechless!"

"Then a voice could be heard coming from the next door veranda. 'They are the ones who set the fire, they did it, I know that they did it! They are a nasty bunch that you have there!' Old Philomena wanted our father to know the truth, and for father to know that she had been doing her job of supervising us as he had asked her to do," said Rose.

"It did not really matter who had set the fire because we would have to move anyway and that is what we had all wanted. The move did occur within hours of the fire. The new house was somewhat smaller than the old house, but we did not mind, it was more peaceful, we were now on the other side of the harbour, more at the center of the village and closer to the church. We would not need to walk for miles to get to church."

"A rumour went around after that," said Rose, "saying that the former owner of that house, an old man called 'Tit Pic' had not wanted the house to be sold and that if ever it did get sold the curse that he had put on it would come true. Some said that at night, around midnight, the dark shadow of a man could be seen sitting where the charred remains had been."

"We did not even bother to go over there, we were too happy to be rid of it!" Rose exclaimed. "Father remained quite suspicious about the fire and thus continued to keep a watchful eye on us. Moving from one house to another had not changed his strict position on dancing, listening to music and playing cards. We were all so happy when he would leave for the fish factory on Mondays. We felt that we could breathe freely once again. The situation in the house would turn gloomy when Friday evening rolled around; father would be due home for supper."

Rose remembered quite clearly that her father had made it known that as he got older he would not go to any kind of nursing home. Since he had had ten children, they would each take a turn looking after him. They always made sure that a place was provided for him in their homes. He did prefer to be with one of his daughters, of course; he felt their attention far surpassed that of a daughter-in-law. He was at his daughter Cecile's house when he died. John was still quite young then, but he remembered his grandfather's answer when Rose asked him one evening if he was afraid to die. He had looked at his daughter with tired, feverish eyes and had answered her in a low but steady voice, "Why should I be afraid to die? I have always done my Christian duty!" It was not long after this that the priest had been called in to administer the Last Rites of the Church to his grandfather. He had remained a stoic, stubborn, unbending Roman Catholic Frenchman to the end. Somehow, John, as young as he was, had understood that he wanted to have that strength and commitment, that stamina but without the hardness and unbending attitude.

It was somewhat ironic that grandfather had spent his last days at Aunt Cecile's house and died there after the way he had treated her in the past. Fr. John had not forgotten his mother's account about the return of Aunt Cecile from the convent. Aunt Cecile had loved the Sisters and would often be with them at their huge convent in the village. All she had wanted was to be one of them, to be a simple kitchen nun, cooking and cleaning in God's service. She had finally applied to enter after grandfather had given his permission. She was unable to provide the dowry required at the time, but the Sisters had accepted her anyway. Aunt Cecile had made the long journey to the town of Three Rivers in the province of Quebec, where the Sisters had their noviciate; in those days, in the 1930's, this was considered a very long and tiring journey. Aunt Cecile had gone willingly, full of enthusiasm to undertake her new way of life. In the course of the noviciate, however, she had become ill; the strict way of life, the long hours of prayer, silence, training and work, took its toll on Aunt Cecile. She would need to be placed under a doctor's care. The Sisters wrote to grandfather to request financial help from the family since Aunt Cecile had entered without a dowry. Grandfather had been furious at such a request and wrote the Sisters saying, "I will not send any money. You are to care for her yourselves. If that is not possible, then she is to come home. This is where she belongs. We will take care of her ourselves." Aunt Cecile had been devastated. She had not wished to return home, however, she had had no choice in the matter.

Upon Aunt Cecile's return, she had gone to live with John's family. As Rose had told them, "She was, in a way, homeless, having had to leave the convent. She truly needed a place to stay until she could get her life organized again. Grandfather had already started living with each one of us and so had really no place for her in spite of the fact that he had told the Sisters that the family would care for her." Aunt Cecile was fine with Rose, but the fact that she had had to leave religious life caused her to have a very difficult mental breakdown. She would often say to Rose when they were doing the dishes together in the kitchen, "You know, I was consecrated at one time, but now I am no longer consecrated." She would then begin to cry. With Rose, Aunt Cecile gradually recovered her health and with time met her future husband, Simon. They married and had four beautiful children. Aunt Cecile remained a good housekeeper and an excellent cook but she kept certain of the ways of life she had learned with the Sisters; she remained faithful to her Church, but ever after longed for what could have been. Fr. John was convinced that his Aunt Cecile's true calling was to be a Sister in the community of Les Filles de Jesus. She espoused marriage because one did not simply remain single; proper young women did not live alone. Aunt Cecile always remained grateful to Rose for loving her as a mother would.

Rose did turn out to be a true mother and housekeeper; she would say to John years later when she was unable to work much because of her health, "You know, I loved housework; that was truly my calling in life, to be a mother and homemaker. I have no regrets about that."

The hard-working, persevering, deep faith and enduring fidelity that was so much Rose's character was all passed on to her children and in a special way to John; he was also a worrier, like his mother. John would have to wage an on-going battle over the years to overcome this. Rose was also quite serious about her faith and her Church, so she had been quite pleased on learning of John's decision to become a priest. She had never fully understood, however, why he needed to go so far away, in fact all the way to Africa!

John had never witnessed openly affectionate behaviour between his mother and father. However, their love showed in their concern for one another and for the family in spite of the problems that existed. Batist was always terribly concerned whenever any of them were sick. He would constantly check on them. John did not feel close to his father and so felt uncomfortable with his fussing over him whenever he was sick.

Batist was a hard-working fisherman. He was not a tall man but rather short with a robust, muscular build. John did gather from the stories others told about him that he had been somewhat of a playboy in his day. He had dressed in quite a dapper fashion when not working at the fish factory. He had often traveled to the U.S. at a time when the border crossings were not too strict and difficult. He was an excellent dancer and knew how to play several musical instruments. He loved a good bottle of wine and enjoyed a good stiff drink of Demerara rum even more. He was not fond of attending church and thought that the clergy were too bourgeois for his liking. It was mainly because of Rose that he attended church at all. He was a die-hard labour man, fully involved in the union at work. His attendance at church lagged whenever he was on union business or on one of his drunken binges. However, he was a good provider and his pay cheque went directly into Rose's hand. He knew very well that she could stretch a dollar miraculously. Batist did not want his children to end up as he had with little education and working in a fish factory. He wanted them to have a better life than he.

They all struggled to create a pleasant, happy home life. They, of course, hoped for a better and brighter future. In spite of life's difficulties, they learned to become outgoing young men and women, who made friends easily and got along well with others. One friend that they liked very much was a friend of Martine's named Lilly Maude. She lived in the section of the village of Arichat called Little Barachois.

One Saturday afternoon, long before Clarisse was born, and not long before Christmas, John was with Martine and Della in the front yard enjoying the warm fall sunshine. John was colouring in his colouring book on the steps of the veranda, something he enjoyed doing very much; his two older sisters were talking about the coming Christmas celebrations. Martine and Della were babysitting John that day since Rose was busy making the Christmas fruit cakes and watching baby Timmy. It was a busy time of the year and Rose depended on Martine and Della to help her. They were happy to do so but this particular Saturday was turning out to be somewhat boring; the weather was beautiful and quite mild for that time of the year. There was still no sign of snow or cold.

Suddenly Martine had a marvellous idea to break the boredom of the afternoon. Lilly Maude had told her that she had many beautiful Christmas cards and that she would give Martine some of them if she came to visit. Martine thought that this would be a good day to do this. Then they would have some beautiful cards to give at Christmas.

"You want us to go all the way to Little Barachois for Christmas cards?" Della exclaimed. "That's at least a mile and a half away and we're not supposed to go out of the yard with John."

"It really isn't very far," said Martine. "We just take the dirt road that joins the high road once we get up Godfrey LeBlanc's lane. We'll simply go and get the cards and come right back. It's only one thirty in the afternoon. We'll be back before supper at five o'clock. Come on Della, let's go. We'll tell Mom so that she knows where we are gone; that way, she won't worry! We'll take John with us of course."

John didn't like the idea. He didn't like to go there even with his mother. He had gone there before with her and there was someone there who was very frightening.

"I don't want to go. It's too far," said John. "There is an old man at that house who is very scary. I don't like him. I saw him when I went with Mom."

"Oh, don't be such a scaredy cat," said Martine. "That's only old Charlie, Lilly Maude's grandfather. He won't hurt you. And it's really nice out and it will pass the time instead of our being stuck here in the yard."

"Make sure that you are back before your father gets home from work," said Rose when they told her what they wanted to do. "Make sure that John is well taken care of. Just be careful, for heaven's sake!"

Martine finally convinced John to go with them by promising to give him two of the Christmas cards. "I want one with Santa Claus on it and one with baby Jesus," said John. "Promise me right now!"

"Okay, okay, I promise," Martine answered. "Now, let's go."

So off they went to Little Barachois for Christmas cards. They climbed Godfrey's hill and turned onto the gravel road leading to that part of the village. To John the road looked very lonely and deserted. Martine, however, plodded on determined to reach Lilly Maude's house. The day was beautiful but the road was very dusty. It seemed to John to take forever to reach Lilly Maude's house. Finally, they could see it in the distance; sitting there on the slope of the hill overlooking the water, a fine Victorian house with a beautiful, white veranda along the front of the house.

"Look we're almost there," exclaimed Martine. "Come on, let's hurry. I can't wait to see the Christmas cards."

They did not go to the front door; they made their way to the back porch of the house. "Come in," said a voice after they had knocked on the door. They entered directly into the kitchen. It was cozy and warm and Mary Jane, Lilly Maude's mother, was baking cookies. They smelled wonderful. Mary Jane was pleased to see them, but very surprised. "How are you all?" she asked. "And how is your mother? I have not seen her in quite some time. I'm sure she must be busy preparing for Christmas?"

"We are fine and so is our mother," answered Martine. "She is very busy with our new little brother!"

"Does she know that you have come all the way out here on foot?" asked Mary Jane.

"Yes, she knows. She said that it would be alright, but we need to be back in time for supper."

"I see. So what brings you all the way out here?" Mary Jane asked.

"Lilly Maude told me at school that if I came out to visit her one day that she would give me some Christmas cards. Apparently you have quite a few left over from last Christmas. We just love Christmas cards," answered Martine.

"Oh dear, Lilly Maude is at her friend's house in Boudreauville," said her mother. "I don't know where she keeps the Christmas cards, and she won't be back before tomorrow. It's too bad that you made the trip for nothing" said Mary Jane. "I'll tell her when she gets home that you were here. I'll make sure that she brings them with her when she goes to school on Monday."

Martine was extremely disappointed but politely refused to show it. "That's alright, Mrs. Boudreau," she answered. "I'll see Lilly Maude on Monday and that will be just fine." Della just glared at Martine in frustration and said nothing. Lilly Maude's mother noticed the disappointment in the children and offered them each cookies and milk in compensation. "Oh thank you, they smell so good, we could smell them when we came in," said Martine.

All had been going well until then. They were about to leave when old Charlie came bustling out of his bedroom. He was a very tall man with a huge mustache. On his cheek was a huge festering sore that seemed to be eating into his face. For some reason unknown to them, he went straight towards John with his mouth wide open and his hands raised in a way that gave the impression that he was going to claw at John. When John saw him, he ran screaming to Martine and hid his face in her skirt. He could not look at this huge monster with the rotting face. Old Charlie continued to come towards John laughing a coarse, raspy laugh. John looked up and screamed "Don't let him get me! The monster will get me. He'll eat me up! I want to go home! I'll never come back here again." John was so terrified that he thought he would die of fear. Out the door he ran, with Martine and Della running after him yelling good-bye to Mary Jane as they went. Mary Jane looked on in total dismay, feeling sorry for John and very upset with her father's behaviour. However, he was an old man and often did strange things. To some of the children, he did look like some kind of ogre.

Outside, Martine and Della had to look for John. If anything happened to him, they would be in deep trouble. Soon they discovered John, hidden behind the porch of the house behind some large water barrels. Martine and Della called to him, "Where are you? Come out for heaven's sake, we need to get home for supper. It's getting late and Dad will be furious if we are not back when he arrives home from work."

John finally came out from his hiding place, looking carefully to see if old Charlie was anywhere to be seen. He was so terrified that he began to cry. He screamed at Martine and Della saying, "I just want to go home. I don't like this place! Why did you bring me here? I told you that he was a monster, but you would not believe me. Now we have to walk all the way back home on that lonely, creepy road. It's even starting to get dark!"

"Stop being a cry baby," said Della. "We need to hurry up. If Dad has to come looking for us we'll be grounded for sure."

They both took him by the hand so they could walk faster. Too much time had passed and they needed to get home.

As it happened, just as they were starting down Godfrey LeBlanc's lane, their father was rounding the corner by the stop sign at the bottom of the lower road. Rose had told him when he got home from work that the children had gone to Lilly Maude's house and were not back yet. Frantic, he set out to look for them. When he saw them coming down the hill, he called out, "Are you alright? We were beginning to worry. Darkness was falling. Supper was ready, and there was no sign of you. Martine, you should have known better than to go off like that on such a long walk so late in the afternoon. What were you thinking of?"

"I'm sorry," cried Martine, "it won't happen again, I promise! It just seemed like such a good idea to get Christmas cards. They are so expensive to buy and Lilly Maude told me that they were very beautiful. I wanted so much to see them and get some for us. Her mother promised that she would get her to bring them to school on Monday."

"Never mind the Christmas Cards! Supper is on the table and you need to be home," said Batist. He tried not to sound too annoyed, especially since it was Martine that he was talking to. He loved them all, but she was his favourite and he always found it difficult to hide that fact. Of all of his children, she was the one who fully accepted him as he was, no matter what the fault.

John would not forget the Christmas card day, ever, but he soon put it out of his mind when time came for him to play with his friends in the neighbourhood. He of course showed them the two beautiful Christmas cards that Martine gave him. Of the two cards, he liked the one with baby Jesus on it best. It had gold and glitter on it.

John often played with the children of the family next door, the Cosman family, as well as the Boutin family who lived across the street. His best friend, however, and the one he preferred to be with most, lived further down the street. Miriam was his age and lots of fun to be with. She was fair in complexion with beautiful, very curly, auburn hair. John loved the way her short ringlets bobbed up and down at the nape of her neck. Miriam did not think that curly hair was so great. She longed for straight, easily manageable hair. John never fully understood this since her hair was so beautiful. She would often say to John, "Oh yes, this head of hair is beautiful, but you don't have the struggle of putting the comb through the tangled mess in the mornings." This would make John laugh. She and John got along splendidly together. She always had new and different ideas to try out.

One afternoon, when visiting at Miriam's house with his mother, he and Miriam went out to play hide and seek in the field behind the house. While playing, John needed to use the toilet and was about to go into the house when Miriam told him to just go behind the little shed that was there in the field. Miriam did not let on that she could see him but she was watching him from the corner of her eye while he went about his business. Before he could finish, however, Miriam said to him, "Do you know that boys and girls are made different?" "No," John answered, "I don't know that". So Miriam suggested that they check one another out to see the difference and to see how true this was. John was reluctant to do this at first, thinking that it was not a nice thing to do, but Miriam answered, "But, no one can see us, we're behind the shed and it's away from the house! It will be our secret!" John finally gave in to Miriam's coaxing; and they, in fact, found out that they were quite different. John was so surprised when he saw Miriam that he simply exclaimed, "Oh my God, you don't have any! How do you pee?" It was all quite funny but they decided it should be their little secret.

They both got tired of playing hide and seek and so went inside. They were no sooner inside the house than both of their parents wanted to know what they had been doing. They said that they had been playing hide and seek and of course, left out the "show me yours and I'll show you mine" event. One of the mothers said, however, "Are you sure that is all you were doing outside?"

Miriam and John looked at each other and remained silent. Then they found out that Miriam's oldest brother, Jeremy, had been watching them from an upstairs window and, seeing what had gone on, had told their parents. The secret was no longer a secret; John felt so betrayed! He wanted to beat Jeremy up for having tattled on them!

Rose was not at all pleased and made John feel that he had done something terribly wrong, that such actions were bad and that God punished children who did such things. "But Jesus loves us!" he would say to himself over and over. So how could this be? He did not understand his mother's reaction at all. This really bothered John very much since he had already learned about Jesus and of course knew that certain things were just not done. This, however, seemed to be such a little thing! The way his mother reacted, however, made him feel awful. For the first time in his life, John felt confused and alone.

Once back at home, he ran to the big bedroom where his parents slept and standing behind the window curtain looked out into the summer sunshine, all the while feeling an awful emptiness inside of him that he could not comprehend. A sickening, feeling that he had done a terrible wrong persisted. He felt so uncomfortable and strange because of his mother's reaction. He had a frightening, hollow feeling in the pit of his stomach. Even if the sunshine was there, it was as if it had disappeared for him! "Would the good feeling that he usually felt ever come back?" he asked himself. He could not understand why his mother had reacted the way she had. His trust in adults was severely shaken. It would later affect his trust of authority. He would also eventually learn that the strict moral and religious upbringing that his mother had received was a factor in the type of reaction that she manifested in the face of such innocent behaviour. It was certainly not that she did not love John. He would realize this more fully with the passage of time.

It was with such an event that John was launched into the realm of prayer. He had learned the more formal prayers of the Our Father and the Hail Mary from his mother and with those prayers the whole of the rosary prayer. He would feel so upset at times about different difficult times in his young life that he turned to prayer for consolation and some type of help. He would just pour his heart out to Jesus as he knelt there beside the hide-a-bed in the living-room or in the big wooden church whenever they were at Mass. He knew that Jesus could help him if he wanted to; it often seemed, however, that his prayer went unanswered. He persevered all the same and there was a kind of consolation that entered his heart even if ever so fleeting. This he shared with no one not even his best friend Miriam and certainly not with his friends, the Boutin children, who lived across the street. He knew that they would just laugh at him and call him a sissy.

The Boutin family had six children. Caroline and Gus were the two that John enjoyed playing with; they were his age and enjoyed having fun. They also often loved to play tricks on other people in the village. John did not always approve of some of these tricks because they could be mean and destructive. When this would happen, John became very difficult to get along with and they would end up arguing. John hated it when this happened because he always feared saying something that he would regret later. Caroline was three years older than John and Gus and she thought that she should be the boss in everything when Caroline's oldest sister was not present. Marion, the oldest sister, was very bossy and very difficult to get along with. John hated it when Marion was with them. She always called him nasty names. Caroline could be just as hateful as Marion when she wanted to be.

One Saturday afternoon Caroline and John were arguing about some things concerning their trick playing. Caroline was furious at John and when she saw that she was not winning the argument, she told John, "Get the hell home you little shit–head before I crack you one over the head." John simply crossed the road and turned to face Caroline and Gus from the other side. He stood there taunting Caroline saying, "Nyin, nyin, you are wrong, you didn't win! You think you're smart but you're not. And I don't care!" Without John realizing it, Caroline had picked up a sharp- edged stone from the ground and threw it at John with as much force as she could muster. It found its mark. John was hit in the head just above the forehead at the hair line; just the right spot to hit and split a small vein. The blood spurted all over John's head, face and chest. He screamed and started to cry as he ran into the house.

"What happened?" John's mother screamed, jumping up from the rocking chair where she sat knitting. "My God, the blood! How did this happen?"

John, crying and trying to wipe the blood from his eyes, kept screaming, "It was Caroline. She threw a rock and hit me."

Immediately, Rose soaked a towel in cold water and wrapped it around John's head. She then got Della to help her take him to the doctor's. But before the doctor's visit she took him over to the Boutin residence across the street and when Agnes, Caroline's mother answered, she showed her the cut that Caroline had inflicted on John. Agnes was not pleased at all and called Caroline to make her apologize to Rose and John. Caroline just blurted out, "He was making fun of me and calling me names, so he got what he deserved."

"You will apologize immediately or you will be grounded for the rest of the week. That is not a way to behave and you know it," exclaimed Agnes. Looking at John's mother, Agnes said, "Rose, I truly am sorry for this, but I will take care of it." Rose thanked Agnes and went on to the doctor's office with John. Della walked beside John and held him around the neck.

Dr. Herbin was an older man and was very kind to Rose and her family. When Rose had found out that she was a diabetic and before socialized medicine, Dr. Herbin had given Rose many insulin samples to use to cut down on medical costs for the family. He looked at John and gently said to him, "Let me see that cut. Yes, she sure aimed right, but it will be fixed in a jiffy." He quickly stopped the bleeding and was able to clamp the wound with a small pin made especially for that; it would hold it closed until the cut healed properly. "That should do it," said Dr. Herbin. "Try to avoid hitting it with the comb when combing your hair and in no time it will be fine. Come back to see me in two weeks' time. You must come sooner of course if it starts to bleed again."

It was not the first time that John saw Dr. Herbin for medical attention. He had been there several times in the past for an iron deficiency. John had very fair complexion with hair so blond that it looked almost white and he tired easily; he tended to look sickly. He would sleep for hours on the living-room sofa during the day and would not be able to wake up. Sometimes he would go a whole day without waking up. This would worry his mother and father very much. One afternoon when one of John's aunts was visiting, she suggested that John needed a tonic of some kind. John's mother did get him a tonic, and he took it regularly.

"Our little wounded soldier will be fine," whispered Della as they returned home from Dr. Herbin's office. John was close enough to Della to hear her. "If it ever happens again, Caroline will have me to contend with. I'll knock her block off." John did heal well and Dr. Herbin was able to remove the clip after the two weeks had passed.

This was the first bad physical wound that he experienced. There would be many others, and not just physical wounds to be sure, as he had already experienced from his mother's reaction to his little escapade with Miriam. It was around this time that another of those emotional wounds occurred; John realized that there was a problem in the family, a problem that would cause him great anguish, the problem of alcohol, a very nasty wound indeed. John gradually discovered that his father, was what he later termed a "sporadic alcoholic." Of course he eventually learned that a person is an alcoholic or isn't one, there is no in-between; one cannot be an alcoholic on the week-end and then not so during the week; it would be similar to saying that one can be a little bit pregnant! All the same it sounded good to John, to use the label "sporadic alcoholic", somehow it didn't sound as bad.

When things got rough at work, or because of money problems, John's father would go on drinking binges. That was when he would be gone for whole week-ends at a time and sometimes for a couple of weeks. He also realized that, luckily, his mother was not afraid of his father. If there was someone who could keep him in line, she was the one. John was always so grateful that his Mom was there; she gave the impression of strength and motherly concern, so her home had to remain calm and peaceful. Being a woman of faith and prayer, she always gathered the family together for the recitation of the rosary each evening after supper. The whole family had to be there unless there was something very important that needed attending to, so Batist was expected to be there for this important moment of family prayer. All would kneel in the kitchen and Rose would lead them in prayer; if someone came to the door, Catholic or Protestant, they were expected to kneel as well or go away and come back later.

One such incident occurred one evening when Martine's special friend came calling. Francis was not Catholic, but a United Church member.

Martine was really taken with him; they would eventually marry. For the time being, however, it was but a budding romance. This one particular Friday night he was to pick Martine up since he had asked her to go to the movies with him. Of course Martine had said yes but had failed to let Rose know about it. They were still at prayer when there was a knock at the door. Martine's eyes opened wide and she looked at her mother with a pained expression on her face. "Do you know who that is at the door?" Rose asked Martine.

"Yes. It has to be Francis. He's picking me up for the movies," said Martine.

"Then you answer the door, Martine"

Martine then called out, "Come in." In walked Francis. When he saw them all on their knees, he was visibly embarrassed and seemed out of place. John stuffed his head under the cushion of the rocking chair where he was kneeling to stop from laughing.

Then Rose spoke, and in French said to Martine, "Tell him to kneel like all of us. You will go when the rosary prayer is over." Prayers in the DeCoste family were always said in French.

Martine looked at Francis saying, "You'll have to kneel with us till the prayer is over."

"That's alright, I don't mind," answered Francis in a conciliatory tone. He awkwardly got on his knees but remained quite silent as they prayed.

John was weak from laughter as he observed what was going on but did his best not to let his mother see him laughing. If she saw him he would be punished.

Rose continued on, undaunted by the presence of a non-Catholic during the prayers. She finished the rosary prayer and launched into the litany to the Blessed Virgin Mary. John at that moment tried to protest saying, "Ah Mom, do you really need to do the litany, it is so long?"

"You be quiet and answer the prayers properly," was Rose's response. John knew that there was no arguing with his mother. She knew every litany prayer by heart. Again Rose droned on with each invocation, "Mother most holy, Mother most pure, Tower of Ivory. House of Gold, Ark of the Covenant, Morning star, Health of the sick, Refuge of sinners," and many, many more. To each of these they obediently answered, "Pray for us." They would only be free to go after the final "Amen" had been uttered!

There were times when Batist was absent from the prayer. When this happened for no good reason, Rose would let her displeasure be known.

John remembered one Friday evening when his father had come home for supper and had his uncle Robert with him. Both were already quite drunk. They were no sooner in the house that they began to argue. John's mother only allowed this to go on for a short time. She told them that there was to be no arguing and goings-on in the house; that supper was ready and they needed only sit and eat and then go to bed to sleep it off. Uncle Robert got on his high horse and started throwing his weight around, yelling quite loudly. He insisted that he needed to argue things out with Batist so told Rose to get out of his way. Although Rose was not a big woman, she was quick-witted, quick-tempered and strong. Without a word, she opened the kitchen and outside porch doors and with both hands swung him around and sent him flying outside into the snow in his bare stockings. Uncle Robert's winter boots then went flying out behind him as Rose threw them out the door. One of the boots hit him in the backside as the other boot thumped against the door of his car. If he wanted to argue, he could do it in his own home.

Batist was quite upset that Rose had thrown Uncle Robert out, so he started yelling at her. By this time John was terrified. His mother, however, without another word, grabbed an empty beer bottle in one hand and Batist by his shirt front with the other hand, throwing him against the corner wall of the pantry. She told him in no uncertain terms, "If you do not calm down and go to bed NOW, so help me God, I will smash this empty beer bottle over your head! Do you understand me?"

John, witnessing this, went running into the bedroom crying, and, throwing himself on his knees below the bed, prayed to all the saints in heaven that they stop. At that moment he heard his father say, "Okay, Okay, I'll go to bed. Let me be." He heard him go to the sofa in the living room and lie down on it. Within a short time, he was snoring.

John stayed in the bedroom sobbing, exhausted from the whole affair. His mother came looking for him. She held him in her arms and said "As long as I am here, you need not be afraid. I'll take care of everything." John wondered if this kind of behaviour would never end. Dread was like a vice inside his chest. His mother brought him to the kitchen for the family rosary prayer while his father snored away in the living-room.

Chapter Two

The loud sound of an airplane flying overhead at the Kavumu airport brought Fr. John back to the present. He looked up and saw a huge passenger plane landing some distance from them. There was a lot of activity with many people milling about near the plane. Some people seemed to be disembarking; others were carrying long boxes. They eventually were told that the plane was carrying passengers fleeing Kinshasa, the capital, and, apparently, the plane was also transporting arms. The fighting and the killing would escalate! These were very disturbing signs. How would it all end? They continued to watch and listen. "Surely our plane should arrive soon," thought Fr. John.

Suddenly, one of the students raised his hand pointing towards the sky saying, "There's another plane arriving, maybe it's ours!"

The group of Xaverian priests and sisters who had been waiting for that plane to arrive shouted to them," Come, this plane is ours!"

One of the Sisters called out to them, "You will probably have to line up with your few pieces of luggage, passports and boarding passes to get on the plane. Have all of that ready!" They all ran to the runway.

A soldier ran towards them screaming at them," Line up, line up now! I want to see your passports, boarding passes and any luggage you have. You cannot get on that plane without your boarding passes!"

"The other soldier in the office, the Civil Guard, checked all that!" said Fr. John.

"No matter," said the soldier, "it must be checked again!"

At that moment Fr. John's thoughts went back to the moment in the Civil Guard's office when he had fallen on his knees in front of them. They had screamed at him that he was a traitor and how could he, a priest, get on his knees in front of them! In a moment of cunning perception he recalled that his kneeling gesture and tears had affected those soldiers. They had screamed at him to get up, that they would get their passports back, but Fr. John would have to find more American dollars for them. He had run to Fr. Antonio, the bursar of the Xaverian Community of priests, in desperation, to see if he had any money to lend him. He would never forget that lovely smile and the wonderful words of Fr. Antonio saying to him, "Don't worry, Father, don't worry. What you need, I have! How much do you need, one hundred, two hundred? "He had then discreetly shown him an envelope filled with American dollars. He had handed a sum of two hundred American dollars to Fr. John, saying, "Here. Go and get your children. If we survive, we will settle the accounts later." Fr. John could not believe what he was hearing but it was music to his ears. He would never forget Fr. Antonio. Because of him, he had gotten the passports back as well as the boarding passes and now they were lined up to board. But this screaming soldier was now insisting on checking everything again.

The soldier noticed that one of the students had a long narrow binder in his hand. "What is that?" the soldier shouted. "Wait, let me see it!"

Fr. John intervened, saying, "It is only a picture album of the student and our school."

"Let me see," screamed the soldier and he tore it from the student's hands to look through it. "No, you cannot leave with this," said the soldier, "It is subversive material." Fr. John went through the album with the soldier pointing out the pictures of the students, the school and the staff. The soldier refused to let it go. They left it with him. Fr. John had to hold back from lashing out at the soldier, both verbally and physically, but held back and just fumed inside instead.

Fr. John then said to the students, "Quickly, board the airplane! Do not waste time!" Under his breath, he told the student who had brought the picture album, "If I had known that you were carrying the album, I would never have let you take it. All is so fraught with danger! Any excuse is good for the soldiers to give us a hard time."

It seemed as if they would never get boarded and fly out. Suddenly, another problem occurred. Sister Theresa, one of the elderly Carmelite sisters, who was crippled and wearing leg braces could not climb the stairs to get into the plane. The plane actually opened from the rear and the stairs were quite narrow and steep. Fr. John and the students were attempting to lift Sister Theresa up the stairs and into the plane. While they were labouring to get her into the airplane, the soldier kept screaming, "Hurry up or else I will ground everyone, stop the whole operation and no one will leave!" With much difficulty, the Sister was finally dragged up the stairs and lay on the floor of the plane for a moment to get her breath while praying and thanking God and everyone. Several of the students helped her into a seat and got her to fasten her seat belt. Everyone else quickly scrambled to take whatever seats were available.

All were finally settled in for take off. Everyone was still on edge and holding their breath, because the signal for take-off still had to be given. The plane taxied out onto the runway of the small Bukavu Airport. There was total silence on the plane. All were anxious to leave. It was already evening. The waiting had been long, since nine that morning. The sun was going down and the take- off had to be soon. After waiting at the end of the runway for five or ten minutes, the signal was given. The plane cruised along the tarmac, gained speed, and lifted up and into the air. Once airborne, all the passengers applauded vigorously and shouted loudly, "Hurrah! Hurrah! Hurrah!"

The small nineteen seater plane pushed on towards Kampala. All were silent, exhaustion had taken its toll. Out of the cockpit, came a young, black woman dressed as an airline hostess. Everyone was surprised to see her since there had been no sign of her at the airport when they boarded. She stood at the end of the aisle closest to the cockpit so everyone could see her and introduced herself, saying, "My name is Angela Makarere and I wish to welcome all of you aboard this flight heading for Entebbe Airport, in Kampala, Uganda. The Italian Consul in Kampala asked me to accompany this flight and to do everything possible to make your flight a pleasant one. I apologize for not being around when you arrived to board the plane but I was cautioned about showing myself outside the plane as my life would have been in grave danger. One of the soldiers guarding the plane told me to remain inside the plane and not to show my face. He said that I could easily be killed since I look very much like a Tutsi woman. I was extremely surprised at this but fearing for my life, I hid in the washroom of the plane. Please accept my apologies. I will serve some refreshments and snacks shortly now that we are airborne. I wish you all a very pleasant flight and welcome to Uganda!" Everyone just stared at her dumbfounded; they could not believe their ears. This was incredible! As all received a drink and a small snack, conversation began to flow. Tensions eased.

Since it was taking time for the snacks to be handed out, Fr. John catnapped as the plane hummed along heading towards Kampala. He dreamed of days gone by when he was at home as a schoolboy. Maybe he would see home once more after all. Different people flowed in and out of his thoughts and dreams. There were many events and happenings that crowded his mind. He could not believe at times that they had been able to get out of Zaire. Only the first year of his tour of duty in Zaire had been somewhat peaceful and almost uneventful. Even in that first year there had been rumours of war and terrible unrest. Besides the threat of an invasion by rebels from Uganda, his own missionary community had been seriously touched by illness and the difficulties that sickness can bring to any group in the service of a struggling church.

Fr. John's thoughts returned to the town of Bukavu where he had worked for the last four and a half years. He remembered being in another airplane at one point, a year and a half after arriving in Bukavu, in the beginning of December of 1993; December was a pleasant month in Bukavu. He had been asked to accompany another Canadian Missionary of Africa to Canada, after he had experienced a stroke. Fr. Conrad Gareau had been working in Zaire for some time and was serving the communities of the Maniema region in the interior of the country when Fr. John had arrived in Zaire. Fr. Conrad was a brittle diabetic and had found it very difficult to keep his blood sugars under control. They were deep in bush country and did not have adequate medical service; all medical supplies had to be flown in from the main centers of the country. This was because interior roads were virtually impassable. The Missionaries of Africa had a very important air service into the Maniema region for supplies and passengers. The six seater airplane of the Missionaries of Africa could be seen at least once a week making its run from the Kavumu Airport to the missions in the interior. It was Fr. Denis Brisson, himself a Missionary of Africa, who piloted the plane. Insulin, was flown in regularly for Fr. Conrad, who would come into Bukavu at least once a month for a medical check up.

It was November 2, 1993 and Fr. Conrad had come to the regional house for his monthly check up with Sister Lucila who was a medical doctor and a cardiologist. She would verify his medication and guide him through all the necessary tests to make sure that all was well. He was given a comfortable room at the regional house and he would be able to visit the different communities and friends in Bukavu.

The Regional House was the main center for the Missionaries of Africa, also known as the White Fathers of Africa, in the town of Bukavu in the eastern region of Zaire. The Regional superior with his regional council lived there and were in charge of keeping all business and relationships with the different missionary colleagues and the local church in good order. They had many rooms available for the colleagues who came to Bukavu from the different mission stations to do business, see the doctor, make a spiritual retreat or just meet with their director and his council about various matters, personal and otherwise.

It was Monday morning and Fr. Conrad had already been at the regional house for a week. It was close to eight o'clock in the morning and Fr. John had come with Fr. Gregory to get funds for the weekly supplies for the school. Fr. John inquired about Fr. Conrad and his health. Fr. Fausto looked at Fr. John and calmly replied, "Oh yes, you probably have not heard the news yet. Fr. Conrad has had a stroke or so we think. He was transported to the Fomulac Hospital in Katana early this morning. We are waiting for news about his condition."

The Fomulac Hospital was a huge medical facility that had been started by the Missionaries of Africa during the colonial era and gave excellent care. There were both African and European doctors working there. The White Fathers and White Sisters both had communities set up close to the Fomulac Hospital and offered their services to the medical facility. Fr. John had already been there several times and had been impressed with the hospital. Fr. Conrad would get very good care there. The area where the hospital was situated was quite beautiful. It had been built on a hill overlooking the valley of the Kivu and one could easily look out on the panoramic view of the lake and the surrounding countryside. A winding road ran down from the hospital to the grounds of both the White Sisters and the White Fathers. Both community houses were surrounded by beautiful flower gardens; the gardens also contained a vegetable section and a few sweet smelling fruit trees. Fr. John loved the area of the Fomulac communities; there was always such a sense of peace there.

"Oh, how upsetting," said Fr. John "What happened?"

"Well, Fr. Conrad had been coming to Eucharist ever since his arrival here at the regional house," said Fr. Fausto. "This morning, as we were about to begin Eucharist, he hadn't shown up. One of the fathers went to see if there was a problem and found his door ajar, but no sign of Fr. Conrad. Several of us came out of the chapel and called to him from the open door of his room, but we received no answer. So I went into the room and found him behind the desk next to the bed where he had fallen," continued Fr. Fausto. "I called Sister Lucila who had come to Eucharist with us and she immediately checked him over. She found that he needed oxygen since he was having difficulty breathing. He was unable to speak or move. His situation was critical and they would need to get him to the hospital as soon as possible! The regional superior, Fr. Joseph, immediately transported him to the Fomulac Hospital in one of the land cruisers. Now we are awaiting news of his condition, as I told you, "said Fr. Fausto.

"Please let us know what is happening and what his condition is when you hear," said Fr. John. "We will want to pay him a visit if possible."

A week passed before any news came from the Fomulac Hospital. One Friday afternoon Fr. Joseph came to the seminary for a visit with the community. And he brought news of Fr. Conrad. "He is doing better now," said Fr. Joseph, "but he has a long way to go. He still cannot walk on his own and his speech has not yet returned. That is worrying Dr. Maartens who is caring for him," Fr. Joseph told the community. "It was definitely a stroke. Apparently the insulin that he was taking had become defective for some reason. We think that the place where it was kept was not cool enough and the heat would have damaged it. He still has another two weeks to go for the doctors to ascertain if he will regain all of his motor skills or remain somewhat handicapped. Apparently it takes a good two to three weeks for a proper assessment," said Fr. Joseph in a worried tone of voice.

"Is it possible for us to visit him?" Fr. John asked.

"That is possible," said Fr. Joseph, "but not for very long periods of time. He tires very quickly. We will eventually have to make a decision regarding his future."

The following Sunday afternoon, Fr. John, Fr. Gregory and Fr. John Paul drove to the Fomulac Hospital to visit Fr. Conrad. He was very pleased to see them although he could not respond vocally to their conversation. Fr. John had a foreboding feeling that Fr. Conrad would not remain much longer in Zaire. He would soon find out that his intuition was correct.

One week went by, then a second week. Then, the regional superior returned to the school one afternoon with news that Fr. Conrad would have to be repatriated; it was necessary to explore the possibilities of his getting some kind of treatment or surgery to try to improve his condition. What he needed could not be done at the Fomulac hospital. Dr. Maartens would accompany Fr. Conrad back to Canada and he would be taken on a stretcher with the proper facilities to care for him on the trip. Dr. Maartens had never been to Canada and had asked that a Canadian accompany him; the Canadian did not need to be a doctor.

"Would you accompany Dr. Maartens on this journey?" Fr. Joseph asked Fr. John. "You are really the only other Canadian left in this region with the stamina to undertake this. Fr. Leopold is at the retreat house with the Jesuit Fathers; however, we feel that he is too old for this kind of undertaking and he also has not been well.

"What would I need to do, exactly, for such a journey?" asked Fr. John.

"Well, you would assist Dr. Maartens in any way necessary; there will be materials to carry, clean clothing and some medical instruments to be sorted and looked after, and possibly phone calls to make and messages to send when necessary. Dr. Maartens will need to be relieved at times to rest. We will also need you to go to Bujumbura to organize the trip with Air France. This has to be done as soon as possible."

Before going to Bujumbura to make the arrangements for the trip, Fr. John returned to the Fomulac hospital to see Dr. Maartens to find out if there were any instructions. He hoped to visit with Fr. Conrad as well and to see how he felt about this undertaking. Fr. Conrad was very pleased that this was to happen. He longed to see his family. Dr. Maartens was pleased to meet Fr. John and they felt quite in tune with one another upon meeting. "It is important that the air lines know that Fr. Conrad cannot walk or do anything for himself," Dr. Maartens told Fr. John. "Once they know this they will know what to do so that Fr. Conrad will feel comfortable and have needed privacy."

Fr. John had been to Bujumbura, the capital of Burundi, to shop, to bring colleagues to the airport for home-leave or for special meetings; however, he had always wondered how things went whenever someone needed to be repatriated because of illness. He was about to find out.

He left for Bujumbura early on a Monday morning, stopping at the regional house to see if there was any mail for the colleagues in Bujumbura. Fr. Gregory, the bursar, had decided to accompany him on the journey; it was always better for two to travel together in case something happened during the trip. They would need to take the escarpment route through the mountains and most areas of the escarpment were deserted, with a very narrow road on which to travel. Fr. Fausto was already up and in his office when they stopped for the mail and messages. "Are you ready?" exclaimed Fr. Fausto. "Have you not heard of the squabbling that is going on between Zaire and Rwanda?" he asked. "They are quarrelling and Rwanda is very upset with Zaire and the ridiculous decisions being taken by our president. Apparently there is a rumour circulating that the Rwandese are putting land mines along the escarpment road. Maybe you should let the taxis go first and they will roll on the explosives before you do to clear the way for you!" exclaimed Fr. Fausto. Then he burst out laughing. This was Fr. Fausto's attempt at dark humour.

"Aren't you nice and encouraging, and so very Christian," answered Fr. John. In spite of the black humour, they set out. Fr. John whispered a prayer as they set out on the road. The trip went well. In fact, it was quite uneventful. They met several taxis on their way back to Bukavu quite overloaded with materials and people. One thing the Africans knew how to do well was to pack their taxis. The passengers all waved and greeted one another with much laughter and many shouts and cries of "Jambo, jambo."

They rolled into the town of Uvira at about ten forty-five in the morning. Uvira was a military town on the shore of Lake Tanganyika facing Bujumbura, the capital of Burundi, situated on the other side of the Lake. At the border crossing on the Zairean side, it was the same old hassle---bribes, bribes and more bribes. Fr. John was prepared for this. He had made sure that he had American dollar bills in each pocket of his shirt and trousers, and a few extra stuck in his socks. Finally they were across. Usually the Burundian border crossing was somewhat easier to clear; but that day two of the Burundian police made signs to Fr. John that he had to stop on the side of the road before crossing the bridge into the outskirts of Bujumbura. He parked the land cruiser carefully.

"Where are you going?" asked the policeman.

"We are going to Bujumbura for a meeting of the Missionaries of Africa," answered Fr. John.

"I need to see your passport, your driving license and the papers for the vehicle," said the police officer. As he examined the papers, his colleague walked around the vehicle examining the wheels and the tires as well as the head lights and the rear lights. Fr. John wondered what they were planning to spring on them.

The police officer who had Fr. John's papers suddenly asked, "Where are you coming from?"

"We're coming from Bukavu," answered Fr. John.

The Officer that had been examining the vehicle approached the driver's side of the vehicle and said, "Your tires are not in very good condition. You are a hazard on the road and a danger for other drivers. I'll have to give you a ticket for driving with defective tires. You'll need to pay that fine immediately before we can allow you to continue!" he exclaimed.

"Really?" answered Fr. John with the best surprised expression that he could muster. "That is certainly amazing! I drove all the way from Bukavu and over the escarpment and did not have one flat tire. How could that happen with such defective tires?"

"I don't know," answered the police officer, "but we will have to give you a fine for such dangerous driving."

He sat there quietly for a moment, mulling this over. Then he turned to the police officer and asked, "How much would that fine be?"

"Two thousand Burundian francs," answered the Officer. He understood. That would be ten American dollars, or five dollars for each of the Officers.

"Alright, I'm good with that," answered Fr. John, "but I will need a receipt for the fine because this is my director's car and he will ask me for a receipt. We cannot use any of the money without proof of what it was spent on."

"We cannot give you a receipt, that's not possible," said the Officer.

"Really!" exclaimed Fr. John. "That's too bad because I cannot give out that much money without proof of what I used it for!"

"I cannot give you a receipt!" the Officer repeated once more.

"Then I guess we'll have to stay here," said Fr. John. "I cannot return to my boss without a receipt. He would be very upset." Fr. John was determined to dig in his heals. A good ten minutes went by before one of the Officers made a gesture to him with his hand saying, "You can go!" Fr. John immediately took off, heading for Bujumbura.

Bujumbura was not a very large city, but a very pleasant one with all the services necessary for food stuffs, goods, accommodations and travel agencies. There was a Center in Bujumbura run by the White Fathers where Fr. John and Fr. Gregory could stay. The Center was quite welcoming and comfortable and was known to everyone as "La Par." This Center provided accommodation for missionaries and other clergy members who were visiting Bujumbura or doing business there. It was a safe spot for everyone. They headed for "La Par" immediately, booked their rooms since they would be staying for a few days and then set out to find the offices of Air France.

Air France turned out to be on the main street. The huge blue, white and red sign of the air lines was quite visible. There were several young women to serve the customers.

"How may I help you?" asked the young woman in a welcoming voice.

"I do hope that you can help us," answered Fr. John. "We need to repatriate one of our priests who is quite ill. He cannot walk and his speech is very affected by the stroke he had almost a month ago. He will be transported by stretcher from Bukavu in a small plane, hopefully to take Air France from Bujumbura to Montreal, Canada."

"How many of you will be traveling and when did you want to travel?" asked the Air France attendant.

"There will be three of us traveling, the patient on the stretcher, myself and a Belgian doctor who will care for the patient on the journey," answered Fr. John. "We hope to be able to travel sometime in the first week of December."

"There is a flight out of Bujumbura on the 7th of December, getting into Charles DeGaulle Air Port, in Paris, on the morning of December 8th and leaving again for Montreal in early afternoon. Would that be suitable?" the young female clerk asked.

"Oh yes, that would be fine," said Fr. John. "What would that entail in seating arrangements to accommodate the stretcher, needed supplies and passengers," asked Fr. John.

"We would reserve nine seats in the rear section of the plane," she said. "There would be six seats for the stretcher with curtains around it that can be opened and closed for privacy; there would be one seat for the doctor, one seat for the person who is accompanying the doctor and one seat for the materials. Do you think that that would be to your satisfaction?" asked the air line clerk. Before Fr. John could answer, she added, "You would each be issued a flight ticket, of course, for the trip and the tickets would be issued for the whole of the trip to Montreal. This would facilitate the formalities for your connecting flight to Montreal from the Paris air port since you would have to wait for some hours at the air port clinic before continuing on to Montreal."

Fr. John thought about the whole thing for a few minutes and then told the female clerk to book everything and to make it for the evening flight of December 7th.

"The December 7th flight is open. I will book everything and make out a memo for the transfer arrangements for the stretcher. I can also give you the flight tickets now and a copy of the memo with all the details of the arrangements. Will that be satisfactory?" asked the air line clerk. Then she added, "For the return trip you will have to make arrangements in Montreal once you know when you will be returning to Africa."

"That will be fine," Fr. John answered. Fr. Gregory, being the bursar of the White Fathers' community, put the charges amounting to fifteen thousand dollars for the whole of the trip through the accounts of the White Fathers. All was set. They would do some shopping and head back to Bukavu the next day.

That evening at the Center all seemed calm enough and they gathered after the vespers prayer for the evening meal. The meals at La Par were always well prepared and it was interesting to chat with colleagues that they had not seen for some time. The conversation always seemed to turn to the political unrest that existed in both Burundi and Rwanda. There had been some demonstrations in Bujumbura over the last weeks, especially by the student population, and the military had made it a point to quell the affair. This happened at times during the day but most especially at night. This turned out to be one of those nights.

Fr. John and Fr. Gregory decided to listen to the news in the T.V. room and then retire for the night since they had a fairly long trip the next day. Fr. John fell asleep rather quickly as he listened to the quiet hum of the ceiling fan in the room; there was also a mild breeze coming in through the partly opened window. Around eleven thirty that night, he was awakened by gun shots and the loud noise of trucks close by; he could also hear shouts and cries coming from some distance in the area of the Center. Fr. John threw himself out of the bed, donned his bathrobe and went out into the hallway. There he met Fr. Gregory who was also awakened by the noise. Then Sister Jacqueline appeared.

"Sister, what is going on?" asked Fr. Gregory.

"It's probably the military again," she answered. "They do this to frighten the people and especially the students so that no demonstrations will take place during the day. It is a warning that they are here and that they will tolerate no rebellious behaviour. The situation is becoming more and more tense due to the upcoming elections. We just hope that there will be no blood shed!" she exclaimed. More people had come out of their rooms and were quietly milling about and talking in whispers. Fr. Gregory and Fr. John returned to their rooms but could not sleep again until the noise had stopped. They got on the road to Bukavu later that morning feeling very tired.

The drive to the border took a mere forty-five minutes. The two Officers they had encountered on their way into Burundi were not on duty; there were two other Officers that Fr. John did not know. The soldiers did not stop them. They continued on and just before coming to the bridge for the border crossing, they received a signal to stop. Once they had stopped, the Customs Officer said to them, "Please follow me into the office." There, sitting at a desk was another Officer obviously with a higher rank.

"I have a question to ask you," stated the Officer looking at Fr. John quite intently.

"Yes, and what might that be?" Fr. John asked.

"When you come across the border, coming from Zaire to Burundi, do you give them something, a bribe for example?" questioned the soldier.

"As a matter of fact I do, but not all the time," said Fr. John.

"Why do you give a bribe there but not here?" snapped the soldier.

"Because you are very correct and honest," said Fr. John, smiling while he said this.

"Oh no, no, no, it doesn't work that way, Father," said the soldier. "You will have to be ready to take care of this the next time you come through here," replied the soldier smiling. Then, suddenly he added, "You are in the same group as Fr. Roberto, are you not?"

"Oh no, I'm not," said Fr. John. "Fr. Roberto is what is known as a Redemptorist priest. We do not belong to the same group! We have different directors, but I do know him quite well," said Fr. John.

"He gives us lots of money when he crosses the border," said the soldier. "You will have to do the same from now on, you know," added the soldier.

"Okay, I will do my best the next time around," Fr. John answered. Now he knew why they were all having such a rough time with the border crossings. Fr. Roberto was throwing his money around.

Fr. John got into his vehicle, driving off pleased that he had got off without paying a penny in bribes, this time!

They finally found themselves on the escarpment road and the long trek through the mountains; they reached the outskirts of Bukavu before nightfall. They stopped at the Regional House to give them the details of the trip and the departure time.

It was decided that Fr. Conrad's contingent would leave for Bujumbura on the morning of December 7th from the Kavumu airport to connect with the Air France flight leaving Bujumbura in the afternoon of December 7th.

The flight with the airplane of the White Fathers' community would leave Kavumu airport around twelve thirty, if possible, depending on the time of its return from the Maniema region where it had brought supplies and was returning with two of the White Sisters who were coming for catechetical workshops in Bukavu. The latest that they could leave was one o'clock, since they needed to be ready to connect with the three o'clock flight arriving in Bujumbura from Paris. All the ticket and passport formalities had to be complete since the stretcher would be the first thing to be put on the Air France flight.

They all arrived in Kavumu by eleven thirty the morning of December 7th to be told that Fr. Denis and the plane had not yet returned from the Maniema region. The day was warming up and they had to place the stretcher with Fr. Conrad on it in the shade while they waited. The Regional Superior and Fr. Fausto had come to see them off. They were chatting for some fifteen minutes when an airplane appeared on the horizon. It was a small plane and it landed smoothly. It was their plane. It taxied to its parking spot off the runway and Fr. Denis got out. He came over to them and greeted them. "Hello everyone! How are you all doing? Good I hope!" He touched Fr. Conrad's hand in a reassuring gesture as he greeted everyone. "We will have to remove most of the seats from the aircraft to fit the stretcher in, leaving some space for Dr. Maartens and Fr. John. Let's get that done immediately. We need to be on our way soon." He chuckled as he said, "Time is flying."

They managed to remove the seats from the aircraft. With some difficulty they were able to get the stretcher into the airplane. It seemed at first that there would be no room for both Fr. John and the doctor. Dr. Maartens did not want to travel alone with the patient. "We must find a way for both of us to be on this flight! Once in Bujumbura we will be boarding a huge 747 aircraft."

Fr. Denis then spoke up, "You sit at the back next to the patient since you are his doctor and Fr. John can sit in the cockpit up front next to me. It will be a bit cramped but it will not be for long. It is only a thirty minute flight."

Dr. Maartens wasted no time in boarding with the necessary supplies. Fr. John got into the cockpit and sat next to Fr. Denis. The seat next to Fr. Denis had been pushed up fairly close to the cockpit dashboard since the stretcher needed a bit more room to fit properly into the aircraft. Fr. John found himself sitting very close to the front window with both of his knees pushed up under his chin. While it was an uncomfortable position, it offered an awesome panoramic view of the landscape spread out in front of them.

They taxied out to the runway and, after a short wait, they were given the signal for departure. Everyone was standing on the side of the runway waving good-bye. The aircraft gradually picked up speed and lifted smoothly into the air. They were on their way! First they scaled the escarpment that Fr. John had taken so many times on his trips to Bujumbura. From the air, all quite breathtaking and, in spite of the height, the hills seemed close enough to touch. As they left the escarpment area they overflew a beautiful green valley. They kept their course through this valley and in a short time could see Bujumbura in the distance. Fr. John breathed a sigh of relief since his legs were cramping from their unnatural position. He looked forward to being able to stretch his legs.

"We've arrived!" Fr. Denis exclaimed. "The first leg of the journey has gone well. I pray that your whole journey will continue in the same way." Several porters came to take the stretcher from the aircraft and wheeled it into the terminal. Fr. John hoped that the guest lounge of the airport would be available. He went to the information desk for the passengers in transit and asked if they could take the patient into the lounge.

"The lounge is not open to anyone for security reasons," he was informed by the information agent.

"Could you not make an exception this time?" Fr. John asked. "This is one of our priests from the White Fathers' community who is quite ill and he needs some quiet rest while waiting for his flight to Paris. It will be a very long flight since we must connect to a flight going to Montreal, Canada, once we arrive in Paris."

"I am sorry, but no passengers are allowed in the lounge area, under any circumstances," answered the agent. Fr. John later found out that there had been a civil disturbance in Bujumbura the night before and that parts of the airport had been affected.

The only free space in the waiting area with enough room to place a stretcher was just below the bar. That is where they placed Fr. Conrad with Dr. Maartens watching him and Fr. John attempting to get needed errands done. As time passed the temperature in the waiting room rose as it became overcrowded with departing passengers. Dr. Maartens used a damp face towel to wipe the sweat off of Fr. Conrad's face, head and neck. The air conditioning was not working. Fr. John wondered if that was part of the result of the previous night's disturbance.

The travelers who walked by the stretcher would repeatedly express their regrets for Fr. Conrad's exhausting, hot and miserable waiting time. Fr. John brought coffee and tea, sandwiches and reading materials to Fr. Conrad and Dr. Maartens. Suddenly a soldier came to Fr. John and told him to follow him to one of the exits leading into the main terminal. There he could see Sr. Jacqueline from the Center holding a bag of what he presumed to be mail in her arms. She wanted him to come for the mail, but he could not leave the International area of the airport. She raised her arms in exasperation. Fr. John said to the soldier, "Please, can you not supervise me while I go and get the bag of mail that Sister has? I'll go quickly, get the bag and come back immediately, as you watch me!" exclaimed Fr. John. The soldier hesitated, then suddenly said, "Go quickly, don't waste any time! This is against all procedures!" Fr. John could not believe his ears. He darted across the main hall, grabbed the bag and darted back again. The mail was on its way.

Fr. John and Dr. Maartens were chatting quietly as they stood by the waiting room bar. Fr. Conrad seemed to be sleeping, although the sweat trickled down his forehead as the warm sun poured in on him. "I do hope the Air France flight arrives soon," Fr. John whispered under his breath. No sooner had he voiced the thought than a huge Boeing 747 turned gracefully into the docking zone of the Air France section of the Airport. Fr. John breathed a sigh of relief!

The stairways were rolled into position for the doors of the airplane to be opened. Two flight attendants rushed down the stairs and into the main international waiting section where the passengers were waiting. The stretcher with Fr. Conrad on it was to be boarded first. Fr. John and Dr. Maartens followed closely behind as they crossed the tarmac, climbed the steps and entered the aircraft. The stretcher was taken to the rear of the aircraft where nine seats had been reserved for them. Six seats in groups of two on one side were used to place the stretcher on and a curtain placed around the section which could be closed to surround the stretcher for privacy. The other three seats were for those accompanying the patient: one for Dr. Maartens, one for Fr. John and one for the medical supplies. Fr. John would assist Dr. Maartens and support Fr. Conrad in any way he could. Fr. Conrad had not as yet regained mastery of his speech, but with some rather exhausting effort he could make himself understood. He was

John DeCoste

also incapable of full use of his right arm and hand. Fr. John noted that he seemed quite calm, but often had a pained frown on his forehead. Leaving the Africa that he loved so much in such a condition was an extremely painful experience for Fr. Conrad. Fr. John sensed this and grieved for him. "Would he ever completely recover?" Fr. John asked himself. Short of a miracle, he did not think so.

Once they were settled the other passengers began to board. Soon the aircraft taxied out to the runway in preparation for departure, and before long they were cruising comfortably towards Paris. Fr. Conrad napped while his companions quietly read magazines. The stewardesses handed out blankets, pillows and head-sets. "Drinks and a hot meal will be served shortly," came the welcomed announcement from one of the hostesses. Fr. John was happy to hear this as he was famished.

Dr. Maartens looked at Fr. John and said, "That is a welcome announcement, I am so hungry! Aren't you?"

"That is precisely what I was thinking," answered Fr. John.

One of the stewardesses came to them and asked, "Is everything alright so far? Is the patient comfortable?"

"All is well, thank you," answered Dr. Maartens. The stewardess then added, "You will be served meals first and please do not hesitate to let us know if you need anything. We want your flight to be as pleasant as possible."

"Oh, thank you. You are so kind," answered Dr. Maartens.

Things were going well as they cruised smoothly towards Paris until Fr. Conrad needed to urinate and discovered that nothing was happening. He looked at Dr. Maartens with a pain-filled expression on his face and with much difficulty managed to say, "I can't go. I need to, I can feel the pressure but it will not flow. I'm beginning to have pain in my groin." Dr. Maartens looked at Fr. John and in utter exasperation whispered to Fr. John under his breath, "This would have to happen and I forgot to bring material with me to be able to catheterize him. I cannot believe that I left that behind! How utterly irresponsible of me!"

"What if I get a pitcher of water and pour water into the bed pan within hearing distance; maybe that will help him to urinate. What do you think?" asked Fr. John.

"There is no harm in trying," answered Dr. Maartens.

Fr. John ran to the stewardess and asked for a large pitcher of water. The curtain giving privacy to Fr. Conrad was partially closed for privacy. Within hearing distance Fr. John poured the water into the bed pan. Amazingly, it was enough to do the trick! An expression of utter relief on Fr. Conrad's face testified to his success. Dr. Maartens rolled his eyes in relief while Fr. John chuckled to himself. The flight continued on without any other incidents. The meals were quite good and Dr. Maartens was able to have two of the grilled chicken dinners instead of one. He was absolutely famished. Fr. Conrad did not eat much of his even with Fr. John's help. He was simply not hungry. They were able to place a headset on his ears so that he could listen to music. That helped him sleep for the remainder of the flight.

The pilot finally announced that they would soon be landing at the Charles DeGaulle Airport in Paris. The stretcher was to be taken off the aircraft first and taken to the infirmary of the airport. They were to have a two hour wait for the connecting flight to Montreal. Both Dr. Maartens and Fr. John breathed a sigh of relief. They would get a bit of a rest and so would the patient. Dr. Maarten would get some catheterizing material in case the need arose on the next leg of their journey. Dr. Maartens and Fr. Conrad were taken directly to the infirmary from the international section of the airport. Fr. John, however, had to go through customs, have his passport stamped and re-enter the international section. He was then directed to the infirmary. They were served coffee or tea and snacks if they wished. Fr. John went in search of an international pay phone and phoned through to the Missionaries of Africa in Montreal to let them know that they had arrived in Paris and that they would be leaving around two thirty that day, December 8th. They would arrive that evening at Mirabel Airport in Montreal.

"Please meet us at the airport with winter jackets, gloves and boots!" exclaimed Fr. John. "We are arriving dressed in short-sleeved shirts, light trousers and sandals.

"We will do that, of course," answered Fr. Pierre, the bursar of the Provincial House of the Missionaries of Africa in Montreal. Then he added, "You could be arriving in the middle of a snow storm since there is a storm warning that has been announced for this evening. We will come prepared!"

All three were grateful for the rest at the airport clinic before departure for Montreal. The flight to Montreal went smoothly without incident, with no problems concerning urinals or catheters. They were very grateful for that. Upon arriving at Mirabel Airport, there was an ambulance waiting for them at the stairway of the plane. The wind had already come up and the snow was beginning to fall. Fr. John and Dr. Maartens gladly put on the winter jackets, gloves and boots. They were taken to a clinic in the city where all had been prepared to receive Fr. Conrad.

The clinic in the city had fortunately made some special preparations for Fr. Conrad. The physiotherapist had already prepared a word and letter chart that he could manipulate to help him communicate. Fr. Conrad was very pleased with this and allowed himself to be guided in the use of this new way of communicating. He would remain at the clinic for a few days and then would be accompanied by a nurse on a flight to Winnipeg, Manitoba, to visit with his family. He would get more treatment there and hopefully in time recover fully from his stroke. The Missionaries of Africa felt that it was important for his health that he be with family during this phase of his illness.

Fr. John and Dr. Maartens left Fr. Conrad in capable hands and were driven to the Provincial House where they would be given accommodations. By this time the snow storm had worsened and it had become quite slippery. It was already eight thirty in the evening before they were each shown to a room of the Provincial House. The Provincial House of the Missionaries of Africa was a large white brick structure on Boulevard de l'Acadie in Montreal; it was the head office of the Canadian branch of this missionary community and had many rooms to accommodate the missionaries who came back from the African missions for a visit with their families or to take up a posting with the communities working in Canada. This kind of work of course was very different from the work in the African missions. It involved a lot of office work, as well as making people more conscious of the needs of the African missions and recruiting candidates for the work in Africa, all work that, although not nearly as exciting, needed to be done.

On arrival they were told, "It is the feast of the Immaculate Conception here and we are celebrating. There is still plenty to eat in the refectory, so come and join us.

"Go with them Dr. Maartens, I'll join you later. I need to make a phone call before I do anything else. I'll be with you all shortly," said Fr. John.

Fr. John went to the nearest house phone and phoned his sister, Della. She would be surprised since no one knew that he was arriving. "Why are you phoning?" she asked. "Is there something wrong?"

"Nothing wrong, not at all," said Fr. John. "But guess where I am?"

"What do you mean? You're in Africa aren't you?"

"Look at your phone line. Where am I phoning from?" Fr. John asked. "I'm phoning from Montreal. I came to accompany one of our priests who is sick. I will not be heading back before the first week of January, which means that I'll be spending Christmas at home! Isn't that great?"

"Oh my God, that's great," she said. "It will be a wonderful Christmas. We haven't been all together for Christmas in years. When do you think that you'll arrive here?"

"I'll know for sure tomorrow, but I think that I will travel by train so that I can sleep; I'm really bushed," said Fr. John. Then he added, "Spread the news to everyone. I should be home in a few days." After he had hung up, his sister wasted no time in relaying the message to everyone.

Fr. John then made his way to the refectory. He was starved. There was plenty of good food left. Dr. Maartens was busy eating and making everyone's acquaintance. Fr. John was very pleased to find a number of people that he had known very well at this feast, amongst whom was Sister Madeleine, a White Sister of Africa, that he had gotten to know well while doing work in Ottawa. Sister Madeleine had worked for many years in the Algerian missions and was a very fine artist. She did beautiful work in watercolours; in fact she had given Fr. John a number of her paintings when they had become close friends. He was absolutely delighted to see her. They had a long chat together until Fr. John started to fall asleep.

"You go to bed. You've had a long day," said Sister Madeleine as Fr. John's eyes began to close. He wanted to stay up longer and chat but he finally had to admit defeat and went upstairs to bed. He noticed that Dr. Maartens still showed no signs of giving up.

"Good, let him enjoy his time here," thought Fr. John.

Fr. John made arrangements for his trip home to Nova Scotia for the Christmas holiday. Before these preparations he made sure that Dr.

Maartens had a place to go for the Christmas holiday. Fr. Benoit, a friend of Fr. John's told him that he need not worry about Dr. Maartens; that he would take him home with him to spend Christmas with his family. With that settled Fr. John made reservations to travel by train. He reserved a roomette so that he could rest and sleep during the entire trip home. It turned out to be a marvelous idea and he fully enjoyed the journey. The storm of December eighth had dumped mounds of snow in Quebec and the sun was shining brightly on the day he left for home. The bright sunshine sparkled on the white covering of snow. They were stopped for several hours some miles outside of Quebec City, since the snow was blocking the train track and still had to be cleared away. Of course, that made them late for their arrival in Halifax. Nonetheless, his brother Timmy was at the train station to welcome him home for Christmas.

Fr. John had not spent Christmas with his family for quite some time. It was a special treat for him. They had the traditional meat pie with freshly perked coffee and delicious fruit cake after midnight Mass. Then they opened their gifts. The following day, Christmas Day, they enjoyed turkey with dressing, mashed potatoes, vegetables smothered in hot steaming gravy. The traditional apple pie with ice cream for dessert topped off the wonderful feast. Of course they all wanted to know what Bukavu was like and what kind of place he was living in. Fr. John explained what kind of school he was in and how beautiful the area was with the mountains and the lake. He talked about the other priests that he was living with and the students that he had in class. He described what they ate and that the food was actually quite good. The people at home always wondered about the food and how difficult it must be to adapt to the diet in those countries. Fr. John answered quite frankly, "The food is very good. The plantain is quite delicious and so is the pounded yam that is called 'fufu'. They even have a small fish that is similar to our smelt and that is deep fried and served with fries. I just love it. I also enjoy the way the Africans cook lentils; they are amazing. No, I have no trouble with the food whatsoever."

"What is plantain?" Della asked. "And what is pounded yam?" Fr. John explained that the plantain is a type of banana that is for cooking. "It is not the sweet banana like we eat here. They have that one also but this is a bigger banana that can be cooked in many different ways. I enjoy it fried and served with the lentil stew," Fr. John replied. "Now pounded yam is similar to mashed potatoes. It is not what we call a yam; that is really the sweet potato, this is white or yellowish and looks like a big root. The yam is peeled and cooked and then mashed or pounded in the mortar and served with meat or fish stew. It is very good." Fr. John enjoyed explaining all of these things to his family but he did tire at times of having to explain so many things. He did enjoy being home and being able to rest and just sleep sometimes for long periods of time in the afternoons. He met quite a number of people at church of course and had many invitations to lunch and dinner. It was difficult to accept them all since his stay was not to be a very long one. They all enjoyed hearing about his work and what Africa was like. It was all so mysterious to them. Fr. John found that the people had very primitive ideas about Africa because of what they would see on television. He agreed that some of it was true but there was more to Africa than what the television showed them. He wanted to make them realize that Africa was very beautiful, that the people were wonderful and that we all could learn a lot from the African cultures. In those visits home from Africa Fr. John often found himself in the limelight for a short time. He managed to get quite a few visits in especially to relatives. After a period of two weeks Fr. John returned to Montreal to make arrangements for the return trip to Zaire. It was all the same hard to say good-bye to the family. Fr. John always went through a lonesome period each time he left home. It was not quite as difficult, however, now that his mother was no longer living.

Upon arriving in the Montreal community, he asked Fr. William at the reception desk, "How is Dr. Maartens doing? Is he somewhere in the house today?"

"Oh, Dr. Maartens has already gone. He was able to get a flight to Belgium yesterday so that he could have a short visit with his parents on New Year's Day before returning to Zaire," answered Fr. William.

"I'm sorry to hear that," said Fr. John. "I was looking forward to traveling back to Zaire with him. It is great, however, for him to be able to spend a bit of time with his parents. He must be thrilled!"

Fr. William then added, "Oh by the way, the Provincial Superior, Fr. Denis, wants to talk to you. Apparently there is a message that arrived for you from Bukavu. He is in his office at the moment if you want to see him right away."

Fr. John went in search of Fr. Denis. He found him at his desk looking over some documents. As Fr. John knocked, he looked up. "Come in, come in Fr. John. Have a seat. A message came in for you from Bukavu asking you to go through Toulouse, France, on your way back to Zaire. Here, read the message for yourself," said Fr. Denis as he handed Fr. John the faxed message.

Fr. John discovered from the message that there was to be a seminar in Toulouse, France, and at least one member of staff from each of the training houses in philosophy was expected to attend. Fr. John knew that this would be beneficial for his center since he would find out what type of programmes were being used and given at the final stage of training for their candidates to the priesthood and to the brotherhood. The training house in Toulouse was for theology; they also had such a house in London, England. It would be a wonderful opportunity to meet the brothers that he had studied with and who were now teachers just as he was; it would be a good up-date on what was happening to all the members of his graduating group.

The return trip to Zaire would take him through to Toulouse, France, with a simple stop-over in Paris. He would not have to stop over in Kampala but would be able to get a connecting flight to Goma. He would wait some two hours in Goma for his flight to Bukavu. He had never taken this route before and it was quite interesting to observe all the goings-on between the customs officers, soldiers and passengers who were very interested in not having to dish out bribe money. One of the particularly interesting events that did happen on this trip, however, happened on the flight between Toulouse and Paris.

Fr. John was comfortably seated in his window seat enjoying a new novel that he had bought in the duty free book shop. The aisle seat was occupied by an elderly gentleman while the middle seat was vacant. A gentleman whom Fr. John speculated to be in his mid-thirties came down the aisle and occupied the middle seat next to him. He buckled up and sat there observing things around him. Noticing that Fr. John was reading a novel in English, he said to him, "You're English, aren't you?"

"No, I'm not English," answered Fr. John.

"You're American then?" he continued.

"No, I'm not American either," said Fr. John.

"But you're reading a novel in English," he answered in a questioning tone.

"Yes, because I'm Canadian and I speak and read both English and French," replied Fr. John.

"Oh, okay, that's cool," answered the young man.

Fr. John had decided a long while back not to tell people when traveling that he was a priest. He did not wear a roman collar or clerical garb, so they could not tell from his dress that he was a priest. He felt that the moment anyone knew he was a priest they became very apologetic about their religious background or felt that they had to talk about religion; some took advantage of the opportunity to air their beefs about religion and about God. He would simply tell people that he was a teacher, which he was, so no lies were told. So the young man whose name turned out to be Jerome, said to him, "You live or work in Paris, don't you?"

"No," answered Fr. John. "I'm going to Paris to take a flight to Zaire, the former Belgian Congo."

"Do you have business to do there?" Jerome asked. "I hear it is a rough place to be, there is much unrest there and some fear that war could develop."

"Actually I teach there," answered Fr. John.

"You're teaching there," reiterated Jerome. "Would you believe that I taught school in Africa as well?" said Jerome in a questioning tone of voice. "I went to Ivory Coast to do my military service and ended up teaching in a secondary school. We, French, can do this rather than do our military service here in France. It is really more interesting and we make money and learn a lot."

"I'm sure you do. We have a lot to learn from Africa and the Africans," said Fr. John. Then Jerome continued in an excited, passionate tone, "I found that the African women were very hot, much hotter than our European women, even hotter than our French women who are supposed to be just great in bed. Man, the women I saw were gorgeous; they had well rounded and beautifully developed buttocks and legs, as well as fantastic breasts. They were really beautiful, man. Were there beautiful women where you were?" he asked.

"I must admit that they are very beautiful." Fr. John answered.

"Hot too I bet?" he questioned.

"I don't know about the hot part, but I can vouch for their beauty," answered Fr. John. Then Jerome quite openly shot back without even a twinge of embarrassment, "I had one in my bed every night, if not one from the town, then one of my students. For a higher mark or a small gift, my students gave it up quite readily. What more did a Frenchman alone and far from home need? Man, it was good!" he admitted freely.

Fr. John did not want to hear more. He knew all too well how the African women and the young secondary school students were being used, especially by some of the European and North American men while they did their "stages" or tour of duty in Africa.

"I think I had better stretch my legs a bit and use the lavatory," said Fr. John to Jerome. When he returned, he resumed reading his novel, realizing with great relief that Jerome had dozed off. He did not encourage the conversation when Jerome woke up later. To his relief, the pilot announced at that moment that they would soon be landing in Paris.

Fr. John said good-bye to Jerome and he in turn wished Fr. John a safe trip to Zaire. "I will need more than a safe trip," thought Fr. John to himself. "The soldiers or customs inspectors must not go through my luggage or else they will certainly confiscate all the cassette recorders that I'm bringing back with me for the students to practice their English with." All the students who joined this missionary group had to know both English and French besides their own native language. The material that Fr. John was bringing back was quite necessary for them to do this and be properly trained. "Please God, let one of the confreres who speaks Lingala, the language of the military, be there to meet me," was the prayer that Fr. John whispered to himself. His prayer was answered in due course. When Fr. John came down the stairs of the aircraft, there, at the gate to the runway, was Fr. Martens, who was already speaking to the soldier there at the gate. By the look of things, all was well. Fr. John gave Fr. Martens one big hug and they both passed through the gate and made their way to the land cruiser parked by the thatched mud huts. Once they were on their way, Fr. John breathed a sigh of relief.

The relief in that instance did not come close to the relief Fr. John was now experiencing as he fled the war torn situation of Central Africa with his students; this sense of relief was deeper and more intense. Fr. John realized quite fully how close his students had come to being stopped as enemies, jailed and possibly killed. He did not want to think about it too much; just the thought of it made him feel ill. He preferred to turn to more pleasant thoughts and so, as the aircraft hummed on towards Kampala, Fr. John dozed and thought of home, a seemingly safer and more secure place.

As Fr. John continued to reflect on the different aspects of his childhood, he could clearly see that there had been too many unanswered questions and upsetting events in his youth; some, in fact, that were not only extremely painful but very difficult to comprehend as well. How could one easily resolve such painful events and memories. Answers would surface as time progressed!

Chapter Three

By the time John reached fourth and fifth grade he knew that he needed to excel in his studies even if he continued to dislike school very much. Having excellent grades became a priority as he knew they would be important if he wanted to further his education.

Grade school turned out to be rough for John; he always felt so alone, so vulnerable. Most of the Sisters were fine, but some could be mean. Sr. Gemma was one of those. She was tall and thin and the black nun's habit that she wore made her appear even thinner. The white "coiffe" that framed her forehead and face and held her long black veil in place accentuated her ruddy complexion and white even teeth when she smiled, which was not often.

One incident in first grade had caused John to hate school; he preferred to stay at home and just play outdoors, to be alone with no one watching him, and laughing at him.

In those days, the students did not have individual seats; there were long benches where two students sat side by side. John sat with Benny. He wasn't really a friend, just a classmate that he sometimes played with or walked home with. This particular day in Sr. Gemma's class, they were doing arithmetic. John did not like arithmetic, especially written problems that one had to figure out about a written situation, and which had to be shown in figures and then a final solution given. On this day, Benny was convinced that John was copying his work for the solutions to the problems. Benny went up to Sister and told her this. At that moment Sr. Gemma was not smiling; she glared at John with a hard, piercing look. Without even questioning the boys, she got up from her desk, grabbed John by the arm and marched him to the front of the class.

"Do you know what is done to boys who cheat in class?" asked Sr. Gemma.

"No, I don't," John answered.

"They are punished!" said Sr. Gemma.

And she took out a large, leather strap and strapped John on the hands until he cried. Some of the students were shocked; others just snickered nastily.

John went to his seat, and sat there sobbing. Mercifully, the bell rang to end the morning session. John walked home alone for lunch that day and it was then that he promised himself that he would never again cry in school, especially not in front of others. He also wondered why Sr. Gemma hated him and would take another student's word over his without even questioning him. In fact, why would he copy Benny's work? He knew even less than John did about arithmetic or any other subject for that matter! His dislike of Sr. Gemma solidified in his heart and mind at that moment, and only grew worse as she continued to terrorize the whole class.

Sr. Gemma would flatly refuse to let anyone go to the toilet during class hours; one had to wait for recess or lunch time. John would rush home to use the toilet because at recess and lunch hour, the older boys were in the toilets bullying the younger children. If one of the children was in the toilet, an older student would force the door open and stand there laughing at the child especially if that child was sitting on the toilet; John found this extremely humiliating. The teachers had no compassion for the students over these incidents and John resorted to rushing home at noon, sometimes with disastrous failure.

"What is wrong?" his mother would ask when he would come in crying.

"I did it in my pants again", he would cry, "Sr. Gemma won't let me go during class!"

"Why did you not go before leaving school?" his mother would ask.

"I can't, the older boys are there," cried John and they frighten me.

His mother would not question further, but patiently change him, try to console him while giving him his lunch and then send him back to school.

John received a very pleasant surprise before going on the yearly Easter break. Ten of the pupils who were in Sr. Gemma's class were told to gather up all of their school things and move to Sr. Madeline's class. Happily John was one of those ten students. They were to complete the remainder of their first grade with Sr. Madeline. She had agreed to teach a split class since Sr. Gemma's group was too large. John could not believe his ears when his name was called for the move! He gladly took his place in the group of ten. He knew that it would be heaven compared to Sr. Gemma's class.

Sr. Madeline was kind, gentle and a very good teacher and John was pleased to discover that Sr. Madeline liked him. She was always in good humour, would smile pleasantly at the students and take her time explaining things so that they would understand, especially in arithmetic. If they did well in spelling and composition, she would give them a beautiful bird with a long curling tail that she had made out of clear, coloured plastic. They were beautiful gifts and John would work extra hard to get one. She never strapped anyone, ever!

In spite of this new development John continued to dislike school very much. Too many incidents had soured him on school and he continued to feel alone, desolate and defenceless. He continued through grade school, disliking every minute of it, hating the smell of pencils, sour milk, unflushed toilets and the dust bane used to clean the classroom floors. He hated most of the teachers; a boy needed to be sports-minded, smart, yes, but excelling in things like baseball, hockey and boxing to be really accepted. Boys who liked to draw, paint, read and listen to exciting adventure stories were considered sissies. Those, however, were what John liked best; he hated sports except for such sports events as racing and swimming.

Time seemed to drag on during school. John loved weekends. He would have two whole days without seeing the smelly, old school. Friday afternoons there were special programmes. These were either a movie or a spelling bee. John loved movies. He would lose himself in his imagination, becoming the main character. Being quite good in spelling he also enjoyed the spelling bees and often won in the competitions. John did feel a twinge of guilt about one particular spelling bee in sixth grade.

There were only three students left in the spelling contest; two more had just fallen, stumped by the word "r e s c i n d." It was George's turn and they had two chances each. George slowly spelled out, "r e s s i n d".

"Not the correct spelling," said Miss De Lacroix. "One more try!"

George once again slowly spelled out, "r-e-c i n d."

"Sorry George, that is not the correct spelling either," said Miss De Lacroix.

They were now down to two, John and Laurie. He had to win this.

When they were down to two students and they were both standing on the same side of the class, they would move to opposite sides of the room facing one another; somewhat of a face off. John was the one who moved to the other side of the room. As he did so, Miss De Lacroix produced two fifty cent pieces. "Whoever spells this word correctly wins the dollar!" Miss De Lacroix exclaimed. Everyone gasped and then clapped.

As John crossed the floor to the other side of the class, he over-heard George, who had looked up the word 'rescind' in the dictionary, whispering to Ricky sitting next to him, "There's an 's' before the 'c', that's what we are missing, damn it." It was just enough for John, he knew the answer. What should he do? Should he do the honourable thing and drop out or should he go for it? These questions ran through his mind. That dollar would buy a lot of potato chips. He just loved potato chips. Then he thought to himself, "I'll wait to see how Laurie does, maybe she'll get it, then, I'll decide what to do." Laurie was next up.

She cautiously spelled out "r-e-c ....then paused for a moment--- everyone waited, then she quickly completed with, "c-i-n-d ".

"Repeat in full please," said Miss De Lacroix.

"R-e-c-c-i-n-d" repeated Laurie.

"That is not correct Laurie", said the teacher. "You have another chance."

"Oh, what the heck," said Laurie. And she quickly spelled out r-e-s-i-n-d.

"Sorry Laurie, that is not correct either," said the teacher.

"John, you have the last chance," said Miss De Lacroix.

Everyone waited. What would he say? This word by now had them all confused. John was not confused. He knew the answer but he must give it in such a way as to not let on that he had heard George. John thought that

George might think that he had heard him as he crossed the floor. John would purposely spell it wrong the first time round. That would throw George's suspicions off. He stood there pretending to think deeply for a moment. Then he quickly spelled out r-e- s-i-n-d.

"That is not correct John" said the teacher. The whole class waited quietly.

This time John took a deep breath and, to create just a little more drama, he slowly spelled out r-e-s-c-i-n-d. There was a moment's silence. The teacher stood there smiling and simply said, "You win. The dollar's yours!"

They all cheered and just at that moment the bell rang to end the day. They all scrambled for their things to go home. John took the dollar but felt very guilty for having been dishonest. He only consoled himself because the potato chips would taste so good. Of course he told no one what had truly happened. He may not have come first in the last semester's results, but he had won this contest.

John's dishonesty in the event had not bothered him much. As he matured he would develop a scrupulous conscience that would plague him, but it would revolve more around sexual matters rather than minor lapses in honesty.

John and his brother and sisters got on well together. He had been pleased when his younger brother, Timmy, was born. As they got older, John realized that Timmy loved sports and the outdoors. This greatly endeared him much more to their father. Truthfully, John always felt that his father preferred Timmy to him. This did provoke some arguments with his brother, even though they did love each other. He was delighted when his youngest sister, Clarisse, was born. John loved them all so very much that he always feared that something would happen to one of them and he would end up losing one of them. He always prayed very hard that God would protect them and take care of them.

He vividly remembered one incident that occurred on a snowy winter afternoon. It was a Sunday and they were going to visit Miriam's house. Just as they were arriving, his little sister Clarisse let go of Rose's hand and darted across the street. Rose called out loudly to Clarisse, "What are you doing, come back here, you will get yourself killed!" Although a car was coming, it was going fairly slowly. The driver saw Clarisse and quickly put his brakes on. As he did so, Clarisse slipped and fell, landing just in front of the car wheels. His mother screamed and rushed to pick her up from under the car wheels. John was frozen to the spot as he watched. His heart was pounding in his chest and he thanked God that nothing more serious had happened.

Clarisse was given a very strong scolding. "Why did you do that? That was very bad, Clarisse. You were lucky the driver of that car saw you in time! Don't ever do that again! Do you hear me?" Rose scolded her in a trembling voice.

Clarisse started to cry, saying, "But I don't want to go to Miriam's house. I want to go back home and play with my dolls. It's too long to wait there at Miriam's."

"We won't stay too long then," said Rose. "We'll just have a short visit and go back home. Mommy just needs to pick up some pickling jars. It won't be long, I promise."

But John kept this feeling of dread over the incident to himself. He couldn't imagine life without Clarisse; he loved her so much. Again John realized how fragile we all are. Once more he felt the foreboding feeling of loneliness and wondered if he would be able to cope with the many challenges of life.

The incident with Clarisse reminded John of one incident which occurred when he was only about six and a half years old, one that he liked to call his "alcoholic incident". This incident certainly showed that he could be as much of an impulsive child as any other and one that could cause much upset in the family. It was the one time that his sisters were furious at him.

It was Christmas time. John loved Christmas. He and his sisters would help his mother to decorate the tree beautifully. Christmas day seemed particularly special for him that year. John had received two special gifts – a cardboard gas station that he punched out and assembled and a small toy truck that he could play with in the sand. He had also discovered that beer with sugar in it was just delicious and, of course, his father had many bottles of beer in a carton near the tree. When his father would open a bottle, John would sneak a glass of it, sweeten it with sugar and just enjoy the frothy brew. This went on for a good part of the afternoon, and when he finally went out to slide in the snow with his sisters and brother, he could not stand up straight. He was too drunk. His sisters had to help him up the hill and keep him from falling off the cardboard slide. That evening they had all they could do to get him into the house. John laughed and laughed and as his head hit the pillow, he fell asleep at once.

One way that his sisters would try to make John obey, especially when it was close to Christmas, was by threatening that Santa Claus would overlook their house. In that case no presents would be placed under the Christmas tree. That threat wasn't too serious because he often did not get what he asked for from Santa anyway. However, he still believed strongly in Santa Claus. It made him feel very good to think that Santa could truly bring him a gift, if he wanted to.

This belief and warm feeling was dashed one afternoon when arguing with Caroline. They were screaming at each other because Caroline once again had nastily spilled a container of sand on Professor Hilchie's doorstep. Professor Hilchie was a French professor at the school. He was very particular about his property and wanted no children near it. He would become very annoyed if he caught someone hanging around the grounds especially at the back of his house where he had a beautiful garden. Caroline decided to play a trick on the Professor; John did not agree and started to protest. Then thinking that it would make a big difference to Caroline, he said to her, "If you keep on behaving like that you will get nothing from Santa come Christmas day."

"Oh you are so stupid, you really still believe in Santa Claus?" said Caroline as she looked at John in disbelief. "There is no Santa Claus! It's your parents and other relatives that give you the gifts. There is no Santa who comes with his sleigh and reindeer to deliver gifts!"

John was struck dumb! He could not believe his ears. He was devastated. He so loved his belief in Santa. He had to find out the truth. He ran home to question his Mom and Dad. Batist was still at work but his mother was there; Della also was at home that day. He entered the house completely out of breath, he had been running so hard.

"Mom, Mom," he cried, "Caroline just told me that there is no Santa. Is that true? Tell me, tell me!" Rose looked over at Della and Della at Rose. At first they were reduced to silence. Then Della said to her mother, "I think he needs to know now, the time has come!"

Rose looked at John with much regret and said to him, "Yes John, it is true. There is no Santa Claus. We are the ones who put the gifts under the Christmas tree when you are sleeping." What a disappointment. He was devastated. How could parents continue to deceive their children like that, he thought? But he would not divulge the truth to Timmy and Clarisse until they were ready to accept the truth. Anyway it was fun to go through all the secretive skulking around and the hiding of the gifts when Christmas rolled around. John would eventually learn through his studies and reading that a true tradition did exist concerning a wonderful saint by the name of Nicholas who was very good to people and gave them many wonderful gifts. It was from this tradition that the Santa Claus phenomenon had emerged.

Time passed and John reached First Communion age. By the age of seven in the Roman Catholic tradition, children were prepared for receiving the consecrated bread at the Eucharistic celebration. This was called "Making your First Communion." One of the events in the preparation process was learning to confess one's sins, so the children were taught how to confess the things that they had done wrong to the priest in the confessional. After confessing, one could go and receive the blessed bread which was considered very special because in receiving the blessed or consecrated bread, one was receiving the life of Jesus in one's soul. The confessional was a small house-like structure in the church that was divided in two parts, one for the priest and one part for the penitent to kneel in; there was a small window with a small screen and a small sliding shutter. A person would just go in and kneel down and the priest would open the little shutter and the person kneeling would tell him all the bad things he had done and the priest would pray a prayer of forgiveness over the person. It was a bit scary for John since the confessional was dark.

By this time as well, the Sisters and teachers at school had made John understand what a sin is and that God does not like sin, or those who indulge in sin, and especially any sin having to do with sexuality. If anything like this happened, it had to be confessed as soon as possible. John became very upset about this because he just did not know how to tell the priest what had happened between himself and his friend Miriam. In fact, he had never, ever discussed it with anyone and had kept it as a safely guarded secret; he had never even brought it up again with Miriam to find out what her thoughts were on it. Miriam's brother had not said anymore about it either; he was just pleased that John and Miriam had received a humiliating scolding over it and then left it at that.

When time came for the preparatory confession before receiving his First Communion, John just avoided the whole issue and did not even bring it up because he did not know how to explain it all. He felt quite awful about it! He participated in communion on the designated day with great apprehension. Instead of being filled with joy and happiness at this special event, John knelt at the altar rail for communion convinced that he was still in the state of serious sin and that Jesus was truly displeased with him. He did not want to make his first communion feeling this way. He felt like running away and hiding some place where no one knew him. His heart was heavy and again he felt extremely alone – alone at the age of seven. How long would he be able to live with such a feeling? How long would this feeling of desolation be with him?

Time, however, seemed to heal many wounds and John put the incident behind him; he even enjoyed going to church immensely. He loved Jesus, he loved the music and the singing, all the activities of the church. The part that John and other members of his family did not like about Church was the obligation to sit in a pew that belonged to the family as a rented space. In those days families rented a seat in the Church and if anyone was seated in a place that they were not renting they could be told to remove themselves from that seat. Their seat was rented by John's grandfather. John hated to sit in that seat when his grandfather was there with them. He had no qualms about breaking wind smack in the middle of the Eucharistic celebration; he would make a real production of it by raising his right buttock and launching the extremely loud, smelly bombshell. John hated this and would, therefore, discreetly look for a seat in another pew that often resulted in his being told to get out of the pew and go to his own. John rejoiced the day that Church pew rentals were abolished.

John did love to go to church and participate in the beautiful celebrations but he was distressed by a terrible feeling of unworthiness. Because of this, he felt the need to do things perfectly so that God would deem him worthy of his love; he would sometimes imagine God saying to him, "You are a very good boy and you do everything very well, so now I do love you!" He would continue to be in the dark about many things for a long time to come. In this state of loneliness, isolation and ignorance, John always longed for love and attention from both God and others and found it so very difficult to constantly desire God's approval and that of others. He never felt that he was truly loved, no matter what happened or how well he performed in and out of school. Already at a very young age he was experiencing the great pain that can be part of growing up, the pain of being alone. In such experiences he would find a place where he could be by himself and would pray to Jesus that he come to help him and fill him with his presence. Even that was quite difficult to do.

John discovered, however, that the pain of loneliness could be alleviated somewhat through the experience of the love of a creature that is not human, through the love of man's best friend, a beloved dog. However he also discovered that this experience could also have its share of pain.

Chapter Four

There was a tremendous silence in the plane as they flew on towards Kampala. Fr. John was suddenly awakened by a nudge on the arm. There, bending down towards him was the cute little black hostess with a drink and peanuts. He thanked her and gratefully took the refreshments. They were cruising towards Kampala and still had some forty-five or more minutes before landing. The students began to talk quietly amongst themselves. Fr. John had nothing with him, not even a book to read. He had left everything in Bukavu, even his toothbrush. He sat and looked out the window. There was still some light on the horizon.

He had been so exhausted from the stress of dealing with the soldiers and thinking about the terrible situation he had left behind in Bukavu that he had fallen asleep and failed to notice who the person was sitting next to him on this flight. That person he now discovered was Francois, the student of mixed ethnic blood whose father was Hutu and whose mother was Tutsi. He turned to Francois, and apologized for his lack of attention, Seeing the little black airline hostess again, with her very Tutsi-like features, offering him refreshments, turned his thoughts to the events that had led up to their running from Bukavu. Looking at Francois pensively, he said to Francois, "It really is a horrendous situation. I am realising now that these terrible events were predicted by a number of White Fathers whom I met when I was a student in the seminary who worked in the Central African region years ago. All that is happening now actually began early in the history of the Central African region. When I was a student, I often heard older colleagues coming back from the Central African missions speak about the volatility in the region, particularly in Rwanda. I can still hear one older missionary telling us during a conversation at dinner, "You will see, one day, there will be a terrible blow-up in Rwanda and there will be great blood-shed. It will be an awful disaster. The situation cannot continue as it is! A people cannot be kept down the way that it is happening in Rwanda. There will be a terrible awakening one day!"

The fear of such a blow up had been expressed within and outside of the community but nothing had ever been done by any government authority to avoid any kind of disaster. Fr. John however, had never forgotten those words of that older missionary. He was now living through this long ago predicted holocaust!

"That does not surprise me, Father," said Francois who was somewhat more mature than the other students. "I often worked with the youth at the mission in my quarter in Kigali and old Fr. Martin would often talk about this when we were sitting outside on the patio at the back of the compound after the evening meal. Even then, Fr. Martin felt that something was going to snap and it would be a terrible blow to the whole of the country."

"In those moments Fr. Martin would speak to me about the White Fathers of Africa, the community that both you and Fr. Martin belong to, "added Francois, "and the one that I am aspiring to be part of one day."

"So he told you about us, all about who we are?" questioned Fr. John.

"Oh yes, he shared with me the origins of the community and the missionary work that it was involved in. Why do you think I applied to be a member of this community? Fr. Martin was quite convincing. He spoke with passion and with love about his adopted family." Francois then continued, "I was very pleased to learn that the Society of the Missionaries of Africa was founded in North Africa. Our founder, a Frenchman, Cardinal Charles Lavigerie, was the first Archbishop of Algiers and eventually became Primate of the whole of Africa. Being a historian, he had the gift of being able to discern what Africa's needs were. He felt that there was a need for a community of men and women to work with the people of Algeria to improve living conditions, agriculture, and to care for the many orphans left after the famine of 1867. So, he started the community of the Missionaries of Africa in 1868 and then a year later he started the community of the Missionary Sisters of Our Lady of Africa. These men and women were to work closely with the Algerian people and see to the education and Christian instruction of the Arab orphans. All this made a very strong impression on me. What also impressed me was the fact that Cardinal Lavigerie had in mind not only the conversion of the Arabs but also the conversion of the peoples of Central Africa. What is also fascinating is that the founder did not have his missionaries dress in the traditional black and white robes of the clergy of that time but he had the men adopt the gandoura or cassock of the Arabs, along with the burnous, a hooded cape that protected the wearer from the wind and the night cold of the desert. A rosary was worn around the neck in imitation of the mesbaha of the marabouts. That was quite an amazing adaptation for the times. I also liked his idea of the rule of three; no one was to be alone in a mission station. There were to be at least three persons together living a community experience. He knew that being alone in a mission station was too fraught with dangers and difficulties. That was a very wise decision on his part," exclaimed Francois.

Charles Martial Lavigerie, founder of the religious Society of the White Fathers

Charles Martial Lavigerie, Founder of the Religious Society of the White Fathers

"I do agree with you," Francois. "Cardinal Lavigerie was a visionary for his time. The first missionary posts were established in Kabylie and in the Sahara. In 1876 and in 1881 two caravans from South Algeria and R'dames, intending to open missions in Sudan, were massacred by their guides as they attempted to cross the Sahara Desert. In 1878, therefore, ten missionaries left Algiers by ship to establish posts at Lake Victoria, Nyanza and Tanganyika. These now form the present Archdioceses of Kampala, Gitega, Tabora, and the dioceses of Kigoma, Lilongwe, and Kalemie-Kirungu. Many more missions were established in time. And at a very early stage, the missionaries of Africa, were baptised in the blood of martyrs. Did Fr. Martin tell you that we were the missionaries who were with the first martyrs of Uganda?"

Young Charles Martial Lavigerie

"Oh yes, in our many moments of sharing he told me all about the fires of Namugongo and the role that Fr. Simeon Lourdel, who was also known as Mapeera, played in caring for the young catechumens and their teachers. It is amazing that twenty-two young Africans gave their lives for their faith. The African Church is truly washed in the blood of the Lamb!"

"It's interesting how Fr. Lourdel got the nickname Mapeera," said Fr. John. "The Missionaries were French, of course, and they would address one another as 'Mon Pere' in French. When the people heard this, they understood Mapeera which means guava, a fruit, in the language of the people; so Fr. Lourdel became known by all as Mapeera, guava. I guess that for the people at the time that seemed quite appropriate."

"That is just as funny as it is interesting," laughed Francois. "Leave it to the people to put their own interpretation on things. Don't you just love it?" chuckled Francois.

Charles Martial Lavigerie with an Orphan

At that moment they launched into a discussion about Rwanda's history and the role that the Church and the community of the White Fathers had played in its development and in the present events. Fr. John felt that it would be interesting to find out what Francois thought about the present situation and the part that the Church had already played.

Fr. John knew there were theories that attempted to explain the arrival of the different ethnic groups on Rwandan soil and how the Tutsis and Hutus had reached this impasse. It was a rather long and interesting, if somewhat unbelievable, history. One would have thought that a country that is comprised of so few ethnic groups and having a common language and culture, would have produced a harmonious, well-governed society. That, however, had not been so.

"Do you have any idea, Francois, what the origins of the first peoples are who arrived in the region that eventually became Rwanda?" Fr. John asked. "Was it a very complicated situation? Was there much fighting or bickering? I did read up on the ideas of some historians and writers, but you may have another take on things from what you studied and read or even from what you may have learned through stories told in your family or in the community!"

"Well, there are different theories and accounts about when the region came into existence," said Francois, "but I don't think that it is known precisely when the country was first established. It is thought that humans moved into the area shortly after the last ice age, either in the Neolithic period, around ten thousand years ago, or in the long humid period which followed, up to around 3000 B.C.(1) Certain archaeological excavations have given us evidence that the earliest inhabitants of the region would have been a group of people known as the Batwa. This was a group of aboriginal Pygmy forest hunters and gatherers, who still live in Rwanda today.(2) These people live a nomadic life in the forest. It is known by the more open-minded Rwandese that the pygmy is often classed as a non-person, so primitive is his life-style thought to be. The other ethnic groups of Rwanda, however, will not hesitate to call upon the pygmies when they need mercenary help. They do not seem to be considered non-persons when it comes to situations involving wars."

Seminarians at the Noviciate of Missionaries of Africa

Fr. John was impressed by Francois' frankness when discussing the peoples of Rwanda. Most of the Rwandese that he had met, even the students, were very private persons, very cautious about what they said to others, especially to strangers, about Rwanda and even more so about their own personal lives. Fr. John remembered having had one Tutsi student at the training center who had written in a school term paper about the Rwandese mentality and culture. In the term paper he had clearly stated that when he had left for the seminary his mother had told him, "My son, remember that you must not let the fathers know what you are thinking!" That kind of advice for a situation where frankness and openness are encouraged is counter-productive if adamantly pursued. Upon hearing Francois' statement concerning the attitude towards the Pygmies, Fr. John felt quite free to continue the dialogue with him about Rwanda's situation.

Seminarians at the Spiritual Year (Noviciate) of Missionaries of Africa

"Would you say that the other ethnic groups in the country arrived pretty much at the same time as the Batwa or were the other migrations different?" Fr. John asked.

"From what I have read and the stories I have heard," said Francois, "the Batwa would have been partially supplanted by the immigration of a Bantu group, the forebears of the agriculturalist ethnic group, known as the Hutu.(3) They were the ones who began clearing the forests for their permanent settlements. You see, the Batwa are nomadic and so move throughout the forest, not having one specific settlement."

"There is a third ethnic group in Rwanda, the Tutsi. Would they have arrived at the same time as the Hutu or later?" Fr. John questioned.

"There was a third major immigration. The exact nature is highly contested, and they apparently didn't arrive in the region until the fourteenth century, which is pretty amazing when we realize how influential they became as an ethnic group. The Tutsi are, however, a predominantly pastoral people, owning large herds of cattle, that we know means wealth in all of Africa, not just in Central Africa," said Francois. "We must also be aware that as these other groups moved into the region, the Batwa retreated further into the forest giving way to the new groups of settlers."

"I had not realized that the Tutsis had arrived in the region at such a late date," said Fr. John. "They must have possessed some kind of extraordinary skills for them to have reached such a strong position in governing the country," exclaimed Fr. John.

"We do know that by the fifteenth century many of the Hutu and Tutsi had organized themselves into at least three small states. The oldest state was probably established by the Renge lineages of the Singa clan and covered most of modern day Rwanda, except for the northern region. (4) The Mubari state of the Zigaba clan also covered an extensive area. (5) The Gisaka state in southeast Rwanda was powerful, maintaining its independence until the mid-nineteenth century.(6) However, the latter two states are largely unmentioned in contemporary discussion of Rwandan civilisation."(7)

"That does not tell us why the Tutsi finally acquired such a strong allegiance with the other ethnic groups."

"The answer to that rests with one person and the position of that person in Rwandese society."

"In a person!" Fr. John exclaimed. "That is quite amazing, isn't it?"

"Why is that so amazing," said Francois, "since the same thing happened over and over again in Europe, and even in the Americas!"

"Oh, how short sighted can I be," said Fr. John. "Such a person could only be that of a king, could it not?"

"There is your answer," said Francois. "In the nineteenth century, the state became far more centralized. Expansion continued, reaching the shores of Lake Kivu.(8) This expansion was especially about a migrating population spreading Rwandan agricultural techniques, social organisation and the extension of a Mwami's political control; the Mwami being the king!(9) The king stood at the apex of the class system."

"How far did the Mwami's power go?" Fr. John questioned. "It had to be quite extensive!"

"Under the monarchy, the economic imbalance between the Hutus and the Tutsis crystallized; a complex political imbalance emerged as the Tutsis formed a hierarchy dominated by the Mwami.(10) The king was treated as a semi-divine being, responsible for making the country prosper. There is a myth that tells of three children who were born in heaven, and fell to earth by accident; one of these children, Kigwa, was the one who founded the most powerful Tutsi clan.(11) The Mwami trace their lineage to this divine founder."

Fr. John knew that it was traditionally believed that Rwanda was so special and beautiful in the eyes of God that after visiting all the parts of the world, his creation, during the day, that he would always return to Rwanda at night to sleep. Belief in these myths would certainly keep all of Rwanda's people loyal to the Mwami since being king he would have a special connection to God.

"Actually, I find that the myths about the monarchy of Rwanda are quite beautiful," said Fr. John. "It is also amazing that the king had such an important power base."

"That the king had an important power base is a real understatement, Fr. John," said Francois. "Let me tell you about the king's power base. The Mwami's power was his control of over a hundred large estates spread through out the kingdom.(12) They included fields of banana trees and many heads of cattle.(13) The most ornate of these estates was home to one of the king's wives, monarchs having up to twenty.(14) All the people of Rwanda were expected to do tribute to the Mwami, and this tribute was collected, in turn, by a Tutsi administrator.(15) Beneath the Mwami was also a Tutsi ministerial council of great chiefs, the batware b'intebe, while below them was a group of lesser Tutsi chiefs who governed the country in districts, each district having a cattle chief and a land chief.(16) The cattle chief collected tribute in livestock and the land chief collected tribute in produce. Beneath these chiefs were hill-chiefs and neighbourhood chiefs."(17)

"Where did the military fit into this scheme of things?" asked Fr. John. "The military had to have an important position of some kind. I'm sure that the country had to be protected."

"Oh yes, military chiefs were also important," answered Francois. "They had control over the frontier regions, protecting the frontier and making cattle raids against neighbouring tribes.(18) Lastly, the Biru or 'Council of Guardians' was also an important part of the administration. The Biru advised the Mwami on his duties where his supernatural powers were involved. They also advised on matters of court ritual. All these posts taken together existed to serve the power of the Mwami, and to reinforce the control of the Tutsi in Rwanda."(19)

"Did the military include both Hutu and Tutsi in its ranks?" Fr. John inquired. "Would the Mwami or King not have feared having Hutu soldiers guarding him since the king was always chosen from among the Tutsis, if I am not mistaken?" asked Fr. John.

"Surprisingly enough," answered Francois, "the military were a mix of Hutu and Tutsi drawn from across the kingdom.(20) The intermixing helped produce a uniformity of ritual and language in the region, and united the populace behind the Mwami.(21) Most evidence suggests that relations between Hutu and Tutsi were mostly peaceful at this time. Some words and expressions suggest that there may have been friction, but other than that, evidence supports peaceful interaction."(22)

"Was it really as peaceful as we are led to believe? Did the Hutu truly express the discontent that they felt or did they feel that they needed to hide their feelings of oppression?" Fr. John asked.

"That is a valid question," answered Francois. "I don't really know the answer to it. I would suspect that over time the Hutus became very discontented and, I think, felt oppressed and manipulated by the Tutsis. There were some moments of accommodation but the control of the situation eventually fell into the hands of the Tutsis," said Francois.

"A traditional local justice system called Gacaca predominated in much of the region as an institution for resolving conflicts, rendering justice and reconciliation.(23) The Tutsi king, however, was the ultimate judge and arbiter for those cases that reached him.(24) Despite the traditional nature of the system, harmony and cohesion had been established among Rwandans and within the kingdom.(25) Through a slow process that was mostly peaceful, the Tutsis took control. They used their ownership of cattle and their advanced combat and organizational skills to achieve economic, political, and social control over any other ethnic group.(26) At the same time, the distinction between the three ethnic groups remained somewhat fluid, in that Tutsis who lost their cattle due to a disease epidemic, such as Rinderpest, sometimes could be considered Hutu. Likewise, Hutus who obtained cattle would come to be considered Tutsi, thus climbing the ladder of the social strata.(27) This social mobility ended abruptly with the onset of colonial administration. What had hitherto been considered social class became ethnic.(28). Over time this Tutsi/Hutu relationship took the form of a client-patron contract, called Ubuhake, which eventually gave rise to a feudal-type class system. The Hutus indentured themselves to the Tutsi lord giving him agricultural products and personal service in exchange for use of land and cattle.(29)

"Do you truly believe, Francois, that the Hutu were happy with such an arrangement?" Fr. John inquired gently. "If that had been me in such a situation, I think that I would surely have rebelled!"

"The Hutu discontent was not so strong in the beginning," said Francois, "since a significant minority of the political elite were Hutu. Before the colonial period only about fifteen to sixteen percent of the population was Tutsi; many of these were poor peasants, but the majority of the ruling elite were Tutsi. It is really the Europeans who simplified this arrangement and applied what is known as the 'Hamitic Theory' to the unfortunate ethnic problem. I have never really understood what this 'Hamitic Theory' is trying to tell us! What does it mean?" said Francois.

"Well, Francois, let me try to explain it to you." Fr. John told him. "The 'Hamitic Theory' is based on a tradition of Old Testament interpretation that identifies the descendants of Ham – Noah's son cursed for his sinfulness – as dark-skinned Africans. This theory was originally used to justify slavery and racism against all blacks, but revised to justify favouritism by the colonial powers – and the Church – of the lighter-skinned Tutsi.(30) They were cast as divinely instituted rulers. Europe had something similar in the divine right of kings."

"Alright, I do understand that," said Francois. "What happened then was that the Europeans decided upon a policy of indirect rule and favoured the Tutsi – taller, thinner and lighter in color – over the Hutu. They centralized power in a single chief and gave the Tutsi control of the judicial system.(31) As a result, the majority Hutu were excluded from participation in Rwandan politics. The ideology supporting this ethnic differentiation was that certain races were born to rule whereas others were born to be ruled.(32) What happened then in Rwanda is not surprising; one ethnic group was elevated over another," exclaimed Francois. "Of course, when the Europeans arrived in Central Africa, there was already a monarchy in place and they needed to ascertain how they would work with this type of government. They were not easily accepted in the beginning, and neither was the Church easily accepted by the elite class. It would be good to take a look at who was ruling at the time and how the Central African region came to be ruled by the European groups who eventually took control in the region."

"Do you think that it is really the colonial powers who eventually ruled Rwanda, who firmly established the distinction between the ethnic groups and the animosity that eventually developed?" asked Fr. John.

"Well I don't think that they created the distinction between the Hutu and the Tutsi, but I think I can say that they certainly aggravated it. The colonialists did do their best to justify and consolidate the rule of the Tutsi elite, I am convinced of that, Fr. John," (33) said Francois.

"In 1894 one of the sons of the elite ruling class and son of the Mwami, Rutarindwa, inherited the kingdom from his father Mwami Rwabugiri IV, but many of the king's council were unhappy. There was a rebellion and the family was killed. One of the elite group of Tutsis named Yuhi Musinga inherited the throne through his mother and uncles, but there was still dissent.(34) This would prove beneficial for colonial powers wanting to firmly establish their authority."

"How could dissent within the monarchy prove beneficial for the colonial powers?" Fr. John asked.

Francois continued, "Unlike much of Africa, the fate of Rwanda and the Great Lakes region was not decided by the 1884 Berlin Conference. Instead, the region was divided in an 1890 conference in Brussels.(35) Rwanda and Burundi, being at the juncture of three empires, became the object of a diplomatic fight for possession. The Belgians under Leopold II, and the Germans and the British wanted possession of the territory. The 1890 conference, however, gave Rwanda and Burundi to the German Empire as colonial spheres of interest, and they in turn renounced all claims on Uganda, in exchange for being given the island of Heligoland. (36) These agreements apparently left Belgium with a claim on the western half of the country. After several border skirmishes, the final borders of the colony could still not be established until 1900. These borders contained the kingdom of Rwanda as well as a group of smaller kingdoms on the shore of Lake Victoria."(37)

"So who were the first Europeans to set foot in Rwanda, Germans or Belgians?" Fr. John asked, puzzled. "I thought we said that the Germans had been given the territory, but then Belgium seems to be mentioned at one point," said Fr. John.

"It was the Germans who first controlled the area," said Francois. "The Belgians appeared later. The first European to set foot in Rwanda was Count Gustav Adolph von Gotzen, a German.(38) He entered Rwanda at Rusumo Falls, and then traveled right through Rwanda, meeting Mwami Rwabugiri at his palace in Nyanza in 1894, and eventually reaching Lake Kivu, the western edge of the kingdom. The next year the king died, placing Rwanda in a state of turmoil over the succession. The Rwandans were divided with a portion of the royal court being very wary of the Germans and the other seeing the Germans as a welcome alternative to the Buganda or the Belgians. The Germans took advantage of the divisive situation and moved in from Tanzania to claim the region for the Kaiser. War and division seemed to open the door for colonialism. At the same time the Germans claimed Burundi, a separate kingdom to the south. The entire area was created as one colony, to be known as Ruanda-Urundi. (39) The Germans ruled indirectly through the King, the Mwami. In the early years, the Germans were completely dependent on the indigenous government; neither did they encourage modernization and centralization of the regime. What is more serious, however, is that during this period many Europeans had become obsessed with the study of race, and this had an impact on life in Rwanda. For the Germans, the Tutsi ruling class was a superior racial type. Because of their apparent "Hamitic" origins on the Horn of Africa, they were thought to be more "European" than the Hutu they oppressed. Because of their seemingly taller stature, more "honourable and eloquent" personalities and their willingness to convert to Roman Catholicism, the Tutsis were favoured by colonists and powerful Roman Catholic officials. They were put in charge of the farming Hutus, the newly formed principalities, and were given ruling positions. The Germans romanticized Tutsi origins, as would the Belgians at a later time.(40)

"In 1895, Rwanda became part of German East Africa along with Burundi and Tanganyika. The following year, in 1896, Mwami Mibambwe IV Rutalindwa was succeeded by Mwami Musinga Yuhi V in the 'coup d'etat' of Rucuncu."(41)

"Was it not at this time that the White Fathers were received in Rwanda as the first group of European Catholic missionaries – they would have been called the 'Peres Blancs' at the time?" asked Fr John.

"That is correct," said Francois. "It was effectively during the German colonial days that the Missionaries of Africa, the White Fathers, came into the area, bringing the Roman Catholic faith to the people, along with hospitals and schools. It was Mwami Musinga who received them."(42)

"You are right, Francois," said Fr. John. "If I remember correctly from my studies, it was a Fr. Leon Classe who was the strong link for the missionary community at the time. He later became the first Bishop of the Roman Catholic Church in Rwanda. Initially, the Tutsi perceived the missionaries as a threat to their established power. The Tutsi chiefs and policy makers agreed that the missionaries should be limited to interaction with the Hutu. The early converts to Christianity, therefore, were predominantly Hutu peasants. This process of evangelization went against the White Fathers' mandate to evangelize from the top down – to convert the purportedly superior Tutsi first; that it did not work in Rwanda was a challenge. In 1907, however, this perception began to shift with the arrival of Fr. Leon Classe, a staunch advocate of the hierarchical method of evangelization. Fr. Classe believed that the success of the Rwandan mission depended on the conversion of the Tutsi; though he did not oppose Hutu advancement per se. In his stance for a Tutsi-led church he applied the 'Hamitic Theory' to theology.(43) Being a Bishop, Classe had the authority to enforce his theory; he was convinced, along with other colonists, that the Tutsis were the only ones who had the intelligence and the capabilities to run the country, and so promoted this idea. This, along with his brutal administration of Church policy and political power did not endear him or the church to many in the population. When tensions arose within the mission itself over its responsibilities, Bishop Classe's argument was decisive. 'You must choose the Tutsi because the government will probably refuse Hutu teachers. In the government the positions in every branch of the administration will be reserved henceforth for young Tutsis.'"(44)

At this point Francois interjected, "It is amazing that Bishop Classe was able to turn things around in the process of evangelization, and a turn around certainly did occur after he appeared on the scene."

"Prior to Bishop Classe's arrival," said Fr. John, "the White Fathers had resigned themselves to establishing an indigenous Hutu church – a goal which required educated clergy. Although there were Hutu ordinations, the vast majority of candidates abandoned the seminaries. With their education, however, many Hutus were able to attain positions as teachers and administrators within the colonial system, thus upsetting the social hierarchy and legitimating Tutsi suspicion of the missions. This might have been the end of Christianity in Rwanda, but an unbelievable event took place that quelled social instability and set church and state on another course."(45)

"I know about the event you speak of," Francois smiled. "It has to be the conversion and enthronement of Tutsi King Mutara Rudahigwa as Mutara III."(46)

"Yes, that's correct," said Fr. John. "The conversion of King Rudahigwa sparked a rush of Tutsi converts to Christianity. With his conversion, conditions turned favourable for evangelization through the chiefs to the masses. Once the leaders converted, there was social pressure for the masses to convert as well. The sociologist Ian Linden noted, 'In a remarkable way, Catholicism became 'traditional' the moment the Tutsi were baptized in large numbers.' Not only did it become traditional, it also became the state religion."(47)

"One of the consequences," said Fr. John, "is that many of the converts were ill-prepared and drawn into the church for questionable motives such as social and economic benefits."(48)

"Add to that, of course, the Germans' need for a streamlined administration," said Francois, "which pushed them to strongly encourage the Mwami to gain greater control over Rwandan affairs. But there were forces that entered with the German colonial authority that had the opposite effect.(49) For instance, Tutsi power weakened through exposure of Rwanda to capitalist European forces. Money came to be seen by many Hutus as a replacement for cattle, in terms of both economic property and for purposes of creating social standing.(50) Another way in which Tutsi power was weakened by Germany was through the introduction of the head-tax on all Rwandans. As some Tutsis had feared, the introduction of this tax also made the Hutus feel less bonded to the will of their Tutsi patrons and more dependent on the European foreigners, any head-tax necessarily implying equality between any of those heads being counted – whether Hutu or Tutsi. Thus, despite Germany's attempt to uphold traditional Tutsi domination of the Hutus, the Hutu were now getting a taste of autonomy from Tutsi rule.(14) This, of course had its adverse consequences over time and on May 4, 1910 the Germans ended up helping the Tutsis put down a rebellion of Hutus in the northern part of Rwanda who did not wish to submit to central Tutsi control."(51)

"I presume that the discontent that the Hutus had felt now started to surface. They must have felt more at liberty to protest and had possibly lost a lot of their fear of reprisals," said Fr. John. "There was also a clear bias by the Catholic church for the Tutsi, who thereby acquired a monopoly on positions of authority and control, not only in industry but in the political bureaucracy as well. The Catholic Church took control of education and their educational policy resulted in clear discrimination against the Hutu in most of Rwanda's Catholic mission schools. The alliance between church and state introduced a more marked stratification between ethnic groups than had existed in the past. And as stratification intensified, ethnic distinctions were sharpened. The mission schools' bias in favour of the Tutsi against the Hutu was a major factor in hardening ethnic divisions and spurring resentment."(52)

"Then the Germans lost power in the course of the First World War. This created a whole new situation," said Francois. "While the earlier agreements had called for the region to remain neutral in the event of a European war, this was disregarded after the outbreak of World War 1. Small forces of Europeans, backed by large numbers of locals fought for control of the region. The main offensive was by the Belgians who in 1916 advanced from the Congo into Germany's East African colonies, quickly forcing the Germans out of the region. A British offensive from Uganda that was comprised of British machine gunners preventing the Germans from mounting a successful counter-attack came next. The German army was now in almost full retreat. The Belgians then released Congolese raiders who proceeded to loot and pillage the region. A great number of Rwandans, who were fighting alongside the Germans, were killed in the long German retreat.(53) The Germans were defeated in World War I, and at the end of the war Belgium was officially granted the League of Nations mandate to administer both Rwanda and Burundi under the name of Ruanda-Urundi along with its existing Congo colony to the west. The Belgian government continued to rely on the Tutsi power structure for administering the country, though their involvement in the region was far more direct than German involvement had been and extended its interests into education and agricultural supervision. This created additional problems because of their insistence on political favouritism and on turning a profit especially in the production of coffee. The Belgians also considered the Tutsis to be the superior race and systematically imposed their authority over the Hutu across the colonial administration and the access to education, engendering great frustration among the other Rwandans."(54)

"You know, Francois, what really interests me is how all of this political, racial and authoritative handling of the population and situation affected the church and its role in the whole scheme of things. It is very disturbing to hear about all that the church is being accused of at the moment and the terrible way that we are being implicated in the present genocide," said Fr. John vehemently.

"If we go back and look at the German and Belgian presence at that time, we see that the church played a significant role in things." replied Francois. "Both the German missionary clergy as well as the Belgian missionaries fully supported a Tutsi church-state alliance. This alliance started to come apart after World War II, when colonial, political and religious support for the Tutsi was gradually transferred to the Hutu. Several factors account for this shift. First, Belgium's exploitation of Rwanda during the war generated anti-colonialist sentiment, and the empowered Tutsi began to rail at their colonial yoke. Because of the alliance between church and state, the church was also implicated in this discontent. Second, the champion of a Tutsi dominated church, Fr. Classe, died in 1945. According to the historian Gerard Prunier, Classe was 'almost a national monument' for his influence on Rwandan politics.(55) Classe was replaced by the White Father, Laurent Deprimoz, who began to address the divisive nature of ethnicity within the Rwandan church. Perhaps inevitably, however, Deprimoz's efforts backfired and only made these divisions more strident. Third, the number of indigenous clergy, the majority of whom were Tutsi, came to equal the number of European clergy, and a struggle ensued for control of the church. The imbalance of power between the White Fathers and indigenous clergy caused great resentment among the latter. This struggle was intensified by new Belgian missionaries who were. Flemish rather than Walloon and from humbler social classes. They did not sympathize with the aristocratic Tutsi but encouraged the downtrodden Hutu."(56)

"I believe, Francois, that you forgot to mention the shattering of one of the final vestiges of colonial control over Rwanda that also occurred around this time!" Fr. John stated.

"Which final vestige are you referring to?" Francois asked.

"The death of King Rudahigwa in 1959," exclaimed Fr. John. "We must not forget that he was the Christian king who made such a huge difference in the Tutsi population by embracing the Catholic faith!"

"That is so true," said Francois. "His death was followed by the investiture of his successor, Jean-Baptiste Ndahindurwa, who took the name Kigeri V. This transition of power precipitated a civil war. Tutsi and Hutu formed factions poised against one another. Pushed by Tutsi clergy, Bishop Aloys Bigirumwami, of the Nyundo vicarate, became the symbolic figurehead of the Tutsi faction, the Union Nationale Rwandaise. At the same time, Bishop Andre Perraudin, of Kabgayi, was perceived as the champion of the oppressed Hutu for his insistence on the church's social teaching. Though they had issued a joint letter calling for peace, the bishops and church were swept into the emerging violence. The powder keg," underlined Francois, "exploded in November 1959, after the brutal attack on a Hutu activist. A peasant revolt broke out leaving hundreds dead and thousands displaced. Thereafter, through political guile and propaganda, the Hutu nationalists gained support and momentum and thus a movement towards independence developed."(57)

At this point Fr. John interrupted Francois to add a personal note of his own to what Francois was saying: "When I was a student I had a colleague tell me about what Bishop Perraudin had told the university students at one point while speaking about the political situation in Rwanda. He said 'Why are you still living as slaves of a feudal system? You have the numbers and the means to establish political parties and so win power in elections! What are you waiting for?' And with that, the independence movement was born."

"Ah yes Father," said Francois, "and we know now that this movement was much stronger in Ruanda than in Urundi. The Hutu leaders published a 'Hutu Manifesto' preparing all supporters for a future political conflict to be conducted entirely on ethnic lines. In the late 1950's, the first outbreaks of the violence that we spoke of were sparked by a group of Tutsi political activists in Gitarama beating a Hutu rival. This resulted in a nation-wide campaign of Hutu violence against Tutsis that became known as 'the winds of destruction.' Many Tutsis fled from Ruanda, including the young Tutsi who was to inherit the Mwami's throne. The young zealous politicians took Bishop Perraudin at his word. In the 1960 election, the Hutu politicians scored an overwhelming victory. Gregoire Kayibanda, one of the authors of the 'Hutu Manifesto', led the provisional government for the interim period to independence. The two parts of Ruanda-Urundi became independent in July of 1962; the United Nations wanted them to remain federated as a single nation, but both opted to go their separate ways. Ruanda became a republic and the spelling of the name changed to Rwanda and Urundi became Burundi."(58)

"Do you know, Francois, what pains me the most about all the events which led to independence?" Fr. John said as he interrupted Francois at this point. "It is that the independence granted by Belgium on July 1, 1962, brought only deeper wounds," he said sadly. "Following independence, the Hutu took over governmental positions from the Tutsi, and the oppressed rapidly became the oppressors. The Hutu turned the 'Hamitic theory' against the Tutsi, who were recast as 'Hamitic invaders and colonialists. Many Tutsis fled north into Uganda from where they staged raids on the Hutu, who retaliated in turn."

"Under the government of Gregoire Kayibanda, the first president of Rwanda," Francois said sadly, "thousands of Tutsis were killed. The new government's platform was clear: it was for the liberation of the Hutu people. In the spirit of Kayibanda's movement, "cockroach" became the favourite slang name for Tutsi. The killing of cockroaches became a too familiar feature of the new government, especially when the Tutsis attempted an invasion from across the border. One such attempt was made by Tutsi guerrillas in December of 1963; however, they were massacred by the Rwandan army. A state of emergency was declared; a horrendous massacre of 14,000 Tutsis in the region of Gikongoro ensued. In the interim, there was a coup within the Hutu regime and in 1973 Kayibanda was removed from power and a Major General Juvenal Habyarimana was placed at the head of the government."

"What is unbelievable," said Fr. John, "is that Habyarimana remained in power for twenty-one years! That is a long time! I believe, however, that his biggest mistake was in running a conventional military dictatorship.

Add to that, the fact that he was governing in this way with the enthusiastic support of several western countries, especially France. We must admit that he was not vigilant enough about the dissent that was rampant inside and outside of his own government even after having governed for so long a time. He tried to initiate changes too late; it was really a case of too little too late. His Hutu electoral policy created an increasing problem on Rwanda's border. There were vast numbers of mainly Tutsi refugees on the other side of the borders; they became increasingly unwelcome in their host countries. Efforts were made to send them home to Rwanda, but Rwanda rejected them as well. In 1986, however, President Habyarimana stated that as a matter of policy there would be a right of return for Rwandese refugees. The RPF or Rwandese Patriotic Front had already been formed and was growing in numbers. They became committed to armed struggle against the Habyarimana regime."(59)

At this point, Francois interjected, "In October 1990, the Patriotic Front moved from the Ugandan southern territory into Rwanda. The invasion had begun, the country was at war, though many did not realize it; a war that would eventually result in the terrible genocide that we face at the moment. First, there is the wave of Tutsi refugees, fleeing the killer militia known as the Interahamwe; these killers incited many of the population to help in their massacre of the Tutsis. Secondly, there is now the wave of Hutu refugees, fleeing the Patriotic Front that has finally taken power. The Patriotic Front is comprised mainly of Tutsis from the southern territories of Uganda, from certain areas of Zaire, from Burundi, and from Rwanda itself. Their training has taken place mainly in Uganda. This well-trained army is intent on revenging the killing of its people; they want the world to believe that they have come purely to liberate their people from massacre and oppression. However, their arrival and take-over is going much deeper than simple liberation!"

"We must not forget the intervention of the Catholic church in November of 1991," said Fr. John. "The Catholic bishops of Rwanda issued a letter to priests on the 'Pastoral Role in Rebuilding Rwanda.' A central theme of this letter was the need to overcome ethnic divisions. Thaddee Nsengiyumva, bishop of Kabgayi and president of the Rwandan Episcopal Conference, acknowledged the church's complicity in perpetuating these divisions by declaring in a public letter dated December 1, 1991, that 'the church is sick.' Was this also too little, too late? Certainly too little to prevent the present genocide when Habyarimana's murder gave Hutu extremists within his regime free reign to execute their 'final solution.'(60) Was it not too little as well to prevent the Patriotic Front from exercising their belief that they still possess the Divine Right to rule?"

"As we flee," answered Francois, "we know that the war and the violence are going much further than the Rwandese situation! We know that it continues to escalate and that it has spilled over different borders, including into Zaire; we now know that many from the border towns have to flee the violence and the killing, and so it is that we find ourselves in this nineteen seater airplane fleeing to Kampala, Uganda, to escape a very possible massacre! I pray, Fr. John that all turns out well for us and that Zaire, especially Bukavu, will not be too devastated"

Chapter Five

John hadn't had many pets in his young life. The family was too poor. There had been a number of cats born in the old stone root cellar behind the house but they never stayed around for long, being undomesticated. However, to his utter joy, John received a puppy for his tenth birthday. He was overjoyed. He could not believe that this was happening to him.

John's dog, Buddy, was a black Cocker Spaniel given to him by his godfather. He was elated by this gift. Buddy would run to meet John when he got home from school each evening. He would jump up on John barking and yelping with excitement. John thought it was almost worth going to the school he hated to be able to come home at the end of the day to his much loved Buddy.

As time passed, Buddy became very aggressive and would not just jump on people, but would snap and bite them. John tried to hide this since he feared the consequences if his father found out; this would be intolerable. They could not own a dog that bit people! John's father did find out about Buddy soon enough since many people who came to the house complained about the dog's biting. John's father threatened to get rid of Buddy. John tried everything to get him to stop; he was afraid that he would lose Buddy. He often came home from school dreading to find that Buddy had disappeared.

One morning as John left home early for school, he did notice that his father had a burlap potato sack in his hand as he opened the shed door to let Buddy out. Of course, Buddy came running to John, jumping all over him as he usually did. His father threw the bag behind the shed door, suspecting, of course, that John had seen it in his hand. As John closed the front gate he was filled once again with a foreboding fear, fear for Buddy and what might happen to him. What was his father doing with that burlap bag, John wondered? He was troubled that whole day at school.

When John returned home that evening, there was no Buddy to meet him. What had happened? He was beside himself with worry and he insisted on knowing from his mother and father what had happened to Buddy. His mother insisted that she knew nothing; his father denied having even touched the dog! John was totally devastated. Where could he have gone? Maybe someone had hit him with their car and killed him; he sometimes did get out of the yard if the gate was left open. However, there was no evidence of that whatsoever. Maybe someone had stolen him. John could not believe this! Who could do such a thing!

Time passed and the pain became just a dull ache. He prayed that he would overcome this loss. It was John's first real experience with grief. John, however, was not yet mature enough to put the whole experience in such terms. What he did know was that he was painfully sad. He was a young boy mourning the loss of his dog.

One month and then a second month went by and Buddy did not return. He was often in John's thoughts. One afternoon, John and a few of his friends were playing on the shore. They loved being close to the water. They also had permission from their parents to use the small dinghy that was tied to the wharf, as long as they did not go too far from the shore. John at first hesitated to get into the boat, fearing that it would tip over. He was not a very good swimmer. Ricky, a classmate, pushed the dinghy from the wharf and was watching the flatfish swimming on the ocean bottom. Suddenly, he shouted out, "Hey, there is something on the floor of the ocean here. It looks like a bag of some kind! I wonder what's in it?" John's suspicions were aroused and he did not hesitate to get Ricky to help him get the bag to the surface. They both managed to use the oars to bring the bag up. It was quite heavy and took several attempts before they managed to get the bag near enough to the dinghy to grasp it. Ricky quickly untied the rope holding the bag closed and without fear emptied the burlap sack into the water. There, floating on the ocean was the bloated body of John's dog, Buddy. John stared at it, speechless. Then he began to scream and cry to be taken to shore. Ricky, horrified, obeyed immediately. What John had feared most had happened! Buddy had been drowned! He felt sick to his stomach.

John now suspected what had happened. He remembered his father holding the burlap bag in his hand and quickly throwing it behind the shed door when he realized that John was looking at him. He had drowned Buddy that morning. John ran home and confronted his father who was just getting home from work. He stormed into the house and screamed, "You killed him! You drowned him! How could you do such a horrible thing?"

"What are you talking about?" asked his father as he looked at John incredulously.

"I'm talking about Buddy. We found him this morning in the burlap bag you used to drown him! Do you hate me so much that you would do such a despicable thing? I can't believe this! I will never forget this as long as I live," cried John. John was inconsolable. His mother tried to calm him down but she was lost for words. All John's father could say was, "I'm sorry it had to be that way, but I had to do what needed to be done. Buddy would have eventually brought us a lot of trouble and that was the only way that I was able to deal with it. Maybe you will understand better once you are older. Right now, all I can say is that I'm sorry for your pain. I know that you are hurting. It will pass."

John's hatred for his father grew even more. He would eventually see things differently but that would take a long time. He still had many years to go to mature; the road would be a long and rough one.

Not long after the horrendous experience over Buddy, an incident occurred for which John received a great deal of attention but no approval from anyone. In fact many were quite furious with him, especially his father. It was also an incident that was of John's own making.

The Cosman family, who lived next door, had a son named Billy and John enjoyed playing with Billy very much. Billy enjoyed the same things John did and they would often read adventure comic books together; Billy also had many Hardy Boys mystery novels and he would lend them to John.

They both loved the Hardy Boys adventures. Billy's father, Gerry Cosman, was a bank manager. Their better financial means made it possible for Billy to have things that John's family could not afford, like good books. Billy, being a true friend, did not try to pick fights with John and never ridiculed John; he would share with him all those things that he loved best.

One afternoon during the summer holidays while John and Billy were playing in the field behind John's house, John had an idea for an adventurous experience. He thought that it would be fun to hide somewhere for a long while during the day, pretending that they had been captured by smugglers somewhat like an adventure in their Hardy Boys novels. John also felt that it would be interesting to see how their Dads would react. Billy was not too keen about this in the beginning. He did not want to make his parents worry. "How long would we stay hidden?" Billy asked.

"Oh, for two to three hours," answered John. "We have to give everyone a bit of a scare! Then we'll suddenly reappear! It will be a great adventure and I know the perfect place to hide. There's a space just behind the chimney of my house that is perfect for two people to stand in. I have hidden in that space many times before. When you are there no one can see you. The chimney of my house goes from the ground right up to over the roof top and there is that space where the chimney comes close to the corner of the house. Come, I'll show you."

They brought some comic books with them to read while hiding. It was already three-thirty in the afternoon when their adventure began. At first they talked about school and what they liked and disliked about it. There were teachers that Billy did not like either and, like John, he did not like Sr. Gemma. Once in a while they would stick their heads out around the chimney to see if anyone was around. Things seemed pretty normal and so they started reading their comics. It was a bit warm in the niche; the sun had been shining all day and they were enjoying their summer holidays.

Supper time came and John's father arrived home from work. Batist always looked at the wood box and the water buckets that were in the porch when he got home in the evening. Those were John's chores to be done before supper, filling the wood box with kindling and the water buckets with fresh drinking water from the well. They were not done and John was not around! When they sat down to eat, everyone was at the table except

John. Batist sent Tim to call him for supper. He came back saying that he had called but got no response. None of his sisters had seen him since early afternoon. Where could he be? Batist ate quickly and went out looking for him, but he couldn't find him. At the Cosman's house, he discovered that Billy was also missing. They were not too worried since they ate late, waiting for Mr. Cosman to come home from the bank. Batist continued to shout for both boys, but in vain. Batist decided to check the wells; there were two on the property. They had not taken the small row boats since they were both tied to the wharf at the shore. He even checked the four village grocery stores, and still nothing. John, of course, had watched his father as he had checked one of the wells in the field.

"My Dad is checking the well," he told Billy. "They really cannot find us! This is a perfect adventure!"

"They will be very angry at us. They must be so worried about us!" exclaimed Billy. "We had better show ourselves!"

"We'll wait another ten minutes," said John. "It should be close to six o'clock by then."

Suddenly they came out just as John's father was coming back from checking the old ice house that was down by the shore. The children often played there but there was always the possibility of their getting hurt there as well.

"We're here, we're here," John called as he came running from behind the house with Billy in tow.

John's father stopped short, fury written all over his face. "Where were you? I have been looking for you frantically everywhere! Didn't you hear me calling you? I thought you had hurt yourself or fallen into one of the wells!"

"We were just behind the chimney," said John. When Billy saw how angry John's father was, he ran for home. Batist told John to get into the house immediately. He was to do his chores and then go to bed without supper. On top of that, he was grounded for a week with no visitors. John's brother said to him, "Why did you do that? We were really scared something had happened to you! Mom was crying. I saw her. That was mean of you!"

John felt bad for his mother. He hadn't meant to hurt her or anyone. He noticed that his sisters were very cool towards him and had no sympathy for his punishment. They thought that he had been an insensitive little jerk. But he had simply wanted to have his very own adventure!

It was a long, difficult week for him especially since the weather continued to be beautiful and his father was unrelenting about his completing the full punishment. He was a prisoner in his own house and yard. He also missed playing with Billy very much. He hoped Billy wasn't too angry with him!

John did wonder as he got older and reflected on some of life's events, if he had not concocted such a nasty adventure to get back at his Dad for the loss of Buddy. Life continued on and there would be many more adventures, pleasant ones and not so pleasant ones to be sure.

One episode that turned out to be hilarious was the chamber pot episode. As John got older his mother and father gave him more responsibilities. Besides his regular chores of filling the water buckets and the wood box each day, John also had to fill the coal bin since the family used some coal for heating the kitchen stove for cooking, and he had to empty the chamber pails that were kept in each bedroom. One summer afternoon when he arrived home from the post office, John's Mom told him that the chamber pails needed to be emptied. This was usually done at bedtime. "You can do that now if you like or wait till it's dark if you wish," John's mother told him.

"I'll do it now," said John. "I really don't care who sees me carrying the chamber pails into the field to be emptied. That is a bodily function that everyone does!" John would take the chamber pails to a place in the field where there were big trees and where a deep hole had been dug for this purpose. He would empty the pails and then throw lime over top and place a cover over the hole.

John picked up the two white and blue enamel pails by the handles and was making his way towards the side porch entrance to go out. When he reached the doorway to the kitchen from the living- room, his mother made signs to him to go back into the bedroom and quickly whispered to him that Mrs. Bruneau was coming in, probably collecting for the March of Dimes or the Red Cross. John knew that Mrs. Bruneau was quite haughty and would have been highly insulted to have chamber pails paraded before her. She would also have made sure that the whole village would know of the incident. Therefore John turned quickly on his heels and headed back for the bedroom to wait till Mrs. Uppity was gone. But when he turned to go into the bedroom his feet slipped on his mother's well-polished floor and down he went. As he fell he tried to stretch out his arms as he held tightly to the pails to prevent them from spilling. But the covers of the chamber pails flew off and the sound of the enamel covers clanging on the floor rang out. Of course, some of the contents spilled. John just stayed in his extremely uncomfortable position, hoping Mrs. Bruneau had not heard the clanging noise. That was not to be!

"Oh my, did someone have an accident?" inquired Mrs. Bruneau.

"Oh it's simply John fooling around in the bedroom again!" answered Rose. "He is always up to some kind of mischief!

"Oh dear, oh dear," exclaimed Mrs. Bruneau. "Boys will be boys, won't they?"

"Yes, it is not easy bringing them up for sure!" answered John's mother.

Once Mrs. Bruneau had left, Rose came to see what had happened. John was still sprawled out on the floor, pleased that he could now get up.

"What did you do, for heaven's sake?" asked his mother. When she saw what had happened, she did not seem too concerned about John having hurt himself in the fall but was more concerned about the spilling of the chamber pail contents. "If you got pee all over my new wall paper, I'll beat you over the head with the chamber pails," said John's mother.

"Oh sure, you're more concerned about your wall paper than whether I hurt myself or not! Thanks a lot!" said John. "I'm sure Mrs. Uppity wondered what was going on!" declared John.

"Well you know these people. They can afford servants so they have lots of time to be collecting for all kinds of things. There is always one of them in the doorway looking for money that we don't have," said Rose. Then they both looked at one another and burst out laughing. Nothing had spilled on the precious wall paper but some had landed on the floor.

"You'll clean up that mess. I'm not doing it. I have to get the supper on the stove! Make sure that it is properly cleaned and that there is no smell. You can use some of the deodorizer that is on my dresser," Rose informed John.

John could never remember this incident without a chuckle. He only wished that all episodes and events in his youth could bring such smiles to his lips. Unfortunately that was not so.

John remembered that the ice floe-hopping event was one such incident. It turned out to be a dangerous, frightening and tense event that had involved the police. Ice floes or "clampers" gather along the shoreline during the winter months, swept in on the tides. They are not as big as icebergs but can be fairly large. In John's youth they came from the open ocean, easily floating into Chedabucto Bay, since the Canso Causeway had not been built yet and so allowed the ice to float freely through the icy waters. John just loved to see how daring he could be as he jumped from one ice floe to another as he made his way home from school in the evenings. This activity was very dangerous. If he slipped and fell between the floes, it would be a miracle if he managed to be able to get back on; he would more than likely be dragged under water. But, for John, the danger was attractive.

One Saturday afternoon in the winter, John decided to do a bit of 'hop-wetting' as the activity was often called. He wanted to see if he could hop on to a floe that was at the periphery of the row and so be facing the open water. The danger was that he could find himself floating out into the open water on the lone floe. He had the urge to try this no matter what the outcome. The row of floes was about five wide to the periphery. He managed to clear the first three. The fourth one was a bit far and he was not sure that he could clear the jump without falling into the icy water. He jiggled the floe that he was on a few times with his feet in an attempt to get it closer to the fourth that was close to the fifth. He leaped onto the fourth almost falling headlong into the water. He fell on his backside and fortunately did not slide further but held on. Then he jiggled the fourth floe moving it closer to the fifth. He jumped, held and realized that he had sent the fifth floe too far into the open water. Immediately he began to jiggle the floe to bring it back closer to the others. As all his attention was on getting this to work, he didn't notice the R.C.M.P officer making his way down to the shore. Constable Poirier had seen John from his cruiser as he was pulling into the service station for gas. John was so busy that he had not heard the Constable calling to him to get off the ice. Finally, John heard a booming voice shouting out to him, "Get off that ice now. You are putting yourself in grave danger. If I have to get a boat to go and get you, you will be arrested. That is an order! Do it now!"

John stood there on the ice floe, totally surprised by the Constable's outburst. "Oh my God, I'm trapped," he thought. "I must get myself off this ice quickly. So he shouted back, "Okay, okay, I'm coming in." He continued to jiggle the ice floe with his feet so it would move closer to the remaining floes. He did not want the constable to have to come for him. His mind was racing and his heart was pounding as he continued to jiggle the floe. Of course, by this time a group of people had gathered along the shore and were watching him to see how he would manage. John was totally embarrassed; he had not expected to attract an audience. His father would be furious with him.

Eventually he managed to get the ice floe closer to the remainder of the ice, jumped quickly onto three floes in succession and cleared the fifth one and onto the shore. He could not believe it when those watching broke out in a loud cheer. John did not feel like cheering whatsoever. He knew that Constable Poirier, standing there glaring at him, was not happy. "What is your name young man?" he asked John. John told him. "If I ever see you on those ice floes again, you'll spend a couple of nights in the local jail. Do I make myself clear, young man?"

"Oh yes, I hear you," answered John. "I will never do it again. I promise." John could not believe that he was not taking him home to his parents. John feared more what his father would do to him than what the constable had to say. John thought, "Too bad I got caught. It was such fun. And I did get to the outermost floe, as I wanted to. The victory is mine!" But he could not openly show the pleasure of his victory. He had to enjoy it all by himself; neither did he mention anything about it that evening at the supper table. John had been very relieved at not having been taken home in the police cruiser; that would have been too humiliating.

This was not John's first run in with Constable Poirier. He had gotten into trouble the previous summer with the famous ice-house incident. This incident had not turned out as smoothly, as John recalled.

The ice house was so named because huge ice blocks were kept there with saw dust on them to keep them from melting too quickly since the fishermen would use the ice to preserve their fish before it was sold. The building was made of huge stone blocks and it had a wooden roof. This ice house stood on the shore and next to it was a small wharf where some of the fishing boats could be moored. It had recently fallen into disuse and the fishermen had stopped storing ice blocks in it but there was still a lot of sawdust inside it. It was getting very run down and part of the roof had rotted leaving a gaping hole. There were several windows in the walls of the building that had been boarded up. Some of the boards had been smashed in, leaving holes there as well. This was how John and a few of his friends would get into the building to explore the inside of it, to play games and pretend that they were in the process of solving some thrilling mystery as the Hardy Boys would do.

One afternoon John was looking at the hole in the roof as he sat on the small wharf with his feet dangling over the side. Billy Cosman was with him. He turned to Billy and said,

"Do you know what we should do?"

"No I don't but if you tell me, then I'll know," answered Billy.

"Okay, okay, don't be a smart ass," answered John. "You see that gaping hole in that roof? Well, I think that we should get ourselves some rope and just tear the whole of that roof down. Then it would be easier to jump from the wall into the sawdust. Let's make that our week's project, to tear down the ice house roof. What do you think?"

"I think that we'll end up getting into trouble again," answered Billy. He had not forgotten the chimney adventure that had ended being a far cry from a Hardy Boys adventure.

"You're such a scaredy cat, Billy. You are afraid of your own shadow," said John.

Finally John, Billy and a couple of other friends decided that they would tear down the ice house roof. They would start that afternoon since it was a beautiful day and there was no sign of rain. "What tools do you think we'll need?" John asked Billy.

"We'll definitely need a rope and a hammer, maybe even a crowbar if we can get one," answered Billy.

"That won't be too difficult. We have those tools and the rope in the little shed next to the root cellar, just behind our house," said John. The little shed that John was referring to had been a chicken coup at one time but now it contained wood and coal for heating the house during the winter months and one section of that little shed had different types of tools and gardening utensils; John would get what they needed.

Once John had brought the different tools from home, he and his friends got started. For several days they tugged, pulled, chopped and hammered at the dilapidated roof. It proved to be a very difficult task. When they became tired of it and the roof strongly resisted being torn down, they would take a break by exploring the inside of the building. It had numerous interesting nooks and crannies. They would also find chunks of ice under the sawdust and would throw these pieces of ice from the top of the ice house wall into the harbour. They would also change into their swimming trunks and dive off of the small wharf that was close to the ice house. This was lots of fun.

One afternoon as they were tugging on the rope that they had tied to a small beam jutting out through the hole in the roof, Constable Poirier appeared on the scene. He had been alerted to the goings-on at the ice house by Mr. Bruneau whose garage was just next door to the ice house. Mr. Bruneau was convinced that the young boys would end up by injuring themselves and had called Constable Poirier to investigate.

John had just returned from having his lunch and was tugging on the rope in an attempt to tear down the remainder of the beam that had been stubbornly refusing to fall, when a voice behind him said, "And what do you think that you are doing, young man?"

Without turning around immediately, John instinctively exclaimed, "Tearing down this stupid old roof!" As he said this he turned around and there stood Constable Poirier. John quickly let go of the rope as if it were on fire. He stood there speechless and very embarrassed. He could certainly not deny what he was doing since he had blurted it out and had been caught in the act.

"Get into the police cruiser," instructed Constable Poirier. John was the only one who was made to get into the police car since he had been the one who was caught in the act. "We will go and see your father and see what he thinks of all this," said Constable Poirier to John. "Where do you live?"

"Just there on Main Street, the third house from the American House Hotel," answered John. Of course all of John's friends who had been tearing down the old ice house with him fled the scene, all of them terrified to death. All the neighbours along the street were looking at John wondering what was going on. John just wanted to die. He was in deep trouble and figured that he would be grounded for at least a month this time.

Just as they were arriving at John's house, Batist came out of the house. John's father had come home from work for lunch and was getting ready to go back. He was just coming out of the yard, when the cruiser pulled up to the gate. John and Constable Poirier got out of the police vehicle. John's father looked at one then at the other.

"What is going on?" Batist asked Constable Poirier.

"Are you Mr. DeCoste?" asked Constable Poirier.

"Yes, I'm Mr. DeCoste, Batist is my name," answered John's father.

Constable Poirier explained the situation mentioning that Mr. Bruneau had reported the goings-on at the ice house fearing that the boys would get hurt. The one mistake that Constable Poirier made, however, in his explanation was to make it sound as if he was telling Batist how to bring up his child. That did not sit well with proud Batist.

"Leave him with me," he told Constable Poirier, "I'll take care of matters. However, I do not need anyone, you included, Constable Poirier, to tell me how to raise or discipline my child. Mr. Bruneau could have let me know about this directly without involving the police. He has children of his own. He did not have to call you. I do not appreciate that one bit. I thank you for your trouble and I'll take things in hand from here."

Constable Poirier knew better than to argue with Batist. He told him that was fine by him since the child was in his father's care. They parted with a simple, "Good day to you, Sir," and Batist took John into the house. John was sure that he would be grounded forever, but to his amazement, all his father told him was, "Stay away from that ice house! I'll not tell you again. You don't need to play there; the village is big enough for you to find things to do elsewhere." Then, he left for work without another word.

John later found out from his mother that his father did not like Constable Poirier very much because of a run in with him at an earlier time concerning a dog that the Constable had. There were times when the Constable's dog, a Doberman, would get loose and run around the neighbourhood terrorizing people. John's father had been bitten by this big dog and Batist had never forgotten it. He did not want to have any dealings with Constable Poirier and did not want John to have to deal with him either. Apparently, Batist had gone to see Constable Poirier after having been bitten and had told him that he needed to pick up his dog since the dog was terrorizing people in the village. Constable Poirier had answered Batist saying, "You are the first person to complain about being bitten. Why have I had no other complaints about this? Are you exaggerating the whole thing?"

"People are not coming forward because you are the police and they are frightened of getting into trouble," answered Batist. "But I don't care about that and the police do not frighten me. So I am telling you now and you can also see the bite that I got from your Doberman, so I am telling you that if it ever happens again I will bring my hunting rifle and shoot that vicious dog. I hope that I have made myself clear!"

John could not believe it. His father truly had guts! Although it had been fun at the time, he really regretted becoming involved with the ice house. He was completely humiliated at having been brought home in a police car with everyone looking at him. He felt so disgraced! He wouldn't try a thing like that again!

The summer continued and John and his friends played in the row boats on the shore, and went swimming in the ocean. They would sometimes hitch-hike out to the beach and tease the many girls who were swimming and sun bathing there; they would also try to see who could stay under water the longest without coming up for air. Daring and taking risks gave more pleasure to their everyday activities.

When August rolled around, the blueberries ripened in the fields. John loved to go blueberry picking. He and the Boutin children would go to Mr. Bruneau's blueberry fields. The farm was called the Rock Loaf Dairy Farm because it had a huge loaf-shaped hill at the end of the long driveway close to the farm house. There were acres of blueberry bushes next to a small lake behind the green rolling hills of the farm. The children would pick there for hours, then break for lunch and continue picking until early evening. When none of the girls had accompanied them, the boys would make there way to a nearby isolated beach on the ocean. The water of the ocean was often very cold even in the depth of the summer, but there were fairly large pools of water in the sand that were very warm. In these, John and the Boutin boys would skinny dip. It was great being able to swim completely naked in the warm water; the sense of freedom was exhilarating. With the Boutin boys John did not feel that sense of fear and trembling because they were naked. They were simply friends, quite used to one another like brothers, having an innocent and free time in the warm sunshine, sand and water. If one of them became aroused, which could easily happen, they just laughed it off. They wouldn't dream of voicing any fantasies that may have been the cause. The great sense of freedom that they experienced was more important somehow than any fantasizing that could be taking place. John did not always understand what all these innuendoes meant but laughed as well pretending that he did; Robert and Andrew, the two older brothers of Gus and Caroline, would tell them things that they did not always share with John. He would gradually learn some of those rather sordid ideas from the older boys at school. He would be very upset by some of the things he learned and often wondered if they were really true. He would eventually come to realize more and more that he had a great deal to learn. Later, when John developed an overactive sense of morality, as many young people do, he would look upon these incidents differently; a sense of having indulged in wrong-doing would cause him great anxiety.

When the Boutin girls, Caroline and Marion, and his sister Della were with them they did not go to the private beach. That spot was private for the boys alone. There were many times that the girls were with them, especially Della, since John's mother did not like John to go that far without an older sibling with him. John enjoyed the blueberry excursions when Gus and Caroline were with them but he just hated it when their oldest sister, Marion, was with them. She was very selfish and domineering, wanting her own way in everything. She thought that she could control everyone. She thought that she should be the boss over everything and everyone.

As they started to pick the blueberries, Marion would begin. She would declare a certain portion of the blueberry bushes as her territory, and demand that no one pick from her bushes.

John and Della refused to accept this. John would say to her, "Since when did you become the owner of these blueberry bushes? You must have a bill of sale and some kind of paper showing us that you own this land. Show us the proof that it all belongs to you," said John furiously.

"You mind your own business," answered Marion, "I'll kick your ass for you if you try anything!"

"I'll pick wherever I please and you can't stop me!" answered John, screaming at the top of his lungs.

Just when they were about to come to blows Della piped up, "Come, John. Let's go home. We don't need this foolishness. We'll go across the harbour to Robins to pick our own blueberries. We're very close to Robins from here. The hills at the back of the village have plenty of blueberries." They began to pick up their lunch boxes and cans and head for Robins.

"No, don't go," said Caroline and Gus, "we'll all pick where we want. She can't stop us and we'll tell our mother when we get home; she'll be grounded for sure."

Marion became furious and cursed them all, but she gave in knowing how ruthless her mother could be.

They picked for most of the day. Their first break from picking was for lunch. They brought out their lunch boxes and ate their thick peanut butter sandwiches made with home-made bread; John and Della were often embarrassed that they had home-made bread for their sandwiches and not store bought bread, what they called "baker's bread" that looked daintier but really had no taste. Their half-gallon cans would easily be filled by three o'clock in the afternoon; then they would head for home, hoping that their mother had made a depression stew or a garden stew for supper.

John loved depression stew. It was a simple mixture of onions sautéed in butter with lots of different spices, diced potatoes and green peas added to it along with bits of bologna, the cheapest meat available. The taste depended on how Rose put the ingredients together, the exact combination of food and the length of time it simmered.

Garden stew was a simple combination of spices, onion, butter and a medley of all the garden vegetables they had grown in their garden throughout the summer months. Again the taste depended on how Rose had combined and sautéed all of these ingredients. John's mouth would water just thinking of it. Of course, once they had brought home the blueberries, John's mom would bake them a blueberry pie. It would melt in your mouth and was even more delicious when it was eaten with thick, fresh cream. It made the effort of blueberry picking worthwhile, even when they had to put up with Marion.

Rose only used a portion of the blueberries picked by the children. The remainder they took door to door to sell to the neighbours for fifty cents a half a gallon. They would use the money that they collected to buy their school supplies for the coming academic year.

There were times when people didn't want to buy blueberries. When they did not have much success in selling their produce they would make their way to Brigitte Landry's house. She was a sweet little old lady who loved to help the children and would almost always buy some of the blueberries. She very often forgot that she had bought some the previous day and she would buy them again! The only time that this did not work for them was when old Albert, her husband, was at home and not sleeping. He would never answer the door; however, when Brigitte answered he would call out to her, "Who is that at the front door? Tell them to go away!"

"It is the children selling blueberries today. Albert come and see, they are just beautiful! I believe that we should buy some at such a reasonable price!" exclaimed Brigitte.

"No, no blueberries! All the pots and pans are full of them and you forget to bake pies with them. They will rot in the pots! No more! Send the children away!" Albert would shout in a very angry voice. He was a man that was very grouchy most of the time. Brigitte, his wife of many years, was a sweet bit of a thing always dressed in a beautiful frock with a cameo broach at her neck. Her snowy white hair was pulled back into a bun and held in place by beautiful silver coloured combs. She always had an angelic smile on her lips.

With a twinkle in her eye she would say to the children, "I'm afraid that Albert is not in a very good mood today. I must try and bake those blueberry pies tomorrow." Then as she stretched out her closed hand towards them, she would whisper, "Here is fifty cents to help you with your school supplies. Don't let Albert see the money. I know that you need many things for school." She would then give a little laugh, pleased as punch that she had fooled Albert.

John was always so happy when this happened. It proved to him that there were good people in the world.

Next door to dear old Brigitte and Albert lived Mrs. Lenora Lassiter, who never agreed to buy blueberries, although it was known that she had lots of money and travel ed abroad every year. Lenora lived alone, having lost her husband many years before. Even though she did not buy any blueberries, John would always greet her politely whenever he saw her sweeping off her front porch when he went by after his post office work in the evening. On one of those particular evenings, Lenora stopped her sweeping and looked at John as he was slowly walking home from the Post Office. She suddenly said to John, "Come here young man. I want to talk to you." John politely came over to the steps where she was standing and said to her, "Is there something that you want me to do for you, Mrs. Lassiter?"

"No my dear boy," Lenora replied, "but this is for you!" And as she said this she grabbed John's head into both of her hands and landed a great big kiss on his cheek. John was stunned. He stood there looking at her dumbfounded. "That is for being such a good boy," she exclaimed. John grabbed his cheek and kept rubbing it up and down with the palm of his hand.

"Don't rub it off now my dear that is a special kiss for you! You are quite fine you know!" she exclaimed.

John was speechless and hoped that no one had seen her do this. He rushed home for supper and of course did not breathe a word of this to anyone. He felt disgusted. Why did these things happen to him! John knew that she would not have done that to him if she had known what he and the Boutin boys did on their way to Sunday evening services. They had discovered that Lenora did not lower her blinds at night when preparing for bed. They would stand at the corner of her house and peer through her window and watch her getting ready for bed. She would first remove her wig revealing a head of wispy, scraggly looking hair. Then she would remove her dress to reveal a very complicated looking corset that was a total mystery to John. This corset seemed to be made up of wooden stays that took the form of the body. What was even more fascinating was the number of laces coming out of the corset that apparently could be tightened for the corset to take the form of the body, or so Caroline had told them. According to Caroline, this was truly an old lady's corset and no modern woman would have been found dead in one. Gus and Caroline would laugh heartily as they watched. Caroline would say nastily to John, "There now, isn't your girlfriend just a beauty to behold?" John would not say a word because he knew that if Caroline thought that this irked him, she would keep up her insulting comments for the remainder of the evening. He would, therefore, remain silent.

One incident that was not very amusing and in fact still sent shivers up and down his spine was the episode with Colin Boulanger, the village undertaker. This happened one dull, but warm Saturday afternoon.

John had gone to pick up the mail at the village post office and was returning home for supper. The post office was a Victorian building on the ocean side of the street. There was a driveway to the left of the building that led to a small wharf where fishing boats and small freight ships docked to deliver fish products and various supplies. On the opposite side of that driveway stood a blue-grey building that belonged to Colin Boulanger, the village undertaker. This building was rumoured to be the coffin shed where Colin kept his caskets. John had never been in this building and so was not entirely sure what was in the building, but on this particular Saturday he would find out.

As John was walking across the driveway that led to the wharf, he noticed that Colin was standing in the doorway of the building. As he neared the open doorway, he said hello to Mr. Boulanger, who answered John with a question, "You're the DeCoste boy, aren't you?"

"Yes, I am," answered John, stopping. "My name is John."

"That's right, that's right, you're John DeCoste, the son of Rose and Batist. Now I remember. Do you think you could do me a favour? You're not in a hurry, are you?"

"Not really, it will soon be time for supper so I just picked up the mail and now I'm on my way home to eat," answered John.

"It's the darnedest thing. My helper, Roddie, was supposed to be here by now to help me and he hasn't shown up yet," said Colin. "I need to take one of the coffins into my work room across the street but I can't do that alone and I don't want to wait any longer. I don't know where Roddie went. Do you think you could help me carry the coffin across the street to my work room? It won't be too heavy with two of us carrying it."

"Okay, I can help you with that," answered John. As John entered the shed, there on the clean, well-swept floor was the coffin. There were many other boxes stacked in the large room of the building. Now John knew first hand what the building was. He took one end of the coffin and Colin the other end. John backed out of the building and was on his guard for on-coming cars as they crossed the street and made their way to the work room. John was the one with his back to the work room door. As he backed through the door of the work room, he looked back to see where he was going. Mr. Boulanger kept telling him that he was doing fine and to keep going. Once they had cleared the doorway, John realized that there was a fully clothed dead body lying on a table in the work room. John immediately recognized Robert Gordon who had recently died. He was dressed in a powder-blue suit with white shirt and tie but was barefoot.

"You're not afraid of the dead, are you?" asked Colin.

"I don't know. I've never really thought about it before," answered John.

"Well, you know, Roddie is still not back and I need to get things completed with Mr. Gordon. Do you think you could help me get him into the coffin? With two of us lifting he shouldn't be too heavy. You take him by the legs and I'll take him by the shoulders and that should do the trick." They placed the open casket just below the table that Mr. Gordon was lying on. John wrapped his arms around Mr. Gordon's legs; they felt hard, rubbery and lifeless. John did not like the feel of them. Colin took him by the shoulders and looking at John said, "One, two, three, lift!" Into the coffin went Mr. Gordon. Colin arranged the satin interior more neatly around the body. Just then Roddie walked in. He smiled and nodded to John. Mr. Boulanger looked at Roddie and exclaimed, "Where have you been? I've been waiting for you all afternoon! It's a good thing the DeCoste boy here came along or I would still be waiting. What was so important that you had to leave without telling me?"

"My brother had a stroke around noon time and I had to rush him to the hospital," answered Roddie.

"Oh, geez, I'm sorry Roddie. Will he be alright?"

"The doctor seems to think so, but then, time will tell. We won't really know for a couple of weeks or so."

John told Roddie as well that he was sorry for his trouble. Then he said to Mr. Boulanger, "I really need to go now, or I'll be late for supper."

"That's fine, that's fine. Thanks for the help. Roddie is back, so I'll manage just fine now. You're a fine young man. Keep on being so," said Colin.

As John walked home he found that there was a strange smell on his hands. It smelled like death, he thought. "It must be the kind of make-up or powder that they use to prepare the bodies for burial," he thought to himself. In any case, he did not like the smell. He was still smelling his hands when he came into the house.

His mother looked at him and said, "What is wrong with you? Why are you smelling your hands like that?"

John told her what had happened with Mr. Boulanger on the way home from the post office.

"Don't be so silly," she replied. "Go and wash your hands and come and eat. I have cooked one of your favourites today, baked beans and Johnny cake. That smell on your hands is only the smell of the make-up that the undertaker uses on dead bodies. It's nothing. It won't kill you."

John sat at table gladly after having washed his hands with lots of warm, soapy water. They smelled much better now.

John had just recently turned thirteen years of age. The incident with the dead body had been somewhat of a jolt for him but he was not yet finished with having to deal with dead bodies.

Little Marylynn had been born into a very caring, warm, friendly and very Catholic family. From birth she experienced serious health problems. Of course her mother and father, Marion and Francis Brandon, made sure that she received the proper medical attention. Many tests and check-ups were done on Marylynn and finally the doctors in Halifax had to break the news to her parents that she had cancer, that dreaded and terrible disease that most people feared. Everyone was stunned! Cancer at such a young age! How could this be? Not much was known about cancer in the nineteen fifties. Nonetheless, little Marylynn would certainly be loved to the utmost and given excellent care. Unfortunately the cancer manifested itself in her little bum. Consequently, having such a painful monster festering in her buttocks made it almost impossible for her to be placed for long periods of time on her back when in her crib. She most often had to be placed on her side or on her stomach when lying down; in fact, it was just about impossible for her to sit up.

Marylynn succumbed to the disease after only two and a half years of life. God in his great mercy took her back. It was a horrible tragedy for the family but they would now have their own little saint in heaven,

St. Marylynn. For some this was too great a loss, but for her parents, it consoled them greatly in their grief.

The arrangements were begun for her burial. Since Marylynn had brothers and sisters in school but who were still quite young, the family decided to ask some of the older students to carry the small white casket containing the remains of this beautiful little child. Four young men were needed and it was decided that four of the altar servers would be chosen. John was an altar server at the time, yet he was totally surprised that he was approached for this service; he knew that there were other servers who were stronger and older than him who could do this job. He had mixed feelings about this task; he felt honoured, yet he was also extremely frightened. He agreed to render the service but thought about nothing else for days. He would wake up in the middle of the night shaking with fright. There were many "what ifs" going through his mind. One of these came from a previous experience involving a pall bearer.

John remembered vividly when his grandfather, Frederick, had died and the terrible incident at the graveside. The family could not afford the automatic lowering device for the casket and so the more primitive poles and ropes were to be used to lower the coffin into the grave. John had always disliked this part of the burial ceremony and was watching the whole procedure very closely. The ropes were placed under both ends of the coffin and since they were fairly long could rest on the ground while waiting to be used. Fr. Alexander said the final prayer over the grave and threw a handful of earth on the coffin as he uttered the words, "Remember, Frederick, that thou art dust and unto dust thou shall return." The undertaker, Mr. Boulanger, made signs to the pallbearers to lift the coffin with the ropes so that the poles could be removed. Then they carefully lowered the coffin into the wooden box that had been previously placed in the grave. This had to be a careful balancing act. Suddenly, to John's horror, one of the pall bearers accidentally dropped his end of the rope and the coffin went tumbling down into the grave. As it hit the wooden box, the cover flew open and John looked squarely into the face of his grandfather. He stood there riveted in fear as he looked at the already swelling and yellowing face of his grandfather. Nausea welled up inside of him; a sour taste came into his mouth, but he fought to keep from vomiting. This scene remained engraved in John's thoughts and he knew that he would never forget it.

He continued to watch as two of the pall bearers jumped down onto the sides of the wooden box, quickly closed the casket and with unbelievable strength and deftness straightened out the casket so that it fell neatly into the wooden box, this time without opening. John had not been able to keep his eyes averted from the whole ordeal no matter how frightening it all was.

What did this have to do with his being a pall bearer for little Marylynn? It was simple. He feared dropping his end of the little white casket and having her go tumbling down into the grave! And this was enough to disturb his sleep the night before the funeral service. On his knees he prayed that night for this fear to be taken away. The following morning as he dressed to go to the service, his stomach was filled with butterflies. He wanted to run away and just not have to do this. Yet he knew that he could not turn his back on the promise made; he had given his word. Everyone thought that he was so strong, so brave, yet he knew better and felt like such a hypocrite.

He and another altar server, Donald Boutilier, who had also been chosen to be a pall bearer, walked to little Marylynn's house, dressed in their Sunday best. Marylynn's mother and father had chosen to have her waked at home rather than at the funeral parlour of Mr. Boulanger. It was still the traditional custom in the village for the people to wake their loved ones at home. John and Donald and two other altar servers stood as sentinels, two at the head of the casket and two at the foot in readiness for the start of the short journey to the Church. John looked at Marylynn as she lay there in her little white coffin, her head resting on the white satin pillow, a picture of peaceful repose. She was absolutely beautiful in her white satin and lace dress.

She truly looked as though she was simply sleeping. As John looked down at her beautiful, peaceful face where all pain and suffering had been removed, his own fear and doubt left him; at that moment he would carry her to her final resting place with utmost care and gentleness. He was glad now that he had accepted the invitation to render this service. "Dear Marylynn," whispered John to himself, "may the angels gently carry you to Jesus!" John had taken one more step towards growing up, no matter how difficult it had been. Would it continue to be such an ordeal for him each time he encountered a new experience? Did growing up need to be so difficult? He did not realize that he had far from finished with the extremes of growing up! One blow would soon hit him that he would be totally unprepared for; it would shake him to the very core of his being!

John soon experienced another of the unexpected extremes of growing up, that of the changes that occur in a young man's body as puberty approaches. What an ordeal for him once again! Knowing little or nothing about sex, since his parents had not prepared him for this, his mind and thoughts were riddled with many questions, many of which came from the stories and expressions he heard from the older boys at school. They spoke about girls and their "bleeding cycles". Some spoke about the "hand job" and jokingly mentioned that that is when you "go off" and end up with a discharge in your hands. It was supposed to be a big joke. What did it all mean? He shied away from questioning the older boys for more information because he knew that they would simply laugh at him, call him stupid and a "queer" or a little sissy. This was all very frightening for John especially when he was also made to understand that there were boys who loved boys and girls who loved girls and that this was just not acceptable behaviour. What if he was like that? He wondered about this because now when he heard talk about sexual things, and even saw another boy or classmate naked when changing for swimming, John got all frightened and weak, sensing an empty feeling in the pit of his stomach; there was a stirring in his genitals and he became aroused. This was very upsetting and he felt that maybe there was something wrong with him. It was also very annoying when he would be sitting in class at school and suddenly he would find himself with an erection. He dreaded being asked to go to the black board at that moment or to stand up for any reason. How could he know, how could he find out if there was something wrong with him? Who could he ask without being embarrassed about it? What was he to do with all this? Alone again and with no one to turn to for answers!

One morning, while lying in bed, he was thinking of all of these things and agonizing over how to talk about these things to his friends or even how to bring them up to the priest when speaking to him in the confessional. It seemed to John that maybe he would be able to explain some things to him. But he always felt too embarrassed and frightened as to how the priest would react to his questions. He always seemed in such a hurry and in bad humour. John just did not know what to do. As his thoughts raced and many images went through his mind as he lay there, he became aroused and suddenly to John's utter surprise, a white, sticky fluid squirted out of him. John was stunned, shocked! How could this be? Where did this come from all of a sudden? Could it be the "discharge" the older boys had joked about? Or, maybe, somehow he got toothpaste on himself? But it did not look like or feel like toothpaste. How could that possibly be? He just lay there horrified with the sticky fluid all over himself. He got up quickly and washed himself, afraid that someone in the family would catch him! What would they think? Alone once again with his thoughts, with an experience he did not understand.

John wondered if some of his friends his own age had experienced such an upsetting situation. He had to ask his friend, Gus. He would be the safest one to ask if such a thing had happened to him. John did not realize that Gus, being a year younger than him, had not yet reached that frightening stage of growth. With much apprehension, he asked Gus, "Did you ever have white sticky fluid squirt out of you all of a sudden, down there I mean as he pointed towards his crotch?"

"No, I didn't," said Gus, "but my older brother did. He told me. His friends told him that now he can make babies. That's the stuff in the man that makes babies."

"Are you sure?" asked John, totally amazed and somewhat frightened at this distressing news.

"That's what he told me!" exclaimed Gus.

John did not question further. His thoughts were filled with questions. The most important was, "How was that baby made? Was there something else that was needed with the white stuff to make the baby?" John was confused. He had always been told that the doctor brought the baby with him in his black bag. There was something fishy in all of this. In time he would find out. The next school year, that of the eighth grade, would give him some answers to his great and pleasant surprise.

John had already realized that he needed to excel in his school work if he was to move on to better things and not end up in the fish factory like his father. That was one thing that his father did not want. Batist wanted his children to have a better life.

John was now more determined than ever to do well in school, even though he continued to hate many things about it. The one event that gave him the motivation to accomplish this came in eighth grade. As the students entered the eighth grade classroom on that first day of the new school year, whom did they find sitting at the teacher's desk but a handsome male teacher! John had never had a male teacher before. He was elated. All his teachers had been Sisters or lay women. He could not keep his eyes off him. Who was he?

Mr. Don David had just recently graduated from University and Normal School as a teacher. He was from one of the neighbouring villages and all the grade eight students were thrilled to have him as their teacher. This would be a new experience indeed. In fact, John actually enjoyed that last year at the Richmond Academy.

Mr. David was a teacher who believed in practical work projects, field studies and excursions to help the students to better understand what they were learning from their text books. He often did this for the science, history and geography classes. The students loved the outings. Sometimes they would go to the fish factory, to some historical sight of the region or to the forest to study the trees and various plants.

One of the excursions took them to the shore to look for seashells and starfish, as well as jellyfish. As they searched, Mr. David came upon a length of thick rubber that looked somewhat like the strap that once was used to discipline students. Jokingly he picked it up and looking at all of them said, "Well, well, what do we have here? A good sturdy disciplinary tool, maybe, what do you all think?" No one answered! "I think I will keep this. It may just come in handy one day for some unruly miscreant!" They all just laughed of course. No one thought for a minute that such a thing would happen. Not at that time!

Mr. David's classes continued to be very interesting and the students learned a lot from all of his courses. Mr. David was also easy to talk to and the boys often talked with him about private things. This was a resource that John had never had. He had always shied away from discussing things about sexuality and women. But with Mr. David there was an ease that had not existed before. Could John come to be relaxed enough in school to just be himself for a change? He was always so frightened of making a mistake and being laughed at by the other students. To his amazement, he now had this freedom.

One incident set back his ease with this new teacher. Surprisingly, it happened during prayer time. Each day before going home for lunch, the students took turns reciting the Angelus. The Wednesday of the second week in June was John's time to do the Angelus. What Mr. David did not know was that the students had been passing jokes to one another during the exam review that had just finished. One joke in particular had struck John as extremely funny and each time he thought about it, he laughed to himself even after everyone else had calmed down. Miriam kept signaling to him that he had to stop, that Mr. David would catch him. Nevertheless, time came for the prayer and John thought that he had calmed down sufficiently to do the prayer properly.

"John would you please lead us in the prayer of the Angelus," said Mr. David.

"Yes of course, Sir," answered John. John began the prayer. Halfway through the prayer he burst out laughing. Everyone turned to look at him in disbelief.

"You will be more serious, John, and start again," declared Mr. David.

"I'll do my best," answered John. Once again he launched into the prayer and once again, halfway through it, he burst into laughter. This went on for at least three more times with John having to start over. By this time Mr. David was completely annoyed and told the class, "None of you will leave this classroom until the prayer has been completed properly. You will also have to be back here on time for the afternoon classes no matter what time you leave. Those who show up late will be sent to the principal's office," said Mr. David in a tone of voice that he rarely used with the students.

"Come on, John. Get on with it," the students yelled. "You're wasting our time and we'll all end up being late!"

John remained silent and refused to say another word. When Mr. David saw that John had clammed up, he took out the long piece of rubber that he had picked up on the shore. He had said at that time that it might come in handy as a strap one day.

There was now total silence in the class. Some were holding their breath, wide eyed, while others just glared at John in anger. John refused to open his mouth. Mr. David knew that he had to deal with this and to do that he needed to calm down. This he did and all the students were dismissed with the exception of John. Mr. David left John standing and remained silent for a while longer. He then looked at John and said,

"You are a very serious and good student! What is this all about? Can you explain your behaviour to me? Otherwise, I'll be forced to use this strap on you!" Mr. David said sternly.

"I'm sorry, Sir, but we had been passing jokes to one another during review period and one got stuck in my head and I kept remembering it when I tried to do the prayer. I really did not mean to be so disruptive and disobedient," answered John in all honesty.

"Oh that is what happened! Why didn't you say that immediately?" asked Mr. David.

"I guess I was scared that everyone would get into trouble!" answered John

"You do know that this strap would sting, don't you?" Mr. David asked.

"Yes I know that!" John answered. "But no matter how much it hurts you will never make me cry! I'll pass out first!" John told Mr. David.

He looked at John in surprise. "Where is that coming from?" he asked John.

"I made myself a promise after Sr. Gemma strapped me in grade one when I first started school that I would never again cry in school even if they killed me and especially not in front of others," replied John

Mr. David could not believe his ears. He immediately put the strap away and told John to go home for lunch and to do his best to be back on time for afternoon classes.

"Thank you, Sir," answered John.

Of course when John came out of the school, who was the one person standing on the school steps? None other than Miriam herself! She was dying to know what had happened! She was so worried! John told her what had gone on and they both agreed that they had never had as good a teacher as Mr. David before. He was absolutely the best!

John was to leave Richmond Academy that year at the end of grade eight to go to the Convent School just up the road. Before leaving, however, he would get another pleasant surprise. Through the intervention of Mr. David he would get some answers to some of his questions on sexuality.

The grade eight class took biology that year. When they reached the section on reproduction the questions were fired at Mr. David from every corner of the class. One of the students, Cyrille, had many different theories concerning reproduction. He bluntly told Mr. David, "We need some answers. These old wives tales about the stork and the doctor's black bag are all ridiculous! We need to know how babies are made; the facts, not stories! My aunt just had twin boys; how does that happen? We don't want to remain ignorant. You must help us."

"Well, I do agree with you that you shouldn't remain ignorant. But I can't tell you all of this in class. I'm not permitted to do that. However, if you wish to stay after class I'll answer any questions you have! How's that?"

The whole class was in favour. They would know when the bell rang at the end of the day; and at three thirty, it did ring.

No one moved towards the door, everyone stayed in their place. Mr. David looked around the classroom and then said in a questioning tone, "I guess everyone is interested in this session, right?"

Suddenly there was movement at the back of the class and shuffling of feet. Anita Russell, a boarder at the Sisters' Convent and an intelligent but very shy student got up from her desk and made her way slowly to the classroom door.

"You don't wish to stay, Anita?" asked Mr. David.

"No, I'm fine," answered Anita. "I do need to get home. I'll be fine." And she disappeared out the door. The students knew of course that they were free to leave at anytime.

Mr. David decided that he would proceed by first making a list of the various questions the students had. He wrote diligently and quickly on the board, not wanting to keep them too long. However, he knew that it would take some time to answer all the questions. Some questions were similar and could be grouped together. Then he would proceed in a logical order.

The first point he dealt with was what the students were calling "making love." He described the male and female genitalia and what happens when people are making love, or having intercourse. He also distinguished between intercourse and making love; there was quite a difference, which he emphasized to them.

John then realized why Miriam did not seem to have anything there when they examined one another. She had the room that welcomed his instrument. He sat there mesmerized as Mr. David explained all this. Then it dawned on him that this was what his Mom and Dad did at one time to make him. That idea horrified him. "Oh my God, my parents did that to make each one of us!" he said to himself. He was stunned!

As Mr. David explained what the sperm was and how it needed to join with the egg inside of the woman, John realized that this sperm was the sticky fluid coming out of him, and that now he too could make babies. He was shocked but also somewhat relieved. He need not worry, it was all part of becoming a man; his body was just changing. Physically, he was growing up. Emotionally, he was very far behind, which oddly, he did realize.

Cyrille, whose aunt had had twins, was delighted to learn how this process occurred with the two sperms managing to join up with two eggs. It was all quite awesome. Knowing the real truth was so much better than believing silly stories about storks and black bags.

Mr. David promised to meet with them for more questions. They had already been talking for over an hour. They all needed to get home since most of them had after school chores to do.

Some of the students mentioned this out of class session to their parents who were very upset with Mr. David. The following week Rose asked John if it were true that Mr. David had kept them for a special session about sex. "Yes, he did," answered John, "and I thank God that he did."

"Well some of the parents are very upset about it and are going to report him to the school trustees," said Rose.

"Mom, if they do that they are stupid. Don't be part of it, Mom. Someone has to inform us. You are not doing it as parents! So how will we know the truth and not be told just Old Wives' Tales?" John said.

Rose had to agree with John and again she just smiled at the thought of it.

John, however, remained somewhat upset because he knew that it was from his experience with the white sticky fluid that the awful dream had begun. That was a mystery that he would need to resolve. How would he be able to resolve it?

Chapter Six

Fr. John was brought back from his reflections and his exchange of ideas and theories with Francois when the pilot announced that they would soon land at the Kampala Airport in Entebbe. The landing was smooth and they filed out of the plane and into the terminal. The Kampala Airport was certainly different from the Bukavu Airport. It was a well maintained building, clean and welcoming with all technical apparatus functioning properly. Flights were steadily arriving and departing and they had the needed personnel to accommodate all passengers to and from the planes. One had a sense of being in a safe place, even though soldiers were in view with arms slung across their shoulders. One knew that it was to safeguard the people entering and leaving the country. Uganda had had its share of revolutions and upheavals but there now was a feeling of stability and order. Time of course would reveal different problems that still existed, but the safety that Fr. John felt in that instant was necessary and important.

The Italian Consul was at the airport to meet and welcome them. They were grouped together and a customs official came to meet them. They were given forms to fill out and they would soon be processed for visas. It took time, of course, to get them filled out properly. There were many questions to be answered. Once all the forms had been filled out and checked, they all received a three-month provisional visa that was to be extended with time. The Consul chatted with Father John as they waited to be processed; he wanted to know what had happened in Bukavu and at the Bukavu Airport Fr. John went over the events as best he could.

"We had a very difficult time leaving that airport. The military personnel at the different desks gave me a hard time and were angry that I was attempting to protect the enemy. I had to pay a considerable amount of money before they agreed to give me back all the passports. Then another soldier insisted on going through all the hand luggage once again and then was very upset that it was taking us so long to board the aircraft. He threatened to stop our departure. It was terribly stressful!"

The Consul was furious at how they had been treated. "They are a disgrace to the military profession," said the Consul. "Unfortunately, there is not a lot that we can do about it. We are not the masters here at this time in history. That, in my opinion, is a good thing, no matter what kind of treatment we receive. If it gets too nasty, we can just leave."

Fr. John knew, however, that the soldiers in Zaire were very poorly paid, if at all, and were desperate for money to feed themselves and their families. It was really the President and his henchmen who should receive such treatment. All monies were funnel ed to the coffers of the President of the Republic. These high-placed dignitaries were living like fat cats while the population struggled and starved.

It was dark by the time they finished being processed and were finally on their way to Lourdel House, the central residence of the Missionaries of Africa in Kampala. Lourdel House was a fine center where the White Fathers could stay when in town. Once there they could get their meals and accommodations for the remainder of their stay in the city. They would stay there until they could move on to Jinja, to the House of Studies for students. Fr. John began to relax and breathe more freely. He would accompany the students to Jinja and stay with them until they were accustomed to the classes and life at the Centre. He wondered, however, what was going on in Bukavu, how the other priests and students were doing and if the town had fallen to the rebels. He now began to wonder if he had done the right thing, leaving as he had done! But, the students were safe. Keeping them in Zaire would have been too fraught with danger. Maybe he would try phoning or sending a fax to the Regional House in Bukavu or to the Sisters in the morning.

It was midnight before they got their rooms and fell asleep at Lourdel House. Exhausted, sleep came quickly for Fr. John; however, it was a troubled sleep, with many awakenings throughout the night. It was very hot in his room. He could hear mosquitoes buzzing around outside the mosquito net. He finally sat up and propped himself up on his pillows against the headboard, trying to relax and calm down. He noticed at one point as he looked at his watch that it was only 3 o'clock in the morning. He needed to sleep, he needed to rest; there would be much to do in the coming days. He decided to try some breathing exercises to compose himself; maybe then the much needed sleep and rest would come. He found this to be of some help and he gradually fell into a deep sleep once again.

In spite of the difficult night and the eventual deep sleep, Fr. John awakened early the next morning. The sun was streaming through the window of his room. The mosquito net around the bed made him feel a bit claustrophobic, but he pushed the thought from his mind. Jumping up, he went into the washroom, shaved, showered and once ready, went to the refectory for breakfast. The food was ready and being served. Waiting for him was a message asking him to call Fr. John A MacCarthy, a friend back home in Nova Scotia. Without hesitation and even before eating, he rushed to the phone and called directly to Fr. John A., who relayed a message to him that he had received from Jules and Chris, two Rwandese students that Fr. John had befriended while in Bukavu. They had boarded the plane from Bukavu to Nairobi some days before he himself had evacuated. They had managed to reach Nairobi safely but were worried about him after hearing about the fall of Bukavu to the rebels. He gave Fr. John a number where they could be reached. Fr. John decided to have breakfast and then try to reach them by telephone. The first attempt at phoning produced no results. By noon, he had managed to reach them and reassured them that he was fine and would come to Nairobi as soon as possible. Jules and Chris were both overjoyed to get the news and that settled the situation for the time being.

Before leaving for Jinja that same morning, Fr. John wanted very much to know what had happened during the fall of Bukavu to the rebels. He went to the sitting room and turned on the television to see if the early morning news had any kind of coverage on it. All it said was that Bukavu had indeed been taken by the rebels after a fierce battle within the city. The rebels were now in the process of restoring calm to the area. Fr. John wanted to know the details of what had happened to the brothers at the Regional House and at the Seminary. He decided to try to contact them by phone. After the third try, miraculously the call went through. Fr. Lucien, one of the assistants to the Regional Superior answered. Fr. John could not believe that he had managed to connect with someone. Immediately he told Fr. Lucien, "We are safe, we are at Lourdel House. We will soon leave for Jinja. But what is the situation there? How is everyone? Was anyone hurt during the fighting?"

"It was very bad at one point!" Fr. Lucien answered. "The military were confiscating vehicles for their battle with the rebels and, of course, one of the places that they came was here, to the Regional House. We had two vehicles that they wanted but one of the vehicles had a dead battery, so they needed to push it out of the compound and down the hill to get it going. While doing this, one of the soldiers' guns, which did not have the safety catch on, accidentally went off, hitting Fr. Joseph, our Regional, in the leg. We put a tourniquet on it in time to stop the bleeding and we immediately called Sr. Lucilla to look after him. Fr. Joseph is doing fine at the moment. We are keeping a close watch on him."

"And the Seminary, did anything happen there? Why did Fr. Bosco not come back with the remainder of the students?" Fr. John asked.

"When he returned from the Seminary in Murhesa, a group of military came to the Seminary to arrest him!" Fr. Lucien exclaimed.

"My God, whatever for?" asked Fr. John.

"He was accused of having helped a Tutsi family escape into Rwanda and the accusation was made by some of those people who were coming to mass at the Seminary every day! We never know who our accusers and traitors are," said Fr. Lucien. "He was released that same afternoon because a number of the soldiers that he befriended while they worked at the boarder crossing had him released. They said that he was their Father and that he had done a lot to help them. So he came home early the next morning."

"Where is he now? Is he at the Seminary? What if they decide to come back for him?" Fr. John asked anxiously.

"Well that was precisely his thinking," answered Lucien. "So he got a small bag ready and he and the remainder of the students set out on foot to go to the next mission some sixty kilometres away. Apparently they met people on the way who were coming from that direction who told them not to continue in that direction that they would go headlong into worst part of the fighting. So they took another direction. We do not know what they will do. Apparently they have decided that they will try to reach Maniema."

"But that is hundreds of kilometres away!" Fr. John exclaimed.

"That is the only safe place, unfortunately," Fr. Lucien answered

"It will take them many days to get there," answered Fr. John. (He later found out that Fr. Bosco and the students walked for ten days, sleeping in the bush and eating what they could get from the villagers.)

Fr. Lucien also added a bit of news from the Seminary itself. "Those who remained at the Seminary, three priests and the workers, felt terrorized by the shelling and gun shots that came from across the river, from Rwanda. They had to be extremely careful when going back and forth to the different buildings on the Seminary grounds. Suddenly shooting would start and a bullet could easily find its mark. One of the workers was not careful enough and was wounded in the shoulder. They treated him there at the Seminary as best they could. At that point they all realized that they could not stay there and should find a way to get the workers home and that the priests, Fr. Robert, Fr. Michel and Fr. David needed to evacuate. Only a couple of the workers decided to stay so that a presence would be there if the rebels or the National Army came to loot."

"They must have been terrified and feared for their lives," responded Fr. John.

"Yes it was a frightening ordeal and they ended up by leaving just a few workers in care of the Seminary with a word for them to be very cautious about their movements so that none of them would be injured. All others left the Seminary for the time being. What has concerned us greatly, however, is the treatment given to our Archbishop by the rebels."

This was the news that shocked, upset and angered Fr. John the most. Archbishop Munziirwa of Bukavu, a truly holy man in Fr. John's eyes, had been mercilessly slaughtered by the rebels. Archbishop Munziirwa was a Jesuit and had been Bishop of Maniema, Zaire, for a number of years. He had been appointed Archbishop of Bukavu when the former Archbishop had been deposed as a consequence of some illicit dealings. The choice of Archbishop Munziirwa for Bukavu had been, for Fr. John, the true work of the Holy Spirit. He had brought healing to the Archdiocese and a wonderful breath of peace.

Fr. Lucien continued in a very sad voice, "The Archbishop and his chauffeur were brutally executed by those henchmen who conquered the town of Bukavu."

"My God, what happened?" Fr. John held his breath as he waited for the news.

"You knew that the Archbishop was a Jesuit and, no matter what, he always went each week to visit the Jesuit Community at the Jesuit College of Alfajiri?"

"Yes I knew that. In fact, I saw him there a couple of times when I had to do business at Alfajiri," answered Fr. John.

"Well, one afternoon not long after the rebels had taken power, as he was on his way to the Jesuit Community, he was stopped by the rebels in the main market area of Bukavu. He and his driver were made to get out of the car and to kneel next to it. They were then both shot in the head and the bodies were propped up in a sitting position against the wrought iron fence of the Water Systems Office. The reason that we know the details about this execution is that the Xavierian Fathers have a house on the street just overlooking this particular area of the market and they were able to observe all that went on. They relayed the news to all the different mission stations. All were devastated."

Fr. John stood there at the telephone, his mouth gaping open, not knowing what to say. He felt so helpless and feared strongly for the people of Bukavu and their pearl of a town. Before he could respond there was a loud static noise that came over the phone and Fr. John could not hear properly. He kept saying over and over again to Fr. Lucien, "Hello, hello, are you still there? Can you hear me?" But there was no response. Just lots of muffled noises and then the connection was broken. Fr. John stood there in utter desolation, not knowing what to think! But he knew that he could not let this kind of news drag him down. He still had to get the students to the Center in Jinja.

Fr. John needed to get his students settled in at Jinja before all else. They finally managed to find transportation to Jinja; the Training Centre there was very welcoming and had a very calm, quiet, refreshing atmosphere. A semblance of normalcy set into their lives once more. Fr. John stayed in Jinja for about three months to help his students settle in and get used to studying in English. It was not easy, but it was what they needed. He was able to make contact with Jules and Chris again from the Centre and arranged for them to meet in Nairobi at a later date to assess their situation there.

The Jinja Center of studies was relatively new and was still quite beautiful and still seemed fresh and inviting. It had been built on a sloping piece of property facing the road that led to Nairobi, Kenya; in fact, the bus that went to Nairobi each day stopped just outside the entrance to the compound. The Center where Fr. John and the students lived was part of a larger complex that was known as a missionary consortium where students from various missionary communities gathered for theology classes and various other aspects of their missionary training. Two of the large missionary groups forming this consortium were the Comboni Missionaries and the Missionaries of Africa also known as the White Fathers of Africa. There were at least six other missionary communities that were part of the consortium. Each individual community had its own house where students were trained according to that community's spirituality and life style. They were beginning to slowly get back on track.

The morning at the Jinja Center started out with community prayer and Eucharist in the chapel, followed by breakfast. Then they left for classes with the other students from the different communities. Each of the communities provided the professors for the various subjects to be studied. The different classrooms were well equipped. The educational facility boasted a very fine library where the students could do all the necessary research for any theological topic. Once classes were over for the day, around noon, the students returned to their individual houses for noon prayer and lunch. After lunch the traditional siesta was observed. It was a refreshing time of the day for Fr. John. The climate in Jinja was not too hot or humid at that time and he could relax and sleep peacefully. The quiet time gave him the opportunity that he needed to sort out his thoughts and plans. He needed to clearly determine what he would do in the following weeks. At the Jinja Center his main responsibility was to his own students. Each day after the siesta Fr. John would gather with his students to drill them in English since now all their courses would be in that language.

Each evening Fr. John would go to the seminary chapel to have some quiet time and pray in silence by himself. The chapel was beautiful and restful. He enjoyed his quiet time there very much. As he sat there one evening praying, contemplating and reflecting, it dawned on him that he had not contacted Jules and Chris in at least three or four weeks. He had not heard from them either, so he presumed that things were going well; as he often said to himself "No news is good news." He would make a note of it to get in touch with them the next day.

Jules and Chris were two young men, one 19, the other 17, who were students that Fr. John had met through the Sisters of St. Francis. These young men, who were from a Tutsi/Hutu marriage, had fled Rwanda during the horrendous war and genocide. The Sisters had had their mother, Jeanne, as a student in their high school in Kigali and she had kept in friendly contact with them ever since. When Jules and Chris contacted the Sisters in their terrible need, they responded immediately and so began a better time for them with help from the Sisters. Jules and Chris had been living in dire straits for months, sleeping in doorways of stores, begging for food and trying to pick up a bit of money to continue their schooling. Sr. Ariana, one of the Sisters who had taught their mother, was very sympathetic to their cause and would attempt to find funds for them to get into school and have better living conditions in Bukavu. Jules and Chris were not from a poor Rwandese family. Their father, Emmanuel, had had his own accounting business and their mother had worked for a large company before falling ill. Sr. Ariana remembered their mother as being a very fine woman, very capable and concerned about her family. She would have been devastated to know that her boys were living in such appalling conditions. Sr. Ariana, however, lived on the Rwandese side of the border and the two young men were refugees in Bukavu, having fled Rwanda. Their situation was becoming desperate and Sr. Ariana tried ceaselessly to find a way to get money to them.

Finally she decided to ask Fr. John to act as a go-between for the two boys. When the Sisters would come to Eucharist at the Formation Centre, Sr. Ariana would bring money and give it to Fr. John, so that he could see that the boys got it. Fr. John accepted this responsibility, not knowing how long he would be able to continue.

Sr. Ariana sent the boys a message through the High Commission for refugees that they were to go to the School to meet Fr. John and get money for their needs.

Sure enough, the following week Sr. Ariana brought money for the boys and they eventually came to get it. When Fr. John met Jules and Chris for the first time, they spoke a bit about themselves and what was non-threatening for them. They seemed very happy to meet Fr. John and have someone that they could come to for help. They made plans to come and see him again in the course of the next week. He was happy to help but unsure where it would all lead. They seemed like two fine young men, but they had been through horrors unknown and taking responsibility for helping them was very frightening.

A couple of weeks passed before Jules and Chris returned to the school. They came one late evening, not a usual time for visitors at the school. The night watchman had already come on duty and came knocking on Fr. John's office door, saying that he had visitors. Somewhat annoyed that visitors were there so late at a time when he was trying to get some work done for the following day, he yelled out to the night watchman, "Who is it?"

"I don't know them," answered the night watchman.

Fr. John stormed to the main entrance of the school, to the visitors' parlour. There sat Jules and Chris, who looked at him with a terribly embarrassed expression on their faces; they were very apologetic for coming so late. Fr. John felt bad about his reaction and in turn was as embarrassed as they were.

"I'm very sorry," he blurted out. "I did not know it was you! But it's alright. I did tell you to come at any time. Don't worry about my yelling! My bark is worse than my bite."

"We were scared when we heard you. We are sorry to come so late, but with school and trying to get food for ourselves, it is not so easy," they answered.

"Yes, I'm sure," answered Fr. John. "Apart from that, how are you both? How is school? Have your conditions improved any?"

"No, things have worsened. The family we are staying with wants to get rid of us, especially the wife, that is. Her husband who invited us to stay there is away on business and she wants us to leave. She wants us to move into a smaller room that's very dirty, has no bed and we can't even stand up properly in the room, the ceiling is so low. We don't know what to do. This new place is worse, just a cubbyhole. We have nothing to clean with and no bed, nothing." Fr. John told them not to worry about cleaning materials and beds. He could get those things for them. He would give them the cleaning materials that night since those were available at the school, and in the course of the week he would look into finding decent beds for them. Fr. John also gave them a small sum of money that Sr. Ariana had given him for them.

Taking the money and the cleaning materials with them, they got into Fr. John's land cruiser. He drove them home since it was already beginning to get dark out. On the way, he stopped at a roadside stand to get them bread. They would be able to have that with the cheese and jam and milk he had taken from the priests' refectory fridge. They were both very grateful for this. Being out in Bukavu after dark was very dangerous, especially if you were on foot. There were always soldiers and police prowling the streets and a person could easily get mugged or stopped and taken to jail for questioning, especially if the persons resembled Rwandese in any way. The situation was always very unstable and extremely dangerous for Rwandese. Anyway, he set out with both of them hoping that they would not be stopped along the way and taken for questioning.

Jules and Chris wanted Fr. John to see where they were expected to stay. They first made sure that no one in the family was still up. They would be very upset if they knew that Fr. John was visiting. All seemed quiet; there was no one stirring. Into the cubbyhole of a room they quietly went. Fr. John was extremely surprised at what he found. Jules and Chris were expected to live in a small, mouldy smelling room that one could not stand up in. When sitting on a chair, one could put one's hand to the ceiling. It really was a mere cubbyhole, but it was better than being out on the street. Jules and Chris informed Fr. John that the mother of this family was doing this because her husband was away on business and she wanted to get rid of them before he returned. They were at present sharing a room with one of the sons, but both Jules and Chris were sleeping on the same single bed. To manage this, they slept one with his feet at the head of the bed and one with his head at the foot of the bed, somewhat like a pair of shoes properly placed in a shoe box.

Fr. John told the boys to clean the room and that by morning he would have two beds for them and a Coleman stove for them to cook on. They were quite pleased. The next day, again at night when the family was asleep, Fr. John brought the beds and Coleman stove in his land cruiser and an order of food for them: rice, potatoes, tomatoes, onions, maggie cubes, all that was needed for cooking. The one good point of this was that the father of this family, Mr. Mubresa, was not charging them rent; they were able to stay there free of charge.

Eventually, Rosett, the mother of this family, found out how well set-up the boys were, and devised another plan to get rid of them; soon food and other items began to disappear from their room.

Jules appeared one morning at Fr. John's school, pleading with him to do something because the situation had become extremely tense; there was a threat of reporting them to the police as genocide perpetrators from Rwanda. Fr. John told Jules to go with Chris to look for a place to stay in the town of Bukavu. By evening, they had found a place, ironically enough called the Canadiana. It had been a centre where people came for meetings and sessions in the days when things were prosperous in Bukavu. They were able to get two fairly large rooms with a place to bathe. Unfortunately, it was the equivalent of $20 per month, a rather high price for Fr. John to handle. He told them to take it anyway and that same night they moved into their new quarters. It was not a 5-star hotel, but much better than what they had been living in for the last few weeks. They were now free of the threat of being falsely accused and reported to the military or police as fugitive killers.

Fr. John helped Jules and Chris settle in at the Canadiana. They were happy and it restored his peace of mind to know that they were safe. The next thing to be done was to get them into a proper school. He realized that Jules had finished his high school and wanted to do some University studies. Chris was still in high school with two more years to complete. Fr. John was able to help Jules get into the Catholic University of Bukavu and Chris into Hope High School. These schools were not ideal, but they were better than a lot of other educational facilities in the town. The big question was what option to choose for Jules, law or medicine? Chris was completing the program that would eventually take him into a business management option. What was important was that they be placed into a half decent educational facility, have a decent place to live and proper food to eat.

At different times Fr. John visited Jules and Chris in their new living quarters. It was so much better than the cubbyhole that they had been living in. They could now breathe easier and they had adequate room for their beds with space enough to have a cooking area. Fr. John told them that he was pleased with the new accommodations and they admitted that it was a great improvement. To Fr. John, they seemed happier.

School life at Fr. John's center continued its normal course each day. There were classes, meals, manual work, prayer, recreation, meetings and many other activities related to seminary life. They always had recreation in groups after the evening meal and Fr. John had found it hilarious how the students had enjoyed being introduced to the game of bingo. Fr. John had found bingo cards and markers in a box in his office. He wondered who could have possibly brought this bingo game to Zaire. It could have been one of the Canadian White Fathers who had been in charge of formation at one time. Nevertheless, he brought the game with him one evening and asked his group, "Who has played the game of bingo before?" No one had ever played. "Well, now is the time for us to learn", said Fr. John. He, therefore, proceeded to explain what the game was about. They would each have a card with numbers on it and from a bag he would pick out balls with the numbers on them. He would call the number and if they had that number on their card they would cover it with a marker. Once they would have a row covered either across the card from left to right or up and down from top to bottom they would shout Bingo and win a prize. Of course Fr. John had prizes all prepared for them. They thought this was fantastic. He eventually introduced the covering of the numbers in the form of an X or what was called "around the world" which was the covering of all the numbers on the outer edge of the card. This proved to be more difficult, but definitely more challenging. They of course came to love bingo very much and the prizes were quite fantastic. They enjoyed it immensely. They always had a good laugh during bingo.

Then, Fr. John realized that three weeks had gone by and Jules and Chris had not dropped by to see him. He wondered why. They had given him the impression that they would drop by at least once a week to report on how things were going and how life was treating them. The mystery of the long absence, however, would soon be solved.

One afternoon Fr. John had dropped in to visit the White Sister's community in the Nguba quarter of the town. Sister Ghislaine, a Canadian White Sister of Africa, had been appointed to that community and had been there now for close to a year. She was on the Provincial team of the White Sisters, so traveled to the different communities all over Central Africa. Therefore she often went by air to Goma, Kisangani and Kinshasa.

This day as usual she was there to greet Fr. John and to offer him a cup of coffee. He accepted gladly. Sister Ghislaine often had news from Canada and he always enjoyed hearing about what was going on at home.

"What's the news, Sister? Any developments at home?" asked Fr. John.

"Just the usual discussion about the coming referendum on the independence of Quebec, but apparently the 'no' vote just barely squeezed through. There was a lot of uproar over the whole process. It makes me ashamed of my own country."

"That is an ugly story, this independence deal, I must admit. You have been away for more meetings recently, haven't you? I was here a week and a half ago and you weren't around?" he questioned.

"Yes, I went to the Sisters in Bunia, Kisangani and Kinshasa. All went well. What have you been doing besides teaching and taking care of your seminarians?"

"Well, now that Fr. George is back from his sabbatical in the U.S.A. he has been giving us sessions on the enneagramme. I knew about it from before but it is interesting to learn more about it from someone who has studied it more extensively. I have also been meeting with a couple of Rwandese students that Sr. Ariana asked me to supervise, with her help of course."

"Oh, what are their names?"

"Jules Mpamo and his brother Chris," answered Fr. John.

"Oh yes, I don't know the brother, but I know Jules. We met on the plane coming from Kinshasa, and we talked together at the Goma

Airport while waiting for our flight to Bukavu," said Sister Ghislaine, quite unaware of the jolt she had just given Fr. John.

"So Jules was on the same flight as you coming from Kinshasa?"

"Oh yes we had a long talk together. It is amazing all that they have been through and all that they have lost. It is certainly an unjust world," she said in a very sad tone of voice.

Fr. John did not allow his surprise to show regarding what she was telling him. Now he knew why they had not dropped by in the last three weeks. He would find out what went on the next time that they dropped by. It was a real puzzle for him and he was rather anxious to find out why Jules had gone to Kinshasa and had not taken Chris with him. What was it all about?

One evening not long after Fr. John had spoken to Sr. Ghislaine, Jules and Chris came to see Fr. John. He met them in the usual place, the visitors' parlour at the entrance to the school. He greeted them and then said, "Hey, it's been a long time. Where have you been? I was getting worried! You are both well I hope?"

Both of the young men made their excuses for having taken so long to come back. No mention was made, however, of the trip to Kinshasa.

After they had chatted a bit Fr. John said to Jules, "I met someone the other day who knows you."

"Oh, who might that be?" Jules asked.

"Well, her name is Sr. Ghislaine and apparently you met when traveling back from Kinshasa," said Fr. John in a questioning tone.

The two boys looked at one another. "I guess we'll have to tell him, don't you think?" Chris said to Jules.

"I think it would be better for us to do that," answered Jules.

"We saved up some of the money that you gave us so that I could go to Kinshasa to see if anything was left of our father's properties and possessions. We know that he left some things in the hands of some business partners," said Jules. "We just don't know what."

"Did you have any luck in finding anything out?" asked Fr. John.

"Not much, in fact one of those men was very nasty to me, once I was able to track him down," said Jules. "There is something fishy that went on because Philippe, the first partner that I encountered, was visibly upset when he saw me." He asked what I was doing there and told me there was nothing left from our father's business; that all had been dissolved when he died.

But who would have dissolved it?" I asked. He would not tell me. He told me then that he would get me a hotel room for the night and that I was to leave for Bukavu the next day. So, I had to tell him that I had no way back since I had come on a one way ticket. He was not at all pleased. He did find me a hotel room. The next day he did not show up and I was afraid that he would leave me there without paying for more days at the hotel, so I checked out. It was then that I realized that he was sending the police after me. He had told them that I was one of the genocide perpetrators and very dangerous. I wandered around Kinshasa trying to find another of my father's partners, a guy by the name of Jean-Louis. I went to the residence where my father's business had been and found him. He had the same reaction; he wanted to know what I was doing there. When I told him, he was very angry with me and said, "You cannot stay here, you must go back to Bukavu. There is no longer anything here belonging to your father."

"But, what happened to everything, the business and the properties?" I asked.

"He said everything was sold to settle the business debts. I was very disappointed because my father had told us before he died that he had left money in the World Bank for us for our education. I just could not believe all this. They were all such crooks. I just wanted to die. I knew now for sure that we were paupers, poor sons with no money, no property, nothing."

"Then he told me he would take me out to the airport and get me a flight back to Bukavu and send me money later to help us."

"What else could I do? I had hit a dead end. Before boarding the plane, he gave me a bit of money to get something to eat during the journey. On that flight I met Sr. Ghislaine; we ended up sitting side by side. I just had to go and see what was in Kinshasa, to see if there was anything there for us. Now I just want to get out of here, leave this country and this continent, if possible. There is nothing here for us. Please, Fr. John, get us out of here! Send us to Canada or somewhere."

What could Fr. John do? It was quite the dilemma!

It was at that moment that Fr. John made the commitment to do something to get them out of the situation that they were in and to make it possible for them to continue their education and be in a safe place.

How would he do this, he did not know, but he would find a way. The next time that Jules and Chris came to see him he embraced them in the Rwandese fashion by a simple accolade on both cheeks with the side of his head, indicating that they had become family for him. This made them very happy and they promised to discuss what steps could be taken for them to continue their life and education in Bukavu and then to see how they could leave the country to go to a safe place to continue their lives in relative ease and peace.

Fr. John went on home leave that June of 1994 and in doing so brought back clothing and proper footwear for Jules and Chris. They were in great need since much of what they had was worn out and in poor condition. Fr. John also brought back a large sum of money for their schooling. They could come to visit Fr. John at his school when they wanted to and were even able to swim in Lake Kivu if they so wished. Fr. John's school was built next to a volcanic lake and one could swim there without developing health problems (from the water) such as bilharzia Since the school was on the border with Rwanda, they could observe the activity going on across the Ruzizi River, the river that formed the border crossing with Rwanda. Jules and Chris continued to visit Fr. John at the seminary and often came to swim in the lake and also to attend services on Sundays. They would come to chat in the evenings when Fr. John was not too busy. Life continued at the seminary at a normal pace but news often filtered through about how the situation in both Rwanda and Zaire was deteriorating. In the town of Bukavu danger lurked at every turn and life became more and more difficult for the two young men.

They did their best to live their lives as best they could in Bukavu. They studied and kept their living space neat and tidy. They shared the buying of food in the market and the cooking. They came from time to time to watch a video with Fr. John since the seminary had a fairly good repertoire of movies.

Jules and Chris continued their studies, thanks to the help of Fr. John. Jules was in the pre-med programme at the Catholic University of Bukavu and Chris was in a private school called l'Ecole Espoir to complete his secondary school courses. This school had school fees that needed to be paid. Fr. John managed to provide the money for these school fees from the money that he received from the seminary each month for his stipend. Fr. John was determined not to leave them on their own.

The situation in Zaire remained somewhat stable in spite of the danger that existed but deteriorated horribly and considerably as awful news leaked through about President Mobutu's attitude towards the Rwandese population that had been living in Zaire for years. There were two main groups, the Banyamulenge from the Uvira Hills and the Banyarwanda from the Masisi area close to the town of Goma, further up the northeast border of Zaire. The Zairean President, who was pro-Hutu, decided that these people were no longer citizens of his country. This was appalling after 300 years in that country. A truly earth shattering declaration!

This caused a terrible reaction from the Banyamulenge, the people living in the Uvira hills. Uvira was a town on Lake Tanganyika bordering the country of Burundi. These people were a warrior people and many of the young men had gone to Rwanda for the war effort there, since their roots were Rwandese. They had returned with arms in well-hidden parts and packages and the Zairean military and police had let them through since they gave the Zairean soldiers and police money for food for their starving families. President Mobutu was not paying his soldiers for the most part, so there was much discontent in their ranks. When these young rebels heard this terrible news about their rejected citizenship, they organized themselves once again and attacked the military camp in Uvira; it was the beginning of a revolt that would have disastrous consequences. They formed a strong army and, with the help of the new Rwandese regime across the border, they swept up the eastern border, taking the towns as they made their way north. Bukavu was for the taking. This was when it became extremely dangerous for Jules and Chris. The military in the area would recognize them as Rwandese and would arrest and jail them, or simply kill them. They would be suspected of being part of the rebel group. They came one Sunday afternoon to see Fr. John, fearing for their lives.

"We need to get out!" they said. "Chris cannot study at his school. He is suspect, and it is too dangerous for him to walk through the town. His features are too Tutsi. Where can we go?" Fr. John stood thinking for a moment.

"Is the plane that comes from Nairobi to take refugees from the camps if they are able to pay the $500 US fare still operating?" asked Fr. John.

"Yes, I think so," answered Jules.

"Well, go and check it out. Find out when it is coming again and get yourselves ready to go to the airport to see if you can board the plane". They both had their old Rwandese passports that Fr. John had gotten them through the refugee camp. It had been expensive, but worth it; they now had a necessary travel document. The passport also indicated that they had been born in Kinshasa, the capital of Zaire since their parents had been living and working there when they were born.

"You'll have to try and take the flight with your existing passports. You will need to show some kind of document to board the airplane; it's a chance you have to take!"

The following morning Jules came to Fr. John to tell him that there was a plane flying out the very next day, Tuesday. They had to be there as early as possible. They did not know if they would get on the flight; they had to chance it. Fr. John went to the Canadiana with them and helped them pack. They packed what they could that day in clothing and footwear. All the pots and pans, they gave to a family living at the Canadiana. Fr. John would take the beds to the Sisters convent and boarding school. They would certainly find use for them. The clothes they did not need they gave to a young man they had befriended at the Canadiana. Fr. John met them the next morning to drive them to the market. He told Jules to find a taxi in good condition that would not break down on the way. They had to go 30 kilometres to the airport and Jules was to negotiate a price for the trip. Fr. John did not go with Jules because he knew that the minute the taxi driver saw his white face, he would double the fare. The night before, Fr. John had given both of them instructions on what to do once they reached Nairobi. He put the money he had gathered for them while on home leave into two money belts and had them strap the money belts inside their underwear. They were then to keep only enough money in their pockets to pay the plane fare and cover bribes at the Kavumu airport and once in Nairobi. After getting their entry visas they were to take a taxi, not public transport, to the YMCA. They were to stay there until they could find a bank to deposit their money in and a school where they could study English. They could then look for a small apartment to settle into. Fr. John would join them when he could to arrange for immigration to Canada. Fr. John was not able to accompany them to the Bukavu airport since he had to deal with the situation at his school. He told them that once they had found a room at the YMCA and a bank for their money, they were to fax him at the Central House of the Missionaries of Africa in Bukavu. He would then know they were safe. Fr. John watched them enter the taxi from a distance, praying that all would go well. "Please, God, be with them!" he prayed. But still, he wondered if he would ever see them again.

The whole of that night Fr. John stayed awake praying this time on his knees on a small mat in his room facing the direction of the Kavumu airport, imploring God to take them to a safe place.

Chapter Seven

So many of the incidents that happened in Fr. John's life reminded him of the days at home when he had been trying to get his life established and get his education completed. There were incidents that underlined how fragile our lives are and that a loved one's life can be taken away so quickly and easily. It was a frightening realization. He learned that there are many things in life that we cannot control and that we must not take for granted.

While growing up, John learned and experienced all that their village life had to offer. What he learned at school in the history and geography books intrigued him greatly and he hoped to be able to experience some of those beautiful and interesting places one day. Before all that could happen, however, he was to continue to experience the many joys, surprises and difficult moments of growing up, in family life and school life. It was all part of the fabric of one's existence.

John was one of those young men who seemed to remain oblivious to the outward physical changes that were taking place in him as he grew older and entered more fully into young adulthood. Those who knew him and had contact with him each day did notice the changes. First of all, he was becoming taller and was developing into a fine-looking young man. He was always neat and clean and quite pleasant to talk to. One bright and sunny Saturday morning his mother sent him to the grocery store across the street to pick up butter, eggs and milk. "Tell Agatha to put it on our grocery bill and that I will be in to settle the bill on Monday," said Rose.

John had already washed up, combed his hair and had put on fresh, clean jeans and a green v-neck sweater over a beige shirt. He looked just fine. He walked over to Agatha's and found Yvonne, Agatha's daughter, behind the counter. "Hi John, my, don't you look nice today," said Yvonne.

"He sure does look good," said Agatha as she came into the store from the kitchen area of the house.

John said thank you to them and smiled shyly. He was really not used to having people say things like that to him. Yvonne asked him, "What can we do for you this morning?"

"My mom needs milk, butter and eggs. You can just put it on the bill. She'll be in to settle it on Monday," answered John.

The two women looked at John strangely; then Yvonne said, "You sound different today. Do you have a cold?"

"No, I'm just fine," answered John, surprised at Yvonne's comment.

Both Yvonne and her mother looked at one another and burst out laughing. John did not understand this outburst and just looked at them inquisitively. Then Yvonne said to John, "Oh, my goodness, your voice is changing! You have lost your little boy's voice and now you have a man's voice. You have become a man!" they exclaimed laughing merrily.

John did not think it was funny at all. He was totally surprised, not having realized that his voice had changed. He guessed that it probably went part and parcel with the sticky fluid change. 'Why could I not have awakened one morning to find myself as a grown up adult," said John to himself. He hated all of this. It made him feel awkward. When he walked into the house with the groceries, he said to his mother, "Don't send me there for groceries again! They are crazy women; they were laughing at me and I didn't like it!"

"Why were they laughing at you?" Rose asked.

"They said my voice was changing and that now I had a man's voice! What's so funny about that!" John exclaimed.

John's mother did not comment and just smiled to herself.

John was certainly growing up. He was discovering, and facing his own likes and dislikes. What would he do in life? This question came to mind often. He wanted to do something that would help his family. He also had the thought of becoming a religious person of some kind, like a priest maybe but not a priest like the ones who were in the parishes here at home but a missionary priest, one who would go and help the poor in foreign lands like Africa. He had understood well the message of Jesus that the Sisters passed on to him, that God calls us to give and share our lives with others especially the poor and the needy. He gives us a special love and invites us to give that love back in the form of loving service. He knew that he could begin doing this by the service he could render in his family and by helping others in small ways. He knew that this was not easy to do because people often interpreted your goodness to them as your way of taking advantage of them. Such a reaction was quite discouraging. He knew that he needed to resolve a lot of the tensions and turmoil in his life before he could do any of this. As well, his father was the only bread winner in the family. John's mother was a very brittle diabetic and it was simply too much for her to work outside the home. The family had many needs. The house needed repairs; his father needed transportation to and from work; there were now too many mouths to feed on one income. The children would need to help, but how? John would have liked to do more for the family but he needed to finish high school and be allowed to choose a career and take the time needed to complete the necessary education required for that. He knew also how hard it was for his father to be the sole provider for the family. Martine had just recently started to work part-time while going to school. Della would soon be old enough to work part-time. Della had no desire to pursue an education beyond high school; in fact, she hated school. They all continued to struggle courageously and help each other in the best way that they could.

John knew that to be of some help to the family and to his father, who was working very hard, he would need to do his best to get odd jobs here and there to at least get some pocket money for himself and be able to pay for certain small things that he might need. He regularly made the rounds of the village businesses, such as the grocery stores and the clothing stores, to see if there was any kind of work that he could do. Since he had now entered his teens, he knew that they could give him work and he always did the work quite well, especially since he was already becoming extremely meticulous. He most often got the job of cleaning out the storage areas of the stores, putting order in those areas and making sure all was clean and neatly arranged. He did not make a huge amount of money but a couple of dollars went a long way in those days. Note books and pencils were only five or ten cents each. Comic books were only ten cents each and he just loved reading comic books; he had a small collection of them neatly stacked next to the sofa in the sitting room where he sometimes slept. There were times when his daily chores were completed, when he would sit quietly just reading his comic books. He enjoyed doing that just before supper.

One afternoon on his way home from school, John decided to stop in at the post office to see if there was any mail for the family; he had not picked up the mail on the previous evening. The family did not have a mail box, it being too expensive, so John would go to the general delivery wicket and ask for the mail for the DeCoste family. On that particular afternoon, Mrs. Duquesne, the post mistress, was the one serving people at the general delivery wicket. As she gave John the few letters for his family, she asked him what grade he was in at school. He answered proudly, "I'm now in grade nine. I just recently turned fourteen."

"Well good for you," answered Mrs. Duquesne. Then she added, "How would you like to work here in the post office part time? We need someone after school and on Saturdays. It would entail sorting the mail when it comes in around four o'clock in the afternoon and selling stamps and giving out parcels. Do you think that you would be able to do that?"

John could not believe his ears. He immediately said, "Oh yes, for sure I could do that. I would love to do that."

"Good," answered the post mistress. "Call in here after school tomorrow afternoon and I will fill out an application form with you and we can see when you can start working."

"I will be here, Mrs. Duquesne, and thank you so much for this job offer. I'll do my best to do good work." John rushed home to tell his mother the good news. He knew that his father would be very pleased. It would be such a big help to the family budget.

John started his new job the following week and was trained to sort the letters and put them in the different mail boxes. Any letters that were posted were to be taken out of the out-going bin and stamped to obliterate the stamp that had been placed on the letter. He would hand out the parcels that had come in each day for different people. He also sold stamps.

John loved the job and did his utmost to do it well. He worked at the post office for the next two years, all through ninth and tenth grade. The most difficult part of the job was Saturdays during the summer months. If his friends planned an outing to the beach, he couldn't go because he worked Saturdays. Since it was vacation time, however, he could go on outings during the daytime because he only worked from four o'clock on. So missing the Saturday outings wasn't a terrible hardship.

One bright, sunny Wednesday afternoon, John's friend Lawrence Dobbins wanted to go to the beach for a couple of hours but didn't want to go alone. "Come with me, John. We'll only stay for a short time and then come back in time for you to go to work. Please, please," he pleaded. "We have a ride with my uncle and then we'll leave in time to be able to hitch-hike back in time for you to get to work."

"We don't have a ride back since your uncle cannot stay. The beach is quite far from here. It's at least two and a half miles. That's too dangerous for me. I could end up being late for work," said John. It was a beautiful day and it would be fun, thought John. Maybe he could chance it. So, without further thought, he conceded, and went with his friend.

They had a very enjoyable time and the water in the swimming hole next to the ocean was quite warm. There was a pond not far from the ocean that flowed under a small bridge that gave access to the beach. One of the villagers had widened the area just before the bridge with his bulldozer and this became the swimming hole. The water was very warm and it continued to flow further downstream and into the very cold ocean. There was beautiful sand all around the swimming hole and most people enjoyed swimming here rather than in the cold ocean. John fell asleep on a towel spread out on the sand. It was so warm and comfortable that he hated to wake up. Then suddenly he threw himself up off the towel, exclaiming, "Oh my God, what time is it? I'll be late for work!" He looked at his watch and it was already three- thirty in the afternoon. He had to be to work by four o'clock. He dressed quickly and yelled to Lawrence that they had to go. For some reason that John could not understand, Lawrence seemed to be taking his own sweet time.

"What's your rush for God's sake, you'll get there. It's not that far!" said Lawrence snidely.

John felt very hurt by this remark. It was as if Lawrence didn't care and wanted John to be late. John felt very hurt by his attitude. They finally reached the highway into the village and the cars whizzed by them but none would stop. Four o'clock rolled by and John was still on the road. Five o'clock rolled by as well and still no car would stop. Finally at five-forty a car stopped. It was John's math teacher, Mr. Boyd. "Hey, you guys, hop in. Where are you headed?" he asked.

"I'm headed for work at the post office," John answered in desperation, "and I'm already very late."

"I'm just going home for supper," said Lawrence laughingly.

John could not believe that he could be so mean. It seemed as if Lawrence wanted him to lose his job. Mr. Boyd gladly let John off at the post office. He quietly and slowly walked into the work area. Mrs. Duquesne and Mrs. Elvira were sitting quietly, patiently waiting for the mail truck to arrive with all the mail for the region. John was pleasantly surprised to learn that the mail had not yet arrived. It would make the situation less disastrous.

"Where do you think you're going?" asked Mrs. Duquesne, obviously quite annoyed at John and not at all pleased with his extreme tardiness.

"I'm coming to work," answered John calmly. "I'm really sorry that I'm so late, but I foolishly listened to Lawrence and went to Pondville Beach with him to swim." He told them all that had happened.

"Well okay," said Mrs. Duquesne, "but don't let it happen again. Your father was also looking for you. He came in here wondering where you were and what had happened to you." Just at that moment, John's father walked into the post office. He was visibly upset and said to John, "Where the hell have you been? We were worried when you didn't come home before work. Your mother was frantic!"

John explained the situation once again to his father. He was no sooner finished when Martha McClusky, an elderly woman of the village who carried the mail for many of the village people, called out in her very French accent and poor grammar, "There the mail!" She did this each day, warning everyone that the mail truck from Port Hawkesbury had just crested the hill on its way to the post office. John breathed a sigh of relief, saved by Martha's warning. John told his father that he had to go and that he would see him at home. Batist nodded quickly with a very displeased look on his face. John lowered the wicket in preparation for the sorting and distribution of the mail.

Mrs. Elvira whispered to John as they dragged the bags of mail into the sorting room, "I was worried about you! I thought she was going to fire you. You certainly got off easy."

They both laughed merrily at John's good fortune. Mrs. Duquesne didn't notice what was going on since she was busy wrapping up the day's money orders to be sent out with the returning mail truck.

John had managed to get a job that could help out with some small money matters in the household. He did not want to think about what his father's reaction would have been if he had lost his job. That kind of incident would not happen again. Lawrence was somewhat of a nut case and John needed to be careful of his suggestions even if he was a friend. He knew that it was important to the family that he keep that job. He could even give a bit of spending money to his younger brother and sister, something his father could not always do with just one income coming into the house.

John continued to work at the post office until the end of tenth grade. He decided at the end of that year that he would go to Halifax to help his sister Martine who now had two children. Mrs. Duquesne asked John who he could recommend to replace him while he was gone. With a certain amount of misgivings, he did recommend that she hire Lawrence. He was a good and capable worker; John knew that he would do the work well. He could not vouch, however, for his total honesty and discretion. Lawrence had no qualms whatsoever about lying and exaggerating. He also had sticky fingers: at times ending up with things in his shopping bags that seemed to miraculously appear without John knowing how.

John could not forget the incident that had taken place one December afternoon at LeBrun's General store in the village when he had gone shopping with Lawrence for Christmas gifts. John had been totally shocked by what had taken place and would never forget it.

They had gone shopping for Christmas gifts. Lawrence also had a baptismal gift to buy for a very good friend who was having his baby boy baptized just before Christmas. Lawrence wanted something beautiful and appropriate but at the same time practical and useful. They looked at many baby things and he finally decided to give them a whole bundle of diapers, not necessarily a beautiful gift but a very necessary and useful one. They did look at one beautiful pyjama ensemble that would have been ideal but it was very expensive since it also had a set of booties and a beautiful little baby cap with it. Lawrence, however, settled for the diapers even though he really loved the pyjama set. All was paid for and John accompanied Lawrence to his home. When they arrived, Lawrence emptied the bag of gifts onto the dining-room table since he wanted to wrap the baptismal gift immediately. Out of the bag came not only the diapers but the pyjama set as well. John looked at Lawrence stunned. He said to Lawrence, "How did that get there? I don't remember you buying the set when we were at the cash register?" Lawrence simply burst out laughing and said to John, "It's a simple case of the hand is quicker than the eye! The cashier did not catch it. It's my gain!" John felt a cold shiver go through him.

Lawrence was hired for the post office position and John left for his sister's in Halifax. When he returned the following year to take grade twelve at the Convent school, Lawrence was still working at the post office. He remembered that Miriam had written to him while he was in Halifax telling him that a number of people had complained to the post office that mail destined for them had gone missing. John did not think too much of it. Mail often went missing, especially letters.

John started grade twelve and often walked to and from school with Lawrence. There were times when Miriam was with them. One Monday morning John stopped at Lawrence's house to see if he was ready for school. To his surprise he found Lavinia, Lawrence's mother, sitting at the dining-room table crying silently.

"My goodness, Mrs. Dobbins, is someone sick, you seem so upset?"

At that moment, Lawrence's father came into the dining-room from the kitchen and tried to explain to John what was wrong. It was a bit difficult because, Mr. Dobbins, had a very bad stutter.

"I-I-I-It's Lawrence! H-H-H-He's in jail! They c-c-c-came to a-a-a-arrested him this morning!' he exclaimed. "He's a-a-a-accused of theft by the p-p-p-post office."

"I am so sorry, I didn't know," answered John. "Which jail is he in?" John asked.

"Oh, h-h-h-he's j-j-j-just over here a-a-a-across the w-w-w-way in the C-C-C-Court House jail. There will p-p-p-probably be a trial d-d-d-date s-s-s-set since h-h-h-he is to a-a-a-appear b-b-b-before the m-m-m-magistrate this a-a-a-afternoon. We d-d-d-don't know w-w-w-what to m-m-m-make of it!"

"I don't know what to say," said John, "but please tell Lawrence that I will come and visit him as soon as I am allowed to do so."

He continued on his way to school. Once at school everyone was talking about it. From what John could understand he had been caught red-handed stealing mail. John would call into the post office that afternoon to see if he could find out more about what had happened. Throughout the day he thought about it a lot. It was a frightening thing. What if Lawrence implicated him since they were close friends. Miriam sought John out at recess with a worried look on her face.

"I wonder what they'll do to him?" she asked more to herself than directly to John.

John answered pensively, "God only knows but it is a very serious offense to tamper with the Royal Mail."

John called into the post office after school and was pleased to find that Mrs. Elvira was alone at that moment. Mrs. Duquesne had to go to a meeting concerning the whole sordid incident. Mrs. Elvira got John to come into the work area so she could tell him what had happened privately. The mail truck wouldn't arrive for another forty-five minutes.

"What happened?" John asked. "How did he get caught?"

"Well, two plain clothes detectives came in on Friday morning and spoke to Milly and I. Apparently an investigation had been made into the disappearance of mail and it was discovered that the mail was going missing between here and Port Hawkesbury. So they asked Milly if mail was regularly posted in the outside box and if that was checked each day. Of course we said that the outside box was checked each day in preparation for the outgoing mail and that it was Lawrence who checked that box. The detectives told Milly that they would post two letters in the outside box with money in them. She was to ask Lawrence to check the outside box as usual and they would be in the lobby of the post office; then if Lawrence said there were no letters in the outside box, she would signal them. So at four-thirty Milly told Lawrence to check the outside box for mail and when he returned he said there wasn't any. Of course, then we knew. I tell you my heart skipped a beat and I went all cold inside. I just felt so bad for him.

146

After we had delivered all the mail, we left for home. Lawrence went home on foot and the two detectives followed him in their car. Before he went in, they stopped the car by him and one of them said to him, 'I think you have something that belongs to us. We would like to get it back please.' Of course, Lawrence answered, 'What could I possibly have of yours. I don't even know you!' The detectives said, 'You may not know us but we know that you have two letters on you that belong to us. Now you can give them up freely or we can search you right here on the spot.' They showed him their detective badges, evidence that they had the authority to search him. Then he knew that he had no choice but to comply. They discovered that he could check letters and cards with a pin and see if there was money in them. If they had money he would take them. Parcels had gone missing as well so he would take the blame for all of it. They told him to get into the car and questioned him extensively because they wanted to know if there was anyone else in on this with him. But Lawrence told them there was no one else involved. I guess he didn't want to share his ill-gotten gains with anyone. I just get the shivers each time I think of it," said Mrs. Elvira. John just listened in utter silence. Now he knew what had happened to the sport coat that he had ordered.

When John had returned from Halifax he had decided to order himself a sport coat for the Christmas of that year. He loved the colour olive green and there was a beautiful corduroy jacket in the Sears catalogue. He ordered it c.o.d.(cash on delivery) and intended to pay for it with money that he had saved while working at the post office. Christmas Eve rolled around and no sport coat was in sight. For some reason he had not received it and the company had not said anything about it. John found that rather strange since they always told you if it was not in stock. It was now too late to do anything about it. He would check it out after the Christmas holiday. Christmas Eve, on his way to mid-night mass, John had dropped by Lawrence's to wish him a Merry Christmas and was surprised to see Lawrence with a beautiful olive green sport coat on. "Where did you get that coat? The village clothing store did not have anything like that in stock when I went in there so I ordered one from the Sears catalogue but I didn't receive it," said John.

"Oh I went into the village clothing store on Christmas Eve in the afternoon and they had received a new shipment of men's clothes and this

147

was in it so I bought it for Christmas," was Lawrence's reply. John did not think too much of it at the time. Then the week following Christmas when he had called into the post office, Mrs. Duquesne called him to the wicket where c.o.d's were received and paid for. "Did you receive an olive green sport coat from Sears before Christmas?" she asked John.

"I did order the sport coat for Christmas but never ever received it," said John.

"Well they are inquiring about it and so I would need you to sign some forms here to that effect, John," she said.

"That's fine, I can do that," answered John. Then he added, "I was so disappointed that I did not receive the coat for Christmas."

John now realized that most probably Lawrence had stolen the sport coat when it had come in since John had told him that he had ordered it. He could not prove it but with his being caught stealing, John felt that this had to be the case. He felt so betrayed. That he could steal from a close friend was very upsetting to John. The hurt was palpable in him. He would visit him and he felt great pity for Lawrence, but he knew that he would never be able to trust him again.

John visited Lawrence in the local jail many times after the court sentenced him to six months in the local jail. The judge had been lenient on him because Lawrence was an adopted child. He was not the natural child of Lavinia and Charlie Dobbins. They had had a girl and since they couldn't have any other children, and they had wanted a boy, they had adopted Lawrence. It was shown in court that he had had a difficult beginning before Charlie and Lavinia had adopted him. Lawrence took the whole ordeal, the theft, being caught, the trial and the prison sentence as a big joke. He laughed a hearty laugh about the whole thing when John had first visited him. When he came out of jail, however, he didn't continue his schooling but left for Halifax to find work. John heard from him a few times while he was in Halifax but he also heard that he had lost one job in Halifax once again because of his stealing. He had then lost touch with him. John was rehired at the post office until he finished his high school and set out for Teachers' College.

Life continued on its course and there would be many more disappointments along with the good moments. The lack of money and a very tight budget continued to be a big factor in the family but they plodded on in hope. No matter how poor they were, however, and how tight the budget could be, it did not stop Batist from going on his usual drinking binges. These binges were always very worrisome and fearful for John.

John had never forgotten one horrendous drinking binge that his father had gone on when John was still in eighth grade and Martine had just finished her high school and was working as a nursing assistance at the village hospital. It had remained engraved in his mind and would remain so for many years to come. That night his father had come home very late after work; it had been some time after one in the morning. It had frightened John terribly and it had left him with an awful foreboding feeling that the binges would one day end in some horrific accident and even death.

Rose had come to them in their bedrooms and in a frightened voice had said to them, "Come and see your father. He is sleeping so be very quiet so as not to wake him. Something terrible must have happened to him last night, he looks terrible. Come and see, then you'll know what I mean."

They had quietly gathered around the bed when their mother had put the bedroom light on. They had all gasped bringing their hands to their mouths so as not to cry out and wake him. Batist lay on the bed in a sound sleep but what was disturbing for them were the many cuts and bruises covering his head and face. Some of the cuts had been bandaged. His hands and fingers were also quite bruised and scratched. What could possibly have happened, they wondered. Maybe they would find out more come morning. It was all very disturbing.

For some time after high school and long before leaving for Halifax to join Francis, Martine had worked as a nursing assistant at the village hospital to earn a bit of money for her future studies. On this particular day that Batist had decided to go on one of his binges, she was working on the night shift and was totally shocked when the small ambulance brought in a man who had been in some kind of accident, a man who turned out to be her own father. She was told that he had been found wandering the streets of the village in a confused state, not knowing much about his condition, not sure as to how he had gotten into such a mess. He thought that he had been in a car accident or had fallen over an embankment after having been hit by a car. He did not know for sure what had happened. He had cried when he had seen Martine. "That's okay Dad," she had said to reassure him and had helped the doctor and nurse to clean him up and bandage his wounds. He had been discharged and one of the orderlies had driven him home.

When Martine had come home from work early that same morning, her father was still sleeping. "How is he?" she had asked as she came into the house.

"He is still sleeping," they had replied. Martine proceeded to tell them what she had learned from the hospital. It was either an accident or someone had pushed him down a large embankment." Maybe he would be able to shed some light on this once he would wake up. They let him sleep.

Batist finally woke up around eleven o'clock that morning. "What happened to you?" She asked him as he lay there looking up at the ceiling pensively.

"Be damned if I know," exclaimed Batist. "I was at a friend's house and we were having many beers, as well as my favourite, the one and only Demerara rum, that I love so much. By the time midnight rolled around, I was extremely drunk and could hardly stand up. Simon and his wife did not want me to leave but I insisted. Of course, I didn't think I was drunk, just feeling good. I went out into the night air without any kind of light to guide me. Suddenly, I had the impression that I was falling and at the same time something or someone was hitting me. Then I lost consciousness. I don't know how long I was out. I came to when I felt cold water splashing on my face. The water tasted salty. I was on the shore. I finally got up and started to walk along the shore line and came to a clearing that led me to houses that had lights on outside. I knew then that I was on the road. I was in the middle of the road when a van came along and stopped so that I could clear off the road. However, it was Roddie, the undertaker's helper. He realized that I was injured and took me to the hospital and here I am."

"You're sure that it was not someone from Simon's who followed you and beat you up?" asked Martine.

"Well, that could be, but I don't think so. I think I fell off the embankment that is behind Simon's since I could not see in the dark. That embankment is a sheer drop to the shore. Luckily Roddie came along when he did. I don't know what would have happened to me," said Batist as he looked at them.

"What I hope is that you learned a lesson from this! You could have killed yourself and you also could have drowned if the tide had been high. The liquor will be the end of you one of these days," said Rose.

John listened intently to all of it and had that foreboding feeling that one day they would pick their father up dead in some ditch if he did not stop drinking. That night he was on his knees for a good while before sleeping. He continued to realize more and more how important prayer is in one's life and the need for trust in a loving being greater than oneself. He knew that he needed to be in love not just with a loving, human being but with a being greater than any human being.

Martine continued her work at St. Ann's Hospital as a nursing assistant. She also had continued to date Francis, her high school sweetheart. It all seemed very serious and marriage would probably be considered. Francis, having graduated from high school, needed to find work. He decided to go to Halifax to look for a job. He left for Halifax soon after graduation and promised Martine he would write. But Martine seemed preoccupied and worried and hated to see him go. She would have preferred to take the bus with him, but without proper accommodations in the city, this was not possible. Francis intended to stay at his brother's but his apartment was not large enough for two extra people.

John found that once Francis had left for Halifax, Martine stayed at home a lot when not working at the hospital. She had always stayed at Francis' house or at Aunt Laura's, Rose's sister. Suddenly she was very present at home. John wondered why!

One evening, when John came home for supper, he found Martine busy setting the table for the evening meal but he also noticed that she seemed to have been crying and was still trying to stop the tears from flowing. This seemed rather strange. John was worried. He loved Martine very much and he did not want her to be hurt or unhappy. He also thought that she had put on a bit of weight especially around her waist. Since he now knew about the sticky fluid and egg situation in the lives of men and women---Mr. David had informed them about all of this---he wondered if there was not some kind of a situation that had developed between Martine and Francis. After all they had been going together now for some time.

It was all so puzzling and so mysterious. The family did not talk openly about such things.

John ate supper and then went next door to the Babin family's house to watch one of his favourite television programmes. Eleanor, Mrs. Babin, allowed him to come and watch television at their house. She enjoyed his company and he was good friends with her daughters, Jenny and Lenore. He stayed until the programme was over and then went home, still somewhat worried about Martine's situation.

When he came into the house, Martine was lying down on the living-room sofa. His Mom and Dad were with her; they were talking together. John heard his father say to Martine, "You don't have to marry this young man. You can have your baby and we will love it and raise it as our own. You can get more education and make a good life for yourself. You are our daughter and you will always have a place here. This is your home! You are not the first one that this has happened to and you won't be the last."

"But I love him, Dad," answered Martine.

"But he has been gone for three weeks now and has not contacted you! Why? You must try to contact him and find out what he intends to do!"

"I don't like to pressure him like that," answered Martine.

"But he can't leave you alone to face this on your own," responded Batist. Then he asked Martine, "Did he leave you a phone number where he could be reached?"

"Yes, he did."

"Then, you go to your Aunt Laura's and ask her permission to phone him."

"Will Aunt Laura let me do that? It is long distance and very expensive to call Halifax."

"She should, you have stayed with her and helped her enough times," Batist said. Martine decided that she would do that the next day after work. John now knew what was going on. He now understood why Lucy Pond, the barber's daughter, had asked him some days previously if it were true that Martine was pregnant. John told her that he did not know, but that he did not think so. Lucy had replied, "Well, that is the rumour that is going around the village!"

"Of course, that would be the rumour," John had answered. "This village is filled with nasty gossipers. There is also a rumour that you are allowing George Levy to play around with you in the hay field, but I don't ask you if that is true or not, do I?"

Lucy had been very annoyed at him for saying this, but John didn't care.

Aunt Laura allowed Martine to call Francis. She spoke to him quite privately and came away from the phone with a smile on her face.

"It must be good news," said Aunt Laura, "I see you're smiling."

"He hadn't called because he was busy with a series of interviews with a company called British American Oil. He starts work in a week and he wants me to leave my job at the hospital and come join him in Halifax."

"I'm so glad that things are working out for you," said Aunt Laura. "My dear, when it comes to men, you must be very vigilant and you must not allow them to control you, no matter what the situation. You did not put your own self into this situation. It took two of you to tango. He also needs to do the right thing. Do not let love and your emotions blind you to your good common sense and right judgment or else your freedom will just go out the window. Anyway, you should have enough time to leave your job at the hospital and get things organized to go to Halifax. Do you have enough money for the bus fare?"

"Yes I do. I have been saving most of my money from work," said Martine. "He is expecting me a week from today."

Martine did leave for Halifax the following Monday. They were all very sad as they watched her board the bus and leave for the big city all by herself. Batist loved Martine very much, as did John; he could not stop the tears from flowing at that moment. It was the first time that John had ever seen his father cry. It was a sad day. John would never forget Martine's smiling face as she sat in the window seat of the bus. In those days the Acadian Lines buses came onto Isle Madame and went through the four villages to pick up passengers who were waiting for it by the side of the road. They would signal the bus with their hand for it to stop. The bus trip at that time from Arichat to Halifax was a six hour journey.

John could not believe that Martine was leaving. He prayed that all would be well for his beloved Martine. What John did not know was that Rose had made Martine promise her that she would not marry "outside of the Church" when she and Francis exchanged their marriage vows.

Martine had made that promise to her mother. Time would produce a different outcome.

The family heard from Martine several times in the course of the following month. It took time of course for letters to arrive from Halifax. Finally a letter arrived letting them know that they had found a small apartment and that she and Francis would be marrying soon. Martine informed her mother that she was now beginning to show in her pregnancy; it was, therefore, important that they exchange their vows soon. As Rose silently read the letter she made her way quietly into her bedroom. They were sitting down to supper when John had brought the letter in from the post office. As they continued their supper John realized that his mother was not around.

"Where is mom?" John asked.

"I think she went into the bedroom," responded Della.

John went looking for his mother. As he got to the bedroom door, he saw that his mother was standing before the bedroom window, her back to the door and obviously holding Martine's letter in her hand. John could not see her face but he was sure that she was crying.

"What's wrong, Mom? Why aren't you coming for supper? Did you get bad news from Martine?" John asked anxiously.

Rose turned towards John, tears streaming down her cheeks and, without a word, handed him the letter. With the letter was a marriage license to be signed by the parents giving their consent to the marriage since Martine was not yet nineteen years of age. As John read the entire contents of the letter, it dawned on him why his mother was crying. Martine asked her mother if she would like to have her prayer book. In those days, most Catholics had prayer books that they used at Mass; they would follow the prayers of the Mass in English or French from the prayer book since the Mass was celebrated in Latin. Martine told her mother that she would no longer need the prayer book since they would be doing their marriage in the United Church; she would more than likely attend the services there with Francis rather than in the Catholic Church.

"She promised me that she would not do that!" Rose whispered as she wiped the tears from her eyes.

"Let it be, Mom. Martine is there alone with none of us with her. She needs to be able to adjust to life there. She may be feeling pressured by all that she is going through. We will pray for her and hope that all goes well," John told his mom. Deep down in his heart, however, John was extremely saddened by Martine's decision. She would be automatically excommunicated from the Church community and not be permitted to receive communion, the consecrated bread.

Rose could not seem to stop crying. John felt very bad and tried to console her. Batist and the remainder of the family received the news in gloomy silence.

The family knew that Martine's situation would eventually make the rounds of the village. They would be looked upon with curious, pitying stares. Village gossip was always so vicious and rampant. John hated this part of village life, but he would hold his head up and let them talk; he would certainly never stop loving Martine no matter what!

The marriage license was signed and quickly sent back. None of the family wanted Martine to suffer. They wanted her to know that they supported her and loved her, even if they didn't agree with her. In those days it was considerably frowned upon for a Roman Catholic to exchange vows in a Protestant Church without a dispensation from the authorities of the Church to do so. This would eventually change considerably but it was still a long way from happening.

Martine and Francis were married in the Barrington Street United Church. She did not seem to have any difficulties with her pregnancy. She wrote home as regularly as she could; phoning being so expensive that it was pretty much out of the question. The family was overjoyed when a letter arrived from Martine asking her mother and father if she and Francis could come home for Christmas. What a treat that would be for everyone! What Rose could not understand and what pained her greatly was that Martine felt that she needed to ask permission to come home for a visit.

"How could she think that way?" Rose asked. "She is our daughter, we love her no matter which church she married in and no matter if she was pregnant before she married. How could we reject her and stop loving her for that?" In fact Rose had been furious at her sister Cecile's reaction when she had told her that Martine and Francis would be coming home for Christmas.

"You will allow them to come here and sleep together in your house when they are not properly married?" Cecile had asked.

"Yes I will allow it," Rose had answered Cecile. "She is our daughter and we love her. There is also a rule in the Church that tells us that charity comes before all else. Christ would never reject her so why should I?"

"Well, her children will be nothing but bastards as long as she is married outside of the Catholic Church," responded Cecile.

"Maybe you believe that but I don't and anyway it is none of your business, Cecile. You do what you want with your children and I'll do what I want with mine. And, don't you ever bring this up to me again," Rose answered her sister in anger. Cecile remained silent. She had not forgotten how Rose had helped her when she had returned from the convent years ago, very hurt and quite ill. Rose had always been ahead of the rest of the family in her way of thinking concerning many of the beliefs of their faith and she was surely not about to change that way of thinking at that moment.

Martine and Francis came for Christmas and of course Rose, Batist and the family did their possible best to make them welcome and comfortable. Rose and Batist gave them their bedroom so they would have more privacy. Della and Clarisse doubled up in the one bedroom left and Timmy and John made sure that the sofa was ready for them in the living-room and all back in place early the next morning. Rose had spent many hours making the traditional rabbit pies, fruit cakes and doughnuts. It was not Christmas without that food trio. They were all so happy that Martine was home. John found it so strange to see her so big. She did look healthy and the birth of the new baby would be a marvelous event. Martine told them that the baby was not due until April. It seemed long for them to wait; but what was more difficult was that she would not be with them, she would give birth in the Halifax Infirmary.

Martine and Francis stayed a week and returned to Halifax. Their visit gave the impression that they were not so far away after all. Martine had come home; it brought her closer to the family somehow. Martine wrote home quite often and the special day finally arrived. This time there was a phone call. It came through Aunt Laura. The first grand-child was a girl. They had named her Katherine. They were all overjoyed! Mom and daughter were both doing very well.

The next grand-child was a boy, Rodney, a little brother for Katherine. There would be other pregnancies that would have disastrous results for

Martine and Francis. They would manage to save only Katherine and Rodney of the five pregnancies that Martine experienced. John would eventually spend time with Martine and Francis in Halifax and even live with them when he chose to go to Halifax to work.

Time continued on but John could never forget his last three years of high school; they were the most difficult of his school years. First of all he would have to face the dreaded provincial exams in grades eleven and twelve: difficult exams to succeed in. To his surprise, however, the most challenging year of all was tenth grade, when his mother had to leave for Halifax for major surgery. She would need to have the "Big Operation" as it was called in the village, the terrible ordeal of a hysterectomy. This was crucial to her health. Of course, since Martine was in Halifax, she would stay with her and be helped in preparing herself for entering the hospital. She would stay with Martine and her family during the time before the surgery and then for the lengthy time following the surgery. Rose would be away for three months and it would prove to be an extremely stressful and worrisome time for John The stressful aspect would come from having to keep up his studies while caring for Timmy and Clarisse; then there would be the house chores and the cooking to look after since his sister Della and his father were both working at the fish factory. Della would be sure to put the list of "things to be done" on the kitchen cupboard before going to work in the morning. Consequently, John would walk into class in the morning rather late having too many things to do before leaving for school. In the beginning Sister Roberta did not comment on his lateness. She eventually asked John, "Why are you coming into class so late all of a sudden each morning?"

"My mother is away in Halifax for surgery and I'm the only one to care for my brother and sister and the house. I can't seem to keep up very well. I know that my grades are suffering from it. But it is too difficult to study properly. I end up falling asleep."

"Why didn't you tell us? Maybe we could have done something to help you with your studies!" Sister Roberta answered with a touch of regret in her voice.

John just shrugged. It was too late now. The ordeal was coming to an end. His greatest disappointment was his grades, they had come down significantly. It was so upsetting. He felt like crying all the time.

John also had an additional weight on his shoulders that he had to contend with and that he could not discuss with anyone, not even his closest friend Miriam: the terrible nightmare that invaded his dreams since his entry into puberty. This nightmare persisted making John despise those night hours when the nightmare occurred. When it did happen, he would wake up in disgust and exhausted because of what would happen each time. How well John remembered how many times he had awakened during the night when still a teenager, when the terrible nightmare had started. In the beginning, he could not understand what all this meant, but it had all bothered him terribly because it was definitely linked to his sexuality, and something that had happened in the past. He was becoming more and more upset about his thoughts, his sexual urges, his feelings, and the fact that he was so easily aroused, especially when anyone spoke about sexual behaviour, or if he saw another's body or pictures of nude bodies. Some of the guys at school often had magazines of nude women in strange positions with macho-looking men. All that sort of thing would cause him to become so overwhelmed and he would get weak in the knees, his breathing would quicken and he just had to get away somehow. He would try his best to blot this out; he would close his eyes, pray that it would leave him; try to occupy his thoughts with other things. Of course, he would always think that he had committed some ghastly sin, leaving him feeling dirty and unclean, needing to be cleansed somehow. It was all so very distressing and so uncontrollable. John knew that he was becoming increasingly scrupulous about these things, and that the teaching about sin that he had received did not help him. That had left its mark on him. How would he ever get over this? How could one keep oneself pure when one's urges were so strong – and then, on top of all this, came the recurring nightmare. He feared it terribly, not knowing what to do about it.

Each time, in the dream, he would be in a strange place, either outside or inside someone's house. He would get the urge to urinate. When he would find a place, whether in a public washroom, or outside in nature or in someone's house, he would end up having a whole group of people, it could be people he knew or strangers, watching him urinate and laughing at him while pointing their finger at him. He would have such an extreme sense of humiliation and extreme tension that instead of urinating, he would climax and at that moment he would wake from sleep and find himself sticky wet. That awful sinking, unclean feeling would come over him; he would quietly get up, trying not to wake his brother sleeping next to him and do his best to clean himself. He would look for clean, dry pyjamas and get back into bed, dreading the recurrence of the dream. He always felt so desolate and alone after this and would wonder what God thought of him because of this occurrence. His friends would surely laugh at him if they ever found this out. It had to remain his secret. He eventually learned to control this ejaculation process as he got older, but it was always such an intense, devastating experience. He learned to wake up before the release happened fully and so prevented the warm, sticky fluid from going all over himself. He so dreaded his mother finding this all over his night clothes when doing the wash. He often prayed that this disturbing experience would not happen and that the night would be a quiet, peaceful one. He often went to the confessional and would pour out his heart about this ejaculation, but the priest never seemed to understand and never offered a word of advice or encouragement. He seemed doomed to have to endure this alone forever. He could share this with no one.

He continued to feel an overwhelming sense of abandonment. He often stayed on his knees in prayer at night for very long periods of time before finally getting into bed to sleep. The dream persisted and he continued to sink deeper into dark, depressing thoughts. It remained a constant battle to control his thoughts and keep himself pure.

His preoccupation with himself became worrisome because he would do things or become involved in things that he regretted later, or else he could not remember the details of the events, so others could easily accuse him of having said or done certain things that would make them angry at him; then, to defend himself was difficult since he could not remember what had gone on. His preoccupation with himself and his increasing preoccupation with sin entrenched John even more in a very scrupulous way of thinking – all was a sin, all thoughts not totally pure were sinful and were to be confessed. It was as if he was trapped in his own thoughts and, finally, the only thing that could give him a moment's relief was the confessional. He would run and confess sometimes twice a day, if possible, to be cleansed. But the relief and the cleansing were always short lived. John, however, was to experience a small respite once he had finished Teachers' College and was actually teaching. He would become so absorbed in his work with the students, and on doing a good job that the scruples would actually ease. He got into the routine of confession once a week; the agonizing over this lessened, but there were times when it reared its head again. He continued his commitment to prayer, praying long hours before sleeping, especially the rosary. At one point, John promised God that if he healed him of his scruples that he would become a priest. This promise, however, was pushed to the back of his mind since the struggle with his thoughts and urges were to be dealt with first and somehow resolved before deciding on any kind of religious vocation. In fact, keeping these thoughts and urges in check was a hard, full time job on top of any other work that he had to accomplish.

How could he bring about this break, this turnaround, the needed healing? He would sometimes be so distressed with what others were saying, that he would hold his breath, as if that would prevent the thought from overtaking him and invading his body. Whenever anything happened to disturb his inner peace, he would agonize about it and go over and over what he had done and said and how he had reacted to it; he could never see his reaction as a positive one, but simply condemned himself, convinced that he had given in to the horrible thought. He was always in the wrong.

John went to Halifax to stay with Martine after his mother's surgery and recuperation in Halifax. The number of failures in the grade eleven and twelve classes at the Arichat high school in the provincial exams was quite alarming so John thought that if he went to Halifax to school while staying with Martine, he might have a better chance at passing his provincial exams. He would also be able to help Martine with the children and the house chores. It would also be a change from all the stress and tension that he had gone through while his mother had been in Halifax. He left one Monday morning in late August on the Acadian Lines bus. It was an exciting trip and he was doing it alone. He was not well prepared for the way things played out in the long run. Neither the tension nor the difficulties abated. Once again John was too stubborn to admit defeat.

John started his eleventh year in the huge Halifax West High School in Fairview. He was just a number among the hundreds of students in that school. He was the only French speaking Roman Catholic student in his class. If there were others they did not admit such a thing, probably since it was not a very popular category to be in. There were numerous times that the Catholic faith was brought up for ridicule. The study load was also enormous. John was not used to this much extra work at home. He eventually was made to feel that he was not doing an adequate job of his studies. In fact, he was accused of running around with girls at night and studying anatomy rather than his books. It was finally at a parent/teacher evening that Martine and Francis had to straighten things out with his teachers. They did agree that he was a serious student, maybe too serious and too stressed out. John had been used to making high grades and now he was barely passing. He could not believe this; what should he do? To return home at this stage of the game would be too humiliating! He decided to see it through. He was determined not to give up just yet.

The month of January rolled around and winter was upon them with a vengeance. It was very cold most of the time. Then, one Monday morning, they all woke up to a howling winter blizzard. It was snowing terribly and the radio had just started to announce the closure of a number of schools. John was listening closely to see if his school would be closed. Then, just as he thought that this could not happen, the radio announced the one miracle that he was waiting for. His school would be closed as well. What wonderful news! He would be able to get caught up in his school work, so he thought. However, as he was looking for a dictionary on one of the bookshelves in the living room, he came across a thick, grey book entitled "Gone with the Wind." He had not paid too much attention to all that was being said about this book. He began to browse through it. After a few pages, he was captivated by the story. He continued to read and could not put the book down. The storm lasted all that week. They could not go out; everything was at a standstill. The wind howled and the skies dumped tons of white snow on the city and throughout the province. John read on and on and did not even look at his school books. This story was so interesting! It just grabbed him by the heart strings. It was the following Sunday when he came to his senses and realized that he had been reading the book now for the entire week. He was just unable to put it down. He had completed the book, this wonderful story, by the time Monday rolled around and the city had begun to move again.

Sunday afternoon the weather had cleared and the city was beginning to dig itself out of the huge mounds of snow. The snow around the house at Francis and Martine's was over half way up the front door. The aluminum door had a removable window in it so Francis undid the window and pushed the mound of snow away and crawled out. It took him part of the afternoon to clear the snow from around the house even with John helping him. They shoveled a pathway to the street. When the sidewalks eventually were cleared of snow, it was not possible to see the street from the sidewalk because the snow bank separating the sidewalk and the street was so high. People had not seen such a snowfall in years.

The snow had come in huge amounts that winter but with the arrival of spring it was soon all gone and everything began to bloom. One beautiful, sunny evening John decided to go to the Halifax shopping center to browse around and maybe drop into Simpson Sears to look at the car and airplane models in the hobby department. He browsed for some time. Suddenly he realized that darkness had begun to fall, so he headed for home on foot. It was a good distance but not too far to walk. He would probably be home by nine thirty. As he was walking along Bayers Road, then up onto the road that would bring him to Dutch Village Road that was close to home, a police car passed him quickly and swerved to cut him off not too far from him. "Hey you!" shouted the policeman. John jumped quickly to the side of the road.

"Are you speaking to me?" John asked.

"Who do you think I'm speaking to, the sidewalk?" answered the policeman.

"Were you just in the used car lot on Bayers Road?" asked the policeman.

"No, I wasn't. I'm just coming back from the Simpson Sears store," answered John.

"Explain to me the route that you took from there young man," he said to John.

John was very upset that the policeman was questioning him when he had done nothing wrong. But he tried to keep his cool and answered, "I took Romans Avenue, then turned onto Bayers Road and walked up from Dutch Village Road to here. May I ask why you are asking me this?" John asked politely.

"We were just called to investigate a possible vandalism at the used car lot on Bayers Road and one of the suspects was dressed in a hoodie like you are wearing," said the officer.

"Oh, well I was nowhere near that used car lot. It was getting late and I was rushing to get home. My sister is going to wonder where I am," said John.

"Where do you live, which street?" the officer asked.

"I live on Main Street, the graveled part of the street that hasn't been paved yet," answered John.

"OK, young man, you can go, but keep your nose clean!"

John rushed up Main Street and into the house. He was visibly trembling now and had to sit to catch his breath. "What's wrong with you?" his sister asked.

"I was stopped by the police and questioned."

"Whaaat! What the hell for?" asked Martine.

"They thought I was one of the hoods who vandalized the used car lot on Bayers Road," said John.

"What proof did they have?"

"They said that I was wearing a similar hoodie."

"That's pretty skimpy evidence. There must be hundreds of people in this city who are wearing a similar piece of clothing. They had to let you go. The evidence was too skimpy. They would have needed to catch you red handed in the used car lot. Don't worry about it! I know it's scary but you'll get over it. Chalk it up to another experience of life," said Martine laughing. John felt relieved.

The school year continued and the scariest part of it all soon arrived, even more frightening than the episode with the police on that beautiful spring evening: the end of the school year Provincial Exams. The day of the exams he was extremely nervous. However, the first exams went well. The disaster for him came on the last day with the two exams that he dreaded most, Economics and History: Economics because he hated all things about banking, the economy, percentages and advertising. He also had been caught working on another subject in the economics class by the economics teacher whom he hated, and had been humiliated by him in front of all the other students. He had been in the wrong and had been warned that he would be expelled from the class if that happened again. History he enjoyed immensely but he always ended up being too long winded in an exam and not completing all the questions. He knew that he had failed the Economics exam after he had finished writing it; this did not bother him too much since it was a spare. The History exam was the one that threw him into the throes of despair. He had to pass History; it was a compulsory subject. He fussed too long over certain questions and didn't have time to finish. He was sick to his stomach; he had failed through his own stupidity in not properly budgeting his time.

The first day of July of that same year he returned home to Arichat with a lump in his throat and the urge to cry his heart out. As the summer wore on things settled and it did not seem like such a disaster. By the beginning of August the results came out and he had missed passing his grade eleven by six points only. He could not believe it. He had to put it into God's hands as another suffering to be endured. There was still hope, however, he was eligible to write the supplementary exams. He would spend the remainder of the summer preparing for them in both History and Economics. The results were quick in coming since the students had to prepare for the new school year and for college and university. John moved on into grade twelve. He would do that school year at Our Lady of Assumption Convent in Arichat. It was good to be back home. His mother was doing well, although she now knew that she was a very bad diabetic and needed to take better care of herself for her health to last. Family life returned to a more stable and familiar routine.

John and Miriam did a lot of their studying together, he for his grade twelve provincial exams and she for her grade eleven. They would sometimes study late into the night, breaking to listen to the hit parade and have tea and toast with lots of peanut butter. The school year went smoothly and in those days John often used the brown metal crib in the girls' bedroom when the sofa was not available. He would jump into the crib after throwing off his clothes and would be up the next morning to attend morning Mass in the Convent chapel. The negative thinking and events that plagued him and went through his head did not stop John from going on for further studies. In the course of his grade twelve he decided to become a teacher. The Sisters who taught him wanted him to go to university immediately. John decided against this. He would go to Teachers' College first and teach since he wanted to help at home and have time to find an inner peace that he did not as yet possess. He had been able to get his job back at the post office and the day that the provincial exams came in, he hid the letter in his pocket and after work went down to the government wharf behind the post office to open it up. He again was terrified that he had failed. As he opened it, however, he immediately looked at the top of the certificate before even looking at the grades; there, he saw in large print GRADE XII CERTIFICATE. He knew that he had passed. His heart stopped thumping inside of him. He took time to inspect the grades and was pleased with the results. He had failed Social Problems, which did not surprise him, but the rest was just fine and this time he had made a half decent grade in History. He returned to the post office to tell Milly and Elvira the good news. They all laughed together as Milly said to him, "We saw you go down to the wharf and we wondered if you were going to jump in the ocean if you had not passed! We knew it had to be good news when you didn't jump!"

His was the only name that appeared on the list of results for Arichat when they came out in the newspaper. All the other students had to write supplementary exams. He had redeemed himself for the terrible performance of the year before. His results both of grades eleven and twelve gave him a sufficient average to be accepted into Teachers' College. He was even eligible for an eight hundred dollar bursary to help him with his studies. He would be leaving for Truro, Nova Scotia, come September.

September turned out to be a different sort of month. Not only was John leaving for Teachers' College but John's sister Della had planned her wedding for September second. It would be a time of change once again for the family. The whole family would help with the wedding preparations, even the aunts and the uncles would be involved. Della and her future husband both worked at the same fish factory and both had made sure that their new home was built before they even pronounced their marriage vows. After the wedding festivities they would go to their new home to live. Della had asked John to be her best man, her witness for the marriage vows, and Jeffrey, her future husband, had asked his youngest sister, Ella, to be the maid of honour. The church preparations were put in place and then the aunts and uncles were to prepare the food, the drinks and the decorations. The meal was to be a hot, sit-down meal at Aunt Cecilia's house. It would be of traditional Acadian cuisine: meat pie and salad, with deep-dish apple pie for desert. There would also be wedding cake. Drinks would be served in the basement; several large tables had been set up in the large dining and living room of the upstairs and people would be served in groups. Since it was a beautiful, warm sunny day, the children would be served at a table set up on the veranda. Della wore a white wedding dress, the maid of honour and bridesmaids wore deep rose-coloured short dresses with white velvet bands and bows in their hair and the bridegroom and the other attendants all wore black suits, white shirts and ties. All went quite smoothly and everyone enjoyed the meat pie; there had even been enough for people to have seconds, if they wanted. That evening the couple left for Boston on their honey moon.

Della and Jeffrey had built their new home in the village where Jeffrey's family lived. It was a good distance from Della's parents' home. It was a fine bungalow and when John was home on vacation and then when he started teaching in the new school in Arichat, he often went to Della's to visit. He enjoyed spending an evening at Della's.

Della and Jeffrey's three children were born there and there were times when John would babysit them when Della and Jeffrey wanted to go out. They had been living there for eleven years when they decided to move from that village and establish themselves in Arichat. This was because their third child was a boy who had very serious allergy problems and breathing difficulties. Della felt that they were too far from the doctors. Since she did not drive, she was afraid to be caught in an emergency situation with the child and have no one to take her to the hospital if her husband was still at work. They had become too isolated in the village where they were living. One evening at supper, after a close call with an asthma attack, Della had told her husband, "I will burn this house down if I find myself in such a dangerous situation again. We have to sell this house and move to a place that is more accessible to the doctors and hospitals. They both discussed this with Batist who had a very large piece of land behind the family house. Batist and Rose decided to give a portion of that land to Della and Jeffrey for a new house. They would have to sell their home in order to be able to establish themselves in their new place. The new place they decided would be a trailer type house that came in two sections, fully furnished; a foundation would need to be built to place the house on. The foundation would be built once the old residence was sold. In the meantime they would live with Batist and Rose. It was not as easy as it seemed. Rose was very fussy about tidiness and the children often left their things cluttering the house. Della had to make sure that all was kept neat. The tension could be overwhelming at times. Della would be quite relieved once the house sold and the foundation for the new house completed. That time finally arrived.

The time also came for them to choose which of the homes they wanted. That was done and one afternoon the company arrived with both sections of the house to place them on the foundation. To Della's utter disappointment they had come with a house that was too small for the foundation. It had to be taken back to the company and after three more weeks had gone by, the company arrived with another house, hopefully the correct one in the correct size. Jeffrey and Batist were at work that day; Rose and Della, being at home, watched from the pantry window as the company attempted to place the two sections of the house on its foundation. The sections had arrived on two large flat-bed transport trucks. They approached the section of the property from the high road since there was a driveway there. What they failed to do, however, was to check to see if the ground was firm enough for the huge vehicle to bring the sections to the foundation. That section of the property had formerly been used as a potato field, and it had many ruts and bumps.

As they watched Della said to Rose, "I can't watch this, they are going to tip it over." Rose, however, did not budge, she kept watching the procedure from the pantry window.

"Are they coming into the field?" Della asked her mother.

"Oh yes, they are entering the property now but it looks to me to be pretty wobbly," said Rose to Della. "Come and see for yourself." Della joined her mother at the window.

"Oh my God, they're going to tip for sure," said Della. "I can't watch this," she said as she moved away from the window. Rose, however, continued to watch.

"How is it going, are they able to get it on the foundation?" Della asked her mother.

"It's terribly wobbly, it looks to me as if it's going to tip. There it goes. It has tipped. One piece has gone tumbling over and it is now on its roof. They are removing the other section, they are backing it onto the road," informed Rose. Della just sat in the rocking chair holding her head. This would delay everything.

There was a knock at the door. One of the men in charge of the operation stood there, hat in hand full of apologies. "I am very sorry but we miscalculated. It tumbled and all the furniture has smashed. We will take everything back and tomorrow you will need to come and choose another house. I will make the report to the boss."

"We will be there," said Della. "We need to get this done and settled."

Della and Jeffrey returned to the company office in Port Hawkesbury and chose a new home. They did not have anymore models like the first one chosen, so they had to choose another model, a more expensive one. Della and Jeffrey refused to pay more. This situation was not of their making so they were able to get a more expensive home for the original price that had been agreed upon. It was small compensation for the stress they had had to endure. It took another month before the third new house finally arrived. This time it was properly placed on its foundation with out it tipping over. Della was quite relieved and the family soon moved into their new home. Batist and Rose were very pleased to now have one of their children living very close to them. They also enjoyed having the grandchildren around. John enjoyed going to his sister's when he was home. He became close to Della's children and he enjoyed hearing about their classes and school activities.

When Della and Jeffrey had been married John had just finished his grade twelve and had been accepted for Teachers' College that same year. He had prepared his departure for Truro, the town where the college was. He left one sunny morning in September of 1961. The Acadian Line bus stopped at the door on the morning of September seventh to pick him up. On the bus was Dominique Landry, another student who had been accepted at Teachers' College. He and John would be staying with Dorothy and Jim Tatterie on Lyman Street. Most of the students were housed with families for the college year since the college did not have dormitories. John said good-bye to his mother and father; he felt very bad just at that moment because he noticed that his father was crying. His mother would later tell him that his father had been very sad to see him leave. It had dawned on him that his children were now leaving home and would be on their own. Maybe he would not see them again. John had found it hard to blot out this memory of his father crying. John's mother knew so well that John had always thought that his father did not truly love him, but that, she knew, was not so. This had given John food for thought. It would take many years for this to truly sink in.

The bus driver put John's bag into the baggage compartment and off they went. They arrived in Truro late in the afternoon and were at the Tatterie's in time for supper. Dorothy showed them to their room. They would be sharing the same bedroom but could use the dining-room and living-room to study. She said to them, "I hope you don't mind sharing the same bed! It is a double bed so there should be lots of room for both of you". It didn't matter much to John since he had always shared his room and bed with his younger brother. John did discover that Dominique was not easy to sleep with since he often ended up with Dominique's arms in his face and his feet and legs on top of him. John, however, was up early each morning since he continued his practice of daily morning mass. He was also late to bed since he often used the college library and then spent a good portion of time on his knees praying before getting into bed to sleep. He sometimes stayed up with Dorothy to talk or watch a good T.V. programme. He became close to the Tatteries and their two clever children, Meaghan and Peter.

The first day of class had taken place in the building called the Normal School. At their first assembly they were informed that they would only be one month in the old Normal School building. They would then move to the new Teacher Training College that was due to open before the Thanksgiving week-end. All the students were quite pleased since the old Normal School was very dark and musty smelling. "Better days ahead", thought John.

In the course of their first week they were informed that they would have to do an English and Math test in order to be eligible to obtain the teaching diploma that they had registered for. They would be given four chances to pass these tests in the course of the year. They were not easy to pass and if they failed all four times, they would receive a lower teaching certificate and only obtain the certificate that they had come for after a session of English and Math courses at summer school at Dalhousie University in Halifax. John prayed that this would not be the case for him. However, there was no way of preparing for these tests. You just went and took them and hoped for the best. John put his name down for the first group of those writing the tests in the first week of classes. The tests were written in the afternoon and the results posted the next morning. John was pleased to see that he had succeeded in the English exam on his first try; to his disappointment, he would have to rewrite the Math test. This he did the following week and passed on the second try, even though mathematics was not one of his best subjects. That hurdle was over and he was pleased. Now he would qualify for the class two certificate that he had registered for.

The Teachers' College was a beautiful educational facility that strived to turn out excellent teachers. Besides its beauty and striving for excellence, it was run in a very strict and conservative manner. Dr. P.J. McGivney was a very serious and strict headmaster. He made sure that the students understood that there were rules of conduct in the college and anyone caught in an infraction of those rules would be immediately expelled. The college was co-educational but there were no mixed classes. The men had to wear a tie each day to class. If a male student was caught without a tie, he would be expelled. There were restaurants and places in the town of Truro that were off limits to the students. If caught in those places, the student was immediately dismissed. Any female student who became pregnant during the academic year would also be dismissed, as well as her partner if known to be a student of the college.

Each class was expected to put on a play or variety show at some point during the school year. It was precisely in the creation of their concert that John's class got into trouble with Dr. McGivney. In the planning of the show John suggested that they put on a dance to the tune of the French song "Sur le pont d'Avignon" (On the Bridge of Avignon). During the rendition of the song they would periodically stop to ridicule the rules and attitudes of the college, as well as some of the ideas that were being used in the courses. Everyone thought this was a good idea. Of course some of the students would have to act as the female partners in the dance routine since they did not have any women in their class. John was to be the female partner of Tommy MacDonald. One morning at breakfast with Dorothy, John asked her if she had an old bra that she was not using. She looked at John in total surprise and said, "What in the name of God do you want a bra for?"

"Well we are having this dance in our all men's concert and I am to be one of the female partners and I was thinking of wearing a bra with two grapefruits in it," answered John

"You don't need to use grapefruits, just stuff the bra with Kleenex," answered Dorothy as she laughed merrily. "I would love to be there to see this spectacle. That will be too much!" Dorothy exclaimed.

"Funny that I never thought of the Kleenex," said John. "I guess I don't have much experience in all this. I'm still pretty green, eh?" Dorothy did not comment any further, she just continued to laugh.

The time came for the famous concert and John was dressed in a white shirt with his stuffed bra underneath, black leotards under a flared black skirt and his black and white sneakers. He was a sight. They pranced onto the stage to the tune of "Sur le Pont d'Avignon, l'on y danse, l'on y danse" (On the bridge of Avignon, we dance there, we dance there), the couples all paired off. At certain moments in the dance, they would stop to tell the people what they were dancing about. The first stop was to say that they were dancing because the fine gentlemen of Avignon do things this way: they say, "ing, ing, ing, pudding." John's class was making fun of the English diction drill that they had before each English class. Many of the students did not properly finish the words ending in "ing", such as saying "dancin" instead of "dancing". This was not acceptable English diction; thus the DRILL. The whole auditorium roared with laughter. They went through a whole repertoire of these drills, choosing the funniest ones. The people in the audience were holding their sides from laughing so hard.

They had a variety of numbers, but the final number was an Irish pub skit that included lots of alcohol. Of course it was not real alcohol but ginger ale and black tea. However, some of the Irish jokes were off colour and the make-believe drunks were very convincing. The audience laughed till they cried. However, Dr. McGivney was not laughing; he was as red as a beet and ready to explode. When he came back stage after the show, one of the students asked him how he liked the concert.

"I will deal with all of you in the morning," was his answer.

They were all in big trouble. "Let's hope that the other professors feel differently," said David Courtney from the Annapolis Valley.

They were all seated in class the next morning discussing the variety show when Miss Brooks appeared for her English class. Their first question to her was, "How did you like the show, Miss Brooks?"

"I enjoyed it immensely and found it very creative," answered Miss Brooks. "I believe it is a good thing to be able to laugh at oneself. It is very healthy."

They were all pleasantly surprised at her answer. Then, there was a knock at the door. Immediately after the knock, Dr. P.J. McGivney walked in. They all held their breaths.

Dr. McGivney did not greet them in any way. He had a scowl on his face and his complexion was bright red. He raked them over the coals, telling them that they were unfit to be teachers, that they were vulgar, exhibited inappropriate behaviour, and that they had gone against all the rules of the College. They did not deserve to continue their teaching careers. "You are, however, very fortunate that all the professors here spoke in your favour and enjoyed your concert. This has saved all of you from expulsion," he said angrily. Then he added, "I wish you to know that I overlook this against my better judgement. I would certainly have expelled the lot of you!" Then he quickly left the class.

The entire class sat there in total silence. Then, the entire class rose and after profusely thanking Miss Brooks and all the other absent professors, they applauded with a thundering applause.

There were many students at the Teachers' College from Cape Breton, but not as many as those from mainland Nova Scotia. They, therefore, tended to stick together, always on guard for bizarre kinds of discrimination. Some students came from their home areas with strange ideas about Cape Bretoners; anyone who was Roman Catholic, from French or Scottish background and from Cape Breton as well was definitely suspect and had to be backwards and possess a special type of ignorance. All this was a rude awakening for John, but then he had not forgotten the narrow, bigoted mentality that he had encountered at the school in Halifax. It would take a long time for this kind of bigotry to change, and vestiges of it would remain for years.

This way of thinking would produce a fierce competition in the college between the Cape Bretoners and the Mainlanders. This competition became particularly fierce when it came time to choose a college Prom

Queen for the end of the college year. There were many beautiful girls at the college from both the Mainland and Cape Breton. In the past most of the college Prom Queens had been from Cape Breton. This year the Mainlanders were determined that it was their turn. The Cape Bretoners would not go down without a fierce fight. The Mainlanders did win that year and gorgeous Kimberly Kavanaugh from Antigonish won in a tight race with Grace MacDonald from Glace Bay.

John was quite an outgoing person and made friends easily. Those good friends often met at the week-end dances at the CYO meetings held at St. Mary's Catholic school. John loved to dance and to listen to music. Many of the girls enjoyed dancing with him since he was a good dancer. John Penny, Earl MacDonald, Kathy Bates, Cathy MacMillan and Tony Poirier, all Cape Bretoners, sat together at the same table having chips and coke. John had to be careful not to overdo things financially since he had very little money to spare. He always had to make sure that the rent money was there for Dorothy each month. Once in a while he would take in a movie with a few friends. It was at this time that he had seen the movie "Gone with the Wind" for the first time. He had read the whole book when doing his grade eleven in Halifax. He had not been able to put the book down during a whole week-end. It had been so interesting. Now that the movie was out, he could not miss it; it had to be fantastic.

He had asked Janice O'Donnell to go with him; she was one of the girls who made it obvious that she really liked him. He really would have preferred to go with Mary MacNeil. Each time he saw her, his heart would skip a beat. She, however, only noticed him when they were at one of the school dances because she enjoyed dancing with him. But that was alright. At least he was able to get that close to her. Janice was a very nice girl but John did not really feel attracted to her.

They walked back to her boarding house after the movie and stopped on the boarding house steps to talk for a while. It was so obvious that she wanted him to kiss her. He often hesitated about this because it always seemed that Miriam would come into his thoughts at these particular times. He would often wonder what she would think of this. Miriam was somehow more than a friend but they had never indulged in this kind of behaviour. He would feel awkward during moments like these. On this one night he took the plunge and ended up passionately kissing Janice.

"I really care about you," she had said to him as they came up for air. "I know," was all he had said. He had not been able to commit any more than that. Instead he had said, "Maybe we can meet again and go to one of the school dances, what do you think?"

"I would love that so much," she had answered. They had hugged one another and John had left for his boarding house. But he knew that there was no passion there. He would not be able to continue it. He felt rotten about it. This was the night that he had tried to take a short cut through the train yards. He had ended up getting all kinds of mud and grease all over his good shoes and trousers. It was too late to clean them when he got home and the next morning he wore his sneakers to church. When he got home from church Dorothy said to him lightly, "My goodness. Did you go through ploughed fields last night, what a mess your good shoes are in?"

"Don't remind me of it," he had answered. "It was worse than ploughed fields. I just feel so stupid about the whole thing. Why would I go on like that with someone I don't really care about?" He had told Dorothy about the whole episode.

"Don't commit if you are not ready to. Nip it in the bud now! It is wasted energy and will cause too much hurt," she had answered John. Dorothy was very wise.

He felt so wrong about it. Janice said a big, warm "Hi" to him the following Monday morning at the college. John had responded politely but no more than that. The hurt in Janice's face had been very visible. He did not call her back and she eventually avoided him. He had been relieved when he had seen her some months later at one of the school dances with one of the other boys from his class. They were laughing and having a great time together.

This episode with Janice had brought him back to his grade ten days when things were not too uproarious at home and his father had a good spell of being sober; a situation that was quite encouraging for him. It was the year as well that Grace and Georgina MacKillop had come to the Sister's convent as boarders. John had fallen madly in love with Grace, but the madness of love had also been brought on because he had found out that his friend Gus was also madly in love with Grace. He had been determined to push Gus out of the picture to pay him back for all the times that he had snubbed him when Brett Borden, one of the rich kids of the village, had horned in on their friendship. Many times John had found himself alone because Gus had preferred to go off with Brett in his father's car. But John knew that he had a passionate connection with Grace. When he would see her at school or in the village, his heart would skip a beat and he would become all warm inside. He could not believe it when he had found out that Grace and her sister would be staying with a family in Pondville next to the beach all that summer while their parents settled a nasty divorce.

That summer John had spent many hours at Pondville Beach because Grace was there. Being in the sun every day she had become as brown as a berry which made her look even more beautiful. They would lie in the sand together, swim together and discuss the difficulties of life. And Grace had a good number of problems, with her parents going through a divorce. It was devastating for her. John just wanted to hold her and make it all better. They had arranged many meetings at night on the beach and in the fields in Pondville. They would indulge in passionate kissing and embracing but would not go further. John was too frightened of having Grace end up pregnant. The priest in the parish and the Sisters had also impressed on the students that some of this behaviour was sinful and they needed to be careful. John feared the consequences of their actions and so when he became too hot and light headed he would stop and they would go for a walk hand in hand.

The summer had come to an end simply too soon for John and he could not wait to see Grace at school. He was in for a bit of a shock. The first day of the new school year all the students were talking about John's steamy love relationship with Grace. She had shared it with several of her boarder friends and one of them had spread it to everyone. John was furious. He felt so betrayed. His scrupulous behaviour and way of thinking had been alleviated somewhat over the summer; John had not felt that his relationship with Grace had been in any way sinful, but now he was thrown once again into his old agonizing, torturous way of thinking. The disappointment was great. He refused to speak to Grace and she knew why. Of course, as usual Miriam came to the rescue. He could always discuss many things with Miriam or almost everything! He still felt so wrong, so disgusted with himself.

His disgust also came from the fact that he had purposely gone after Grace once he had found out that Gus liked her very much. He wanted to have some kind of revenge on Gus for the many times that he had left him on the front steps some summer afternoons and had gone off with Brett in his father's car. The disgusting feeling came when John learned that Gus had received very bad news about his health that summer.

Gus had been sent on a serious medical exam to determine what was wrong with his heart. It had been determined that he had a hole in his heart that could not be easily repaired. He would have to be very careful about doing too much strenuous sports or any kind of strenuous activity for that matter. Gus, however, was always very active and could not slow down. His parents would constantly warn him of the danger but he found it hard to listen. He finally ended up having to remain in bed for very long periods of time and not be able to have visitors. He had to even give up his classes at school. John wanted very much to visit him so one Friday afternoon he went to Gus's house which was just across the street from John's and asked Agnes, Gus's mom, to be able to visit him for just a few minutes. "Yes, you may go in to see him," said Agnes. John walked into Gus's room which was downstairs since climbing the stairs would be too much of a strain for him. As he walked into the bedroom he was shocked by what he saw. Gus had lost a great deal of weight and his skin was chalk white. He was lying on the bed on his side facing the doorway. He had his hand tucked under the side of his face and his breathing seemed very laboured. His head of thick, pitch black hair made his skin appear even whiter. A shiver went through John. He quietly said Gus's name. He opened his eyes and looked at John with the saddest expression John had ever seen. It broke his heart.

"How are you feeling?" John asked.

"Not good. I am so very tired and it is hard to speak," Gus answered.

"I just wanted to see you and say 'hi' and let you know that I am thinking of you," John answered as he tried to stop himself from crying. "I'll let you rest and come back to see you when you are feeling stronger," said John. Gus just nodded his head without uttering another word. John left the bedroom and went into the kitchen. Gus's mother and grandmother were both in the kitchen. John looked at Agnes and started to cry as he said to her, "Will he get better?" Agnes became very upset and said to

John, "Don't you come here crying like that, it is already difficult enough to go through this." John quickly left the house. It was the last time that he would see Gus alive.

There was a teen dance that night at the parish hall and John went to it with Miriam and some other friends. They jived, round danced and enjoyed the square sets but at the same time they were very concerned about Gus. Each time that they went to sit at one of the tables his name would come up. "Would he pull through this one?" That was the one question on everybody's lips. It was not to be. When John got home from the dance that night his mother was still awake. She called out to him saying, "Gus died tonight around ten o'clock at the hospital. They rushed him to the hospital around eight thirty but there was nothing that they could do for him."

"I am not surprised," answered John. "When I saw him this afternoon he looked to me like one who was already dying." John got into bed and wept, remorse and guilt eating at him for the cruel revenge he had taken out on him when he had taken Grace away from him. John knew that he could not keep doing this to others. That was not what a life of service and love called for. He needed to be healed interiorly and only a loving God could do that for him.

The funeral for Gus was extremely sad but the wake-keeping before that was even worse. Marion came home from Halifax for the funeral; she had gone away to Halifax to work after high school. The one family member most affected and who made a tremendous fuss during the wake was Caroline. She would go to the casket and lean over into it embracing Gus and rubbing his face all the while crying and screaming out his name and imploring him to wake up. At one point she was leaning so far into the casket that it almost toppled over. They had to forcefully remove her off the coffin. Her mother at that point told her that if she did not stop and calm down that she would phone the doctor for him to come and give her an injection to calm her down. This had some effect. It did not stop her from crying and wailing uncontrollably. John was very glad when the funeral was over. It had been a gruesome ordeal for him. He would not easily forget it. At the same time he found it hard to forgive himself and still felt pangs of disgust over the situation with Grace.

With this very short relationship with Janice he had felt once again those awful pangs of disgust and hate for himself come back. That would need to be dealt with before he could commit to any kind of calling. Maybe teaching would gradually bring him to this.

At one point in his life as a high school student John had not been able to imagine himself as a teacher. That way of thinking changed when he entered grade twelve. He felt that he had to become a teacher, an extremely patient one who would be there for all those students who struggled with studies and needed a lot of help to learn and succeed. He, therefore, found himself in the fall of that year in a class of all male students at the teacher training college in Truro.

There were a number of incidents that occurred at Teacher Training School which did not help him to be positive about himself or his way of reacting and working.

One incident took place in Methods Class. John hated that class! It was boring, dry and complicated and Dr. Shaft, the teacher, was severe in manner and appearance and John felt that he did not like him much. One afternoon in class, John was trying to concentrate on what Dr. Shaft was saying, trying to understand the complicated material being given, when suddenly, Dr. Shaft screamed at John,

"What are you doing, young man?"

John looked up startled and could not understand the outburst. So John blurted out, "Nothing, Sir!"

"Young man, you do not chew your nails in my class, do you understand! No one does such a thing in my class! If that happens again, you shall be dismissed for good! Is that clear, Sir!"

John, stunned, answered, "Yes, Sir!"

Apparently, without realizing it, John had been chewing his nails in class. He was totally embarrassed by this outburst and on being treated like a child. He would remember forever the look of pity he received from the other students. He could still see the expressions of Joe Perkins and Bill Dunn as they shook their heads with regret. The humiliation had stayed with him for days. He felt again that he had done something horrible and disgusting.

John was able to get home for Christmas. He saved his money and took the Acadian Lines bus to Port Hawkesbury and his father and mother picked him up at the bus stop. It was good to be home for a break. He was beginning to get used to life in Truro and the Tatteries were quite good to him. After his return to Truro, studies continued but there was now more practise teaching in the local schools of the town. This frightened John somewhat but he would need to buckle down and get it done. His first teaching practice assignment was in Bible Hill Elementary School; he was to be supervised for a Grade seven General Science class by Dr. Fraser, one of the Science Methodology teachers at the College. Dr. Fraser appeared to be lenient and would often leave his class when teaching to go and take a bit of a nip from the bottle in his office. However, he could be much more difficult than one would suspect when it came to scores on Teaching Practice. When John saw him out in the hall just before his science class he knew he was there to supervise him. He did not feel ready. But he needed to go into it head-on.

Dr. Fraser walked into the class just as John began his lesson. All seemed to be going smoothly when suddenly one student raised his hand. He surely had a question. John just about died when the child asked John, "How are babies made?" John wanted to melt into the floor. How was he to deal with this? He could not imagine where a third grade child would get such a question. Had some older student put him up to it or had he heard his parents speak about this? Children had a way of hearing things without letting on that they were listening. Instead of addressing the question, John told the child that it would be better if he asked his Mom and Dad at home that evening. He was sure that they would give him the correct answer. The child became very disappointed and started to cry and told John that he wanted to know the answer right away. So John turned the question back to the child. "Where do you think babies come from?" he asked the child. "The doctor brings him in his black bag!" the child answered, sobbing. Then John opened the discussion to the other children. All the possible child theories came out and not one hit the mark. The science class fell by the wayside and the lesson ended with the children all upset about where babies come from. John knew that he had flubbed badly in his response to the child and in not being able to keep the class on track.

When John returned to the College and went in to see Dr. Fraser, he looked at John and burst out laughing. "You certainly flubbed that one, didn't you?"

179

"Yes, I guess I did," answered John. "But don't you think that I should get at least an honourable mention for the way I turned it back to the class?" John asked.

"An honourable mention, I did give you," said Dr. Fraser. "You did lose your points, however, because you did not succeed in bringing the class back to the topic at hand, science." John was not surprised by this and felt very down about it. He would have to be satisfied with a grade of C. It was average. He would need to do better, but then the practice teaching period was just beginning. That evening he remained on his knees in prayer in front of the night table that was next to his bed. Dominique slept on as John prayed for guidance, for healing and for inner peace.

As the practice teaching sessions moved on, John began to have more positive experiences that did help him somewhat with acquiring a better self image. Of course, he made sure that Dr. Shaft would not catch him again chewing his nails. It was not easy to do this in that class since John found the class extremely boring. It was even very difficult to grasp what Dr. Shaft was droning on about. He would sometimes find himself nibbling on them again but was on the alert for the shifty, beady, snake-like eyes of Dr. Shaft. There were times when he wanted so much to sleep in that class, but if that happened he would surely be expelled. He had had a very difficult time in Dr. Shaft's Methods Class and had continually been making very low grades; the course, however, involved a practical project that proved to be very helpful for Paul. He did all the art work and fancy lettering for the project. All the different groups in the project had project leaders and organizers. John's project leader liked John's work very much and gave him an A+ for his work. That was what saved John from failing the course. That part of the work was the only thing that John had enjoyed in the whole course and Dr. Shaft was rarely around when they worked on the project. This showed John that somehow a more positive turn of events was happening in his favour. This was confirmed by his next practice teaching session.

It was during the third practice teaching session, once again in the Bible Hill Elementary School, that John scored an enjoyable victory. It was a Wednesday morning and John had been assigned to Mrs. Lawrence Miller's fifth grade class. He was to do a Geography class with the fifth graders after the 10 a.m. recess. When he was in the hall waiting for the students to come into the class, he turned to see if they were lined up properly. Dr. Shaft walked through the main entrance of the school. John's heart almost stopped, so strong was his fear; he could even taste bile in his mouth. "My God," he thought, "Dr. Shaft is here to supervise me. I'm done for!" His knees went weak, he could not breathe properly, and a sense of despair almost overtook him.

Filled with a growing apprehension, John entered the classroom with the students. He kept watching the door. Nothing was happening. He got the students to take out their Geography books. He had spent a good deal of time preparing this lesson about the Great Lakes of Canada. It was also a very interesting section of their Geography Course. Mrs. Lawrence had already taken a seat at the back of the classroom. John was in the driver's seat. He slowly erased the board, and pulled down the huge map that was rolled up above the blackboard. As he turned to face the class, the classroom door opened and in walked, not Dr. Shaft, but Mrs. Bowden. He couldn't believe his eyes. He stood still for a moment riveted to the spot behind the teacher's desk. He could not believe it; he was totally overjoyed.

John launched into his class presentation with joy and gusto. He made the children read, he made them participate fully, getting them to point out certain aspects of the Great Lakes, finding those aspects on the map, the value and importance of the lakes to Canada. All that they could know and appreciate about the Great Lakes came out. The students were attentive, interested and very responsive. The bell to end the class sounded suddenly and Mrs. Bowden was gone.

Mrs. Lawrence came to John and said to him, "Well, that was quite a class, an exceptional performance on your part John. I have never seen the students so engaged and interested. You should do well with this one! Let me know what score she gives you. You were certainly well prepared."

John then filled her in on what had transpired before he had started the class. "I thought for sure that I would have Dr. Shaft for supervision; I was simply devastated when I saw him. There is no love lost between Dr. Shaft and I" said John. "I was stunned when Mrs. Bowden came in," said John. "I could have hugged her!"

"Well she is not an easy marker either," said Mrs. Lawrence. "Don't forget that I am also a graduate of the College and I had Mrs. Bowden at one point. She is fair though."

"And she is pleasant and does not come across as some kind of viper!" exclaimed John. He and Mrs. Lawrence had a good chuckle over that.

John was to meet Mrs. Bowden upon his return to the College. She was in her office when he arrived and, smiling pleasantly, she said, "Come in John. I'm ready to go over your evaluation with you." John sat down and, to his surprise, she added, "And, how do you feel about this Geography class that you gave today?"

Immediately and without hesitation John answered, "I have a very good feeling about it."

"As well you should!" Mrs. Bowden exclaimed. "You did extremely well. You were totally at ease. You engaged your students superbly and you covered the material very well. Most of all you had their full attention and made the material very interesting. I enjoyed it myself. I have given you a B+ for your score; it is the highest score that I give my students. You are well on your way to becoming a very good teacher. Keep up the good work!" John thanked Mrs. Bowden and reassured her that this was a real breakthrough for him.

John had to pinch himself as he walked home. "Did this really happen today?" John asked himself. Something splendid had happened. He was on cloud nine. Teaching practice was no longer a frightening, nerve-wrecking experience for him. He walked into the Tatteries' residence with a big smile on his face.

"Something good must have happened to you today from the smile you have on your face," exclaimed Dorothy questioningly. "What's going on?"

John explained what had happened. Dorothy was a very pretty woman with beautiful auburn hair. She was very fond of John and he got along splendidly with the whole family. At this moment she was extremely pleased for John that he had had such a great breakthrough, especially since she knew how devastated he had been over the nail-biting incident.

"This should encourage you now!" Dorothy exclaimed. "It should help you get over all the anxiety that you have been experiencing these last few months."

John agreed. To underline this occasion and such a victory Dorothy made sure that they had one of John's favourite desserts for supper that evening, a wonderful chocolate cake covered with thick seven-minute frosting. John just beamed as he filled his mouth with delicious chunks of cake.

John knew that he would miss the Tatteries when the time came to leave Teachers' College but, overall, he would not be sorry to leave. He had certainly grown up in many ways and for that he was grateful. Dr. P.J. McGivney was certainly over the top with his strict rules and demands. Not only was he strict, he was also mean and physically ugly. John used to tell Sean Penny, one of his classmates and a good friend, that Dr. McGivney's face looked like it had caught fire and someone had tried to put the fire out with an axe. His friend would laugh and say, "DeCoste, your crazy! It's time you got out of this mad house."

Once graduation came John did not take long to leave. He refused to take any pictures and after having a light lunch with his parents at Dorothy's, they left for home. John didn't look back. He had done it, and it was over!

John had hoped to get a teaching position close to home, but none of the applications he sent out received replies. So he decided to apply elsewhere. The Cole Harbour elementary school was the first to reply. John accepted since it was not very far from where Martine and Francis lived. He would board with them and travel back and forth to work with Francis. He had already received his acceptance letter for Cole Harbour when one of the elementary schools at home responded. John responded that it was too late, that he had accepted a position elsewhere. His disappointment was great but he would make the most of another year away from home, especially since he would be with Martine. Little did he realize what awaited him!

By the time John left for his teaching assignment, Martine and her family had moved from the city to a place called Seaforth, very close to the town of Chezzetcook. They were living in the old farm house that belonged to Francis' family. Martine had two children by this time, Katherine and Rodney. Seaforth was really farm country and John thanked God that he was teaching all day. He had been born in the country but he preferred the city any day. In the city he was never bored.

John had been hired to teach Grades 4 and 5 at Hopewell School in Cole Harbour.

There were two sections to the school, one newer and one older. The older section had been a fire hall at one time and had only two large classrooms. The remainder of the classes were in the newer section. The other teacher working with John was Mrs. O'Shea, the sixth grade teacher. Mrs. O'Shea was an elderly lady who was an excellent, experienced teacher. They hit it off quite well and helped one another in many ways. John's students were mild compared to the group that Mrs. O'Shea had. They already thought that they knew everything and so had no need to be in school. This dear lady had her hands full. John offered to do all the after school supervision, especially of those children who traveled by school bus. This made it possible for Mrs. O'Shea to go home early after school. She was truly grateful for that. John would wait for his ride home and prepare the following day's lessons or correct notebooks.

John traveled home in the same car pool as Francis since neither of them had cars. This gave him an hour's wait, during which he could supervise the students waiting for their bus.

It was while supervising after school one evening that a horrendous incident took place, one that John would not forget in a hurry. That evening, the students were particularly rambunctious and he had to tell them several times to stop throwing snow balls against the school doors. They simply would not listen and persisted in their behaviour. So John went out one last time to see what was going on and who was being so bold. As he came down the steps, one of the students, Mike Moore, was running towards the steps after pelting a snow ball at the school. Of course, the bus was coming and Mike had to catch it. John screamed at him, "Get on that bus now. I told you not to throw snow balls, didn't I?" and as he said this, he slapped Mike on the cheek. Mike stood there in utter disbelief and burst out crying as he got on the bus.

The next evening as John was waiting for his ride home, preparing lessons for the next day and correcting tests, there was a loud banging on the school door. Who could that be, he wondered. John went to the door and, as he opened it, a tall man dressed in the full naval Captain's uniform, punched him in the stomach, knocking the wind out of him, while screaming, "Why did you hit my son?" John sat on a bench in the entrance to catch his breath. He was trying to figure out who this was. It finally dawned on him as he heard the name Mike Moore being spat out like venom. It was Mike's father, the father of the child he had slapped on the cheek while supervising the last school bus the previous day. No, this was no madman or drunk, but a naval Captain that had momentarily lost control. John's fury mounted as well! At that moment, however, the man suddenly stopped screaming. All went silent! The man's face went white as it dawned on him what he had done.

John had been able to catch his breath by then and looking directly at him, shouted "Are you quite finished?" The man did not answer. So John continued, "Well, now listen to me; I'm going to tell you what kind of a brat you are raising. You are screaming at me that I hit your son in the ear and so he was up all night with an earache! Do you want to know why he had an earache? I slapped Mike, yes, but I did not hit him in the ear. He had an earache, Sir, because he was in the swamp behind the school all during recess, a place he was told not to go to and when he came in with the others, I had to put him half naked in the washroom while his clothes dried. Mike is twelve years old, old enough to know better. He was surprised when I slapped him because he had not had that done before! Maybe you need to discipline him a bit more! Well, I'm telling you to do something with him because if he continues his delinquent behaviour, he will get more of the same! Do you hear me? Plus, how do you justify your coming into this school and punching the first person you meet? You did not know who I was; we had never met.! Do two wrongs make a right? You can lose your temper and resort to violence, but I cannot do the same. I must deal with 40 children in this class. And on top of it all, you come and do it in full military dress!"

Mr. Moore, white as a sheet, realized what he had done. He began to apologize. John stopped him saying, "Spare me the apologies. I cannot lose my temper with 40 undisciplined brats to contend with, yet you come here and without question or inquiry, punch me in the stomach. How do you justify your behaviour? How would your military superiors respond to that, Mr Moore – that is your name, Mr. Moore, right? Please leave. I'll pursue the matter further with the School Board. I do not intend to be the punching bag of Hopewell School. This school has a very bad record for keeping teachers because parents do not back the teachers, they are always in the wrong and parents believe all that their brats tell them. Please, just leave this school building NOW!" Actually, not all the students were brats, many were fine children. At that moment, however, John was so upset, so hurt, so angry that he said things that he would later regret; so, he backed off.

John could not bear to stay in the school to wait for his ride home. He went instead across the street from the school to the gas station to wait for his ride home. As he stood there, Mr. Daniels, the owner of the service station, said to him, "I see that you had a visitor this evening."

"Oh yes, I certainly did," answered John. "It was not a nice visit and the visitor was a very angry one."

Mr. Daniels then said to John, "That's what happens when we get good teachers, some need to push their weight around thinking they are the only ones in the right. Then we lose our good teachers. It is very unfortunate." John felt somewhat reassured and therefore, not quite so desolate. His ride arrived and he said good-bye to Mr. Daniels and got into the car.

He said nothing all the way home. As he entered the house, he said to Martine, "Meet the punching bag of Hopewell School."

"What do you mean? What happened?" she asked. John proceeded to explain all that had happened that day. Martine was furious and said, "I would get in touch with the trustees or the School Board immediately and tell them that something needs to be done about this and very soon."

John called the School Board and after explaining what had happened, he informed them that he was breaking his contract if something was not done about what had occurred. He would even go to the newspapers with it and to the military since Mr. Moore was a naval officer. He was told by the trustee with whom he was speaking to be patient and to wait until someone from the School Board met with him to discuss procedure in dealing with this matter. The Director of the School Board was in to see John the next day.

The Director advised John not to allow anyone to tell him that he was entirely wrong. "Stay with your convictions and your story," he advised. "I will back you!"

The Director called a school trustee meeting about the matter. Captain Moore was required to apologize; otherwise the Board threatened to take the incident to the military high commission.

John later found out that Mr. Moore's family had been very upset by it all; his wife had to be placed on tranquilizers because she feared

John would go to the Navy. John, however, felt that Mr. Moore had been sufficiently frightened by the results of this; he had apologized to John at the end of their meeting. John simply wanted an end to the matter. It had all been so horrendous.

This ordeal had negative consequences with the students. The parents, John felt, had talked about the situation negatively in front of their children, so discipline became even more difficult. John ended up being quite tormented by his own behaviour and felt an interior heaviness that was difficult to articulate. He constantly wondered if he had not been too harsh, too unforgiving and too strict with the students, too hardened in his position with some of the parents. Would the feelings of guilt and emptiness never leave him!

Scrupulosity had been part of John's life now for some time, since the age of fourteen. As always, he agonized over his thoughts and behaviour, especially anything having to do with the body and sexuality. He had to avoid touching himself and others, or hearing or seeing anything to do with sex and the human body – in his mind all this was sin. John never felt good or at ease for long. The doubts and agonizing thoughts would always come back very quickly. Any nocturnal emissions since the time of his adolescent years would throw him into agonizing despair and fear – fear of what God would think of him and what God would do to him if he did not cleanse himself. How would he free himself of this enslavement?

Once John had entered his later teen years, he had become an avid reader, not just of novels, but of self-help books, especially psychology books dealing with sexuality as related to one's spiritual life and relationships. There would be glimmers of hope at times, but so, so fleeting. He became very concerned with relationships, not just with women, but also with men. He would get so overly attached, even to male friends, so he questioned himself constantly about his own sexuality, sometimes feeling in a no-man's land, not knowing whether he was fish or fowl. Peace of mind was very hard to come by. This peace of mind would only come much later in life; he did not realize at that time what a long and arduous road lay ahead of him.

John decided not to remain at Hopewell School the following year. The "punching bag" incident had taken its toll and he found that he could no longer be at ease or close to the students. Trust had fled.

In the meantime, Martine and Francis decided to move to a place called Humber Park where the houses were very reasonable to buy or rent. After a number of incidents that had shown Martine that they were much too far from everything, especially doctors and hospitals, she had convinced Francis to apply for a mortgage loan for Humber Park. John had helped them move and he enjoyed being out of the woods for a short time. He would soon be leaving for Cape Breton again.

He found out that a new high school had opened in his home area and so he decided to apply for a position there. Somehow he felt that it would be good for him to be in his own home surroundings once again. He was hired to teach Grades 7, 8 and 9 General Science and English. So he left Hopewell School for Richmond Academy and the eventual tragedy that he would have to face.

Chapter Eight

Fr. John had watched Jules and Chris enter the taxi as they left for the airport. He had been quite upset and concerned that he could not accompany them. At that moment he made an enormous act of trust in God and placed them in his care. "You are the one who can get them through this, my God!" He had whispered this short prayer to himself. Fr. John then had to put his worries aside and turn to other urgent matters. As he rode back to the Seminary School it was so very evident that the town of Bukavu was in a panic! The fighting and shooting could be heard, especially from the southeast section of the town. The rebels were at the door, the town would soon fall. People were fleeing, bundles on their heads, trucks rolled by with wounded soldiers in them. It was a frightening situation.

Fr. John wondered what would happen to Jules and Chris. They would probably get to the airport and find a small plane with 50 or 60 people waiting to board. Fr. John whispered a prayer once again under his breath: "Lord be with them, they are in your hands." All that night, Fr. John prayed. He slept very little. Classes would still continue the next day, but Fr. John called a staff meeting to see what they should do now that the danger was escalating. Some of their students were in grave danger, being Rwandese and Burundian. Shouldn't they get them to safety? That was to be the first priority, but how to achieve it? They waited and wondered.

The staff was divided as to how to proceed. Fr. John and Fr. Bosco were for evacuating the school and having someone take the Rwandese and Burundians out to another country to safety. The remainder of the staff felt that they should stay put and allow the soldiers to enter the premises and take whatever they wanted.

"What if they want to kill or jail our Rwandese and Burundians?" asked Fr. John. "What will we do then? And if we protest, will we not be killed as well?" They were to think this over and in a few days come to a decision. The next day, Thursday, Fr. John went into town, accompanied by Sister Katrina to pick up vegetables for the school. They stopped at the Canadiana to see about the beds and pots and pans. The shooting and the people fleeing continued. One could hear the shooting coming from the outskirts of town. Sister Katrina was very frightened and she let Fr. John know that she did not want to die for a few pots and pans. Fr. John, realizing her terrible fear, quickly put the beds in the land cruiser, stopped at the market and then at the Central House of the Missionaries of Africa for messages.

"Maybe you will have a fax from Nairobi today", said Sister Katrina, encouragingly.

"That would be great and would certainly put my mind at ease", answered Fr. John

When they entered the Regional House, Fr. John headed first for the mail room. There on a shelf for the school was a folded paper with the word fax marked on it. He opened it and the message read, "Arrived safely, did all you told us to do. We're safe." It was signed by Jules and Chris. Fr. John was overjoyed. He whispered a thank you to God once again. He would later find out from them what had happened at the airport and the miracle of the departure.

For the students at the school and Fr. John, Friday of that week was somewhat the same as the other days, with classes, meals, manual work, prayer and services in the chapel. The noise of the guns and the shooting continued, it was all quite alarming. When a shot would go off suddenly, Fr. John would jump or cringe especially when he was sitting in the Seminary Chapel trying to concentrate in prayer. What must they do? They needed to decide if they would evacuate or remain at the school. Saturday morning of that week, the decision was made for them. One of the priests of the school often celebrated the Eucharist for the soldiers in the barracks close by and one of the Captains came to see Fr. Martens, who spoke Lingala, the language used by the military. When he came into the compound that day it was just after the noon meal and some of the students were still washing the dishes. Some were outside speaking with Fr. John and Fr. Bosco. The Captain looked at them and said, "You are still here? What are you doing here, you must leave, evacuate as soon as possible. Do you not hear the guns, the shooting! The town will fall. We cannot hold it and we cannot win. We do not have the manpower or the guns. You cannot flee up the lake, you have no boat; you cannot cross the Rwandese border, it is closed off to you and you cannot go through the town as that is the direction from which the rebels will come. You must leave very soon. You must go to the Major Seminary of Murhesa close to the airport. They will have room there and you will be safe."

"Can you not provide us with a military escort? We have students who are in danger and do not have all their papers. The military escort must be one that has a high ranking soldier in it, such as a lieutenant, otherwise we will be stopped and looted and the students arrested", implored Fr. Martens.

"OK, I will do what I can", said the Captain. "Let's prepare the service; then, I have to go into town. There is a matter that I must attend to and then I will return."

He was gone hardly one hour when he returned and with him a lieutenant to be an escort: one who was carrying a gun. The Captain told them that they must leave immediately, that the town was about to fall and that there were roadblocks everywhere.

Fr. John called the students. The Rwandese and Burundians would be in the first group to go, along with as many others that the vehicles could hold. The Sisters would be part of that first evacuating group as well. Some students were still doing the dishes. Fr. John told them to leave the dishes and to get ready. They were to take a simple overnight bag with toothpaste and soap, the bare necessities. The rest of the luggage would follow in the weeks to come. There were three vehicles, the Sisters' vehicle was first, then the land cruiser with the lieutenant at the passenger window with his arm out, to show his credentials and with his gun quite visible. The third car would hold Fr. Bosco with more students. There were only about seven students left, all Zaireans. They were in less danger than the others. They set out hoping for the best: that they would not be stopped.

At each roadblock, the soldiers tried to stop them, but the lieutenant yelled at them to open up.

Sisters Evacuated with Seminarians

"It is because of you that the Fathers are leaving," he screamed. "Open up, open up, that's an order!" When the soldiers noticed his credentials, they saluted and opened the barriers. They were not stopped and arrived at the Major Seminary in the afternoon. There, they found the Xavierian Fathers, an Italian community that worked at the school with Fr. John. Their students as well were there and they would try to leave on Sunday. The Italian Embassy in Kampala would send a plane to get them out. They invited Fr. John to come with them to the airport and take his students who were in danger along with them. It was a difficult decision to make since he had to leave some behind. Fr. John Paul was with him and said that he would stay with the students who were to remain behind. Fr. Bosco would return immediately to Bukavu and come back Sunday morning with the remainder of the students. All was agreed upon. The plane from the Italian Embassy hoped to make as many trips as possible, at least two per day for as long as possible to get people out, especially the Italians and those involved in their missions.

Fr. John slept only in fits and starts. He was worried. Would they be stopped before getting to the airport? There was a huge refugee camp just before the airport, filled with Hutu people. It was a dangerous undertaking, but it had to be attempted.

The following morning, Sunday, Fr. John got the students to ready themselves. There were two of them with only seminary student cards. He would have to leave both of them behind. He was sick over it; he would have to tell the two students that he could not take them with him because they had no proper papers. The danger was that they could be arrested, accused of being rebels or traitors, or even killed. It seemed safer to stay at the Major Seminary with the other students for the time being. They were extremely upset about the situation and pleaded with Fr. John to take them with him. He truly felt that it would compromise the convoy to the airport. With heavy heart he had to stand his ground.

Jesuit Retreat Centre

They left in a small van that opened at the back; they were crowded together like sardines. About half way to the airport, they encountered a military roadblock. They were stopped. Fr. John's heart sank. They had to all get out. They all needed to show their passports. One soldier took the passports and hid them in a desk drawer. Where were they going and for what reason? Fr. John did not want the soldiers to rifle through the bags. They would discover that some of the students were Rwandese and Burundians. One young soldier was furious at them. Why were they fleeing? They were traitors. Fr. John offered Zairean money to the soldiers, bundles of it since it was quite devalued. But they laughed at him. That was worthless; they needed the green American bills. Fr. John had foreseen some of this and so he had money in his T-shirt pockets, trouser pockets and socks; not huge amounts, but enough to entice them. He offered an American $10 note. One soldier, somewhat more amenable to Fr. John's cause and liking Canadians, took it, but stressed that it needed to be a bit more substantial, since there were several soldiers. One other soldier protested, and insisted that they would have to be jailed and could not leave. Fr. John continued to plead with them, while bringing out another $40 American. This did the trick for that first soldier and he also asked Fr. John to leave the bundles of Zairean money. The other soldier continued to protest vehemently, but the friendly soldier told Fr. John to go, that he was in charge, and he gave him back the passports. Both soldiers got into a violent argument, while Fr. John told the students to get quickly into the car, not to waste one moment. Some of them were standing there in disbelief, not moving. Fr. John in strong words and under his breath told them, "Get into the truck now, before they change their minds." That jolted them back to reality and in they went. They had to pass through the huge refugee camp that was just before the airport. Things were intensifying quickly since the rumour was that the rebels were coming this way and would invade the camp and kill all Hutu refugees. Some refugees were milling around on the road and tried to stop the truck from continuing, but the driver stopped for no one and they finally rolled into the airport, where, after much grief, they eventually took the Italian Embassy plane to Kampala. He would be taking his students to the formation center in Jinja. He would stay there for some time with his students until they felt more secure. He would eventually be able to move on, he hoped, to visit other students and colleagues in the Central African region.

Fr. John had spoken several times to Jules and Chris on the phone from the Jinja formation center. He decided that he would go by bus to Nairobi on the first Monday of the second month into their stay in Jinja. He would visit Jules and Chris and see how they were and if all was as it should be. He would stay with the community of the Missionaries of Africa in their promotion house. He phoned them to make sure that they had room for him and that it was okay for him to come and visit. They were able to get a one room flat in an apartment building called Stella Awinja House, not far from the YWCA, where they had been living when they first arrived in Nairobi. They were taking English classes at the British Council Center and preparing for their departure for Canada. Fr. John would carry on with the remainder of the preparations once he had returned to Canada. It was to be a long journey before they would set foot on Canadian soil.

The bus ride from Jinja to Nairobi was not too tiring; it was long but interesting. The one place they were forced to wait was at the Ugandan-Kenyan border. All the bus passengers had to have their papers checked and stamped. Fr. John had a visa in his passport that needed to be stamped and he was granted a three month pass. They continued on to Nairobi, but before the bus could leave the parking area a group of very aggressive Massai women wanted to sell them different types of handcrafted objects. Fr. John did not wish to buy anything but one woman kept throwing the things at him. He just picked each item up and threw it right back at her. She began to scream at him what he figured were obscenities in her own language. He tried to ignore her. She was boarding the bus while screaming at Fr. John when the bus driver came back from the washroom. He quickly made her get off the bus and in a short time they were on their way to Nairobi again. Once at the bus park in Nairobi, Fr. John got a taxi to the house of the Missionaries of Africa. The taxi driver could not overcharge Fr. John since he had been told by the missionaries at the promotion house how much the cost would be from the taxi park. All went smoothly and once he had arrived and been given his room he took some time to make the acquaintance of the priests who were living in the mission house. He was meeting them for the first time. They had coffee together and talked about their different places of origin and how they had met and joined the Missionaries of Africa. He then asked to use the telephone and called Chris and Jules. They were very happy to hear from him and he learned that the Stella Awinja apartment building was not far from the Missionaries' residence. They came over immediately and the greetings, the hugs and the expressions of joy were many.

One of the first questions that Fr. John asked them was what had happened at the Kavumu Airport of Bukavu. "You must tell me in detail what happened. I need to know. I was on my knees that whole evening of your departure," said Fr. John.

As Fr. John had suspected, there were many people, 50 or 60, to take a nineteen seater plane from the Bukavu Airport when Jules and Chris wanted to leave for Nairobi. From what they told him, the departure turned out to be a real fiasco. Many people were shouting, pleading, crying and already waving their plane ticket to the Zairean who was trying to sort things out. Some were screaming that they had arrived first and should board first. Many were yelling so loud that it was difficult to understand what was being said.

The Zairean airport attendant called for passports; they needed to be checked and stamped for them to board the plane. When it came time for Jules and Chris to give him their passports, he opened up the passports and immediately saw that they had been born in Kinshasa, the capital of Zaire.

"You were both born in Kinshasa?" he asked them.

"Yes", they answered, "our father and mother were both living and working there at the time".

"So, you are our children," answered the attendant. With that said, off he went to have the passports stamped, and cleared. When he returned, the yelling and screaming continued at an even greater tempo, "We were here first, we have paid already, we have been waiting for hours and we have our tickets," could be heard.

The attendant yelled for everyone to be quiet or no one would leave.

"No," he said, "it is our children who go first, and so I call Jules and Chris Mpamo to come forward please."

Jules and Chris did not move immediately, being frightened that maybe it was a trap to stop and arrest them. So again, the attendant called out.

"Jules and Chris Mpamo, please come forward!"

So both young men, incredulous and frightened, went up to him.

"Here are your passports," he said. "Get into the plane. Take all your luggage with you."

Jules and Chris wasted no more time. They boarded the plane amidst shouting, yelling, crying and screaming. They placed their luggage in the back compartment of the airplane and both found comfortable seats. They then waited to see who would board next. Eventually the plane was filled, but many people stayed behind. For some it was the husband, for others it was a grandfather or an older son. They had to choose who was to leave since the places were limited; many people were crying and screaming that this was not fair. Once filled, the plane taxied to the end of the runway and just as the sun was going down, they lifted off into the darkening sky. They breathed a sign of relief. A miracle had taken place and they had escaped.

Fr. John had many questions running through his mind concerning their departure from the Bukavu Airport and how they had been able to settle in once in Nairobi. They were eager to talk about it as well, but there were things that they needed to do first of all because of Fr. John's visit and Fr. John would need to be patient and hold his questions until the two boys had said and done all they needed to say and do.

Chapter Nine

After his horrendous time at Hopewell School, John was happy to be able to return home to teach. In August of 1962 he attended a meeting at the Richmond Academy that had been called as a preliminary preparation for the coming academic year. Richmond Academy was a new school. Everything was fresh and clean smelling. John was given his assignments for that year. It was to be as his letter of acceptance for the position had stated, Grades 7, 8, and 9 General Science and Grades 7 and 8 English at the Secondary School level for his first year. These John found out were very difficult grades to teach, especially 7 and 8. He still remembered the questioning look on Sr. Evangeline's face as she came to replace him for the French language class in Grade 7 once he had finished the Science class. Sister would always ask John "How are they today, as rambunctious as ever?" Most times John's answer would be, "They continue to be almost impossible, Sister." Sr. Evangeline would chuckle softly saying, "You always give them some credit, don't you? You are, I must say, a man of hope." John would answer as he left the classroom, "All the best, Sister. Your reward will be great in heaven!"

Since John had returned to his home area to teach, he found that the older students knew him too well. Among some of the people, even the students, he was just the DeCoste boy from the village; so what could he know? Who was he to tell them how to behave and what to do? Finding this difficult to live with, he requested the 4th grade class in the elementary school section. They were much younger children and so did not know John very well. For them he was Mr. DeCoste, their teacher. He found this more normal and was extremely pleased with the pupils. Of course, he lived at home with his parents and younger brother and sister. He helped a lot with the expenses of the family even if he was not making a huge salary. At one point, when his sister Della's house was smoke damaged by fire, she and her family had to move in with them. As well, John's oldest sister, Martine, had a full term baby boy that was born with deformed kidneys and only lived a short time. Martine had to have a number of blood transfusions to save her life. At that time, her two small children came to live with John's parents, as well. The small bungalow was filled to capacity. John had also applied for a bank loan to build an extra bedroom for him and his brother on the back section of the house. The room was sorely needed, even without the extra company. John received the loan from the bank, but since he was not yet 21 years old, his father had to co-sign for the loan and the insurance that went with it. It almost discouraged John from taking out the loan, but the terms of payment were so reasonable that he decided to go through with it. His own uncle, Thomas, who was an excellent carpenter, did the work and remodeled the living room area of the house to make better use of the space they had. John's mother and the family were quite pleased and in no time, John and his brother had their own bedroom, their own private space. The large brown metal crib that John had often slept in as a youth was in his sisters' room. That crib was used when his sisters came with the younger children. John remembered climbing into the crib at night and having to stick his feet out between the metal bars at the foot of the crib since he was growing rapidly at the time and had long legs. John, however, could sleep anywhere, and the minute his head hit the pillow, he was fast asleep. The days of sleeping in the crib and on the sofa were over and he and his brother had their own space.

In spite of the commotion and overcrowding in the house, things were going relatively well. Martine's children were adapting to the situation; Della's house was being cared for by the insurance and they seemed to be managing well enough. Extra money was coming in from John's teaching to supplement his father's income; this was a tremendous help. His father still went on his alcoholic binges, especially when on Union business; he was the Union President for the local at the fish factory where he worked. In November 1964, a union activity day was the day the tragedy occurred. John's father had been on Union business all day with other union members and was not working at the factory that day. John knew that they would be in for a difficult evening. It was cold and windy that day and John's father dropped him off at Mass that morning. John often started his teaching day by attending Mass. His father was up early as well to prepare for the union meeting, so he was able to drop John off at Church. When he did, John refused to acknowledge his good-bye, being too upset with him concerning the situation that he knew would develop during the union business; alcohol would definitely be part of that meeting. At supper time, his father was not in sight. At 5:30 p.m., the telephone rang and it was the parish priest, Fr. Alexander, asking John if his brother was at home. John answered that he had just finished his supper and had gone next door to his friend's house. "Are you sure?" Fr. Alexander asked.

"Yes, Father, I am sure, he just went out the door. Why, is there something wrong?" asked John.

"Well, there has been a very tragic accident at Jerseymen's Hill, at the entrance to the village, and it is believed that one of the passengers is your brother."

"That is not possible, Father," answered John "He was just here. What model of car is it?" inquired John.

"It is a volkswagon and there were three people in it, two men and one woman. Two are dead, one of the men and the woman. They have taken the other man to the hospital," said Fr. Alexander. "They are not sure if it is your father's car or not, it is difficult to identify the man, and the woman is burnt beyond recognition. I am so sorry to have to tell you this. If it is not your brother, it has to be your father. We thought it was your bother because the person seems to have a brush -cut, but it is hard to tell because of the burnt state of the body and the damage."

John swayed back and forth on his feet and felt numbness in his legs. "It is probably my father, he was out on union business today and he has not returned home for supper yet."

"Well, someone will come for you to take you to the accident scene since an identification needs to be done", answered Fr. Alexander.

"Fine, I'll wait", replied John.

John's mother was sitting in the rocking chair not far from the telephone when John turned around to face her. Immediately, she knew there was something wrong and blurted out, "What's wrong, something has happened, tell me!."

"There was an accident at Jerseymen's Hill and they think it's Dad's car. There were three in the car and two are dead and they think that one of the two is Dad," said John without thinking of how his mother would react.

"Oh my goodness, oh my goodness, is your father dead, killed?" screamed his mother. At that point she began to cry very loudly, screaming and lamenting, "What will we do? What will we do?"

John went over to his mother and held her tightly. He hugged her and tried to calm her down, but she wailed continuously. John's sister was frantically running from the kitchen to the living room, not knowing what to do next. The children started crying, it was total bedlam in the house. Suddenly, there was a knock at the door. It was Richard Babin from the neighbouring village who had been at the scene of the accident. They had asked him to come and pick John up and take him to the accident scene. Once there, John ran toward the stretcher that was being lifted into the ambulance. By now, it was quite dark and difficult to see. Suddenly, one of the paramedics saw John and came towards him.

"Don't go there, please, you must go to the hospital and wait for the police there!" insisted the paramedic.

Richard Babin once again took John into his car and they went to the hospital close to the church. John sat in the waiting room. He could hear the man who had been in the accident with his father screaming for the nurse to come to him. His family came into the hospital while John was waiting there. The man's wife, his sister and other relatives rushed to the second floor where the screams were coming from. John realized that it was Ronald Boudreau who had been with his father in the car and that his injuries were extremely serious. He was burnt through to his lungs and needed to be transferred to the City hospital. He was a married man with four small children. He would die at the City hospital the next day. Suddenly, Constable Poirier came in and told John that he was sorry that they had told him to come to the hospital, that he actually needed him to come to the undertaker's with him, for identification purposes. John went with him and on the car seat was part of the accident report. John realized that the woman in the car had been Llewellyn MacDonald, a spinster who had asked John's father for a lift home. She was burnt beyond recognition. She was the only bread winner in her family, living with her spinster sister Eva and bachelor brother, Ralph.

Once at the undertaker's, Constable Poirier asked John, "Are you OK to do this? We do need to make an identification since we're not certain if this is your father or not?"

"Yes, I'm OK, anyway, there is no one else but me who can do this in the family at the moment", answered John.

"OK, let's do it now, but I'm warning you, it is not a very nice thing to see. Take your time and don't go too quickly."

John walked into the undertaker's work area, and on the table was the body in question, partly covered in a tarpaulin. John went up to the body, but was too close to it at first to clearly see who this really was. He could not make out the features very well, since the person's tongue was hanging out and stretched from his mouth to the side of his neck. Then John stepped back and tried to view the features while blotting out the blood and disfiguration. It was his father!

"It is my father", he whispered to Constable Poirier.

"But this man has a brush cut, did your father have a brush cut?" asked Constable Poirier.

"No, he did not, but it looks like he does because he combed his hair back from his forehead in the style of the 30's and his hair is singed from the fire, but now I see that it is definitely him," John replied. "May I see the remainder of the clothing and what was on him?" John asked. John found his father's cap, part of his belt and his treasured Union pin. It was definitely him; there was no doubt about it.

"What happened?" John asked.

"Well, you know that today we have had the first snow fall. It did not last, but at 5:30 p.m. it was enough to cause slippery conditions and so at the curve at Jerseymen's Hill, your father sideswiped a station wagon coming in the opposite direction. The station wagon went down the embankment on his side of the road, ending up on level ground. Your father's Volkswagon went headlong into the stones on his side of the road and the gas tank exploded. Your father and the other man were apparently ejected and the lady sitting in the back had no chance. Your fathers neck was broken; he died instantly."

"Yes, and now to bring such news home!" was all John could say. He felt sick to his stomach, very much alone with a feeling of deep, tremendous sorrow in his chest. How would they all get through such a tragedy? John knew that he was very angry with his father at that moment but he could not deal with such feelings at present; he would deal with that later.

When John returned home from identifying his father's body, a number of the neighbours were with the family. His mother had calmed down somewhat; one of the neighbours had phoned Dr. Herbert, their family physician who lived four doors down the street, for medication for her. John's mother was a serious diabetic and it was out of control. However, Dr. Herbert was able to provide some effective medication. When John saw all the people there, he was grateful. He didn't think the family could face this disaster alone. He leaned against the kitchen cupboard wondering what to do with such a situation. His best friend Miriam walked into the house at that moment. "What happened?" she asked John. He explained it all to her and to those in the sitting room and in the process of doing this he began to cry. Agnes, Gus's mother was sitting on the sofa and immediately said to him, "Now, don't cry, it will not help your mother for you to cry!" John forced himself to stop crying completely, but realized days later that he had a terrible pain in his lower back. He did not immediately connect this to repressed emotion; but that was certainly the case.

The sharp pain that John felt in his lower back stimulated John's memory into remembering the dream that he had had a good three weeks' previously about his father's death. The details came rushing back to him flooding his memory. John remembered now that the dream had been quite disturbing at the time. In that dream Batist had gone on union business and had been gone the whole day. Supper time had come and there was no sign of Batist. They wondered where he could be. They phoned different places to see if he was there. No one had seen him. John himself had gone looking for him thinking that he may have fallen asleep in one of the local bars of the area or that maybe he had stopped to eat at someone's house. There was no sign of him. It was beginning to get dark and a thick fog had begun forming throughout the village. The wind also came up quite a bit. John was worried. Where could his father be? His brother Timmy who was looking through the living-room window called to John saying, "His car has arrived, he is stopped on the other side of the street!" It was 5:30 p.m., the time for the evening meal. In the dream, however, Batist never came into the house. John had awakened from this dream upset and distraught wondering what it all meant.

John did not tell anyone that earlier that month he had made application to enter the Missionary Community of the White Fathers, also known as the Society of the Missionaries of Africa. The thought crossed his mind that he would have to cancel this application. He was not to leave before September of the following year, so his thought was to cross that bridge when the time came. Now, he had to attend to funeral arrangements. Also, the news had to be broken to his oldest sister in Halifax, who had just come out of the hospital. How would she take such bad news? They would have to speak to her husband first and get him to break the news to her. She took the news quite well, considering, but one thing upset her. She feared that her two children, Katherine and Rodney, who were with their grandparents because of her illness, may have been in the accident with their grandfather and that this was being hidden from her. Her husband telephoned John and wanted him to put the two children on the phone to her so that she could speak to them. This John did and that eased her fear concerning their safety.

All the funeral preparations were completed and the wake- keeping had to be with a closed casket since the impact of the accident and the fire had damaged John's father too severely. John got a wreath marked "FATHER" to place on the casket. In the beginning the coroner suggested that they have just one evening of wake-keeping and do the service as soon as possible. He suggested this take place at the funeral home, but John's mother did not agree to this. She was adamant that the wake would be the traditional three day time period even if the casket had to be closed and would take place in the family home. Many people came to pray and support the family. The following days were difficult ones. John was able to get time off from his teaching and a week later returned to school. The children were very sympathetic towards John and remained as good as gold for a couple of weeks into John's mourning time. He was amazed by them and by their empathy with what he was going through.

Many rumours went around the village because of the woman who was in the car with John's father. There was also a question as to who was driving. It was John's father's car, but the other man, Ronald Boudreau, knew how to drive; they had stopped at a friend's house on the way back from the Union meeting, picking up Llewellyn; her friend, Doris Penny, mentioned that the other man, not John's father, was at the wheel when they had left, taking Llewellyn with them.

One neighbour, Mr. Charles Marchand, told John's mother, one day when he was visiting, "Oh, by the way, the gossip in the village is that Batist had been having an affair with that woman for the last nine years."

Rose did not skip a beat and answered quite assuredly, "Well, if Batist was having an affair with Llewellyn, they are the only ones who know it. We don't! If he did have an affair, it was for him and was his business, no one else's, okay?" "Oh, of course, of course," answered Charles. And that ended that story on the spot.

John later told his mother to ignore the gossip. There were always troublemakers in every village. One incident that could not be ignored and that infuriated John's brother, was the two letters that arrived through the mail, unsigned, bearing some nasty comments about their father and the family.

These people had observed certain things about the family in church. How Christian could one get, using church for their nasty observations and comments. John's brother went to the police with the letters, just to be told that there was not too much they could do. Finger printing them would not do much since many fingers had handled the letters. The family and John just let it all drop, but it remained in John's mind for a long time. It would resurface years later at a parish retreat in one of the neighbouring villages.

Life for Rose as a widow was not easy. It was not easy as well for his younger brother and sister. They needed much support and decisions had to be made by them regarding their education and future. There was a lot of adjusting to do and his mother, being a serious diabetic, could not work outside the home. As long as John was there, all was supplemented by his teaching income, and some help from his older sisters. The widow's allowance provided by the government in those days was quite minimal, $68 per month. As a serious diabetic, John's mother was able to get a $10 supplement but that was still only $78 per month. There was no way a household could be run on that, not even in the 1960's. So John and his mother wrote to the government authorities for permission for her to keep borders, two roomers, who would use the extra bedroom. His younger sister would share her mother's bedroom and John and his brother had their own room. That was the way Rose was able to make ends meet; the lodgers' money would be greatly needed once John left for the Seminary.

John's departure for the Seminary was a very tense and trying time. When he broke the news to his mother about his leaving she began to cry and said to John, "How can you leave now, so soon after your father's death?" It was only a year since the accident had occurred. "I really need you here, it is such a bad time to be going and you are going so far, to the U.S., how will I manage?" she continued.

"But Martine and Della are here with you. They will help, they have told me so."

Martine and Della had told John when he questioned his leaving, "You must go now, it will be too difficult later. Mom will become too dependent on you. She is almost there now and you must make your own life. You will regret it later if you don't go. Mom's only 49 years old; she could remarry!"

So John told his mother that he had to do this now or else he would never leave. His mother just shook her head in disbelief. John went to see Miriam to tell her the dilemma he was in; she felt as his sisters did, that he must go through with his plan. His mother would manage. But John's heart was heavy and he had a terrible, empty feeling in his stomach. The time for leaving was fast approaching. It would be after the Labour Day weekend. He was to go by car with friends as far as Boston and then take a bus to a small place called Onchiota in Upper New York State. It was a mysterious unknown adventure.

That Sunday, the day before departure, it was a beautiful sunny day. The water of the harbour was clear as glass. John had resigned his teaching position and everyone he met was amazed that he was leaving. "Are you sure it is a good thing to do at this time? How does your mother feel?" they asked. John wanted to back out at times. At one point on the previous Saturday afternoon, he had gone as far as the Rectory door to tell his parish priest that he had made a mistake. He was tempted to say that he couldn't go through with this, but ended up turning back without knocking. As he was walking home, a priest friend from one of the neighbouring villages stopped to pick him up. John poured out his soul to him. He looked at John and said, "Well, there is only one thing that I can tell you and that is that your first obligation is to your mother!" John was thrown into an even greater anxiety attack. It seemed as if he could not breathe. He needed to go somewhere by himself. He needed to pray! God only knew how much he had prayed and agonized over his spiritual health and journey and how difficult this decision had been, especially since he knew so well the terrible scruples that he had encountered in his life and the ongoing battle with his sexual urges. But he knew that at one point he had been extremely calm and at peace and had made the decision. He needed to revisit that moment and find that peace again, a peace that no longer seemed to be there. He remembered once again the Sunday before leaving when all was calm and the harbour like glass; he had sat under a tree at the hospital picnic feeling totally desolate. One of the Sisters from the convent that he had taught with came up to him and said,

"It is hard to leave, isn't it? You look totally devastated!"

"Oh Sister," John replied, "It is like a knife cutting through my heart and soul! I cannot put in words how hard this is!"

"We are certainly praying for you because we do know how difficult this is for you and for your family. If you get a chance stop at the convent in the morning as you head out."

"I will do my best to do that Sister," John answered.

Chapter Ten

Fr. John continued his visit with Jules and Chris. It was good for him to be able to see first hand where they were living and to be reassured that the living conditions and the area they were in were appropriate. He also had many more questions to ask Chris and Jules but they would have to wait since they wanted Fr. John to see where they had been living before they had found the Stella Awinja apartment. They walked over to the YWCA. "I thought that you had been living at the YMCA for men? Isn't the YWCA for women?" Fr. John asked.

"It usually is, but they have changed those rules. It is now possible to live in either one and we found that the YMCA was much more expensive than this one, so we moved. When we discovered that the YWCA was not as clean and well-run as the YMCA, we looked for an apartment of our own. We found a bachelor apartment on the top floor of the Stella Awinja building. It is really safer, even if it is twelve floors up. When we wash our clothes we can put them to dry on the roof of the building. We just have to go up one small flight of stairs to the roof and there are clothes lines installed to dry the clothes. We just have to be careful of thieves. Some of the other tenants have no scruples about taking things that belong to someone else, especially good quality things.

After their visit to the YWCA, they went over to their apartment. They had to walk up the eleven flights of stairs since there was no elevator. "I'll certainly get my exercises in during this visit," commented Fr. John to the boys. The apartment turned out to be very comfortable and spacious. They had fixed it up in quite a pleasant way. They had put a carpet in the middle of the floor and they each had a bed on either end of the main room. There was a small table with two chairs against the wall next to the small kitchenette. There was a small fridge in the kitchenette, a sink and a double burner hot plate on the small kitchen cupboard. Two people could easily be together in the kitchenette when cooking and doing dishes. As you entered the apartment, the bathroom was immediately to your right. It was fairly large with toilet, sink and a bathtub with shower. If one person was showering, another person could easily use the sink for shaving and teeth brushing. Both Chris and Jules were pleased with their accommodations. To welcome Fr. John they made coffee and served biscuits. They continued to chat about life in Nairobi and all they had had to do to get settled and organize their lives.

"So you did not have too much difficulty with customs and immigration when you arrived at the airport?" Fr. John inquired.

"No trouble really," they answered. "The agent wanted to know where we were coming from and how long we would be in Kenya. When we explained our situation and which flight we had taken, he stamped our passports giving us each an entry visa of three months. Then, he added, "During those three months you will go to the immigration office to have the visa extended. You are usually given a two year extension. Enjoy your stay in Nairobi."

"As you had told us we took a taxi to the YMCA and not the public transport. That was a good thing since we were able to take all our luggage with us and didn't have to leave anything behind. It was a bit late by the time we got to the YMCA but the guy at the desk in charge of the rooms was quite pleasant and gave us a room for the first three days. According to him it was the last room available. We would be able to extend those three days if need be. We slept very well since we were very tired. The next morning we were able to have breakfast at the Y. We were quite shocked at how expensive everything was. We were no longer in Zaire. This was life in the fast lane and by the looks of things our money would disappear fast if we weren't careful. It wasn't going to be easy. Before going out we asked at the desk where we would be able to register for English classes and which direction to take to get to the city center. We needed to find a bank to deposit our funds. The clerk gave us a small map of the city and showed us where the American University and the British High Commission were; both gave training in English at different levels. Then he told us which bus went to the city center. There we would find many of the things that we would need. Our new life had started. It was mysterious, interesting but also scary."

"So where did you go first?" Fr. John asked.

"Well, we needed to deposit our money in a safe place. We could not keep carrying this amount of money with us; it was too dangerous. We could easily lose it or be robbed. We needed to find a bank," said Chris.

"Once we had reached the city center," said Jules, "we walked around for a while, checking out the different banks in the downtown area. Most of the banks had some kind of African name. One bank, however, had a more British name. It was called Barclays Bank. We figured that it would have connections with the British banking system so maybe it would be safer to put our money in that one. We went into the bank and we told the pleasant lady at the teller's wicket that we wanted to open an account. She directed us to another lady working at one of the desks."

"The woman at the desk told us to be seated, that she would be with us shortly. She continued to check and sign various papers that were on her desk. She finally put those away and turned to both of us and asked, 'What can I do for you?' We need to open a bank account. We will be staying here in Nairobi for awhile and we will be doing some courses here, especially English courses. We cannot keep carrying our money around with us. Can you help us open an account here at Barclays? We are expecting our father to come soon to visit us and we need to have all of our affairs in order."

"It is possible to open an account," she answered. "However, you will need a co-signer for your account. Do you know of anyone here in Nairobi who could do that for you?"

"We have just arrived here from Zaire so we don't know anyone. Can't you help us, please?"

"My name is Martha Lwanga and I'm not Kenyan, I'm Ugandan and I had to come here when things were very difficult in my own country. I know what it means to have difficulty in a new country. I will sign for you and when your father arrives I can speak to him and get his name on the papers as well. Then whenever he needs to transfer money to you we will be able to communicate without any problem since we will have met one another."

"So she signed for us and gave us a temporary bank card until the permanent one arrived. With that card we could withdraw money when we needed it. She even suggested that we come to her house to meet her family. She has grown children our age. We have already done that and she has invited us to eat at her house. She has been very kind to us. We really appreciate what she has done for us. You must meet her now that you are here."

"Of course I will do that," answered Fr. John. "You must find out from her what would be the best time for us to meet."

"We will bring her over to the Missionary residence one evening after work. She does not know that you are white and that you are a priest. She will be shocked for sure."

The following afternoon Fr. John received a call from the boys telling him that they would come over to the Missionary residence around four thirty for Martha to meet him. Promptly at four thirty they arrived. Martha was totally surprised when she saw Fr. John. "How can this be, what is going on?" Martha inquired of Jules and Chris. They explained what had happened through the community of Sisters in Bukavu. Of course she was totally amazed by it all. "You have been very fortunate to meet someone who was willing to help you. It is not everyone who is so fortunate," said Martha. Then Martha invited Fr. John and the boys for Sunday dinner. Fr. John had a chance to meet the rest of Martha's family. That was when he discovered that Martha's husband had disappeared during the terrible years of President Idi Amin. They did not know what had happened to him. They never did find out how he had died, if really he had died or was imprisoned somewhere. Martha had never remarried after that.

"Fr. John," she said, "you must always make sure that the boys have pocket money."

"I will do my best," Fr. John answered.

"I can always let you know through the accounts when they are in need," said Martha.

"That will be fine," answered Fr. John.

They continued to show Fr. John the sights of Nairobi. One of the favourite hotspots of the city was a center called the Carnivore. It was a dance place that combined good food, fraternizing and dancing. Many young people frequented the Carnivore. Both young men enjoyed going there very much. They also took Fr. John to the store where many things could be bought at a reasonable price. They also went to the Cinema a number of times; they knew that Fr. John enjoyed a good movie. During this visit they had seen "The Nutty Professor" starring Eddie Murphy. They had a good laugh which was a good thing for each one of them. It made them feel more relaxed. They shopped in the market, ate together and continued to explore the city.

As they explored the city, they often came upon refugees begging for money as they sat quite forlorn on the side of the street. They wanted food and they could get it from the refugee camp if they agreed to go there. Most of these people, however, did not want to go to the refugee camp. For many of them it was like being in jail. Jules always gave them a few Kenyan shillings. One evening he had no coins to give them so he gave them the boots that he was wearing. Even if they did not or could not wear them they could sell them.

Jules and Chris were very surprised to meet a whole group of Rwandese students and young workers who were trying to find a proper means of living. Some could return to Rwanda if they so wished but others could not, depending on which ethnic group they belonged to. They met Veronica, Teresa, Florence, Robert, James and Nicole. They would sometimes all share a coffee or tea together, most of the time at Jules and Chris' place since the others were living in much more cramped quarters. Certain of these friends were attending Evangelical and Pentecostal churches that were already established close by. They all wanted Jules and Chris to accompany them to these services. Jules went a number of times but was very concerned and disappointed in the message that was being given. The gist of the message was that if all was going well for you and you had a good position and were making good money and were properly married, then God was favouring you. You were to rejoice over it. For Jules and Chris there was something erroneous about this. If God is a loving God then he must love you no matter what your life is, even if you are as poor as a church mouse. Chris only went once to these services. He met Cecelia and they became very good friends and so went to services in her church community. Teresa told Jules one evening when he told her that he was no longer attending these services, "But Jules, you need to be saved. I would not want to see you once we have died suffering down below as I looked at you from my position above in heaven." Jules had quipped back, "Well, how can you be so sure that you are the one who will be 'up there' as you say and I will be 'down there'? It could be just the other way around for all you know, because you see, Teresa, I believe it takes at least a minimal amount of humility to get into heaven which you don't seem to have just now! In fact, your arrogance and self-righteousness is quite striking!" Teresa could not answer. Fr. John had been very pleased at hearing Jules answer Teresa in this way. The way of thinking when it came to matters of faith and the ideas expressed concerning God were very appalling. Jules later found out that most of the time when these friends gathered to pray, it was to pray that they come into lots of money so that all their problems would be solved. It quite disgusted him and so he did not return to their prayer sessions.

During this first visit Fr. John came to realize that Jules and Chris were in danger in Nairobi as well. They needed to leave there as well as soon as possible. He would soon have to get the process of their immigrating to Canada under way. The Nairobi situation was not a healthy one. It was also fraught with danger. As they discussed the political and religious situation in Nairobi one morning, Fr. John asked them if they both wished to be baptized and have a short instruction in the Catholic faith. They expressed their desire to do this. Fr. John took a few days to do this with them and before returning to Jinja, he baptized both of them. Having been born into a family of Seventh Day Adventists, they had never been baptized. They both appeared to be quite pleased to do this. In baptizing them, Fr. John had felt strongly that he was placing them in God's care. That was as much as he could do for the time being. He would need to get the immigration process going very soon.

During this first visit with Jules and Chris they had received a visit from a group of soldiers who were looking for Rwandese or Zairean refugees who did not have proper documents. Jules and Chris always had their papers in order but even with this they still had to give the soldiers a "bribe" to be left alone. Fr. John knew that he had to do all in his power to get them out of this country. The danger here was very present. They only had false, illegal Rwandese passports that Fr. John had managed to get through the refugee camps in Bukavu when they were still there. Since they had been born in Kinshasa, Zaire, he would attempt to get them Zairean passports at the Zairean Embassy in Kampala. Those would probably be safer since they would not be illegal. He would certainly attempt this upon his return to Jinja. They had passport photos taken before Fr. John left. He took some of the photos with him. Fr. John returned to Jinja very worried and determined to get them out of Kenya. Because of this incident with the soldiers that he himself had witnessed, Fr. John decided to pay a visit to the Canadian Embassy in Nairobi to see if there was anything that he could do to get things going for their eventual departure for Canada.

Fr. John was totally amazed at what he witnessed at the Embassy. There were many people in the reception area waiting to be served or to book an appointment with an Embassy agent. Many of those waiting had the features of the Somalian people that he often met on the streets of Nairobi. Many had resorted to begging. Fr. John went to the window. He doubted that the woman behind the thick glass could hear him so he had the urge to shout. When the woman spoke to him she was quite audible and he could clearly understand everything she said. "May I help you?" she asked. "Well I hope so," Fr. John replied, giving her a big smile. It was not a time for smiles, however, on her part. She was as serious as a judge in a law court. "Is it possible for me to get an immigration package here since I have two young men who wish to apply for immigration to Canada?"

"The immigration packages are finished at the moment," she replied. "We will have more by next week. Try us again by Wednesday of next week."

"I would like to speak to an immigration officer today if possible since I am traveling back to Kampala tomorrow," said Fr. John.

"That is entirely impossible," she answered, "They are all booked up with interview appointments for the whole week. You would need to book for a date two weeks from now. That is the best that I can do."

"Well I really have no choice, do I? I will wait till I return to Canada and from there I will begin the process. So be it!" Fr. John was actually quite furious with the Embassy. This would delay things a lot. He would eventually be surprised by certain events that would help in the process.

Chapter Eleven

The morning of September 1, 1965 was upon him soon enough and the time for John to leave for the seminary. He had not slept all night. His two feet had felt like ice cubes as he had tried to sleep. It was early September, warm for that time of the year, but for him it was a cold, dull time. The morning of the departure John got into the car with Ellen Boucher who was returning to Boston after a holiday at the village. John waved to his mother who was looking through the front door window. Her sad face, with tears streaming down her cheeks, would be engraved in his memory throughout the two day trip and for many years to come. In fact, he would never forget that scene, and would remember it again the day of her funeral, years later.

They stopped at the Sisters' convent, as promised, to say his good-byes. They had graciously prepared them sandwiches and fruit for the journey. It was much appreciated but at that moment John felt that he would be deathly sick if he saw any kind of food. The Sisters promised to keep him in their prayers and hoped that they would have a safe journey to Boston.

They did not go straight through to Boston. They stopped at a motel just outside St. Stephen's for the night. Ellen got John to call his mother so she would know that they had come safely this far. Rose was pleased to hear and sounded much better. They arrived in Boston in the afternoon of the next day and John stayed at Ellen's for one week. They picked up the bus tickets for the trip to Saranack Lake where he would be picked up by one of the priests and taken to the Seminary that was situated eighteen miles outside Saranack Lake in a tiny, picturesque spot in the Adirondack Mountains called Onchiota. John did not realize that the trip would be so long. It took the whole day and it was dark before he was picked up at the bus station. Everyone had already eaten when he arrived at the Seminary. Many of the students had arrived, but were in the basement recreation hall. The priest accompanying John showed him to his room. It was a huge room, large enough for four beds. To get to it, they had to walk down a long dark hallway. To John, the place looked like a former hospital and he would later find out that his suspicions were correct. He entered his room with his three huge suitcases and before he knew it the priest, Fr. LeBrun, was gone. He turned around to speak to him and he was not there. He looked out into the hallway and saw just the glimmer of a light at the end of the corridor. He decided that he would get his bed ready and go to sleep as he was exhausted from the long journey. He realized that there were no bed sheets for the bed, simply a couple of woollen blankets. He undressed and before getting into bed, placed one woollen blanket on the mattress as a bed sheet and the other he used to cover himself. He was in the habit of sleeping in his briefs only and realized when he got into bed that the woollen blankets made him very itchy. He slept in fits and starts, with the itching bothering him each time he moved. He was very happy to see the morning light stream through the window. His first thought upon waking was, "What did I get myself into this time? How stupid was I to leave my teaching job and family to come to this?" His heart sank.

Mustering up every ounce of courage that he could, he got up, washed, dressed and went in search of some breakfast. He met one Seminarian at the end of the hall who introduced himself as Tom Quinton. "Oh are you the one from Nova Scotia, Canada? Welcome, I'm on my way for a coffee; let's go together. We didn't see you last night. You should have come down to the recreation room. That's where we were," he continued.

"Oh, I was pretty bushed from the trip!" John answered, feeling that his voice sounded hollow and unnatural.

"Several of us arrived early in the day yesterday. I'm from Bristol, Connecticut and from an Italian family. It wasn't easy to leave the family, but I feel better now that I'm here." John wished he could say the same. He felt more like a fish out of water. But the drama had begun, where would it lead him? He really felt more like crying than anything else, feeling extremely alone.

That first day at the seminary was spent settling in, getting acquainted with other students, visiting the property which was huge and quite beautiful. That was when John learned that the seminary had been a hospital and sanatorium for old retired actors and actresses and so the reason for such large rooms and ornate furniture and accessories in the rooms. Many of the portraits, mirrors and period furniture pieces had been put into the huge attic of the main building. There were numerous cottages on the grounds and all were close to a small lake called Lake Kushaqua. The back of the main building had long screened-in porches with numerous windows. John would end up cleaning those many times with water, vinegar and paper towels.

They assembled a number of times to receive their timetables, instructions, course schedules and prayer times. The main building and the chapel were modeled on what appeared to be a Swiss resort. John had to admit that it was a gorgeous property. That did not keep him from feeling totally empty, afraid, anxious and lost. When not at a meeting or session he would wander about the property like a lost soul. His favourite spot was in the library, where double doors opened onto part of the seminary roof. From there, John could see the lake and it made him feel more at home. Sometimes he felt so miserable that he wished he had the courage to jump off the roof. At one of their sessions called Spiritual update, he learned that each seminarian was to choose a spiritual advisor to whom he could go and bare his soul. John thought about this, but he did not know who to choose; he did not know the priests who were there. Gradually he learned that others were going through similar experiences as himself; they also felt lost. It was only the second and third year students who seemed at home. They were in charge of organizing all the student activities. One student, Sean Burns, a second year student who had family roots in Canada gave him a bit of advice on a choice for a Spiritual Director. Acting on this advise, he chose Fr. John Koppelski, as Sean told him that he was open, understanding and quite experienced in direction, therapy and spiritual psychology. John thought that this might be the help he needed. All he knew was that he desperately needed to speak with someone; the anxiety was almost paralyzing him. At one point, Tom Quinton told him that he looked like he had lost his best friend. John unburdened himself a bit to him and how awful he felt. "Well, I'm not feeling so hot myself," he answered. "So we need to choose a spiritual director who can help us unburden ourselves.

By the end of the week, the programmes were pretty much established and John had given Fr. John Koppelski his name as a candidate for direction. Fr. Koppelski had accepted and they were to meet that weekend. Friday nights were reserved for confessions and eventually each one had his manual labour duty established. Friday morning at assembly, they announced that there would be an outing for anyone who wanted to climb to the top of Loon Lake Mountain

The four Canadians in the group would especially appreciate this since from the top of Loon Lake Mountain, on a clear day, you could see Montreal. John thought that having a glimpse of an area that was connected to home would be nice – he needed to know that he was not so far away as the trip had been so long and somehow so confusing that he felt lost, never to be found again. He needed to hear from home and know that all was well, especially his mother who was alone in a way with his younger brother and sister.

Before the outing, John sat on the roof next to the library and suddenly thought that he had to get out of there. He would smother and die from lonesomeness. He thought to himself that he would go tell Fr. Koppelski that he needed to speak to him and that he was sure that he had made a mistake and that he wanted him to take him to the bus station the next morning so that he could begin the trip back home. It had all been a terrible mistake on his part. This he did. Feeling quite ridiculous, John knocked on Fr. Koppelski's door and told him what he planned to do. Fr. Koppelski simply said, "Oh, so soon! OK, go on your outing and when you come back, come and see me and we will talk." John said that would be fine and felt much better at having taken a decision. He had not even unpacked his suitcases as that had seemed too final.

The outing was quite fine, a bit tiring, but the weather was still warm with some sunshine. It turned out to be quite disappointing, however, since there was too much haze that day to be able to see Montreal. John sat on a rock on top of Loon Lake Mountain and wanted to weep every tear in his body. Then he took heart because in the morning he would be on the bus heading for home.

Once back at the seminary, around 4 p.m., he washed, changed and went to knock on Fr. Koppelski's door. He welcomed him in. It was warm and comfortable in the office. It was an office with a bed and bath just off of it, a small suite of rooms. He offered him a seat and sat opposite him facing him.

"Why the departure so soon?" asked Fr. Koppelski.

"This is just not for me," said John. "I can't believe that I left my teaching position, my home and my widowed mother to come to this. It's like I'm doing nothing. It was such a mistake."

"Do you think there is a problem at home that you should have dealt with before leaving and didn't? Or is it something that is bothering you that you can't seem to unburden yourself about?" asked Fr. Koppelski.

"Well, I did lose my father in a terrible car accident just a year ago and I do realize that there are many unsaid words and messages about Dad and our relationship that are weighing me down. And, of course, I can still see my mother's tear-filled eyes in the window of the front door and I can't forget it. I left them all high and dry with so little to manage on. How could I have been so cruel? I'm realizing that there is a can of worms that needs to be opened and I'm scared to death to open it!"

So John mentioned a few things about his family background, what type of family they were, what his father and mother had been like, the relationship with his brother and sisters. Fr. Koppelski listened intently, interjecting a comment and a question here and there. John seemed to feel better as the talk continued. They spoke for a good hour and then Fr. Koppelski said to John, "I'm going to ask you to do me a favour – you don't have to do this, feel free to say no, O.K.? I'm asking you to stay here one more week, and at the end of that week, if you still feel the same, I'll drive you to the bus myself. We can arrange to meet mid-way through that week to see how things are progressing; what do you say?"

John's heart sank and for quite a moment he remained silent. Then he said, "If I feel the need can I come and speak with you before mid-week?"

"Oh, absolutely," answered Fr. Koppelski, "we can meet at any time."

"It is as if you are driving a knife through my heart when you ask me this, Father, but, OK, I accept – one more week!" said John. Now, John felt he knew a bit more of what the agony in the garden was about.

The first part of that week was agony for John, but strangely enough, by Thursday John knew that he could not leave. He knew that the time had come to open up the can of worms and to take a long hard look at his life and all that had been part of him all those previous twenty-two years, be it relationships, education, religion, wounds or hurts: the whole baggage that he was carrying. God was giving him a time of grace and opportunity. That Friday evening he knocked on Fr. Koppelski's door, went in and sat down and told him just that, "I know that I cannot leave now and the process of growing up and growing spiritually has arrived."

"Good," said Fr. Koppelski. "So there will be no bus trip this weekend?" asked Fr. Koppelski.

"No bus trip this weekend," answered John and both laughed together. John's laugh was the first authentic laugh since he had arrived at the seminary. The next day, he unpacked his suitcases. He also found out that Sunday night that he was to be the morning bell ringer to awaken the students. They were to be in chapel by 6:15 a.m.

Of all the courses, John found Latin the worse. He had had very little Latin and so it was a real chore for him. His meetings with Fr. Koppelski were not too difficult in the beginning, but there were things about his relationship with his parents, especially his father that were painful to tell. He told him his innermost thoughts and all his most bizarre thoughts about sexual matters. When it seemed too horrid to him, he would close his eyes and just say it aloud as if he were alone in the room. Then he would open his eyes and look squarely at Fr. Koppelski and say, "There, I've said it," almost as if the words would eat him up or destroy him. Fr. Koppelski would smile and say, "Well, the world didn't come to an end, did it? We're still here and the room hasn't self-destructed, right?"

John would sigh, a huge sigh of relief and then learn that these thoughts and many others were quite normal for a young man maturing and trying to make sense of his life, his sexuality and his spiritual growth. It was so very good to hear such words of encouragement and such acceptance by another person, especially a priest.

Fr. Koppelski was not only John's Spiritual Advisor, but also his confessor. Each week, if he wished, he would make his confession to his confessor. John always felt that he needed to do this, the scruples were still part of him, but they had calmed somewhat. He was learning more and more what it meant to make an adult confession. His sexual drive still remained a problem, and how to control this whole emotional and affective development was quite a challenge. Sometimes, he felt like a spring wound so tightly that it should pop at any moment. He would seek out Fr. Koppelski and go over this with him. The talking and the laying bare of the feelings and emotions helped a lot. It was during the sessions with Fr. Koppelski that he unburdened his mind and soul about the childhood incident with his friend Miriam. Fr. Koppelski helped John see the possible connection between this incident, his mother's reaction to it, and the nightmares that left him so very upset. John realized then that another liberation had occurred in his life when the nightmares ceased.

John became so open with Fr. Koppelski, baring his soul, his feelings, his every thought in such detail that he eventually felt totally naked in front of him. That became a problem for John. He just felt that wherever he was if Fr. Koppelski was present there that he could see right through him. He eventually got into his head that it could not be possible for Fr. Koppelski to even like him after all the details of his feelings and inner thoughts that he had discussed with him.

John began to confess to Fr. Koppelski that there was a person in the community that bothered him greatly and that he did not know what to do with the whole situation. After about a month of confessing this, Fr. Koppelski asked him one evening in confession, "May I ask who this person is?" "Must I tell you, Father?" replied John. "Well, it could help, you don't really have to mind you, but it may help the situation!" John remained silent for a moment and Fr. Koppelski without looking at him asked, "Is that person me?" "Yes," answered John.

"Well, John", said Fr. Koppelski, "You must bring this up in spiritual direction next time we meet. You must be the one to broach it, because it is a matter that has come up in the confessional so I cannot do it, O.K.? You do understand, John?" "Yes, Father, I do", answered John. Of course, John dreaded their next meeting, but meet they did in the next two weeks, one Saturday evening.

That Saturday evening John had several things to discuss and could not seem to bring that point up. Fr. Koppelski just simply looked at John and said, "Was there anything else you needed to speak about?"

"Yes, Father," said John, "my present relationship with you and how I feel about that."

"What do you feel is wrong with the relationship John?"

"I feel totally naked in front of you, especially when you are present wherever I am. It seems like you can see through me, that I've told you so many things in such minute details that I cannot seem to be at ease when you are present," said John.

"You have been very open", said Fr. Koppelski, "maybe too much, in a way. It was not really necessary to be so to such an extent, but then, you felt somehow that you needed that, and so that is fine. But I do not think of these things when I see you. I see a young man in search of his vocation and a full, mature and healthy spiritual life, and that is what is happening. It is to God that you confess these things when you say them to me in and out of the confessional, and I, on the contrary, admire your openness and your quest for truth about yourself and your life and your desire to be spiritually healthy. If only more were like you! Ah, yes! Be at rest, at peace, you are on the search for the pearl of great price. Continue your journey; you are doing well and I do not think ill of you, but have only admiration for your spunk and determination," said Fr. Koppelski. John breathed a sigh of relief once again and slept a deep and peaceful sleep that night.

Classes and life at the seminary continued to run fairly smoothly with John volunteering each Sunday for visits at the St. Gabriel Nursing Home in Malone. John liked going out there on Sunday to entertain the sick and elderly with his visits and stories. Sister Michelle always appreciated his visits. It was also a way for John to get away from the somewhat closed atmosphere of the seminary that was surrounded by the Adirondack Mountains and Lakes. Winter in this area was one of much snow and cold. It was good to see spring blossom forth with the smell of the pine trees, lush green forests, plants and blossoming flowers. John heard from home quite regularly, got the odd phone call, as well, and his mother was finally adjusting somewhat to her life as a widow. There were many things about his home situation that they did not tell him, so that his mind would be at ease and that his concern and worry would not be so acute. He continued to hear from Miriam who announced to him that she would be entering the Sisters' Noviciate the following September. John was pleased; she needed to know if this was an authentic calling for her. He was also told that he could go home for Christmas, that there was a shorter and easier way to get to Nova Scotia from Upper New York State than the route he had taken to get there. A bus could be taken from Saranack Lake to Montreal, then the train to Halifax, with a change in Truro, Nova Scotia that would take him to MacIntyre Lake. He was elated. He needed that time, that return home, to see what this would mean for him, how he would feel about home and the whole situation that he had left behind.

John continued to empty the can of worms but it would take a number of years to get it all sorted out, especially his feelings of inadequacy, lack of self confidence, his problems in his relationship with his father and how he hated his alcoholic bouts and absences from the family; these sessions also included his too great attachment to his sisters and of course, his whole concept that sex was dirty, not to be indulged in and that anything to do with one's body and genitals was to be shunned and avoided at all costs. This sexual component still held a magnetic, curious attraction for John. Just the thought of it made him turn weak and helpless and he feared looking at it head on.

The time came for him to go home. He enjoyed the trip immensely, going as far as Montreal with one of the other Canadian students. From there he reached MacIntyre Lake and since he had got in touch with his mother, Miriam's father, Gerald, was able to meet him at the train station. Of course, his mother was there to meet him as well. As they were leaving the train station, she turned to him and said, "Oh, by the way, I'm not at home right now. I'm not in the house."

"Where are you?" asked John, incredulously.

"I'm at your Aunt Cecilia's and I'm in the process of moving into the basement there. They will fix things up for us. Your Uncle Allan will help us get the fridge and stove over there from the house."

John sat stunned. He knew the scenario of what family life at Aunt Cecilia's was all about. He had visited many times. And she had four children. He would end up babysitting his whole break. So, he mustered up enough courage to tell his mother what he thought of that situation.

"Mom, take me back to the train station. I'll go back to the seminary. I cannot spend Christmas and my break at Aunt Cecilia's! You know what it's like there. Mom, what are you thinking of, what are you doing? I can't believe this", said John.

"OK," she said, "Now that you're here, we won't move. We'll stay at home. Maybe your being home for a while will help me settle down more and I'll get used to the house and being alone." And so they were able to spend Christmas at home. It was a needed time for John, to see that he had made the right move. His mother did have support and was managing, although with some difficulties. His brother had left for Halifax not long after John had left for the seminary and only his youngest sister Clarisse was at home, finishing her high school. But things were not as extreme as he had thought and he knew that he must continue.

John was no sooner back at the seminary when a rumour started circulating in the community that they would be moving from their present site to a University somewhere in the US. John could not believe it, but since Vatican II had taken place and church reform had begun, seminary training had also been affected. It was rumoured that they needed to be at a University level, actually studying for a degree and not just its equivalency in a traditional seminary setup.

John prayed that this would be so. He found certain parts of seminary training and life somewhat outdated and even strange; for example, the Missionaries of Africa had a rule known as the rule of three. This rule applied especially to their African missions which meant that they should be at least three colleagues to form a community in each mission station; they were not to be alone and if they happened to be less than three they could protest to the regional superior. To get them accustomed to this rule, it was applied as well in the formation houses and John found that he could not do anything or go anywhere unless they were three students together. John found that the application of this rule lacked flexibility and was somewhat exaggerated. Of course, the rule was often violated. Once in the university set up, the rule would fall by the wayside, although they continued to be informed about it. John knew that he had to keep his opinions to himself about any of these things at that present time.

As Easter rolled around, the rumour concerning the move to the university became more than a rumour. After Easter celebrations, they were called to a spiritual conference in the main classroom on the first floor of the school. That is when they were informed that they would all go home for the summer break, and that they had to pack all of their things, and that all baggage and personal effects were to be stored in the basement of the main building next to the laundry room. They were to take home with them only what they needed for the summer. Then at the end of August of that summer they were to make their way to Dayton, Ohio, to the University of Dayton where their studies would be continued. The University of Dayton was for both male and female students and managed by the Marianist Brothers. As many as 100 universities had been studied, visited and looked at and this university offered the best all-round accommodations for what the Missionaries of Africa needed for studies and training. This involved the program of studies, housing, university facilities, libraries, possibilities for living a prayer life and a strong community life. All this was well-balanced at the University of Dayton. John could not believe his ears. That afternoon, he danced around his room, laughing and thanking God for such a gift. As he was packing in his room, there was a knock at the door. It was Tom Quinton!

"How is it going?" he asked John.

"I am packing, I am rejoicing. I am so happy about this decision," John answered.

"I am so upset", said Tom. 'I don't want to leave here. It is this type of life that I need. It is protection for me. I'll be so threatened at the University. It'll be a disaster for me!"

"You feel threatened by what and need to be protected from what?" asked John.

"I am simply not ready for university studies; my high school credits are very weak. As well, I am very weak when it comes to my sexual leanings with both men and women. I will not survive!" Tom said.

"But Tom, you'll have all the services and experts of the university and I'm sure they have excellent psychologists and spiritual directors there that you'll be able to seek help from. And then, many of the students I'm sure will become your friends and will be able to support and help you. It will be different and much more realistic, don't you think?" John said. "I'm terrified," answered Tom. "I just don't like it."

John DeCoste

Nevertheless, John had his bags packed in no time, and when the time came to store their things, he was the first one to bring them to the storage room, ready for shipping.

White Father Students at University of Dayton

Chapel at Onciota Formation House – Upper State New York

226

Chapter Twelve

Fr. John ended his first visit with Jules and Chris in Nairobi and returned to Jinja. His students were very happy to see him back. They got together that evening at recreation and he shared with them the events of his trip to Nairobi. He would return a second time but much later. He would need to wind things up here in Uganda first. His students were doing very well in all the English courses and were not having too much trouble understanding the various professors; they became easily capable of taking notes in English. They were becoming quite fluent in the language. All this was good preparation for them whether they stayed in the Missionary community or not.

Fr. John was fortunate enough to have a White Father colleague at the training center with whom he had worked when serving as a missionary in Nigeria. They had also been students together in Pittsburgh, Pennsylvania when on a sabbatical at the Institute of Formative Spirituality. He and Sean O'Leary would often discuss the present situation in Central Africa, as well as the problems that Sean was encountering at the formation center in Jinja. He felt that there was a very serious clash between himself and their Zairean colleague, Raphael Bipendo. They did not seem to hit it off very well. There was some kind of unexpressed animosity coming from Raphael and Sean could not understand why. Each time he tried to bring up the subject, Raphael would shy away from discussing it. This was extremely frustrating for Sean. He and Fr. John would, often go out on an evening to a restaurant just overlooking what was considered the ORIGIN of the Nile. There was a very fine verandah overlooking the river where they could chat and speak freely.

"If this continues," said Sean one evening, "I'm not renewing my mandate here. This is driving me crazy, this silent stewing of tempers. There is also the fact that he will always oppose whatever I bring up in council. I feel like driving my fist up his nose."

"Maybe it is just a clash of personalities; you are just not on the same wave length. I would let things ride if I were you and wait for an opportunity to confront him about it. And don't fool yourself; that opportunity will present itself sooner or later, "said Fr. John.

Now that the students were more comfortable with the course load, Fr. John went into Kampala on every possible occasion. He wanted to visit the different communities where there were colleagues that he had had as teachers or formators. He had often heard about the parishes where they were working since Uganda was a very old territory for the White Fathers. In fact, it was one of the first areas where the missionaries had come to work. Fr. Lourdel, also known as Mapeera, had worked here with the Martyrs of Uganda and Fr. John wanted very much to visit the Martyrs' shrine in Namugongo.

One Monday morning he had an opportunity to go to Kampala with Fr. Joseph Deckker, the director of the Formation house; he was going to attend a meeting of the directors in Kampala. Fr. John planned on staying for two weeks at least. He would visit Namucongo, the different Mission Parishes in Kampala and look up the Zairean Embassy to inquire if he could apply for Zairean passports for Jules and Chris. Their situation would be much safer and more stable if they had proper Zairean passports. He had gotten them to take passport photos while he was in Nairobi and he had brought those photos with him in case it was possible to obtain passports for them.

He visited the mission where Fr. Ronald was first. Fr. Ronald had been the director at the spiritual year in Washington D.C. It had been a difficult year but a fruitful one. At that time he had worked in a Pilot Project School for handicapped children. Fr. Ronald had encouraged him to take up this work and he had enjoyed doing it. It would be good to see Fr. Ronald again. He must be very happy to be back in his beloved Africa.

Fr. Ronald was very pleased to see Fr. John again. He said as he welcomed him to the mission parish. "This is a far cry from the streets of Washington and the chicken bones hanging from the water pipes, isn't it John?"

"It most certainly is," Fr. John laughed as they embraced each other. "But Fr. Ronald, I had no idea that you knew about the chicken bones hanging from the water pipes in the refectory. That is a surprise."

Before answering this, Fr. Ronald got out the drinks, some cold beer and a few cokes. "Well, I really found it all out by accident just before we continued our spring session the year before you arrived. Your friend, Claude Forgeron, was showing one of the students where the chicken bones were placed and proceeded to explain to him how this came about. They wanted to see if any of the staff would notice that there were dried up chicken bones hanging from the refectory water pipes. I never did let anyone know that the cat was out of the bag."

Fr. John could not stop laughing about the whole thing. They all laughed as they sat together reminiscing about past days and events. Fr. John stayed with Fr. Ronald's community for lunch. It was a good day. They ate delicious frog legs with golden brown fries. They were both cooked to perfection. Fr. John profusely congratulated the cook on such a fine meal.

Fr. John needed to know where the Zairean Embassy was located in Kampala. He asked one of the Ugandan priests if he had any idea where it was. "I do know where it is," said Fr. Cyprian, "and I'm going in that direction this afternoon so I'll drop you there." Fr. Cyprian let Fr. John off in front of a huge wrought iron gate. There were several buildings not far from the gate. Fr. John could not get through the gate and so made noise to attract the attention of someone on the premises. One elderly man appeared and told Fr. John that he would send someone who could answer his questions.

The person who came to the gate was very polite and, looking at Fr. John questioningly, asked what he wanted. Fr. John pleasantly greeted him and asked him, "If I have passport photos of two students born in Kinshasa who live in Bukavu, could I obtain Zairean passports for them?

"Yes, you can do that," he answered. "You will have to fill out these forms; then with the photos and documents signed and $350 American for each passport, they will be processed. You can come back here to pick up the two documents in three days' time."

"Well, the two people in question cannot be here. At the moment they are away at school but I have in my possession the documents and the photos that were taken in Nairobi where the school is and I can sign for them as their guarantor, if that is alright with you? What I don't like is to give you all that money before even receiving the documents and only get them after a three day wait?" said Fr. John questioningly.

The official stood there thinking and finally conceded that giving the money before receiving the completed documents was a bit risky. "Well you can pay then when you come to pick them up," answered the official. "Would that be suitable?" Fr. John knew that the Zaireans staffing the Embassies and other programmes outside of Zaire were starving and hurting for funds. They would break any of the rules to have some American money in their possession. Fr. John did all that was necessary and handed the documents to the official. For the whole of the transaction Fr. John stayed standing outside the wrought iron gate of the Embassy building. As the agent began to walk away, Fr. John called him back to ask him a question. "I already have the money here with me. Do you think that if I waited here for a short time that you could get me those passports and I could pay you immediately?" Fr. John asked. The agent excused himself and went off again in the direction of the partially hidden building. He had been gone some fifteen minutes when he returned to tell Fr. John that the passports would be ready in thirty minutes time. Fr. John waited. Forty-five minutes later he left with both passports in his hands.

Since he was not returning to Nairobi immediately, he needed to find a sure and safe way to get the passports to Jules and Chris. He knew that most likely he would be returning to Nairobi for a second visit before heading out to Canada. However, for security reasons, he wanted Jules and Chris to have the legal passports in their possession as soon as possible. The soldiers and police could eventually catch on that the Rwandese passports were clandestine ones. That evening at the meal he inquired if anyone knew of someone who was going to Nairobi in the near future.

Fr. Ronald mentioned that one of the African priests would be going to Nairobi on the Wednesday of the following week. Fr. Sylvester would be a very reliable person to take those documents and he would do all in his power to get them to the persons they were destined for. Fr. John was very pleased about this. The following morning he went to Fr. Sylvester's mission. He would be most willing to take the documents. Fr. John gave him instructions on how to get in touch with Jules and Chris. He hoped that he would hear from them concerning the passports as soon as they had received them.

By the end of the following week they were able to communicate with him about the arrival of the two passports. They were very pleased and felt much more secure with more authentic documents.

Fr. John returned to Jinja once all of these activities had been accomplished. His intention now was to do a quick review and assessment of his students' situation and, if it appeared that things were still going well and that they were continuing to adjust well, then he would return to Nairobi and from there head back to Canada. Upon his arrival in Canada he would initiate the immigration process for Jules and Chris.

Chapter Thirteen

At the end of June of 1966, John arrived home from the seminary in Upper State New York by rail once again. He felt great and really felt that he had been through quite a hurdle on his vocational journey. His mother and Miriam's mother and father were there to meet him once again. His mother was still in their own home and she had not decided to move into someone's basement. John knew that he had to find work, that he needed to help his mother when at home. He had made it clear to the authorities at the seminary that his mother, being a widow, needed his help more than they did. That was well accepted.

To find work at home was extremely difficult. A new heavy water plant was being built in the area of the Strait and they needed men to transport stones to place at the base of the structure pillars and to use a tamping machine to tamp down the earth around the pillars. This was strenuous work. John applied for a job there and was hired. He was placed on an evening shift that ended around midnight. He discovered that it was easy to get a ride to work, but to get a ride home was almost impossible; a ride that took close to an hour if you had a direct ride, could end up taking all night to accomplish. That first night on the job, he started to hitchhike home. It was pitch dark. He caught a ride part way home, and then was left off on the highway. Finally, one man from the village close to his island home came along and stopped to pick him up. "Where are you coming from so late and where are you going?" he asked. John explained his situation.

"So you are the seminarian studying to become a missionary, right?" asked the man.

"Yes," answered John. "That's me alright."

"It was your father who died in the car accident hardly two years ago, right?" asked the man.

"Yes, that is correct," said John.

"Well, the man they sideswiped was a relative of mine. He was very upset about this, did you know?" asked the man.

"Yes, I knew," John answered. "He came to see us to tell us how sorry he was and wanted to know if there was anything that he could do."

"Aha," said the man. "Well, will you stop at home with me for a cup of tea? Then I'll drive you home. You should not have to be doing such a difficult job and then having to hitchhike home. That is not right!" said the man.

"We need the money," John answered.

When John arrived home, his mother was just getting up, it was early morning and the sun was just coming up. John was exhausted. He could hardly move his fingers from having lifted the stones. His legs, arms and back ached terribly. He got into bed and slept a deep, dream-filled sleep. When he awoke around 11:30 a.m., his legs felt like cement. He could hardly budge them. His fingers hurt and he just could not get up out of the bed. He had terrible cramps and needed to reach the toilet. He was not able to hold on until he could drag himself out of the bed and had to finally let all go into his pyjamas. He called his mother! When she came he told her that he had messed the bed. "You're joking," she said. "Oh no, I'm not joking, can't you smell it?" asked John. "Yes, indeed I can." she said. John burst out laughing and crying at the same time. He was so tired, exhausted and weak. His mother told him that he should not return to that job, that it would kill him and that he would be too exhausted to return to the seminary. "There must be something you can do here in the village," she said. "Some people need their houses painted, you can do that." John regretted this so very much because the pay at the heavy water plant was quite excellent. He would not even get a third of that here in the village.

The paint jobs were short lived. At the end of July, John received a call from Fr. Koppelski in Dayton telling him that they needed help to set up the new houses at the University and they would love to have him there by August first to help set things up. There would be a few other seminarians besides himself and Fr Koppelski. He would send him the money for the trip.

The money soon arrived. The grand total of sixty dollars, just enough for the trip by BUS! From MacIntyre Lake to Dayton Ohio by bus; what an adventure that would be! John went out to Mr. Urquarht's, the ticket agent, to see about a one-way ticket to Dayton, Ohio.

"Mr. Urquarht, I need a one-way ticket to Dayton, Ohio. Can you do that for me?" asked John.

"Never did make a bus ticket for Dayton, Ohio, or so far away," said Mr. Urquarht, as he questioningly looked at John over his nose specks. "I will give you an Acadian Lines ticket and you just get it changed at the line, that's what you can do", said Mr. Urquarht. He gave John a ticket with a portion of it that could be torn off. "Sixty dollars is the cost of this if I understand correctly from the books here," said Mr. Urquarht. Fr. Koppelski had calculated correctly to the penny, John thought. He took the bus from MacIntryre Lake the following Thursday morning. He set out, changing buses in Truro, the hub of the province. Once in Moncton, he changed to the New Brunswick line. They finally arrived at the border and John requested a change of ticket, but was told that this was not necessary. He did not think of his suitcases, however, with Acadian Lines checks on them. It apparently was his responsibility to have them changed to the Greyhound bus line that would take them to Boston. This completely slipped his mind. Arriving in Boston, he needed to change buses and so he waited and waited as the bus driver removed the suitcases from the bus luggage compartment. Finally, they were all out but there were none there for him. "But are there no bags for me?" asked John. "Show me your checks," said the bus driver. "These are checks for a Canadian line", said the bus driver. "Your baggage has to have remained at the border. You need to get in touch with them," said the driver. John could not believe this. All he owned was in those two suitcases. While he was trying to get through to the border bus terminal his bus left Boston for New York City, where he would have taken a bus at Port Authority for

Dayton. He finally got through to the lines from a pay phone. To the lady who answered the phone he asked, "Would you have two suitcases there with Acadian bus Line baggage checks on them?"

"I sure do," said the woman. "I'm looking right at them, right here next to my desk."

"Oh, thank God!" exclaimed John. "They are mine. I forgot to have the checks changed and the suitcases put on the same bus with me."

"OK, what you will do is keep your Acadian Line checks to be able to claim them and I'll put Greyhound checks on them so they can continue their journey to Dayton, Ohio. You'll probably only receive them in another week or so. Good luck, my dear!"

"Thank you so much," John answered. "I do hope that they reach me intact!"

John then realized that he must take another bus and this one would take him through Syracuse, N.Y. So off he went. Once in Syracuse, he was called to the Manager's office of the bus station. As he entered the office, the man at the desk wanted to know where he got this bus ticket and where he was coming from and heading for. John informed him that he was coming from Cape Breton, Nova Scotia going to Dayton, Ohio and that the ticket was an Acadian Line ticket from Nova Scotia. The Manager went to an office to consult some books on different bus lines and surprisingly found that the Acadian Lines did exist and that John was not trying to con them. He returned the tickets to John and told him to continue on his way.

After two days and two nights, John rolled into Dayton, Ohio around 6 a.m. on a Saturday morning. He had been sleeping so he had to ask the driver where they were.

"We're coming into Dayton, Ohio, Sir. We'll be stopping at the terminal shortly." John breathed a sign of relief. He phoned the house of studies at the University and Fr. Koppelski answered.

"I'm at the bus terminal Father, can you come and get me?" asked John.

"I'll be there shortly," said Fr. Koppelski. John sat on one of the chairs to wait. He was really exhausted. Fr. Koppelski arrived in no time and as they were driving to the University John realized that this was no longer the bush country of Upper State New York. They were smack in the city life. He also noticed that there were a number of blacks on the streets as they rode to the house on the corner of Brown Street and College Park. Across from their Brown Street house was a huge, Victorian-looking building that turned out to be a cash register factory. They were renting four of the University houses and John had arrived to help the community set them up for living. One long month of work was about to begin. It was quite warm in Dayton at that time of the year. John, therefore, left the windows wide open in the room where he was sleeping. He, of course, had no extra clothing since his two suit cases were to follow. He ended up having to wash his clothes each night for the next day. That was somewhat of a bore! Also, since it was the week-end, the cash register factory across the street was quite silent. On the Monday morning, however, John woke up to a loud thumping sound coming from outside. He could not imagine what it was and where it was coming from. It seemed as if it was in the room with him. He soon found out that it was the machines from the factory, pounding out cash registers.

Being very busy, the time went by quickly and finally the students started to arrive – old ones and new ones. They had succeeded in setting up beds, had painted rooms, and installed the much needed refectory. Some spoiled brats from the Minor Seminary Schools felt it was quite primitive and ugly. John did not skip a beat at their hateful comments and said, "Well, if you're going to be missionaries, it starts now, get used to it. You obviously did not see these houses and rooms before the make-over," answered John tersely. In spite of the cold reception in the beginning, the students all became friends and a lively community began to develop.

The University academic year started at the beginning of September, after the Labour Day week-end. All the students were expected to take part in the orientation for the new students of the University. This was very helpful in learning where the different departments were situated and to find out how to register for courses. One very important session was the one that showed them how to use the library properly. They were also to make contact with the psychology department. The director of their House of Studies, Fr. Colin, had made it clear that each student was to undergo a psychological evaluation. This frightened some of the students. John was not really frightened by this; but he had never done such an evaluation before and he truly wondered what it would reveal.

Each student was to book an appointment with Dr. Schiedler, the psychology department head. Then, on the designated day, the student was to be given the test. This test turned out to be a multiple choice type questionnaire. Unbelievably, the tests took a whole afternoon to complete. Once completed, each student was to meet Dr. Schiedler to discuss the results.

John did the test and was to meet Dr. Scheidler two weeks later. He did not dwell too much on it, but he hoped it would enlighten him further on the type of person he was, his character, personality traits, compatibility or incompatibility for his vocational choice and, of course, where he needed growth and change.

The afternoon of the evaluation arrived. John sat next to Dr. Scheidler to better see what the report said. Dr. Scheidler opened the file in front of him and gave John the positive feedback first. He told John that the test did indicate that John was most probably in the correct vocation. He had a good sense of community and got on well in relationships with others. He needed more openness, flexibility and growth in all that touched on sexuality and the human body. He was too rigid and fearful of this. He was advised to do his best to delve in more depth in this matter with his spiritual director.

Dr. Scheidler then asked the question that floored John. Looking at John directly he asked, "Did you hate your father?" John was stunned by the question! He had never thought of his relationship with his father as a hate relationship. The word "hate" sounded so harsh, hard and inhuman! Hearing it stated aloud was like a knife going through John's heart!

Looking at Dr. Scheidler, John said, "Well, I don't know! It is the word 'hate' that bothers me. It sounds so extreme, so strong! We had very deep differences; there was a very deep animosity that existed between my father and me, but I have never used the word 'hate' to describe how I felt about him. That is a very disturbing thought!"

John at that moment remembered all the screaming bouts that had occurred when his father came home drunk, the violent arguments with his mother and, of course, the horrendous incident with his dog, Buddy. It all made John feel so smothered somehow. He knew that he did need to share in more depth about this with his spiritual director. He knew that he had to come to terms with two things in his life before ordination could happen: his attitude with regard to sexuality and his relationship with his father. He needed to be at peace with both of these in order to experience a deeper and greater personal inner peace.

His coming to terms with his own sexuality and sexuality in general would be difficult, he knew, but in the long run would not prove as difficult as making peace with his father since his father was already gone; he was not physically there for John to speak to and touch! This would have to come about through some form of vicarious experience. The road ahead appeared long and difficult but, then, he wanted so much to reach his goal of becoming a missionary priest. John was to eventually know both the pain and the joy of coming to terms with these two life experiences.

Through his scripture courses, certain of his theology courses, especially those on creation and the attributes of God, as well as all his spirituality courses along with the in-depth spiritual direction and therapy that John experienced, encountered and applied, John did come to accept his own sexuality; it was a mystery to be experienced and appreciated. It was to allow it to embrace him and he to embrace it. Through all of this, he also came to forgive his father and to see the wonderful qualities that his father possessed. All this was so necessary to becoming a seasoned, mature missionary priest.

Change for John did not come easily, but change was necessary. He would, therefore, find a place where he could be alone and be in prayer and in that space give the whole of himself to God. In these moments he would concentrate on his own body. He would take each part and offer it to God, thanking God for that body part and its life function. Many times he did this offering while alone in his room sitting on his bed totally naked. At that moment and in that way John felt free and unencumbered. The acceptance, liberation and feeling of well-being that resulted were unbelievable. He would thank God profusely!

At these times he would also imagine his father present there with him; he would imagine his father taking him in his arms and hugging him closely. He would hug his father back and just allow the warmth of the imagined closeness envelop him. He would at the same time talk with his father, telling him that he was sorry that he had been so cruel to him, sorry for not having said good-bye that fatal day that he had left him at the church before he had been killed in the car accident. He would explain aloud, as if his father were present, that it was because he thought that he did not love him and preferred his brother Tim to him that he had acted as he did; the hurt was so overwhelming! He would lash out in the way he had. John would then ask his father for forgiveness. This was always a liberating moment.

John would then imagine his father taking him in his arms and caressing him and he would tell John over and over again that he was forgiven. He would then ask John for his forgiveness for all the times he had been absent, for all the times he had terrorized them with his drinking, and for having left the family in such a brutal way, without even a good-bye! John would cry himself to sleep during each of these episodes, but he would wake up refreshed in mind and body; he would awaken with a greater sense of acceptance of himself and his sexuality. The experience was like a miracle gradually unfolding in John's life.

It was during one of these imaginary, yet very real sessions that John discovered the wonderful qualities that his father possessed. John had always been secretly concerned that his father had died suddenly, while drunk, without the sacramental preparation of the Church. During these vicarious experiences with his father and in remembering what type of man his father was, John discovered that his father had been a man who had shunned and rejected no one. For Batist, it did not matter if you were sinner or saint, a prostitute, a drunk or the finest man or woman on earth, he treated you in the same way, with utter respect, care and concern. He would have been only too glad to give Llewelyn a ride that evening of the accident. Batist accepted others as they were. John had never heard his father criticize or say an unkind word about anyone. He would become very upset when anyone of the family did that at home. He would often say, "If you can't say anything good about someone then don't say anything at all. Just be silent and hold your peace!" What he did dislike intensely was any form of hypocrisy and he knew that there was no lack of it. He often found that certain members of the clergy displayed this far too often, especially in their homilies at Church. John remembered how silent they all would be at the dinner table following the Sunday Church service. Batist would really have his knickers in a knot when the pastor on a Sunday would criticize those who bought liquor during the week and then put very little or nothing in the collection plate. John's father would passionately voice his concern about this. He would vehemently question the mercenary attitude coming from the pulpit; all knew that the clergy took their fair share of drink; they also drove big cars while the fishermen and workers struggled to make ends meet. Was the fact that the ordinary people sometimes indulged themselves such a terrible thing? Life carried its own share of suffering. The clergy should have been encouraging the people in what they were accomplishing, great or small and not running them down. John would always remember his father's words, "What does this priest know about the trials and sufferings of raising a family? He smokes huge cigars and drives a big car that is given to him by rich friends while we struggle with feeding, clothing and providing for our families as best we can. We have to be satisfied with roll-your-own smokes, a used jalopy and a house that has no indoor plumbing! What does he know about that type of life?"

The silence would be broken finally by John's mother. She would say the word that was needed to ease the tension: "That is enough, Batist! We do what we can and give what we can and we are none the worse for it! Let's try to enjoy our Sunday meal and let the priests take care of what they are supposed to! Enough is enough!"

Batist would stop. Mother had spoken. They talked of school and other matters. John always felt that his father needed that prompting from Rose to get back on track.

Batist had in fact been a good man, hard-working, concerned about others and providing in his own loving way for his family. He had not deserved to die such a violent death. John was now learning to love him. John hoped that his father could hear him as he told him that he did love him and forgave him whatever was to be forgiven.

John made close friends with a number of the other students. They became quite open with one another after sharing quite intimate thoughts and feelings. Tom Quinton was one of John's very close friends and eventually revealed to John that his fear of leaving the closed atmosphere of Upper State New York to come to the University in the City was because of his strong gay tendencies. He eventually revealed his nights of cruising the city for a sexual encounter. John would get quite upset with Tom because he feared something would happen to him or that he would get sick. They went through much together and Tom eventually decided to leave the seminary and just move into an off-campus student house. He came to John one afternoon to tell him that he had met quite a fine girl on campus and that her name was Christina. Christina was Polish and had flaming red hair. She was brilliant and had tried many disciplines on the University curriculum. She was at present in the pre-med program. Tom and she had a very passionate, deep and sexual relationship. Tom was smitten and did not need the nightly escapades he had indulged in, in the beginning. They decided to marry and John agreed to be their best man with Christina's sister as maid of honour.

Another close relationship that John had was with a student from California. He was of Polish decent, quite fair with very blond hair. Randy was very interesting. He enjoyed different cultures and customs, loved being a member of the International Club and he and John enjoyed going to their different events. It was in the International Club that Randy met the woman who would eventually become his wife. She was quite beautiful and from a mixed racial marriage. Sonia's father was black and her mother white and she was their beautiful daughter. Randy was so smitten that he also moved out of the community and into a student off-campus house. They were married after graduation at the Church of the Holy Angels that was part of the off-campus parishes and close to the community houses of the Missionaries of Africa. Randy and Sonia's wedding was influenced by the East Indian culture. Sonia was dressed in a beautiful white Indian sari with gold brocade trim. The maid of honour and bridesmaids were dressed in green silk saris, while the groom, Randy, and his attendants were dressed in Nehru jackets that were the rage at the time. John agreed to be Randy's best man. The director of the House of Studies for their community, Fr. David, agreed to officiate at their wedding. It was a beautiful experience. John, however, kept seeing his closest friends leaving the community and he felt the loss acutely.

Another close friend, Sean Dean, who had been quite a number of years at the Benedictine Minor Seminary, was also having second thoughts about community. This was very hard for John because they had become very close. With Sean, John had become very possessive, somehow, because he had opened up to Sean in a very intimate way and Sean had been surprised at learning of John's questions and problems of faith. He had thought that John was really "Sammy Seminarian" having all the right answers, a rock of Gibraltar in his vocation, with unwavering commitment to his vocational training. It was as if John had lost something or disclosed too great a secret part of himself to Sean; John feared that this would damage their friendship. There was a sense of loss of self that John found extremely difficult to grasp. He had to go into therapy about it, besides discussing it with his new spiritual director Fr. Jan Van Cleves. It was an extremely difficult time for John. Fr. Koppelski had left the seminary for Africa the previous year and John missed him immensely although he had been able to open up quite well to Fr. Jan, too.

Fr. Koppelski had been instrumental in helping John see certain areas of himself that needed maturity and growth. John always thought that a good Christian, a good Catholic, a good seminarian never got angry, accepted all, endured all and should never show smouldering passions. It was quite a false way of living. John had become very dependent on Fr. Koppelski and often needed to talk to him for direction. However Fr. Koppelski knew that John needed to break through certain ways of thinking; he often put John off and made him wait for their meetings. He wanted John to see that he did care about him and that in many ways he could fly on his own. Each time he put John off for their next meeting, he would excuse himself, saying that he had been held up by a meeting or a talk with one of the other priests on staff. John always told him that it was OK and that he understood, all the while seething with anger and indignation and just glad that finally he had Fr. Koppelski all to himself. One weekend, Fr. Koppelski made John wait to see him for the duration of the weekend, putting him off for days. Finally, later in the week he was able to see Fr. Koppelski. He entered Father's room and as always Father said, "I'm sorry, I was just so busy. There were too many holdups and meetings with the priests in the College Park house."

"Oh, that's OK Father. I understand," said John, giving his usual answer. Suddenly, John stopped and looking squarely at Fr. Koppelski said, "Why am I saying this? Why am I saying that I understand and that all is fine when it isn't. I am so angry and I am so upset that I could just throttle you. In fact, Father, I could just strangle the life out of you. I continue to feel that you don't care for me and that you do not love me because of all that I have told you; I am so upset." John broke down and cried.

"At last, you are getting angry," answered Fr. Koppelski. "You are being you and expressing what is going on inside you and not just being nice. It is OK to be angry, you know, even with me. And I still care for you and love you no matter what."

John experienced a marvelous catharsis again and another great shift in himself that evening. The relief was great. One needed to be oneself and to admit one's anger and frustration. When the frustrations and the lack of insight became too great, John would go into dark moods and bouts of depression. He was very much like a manic depressive at times. He knew that this must change and that he must be entirely free. Of course, these thoughts were made even more difficult because of his strong sexual drive and his fear of his sexuality. He discussed this at length with Fr. Koppelski, and also with Fr. Jan. He needed to free himself of the strong attachments he formed in friendships. It was as if John needed the constant approval and support of those he loved, but it was stifling him; the danger was also that he would smother his friends and end up alienating them. He was now facing this head on.

John knew that one area of his life that he needed to liberate was the terrible fear that he had of his sexual urges. He could now face them differently and knew that he had to take certain measures to come to the desired freedom.

He took the plunge in allowing himself to feel the urges coursing through his body, through his genitals, the feelings that came when he thought of another's body, the feeling that overcame him when he was aroused. He allowed his hands to touch and stroke his body, let the full extent of the feelings overcome him, allowed himself to climax if it came to that. Afterwards there was a sense of relief physically and emotionally, but at the same time he would feel awful, dirty and sinful. One thing he would no longer do, however, was to run to confession before receiving Eucharist. He disciplined himself in going to confession once a month only, and always went to communion no matter what had happened. Even when he deliberately caused himself to climax, he still received without going to confession and simply offered all to God. At one point, he decided to take four consecutive week-ends and on those particular week-ends buy a number of pornographic magazines and go through them, looking at the photographs, reading the articles and just simply finding out what these magazines were about, thus satisfying his curiosity. It was a powerful liberation and he could now pass the newsstand magazine racks without that strong element of curiously overtaking him.

All these bouts of desire, turmoil, doubt and anger threw John into agonizing questions about his faith and vocation. It was during this time of turmoil that John's thoughts turned to his relationship with his best friend, Miriam. He and Miriam had continued to keep in touch and had written each other fairly often. They would meet at times when he was home for summer breaks. He had continued to share many thoughts and the events of his life with Miriam. She, herself, had entered a religious community to try her vocation but had decided to leave after a period of two years since she felt that that type of life was not for her. She had returned to the job that she had had at the bank.

John wrote Miriam during his excruciating turmoil. What he said in that letter made her reply immediately. She wrote him saying, "I don't know whether you realize it or not, but your last letter is very different from any other that you have written me! You make allusions to our beginning a relationship that would lead to more serious matters, such as a possible life commitment together. I want you to be aware that you have done this in your last letter! I am willing to pursue this, if it is what you want. I must admit that when I date anyone it is you that I am looking for in that person, but you must be sure that this is what you want. I do not want to be the cause of your leaving the seminary and your missionary dreams, then to have you regret it later. That can make for a miserable marriage and a very unhappy life together, heaping blame on each other for missed opportunities!"

John knew that if ever he married anyone, it would be Miriam. Yet her reply jolted him into reality. He realized that he needed a quiet time of prayer, thought and reflection to come to terms with this whole situation. He also discussed it in depth with Fr. Jan. Fr. Jan also felt that John needed to give this more reflection and a good deal of time to mature. He needed to question himself about the reasons for bringing Miriam into the picture. What were his true reasons for wanting to leave and pursue a romantic, intimate relationship with his best friend Miriam? Was he simply running away from the pain of doubt, insecurity and turmoil? Did he really believe that the grass was greener on the other side of the fence? He needed to find a peaceful space where he could seek inner peace and calm and then revisit what decision he should take, rather than try to do this in the throes of turmoil. When John shared all this with Fr. Jan, he answered John with such gentle understanding. "No. Do not give up so easily," he told John. "It is not a bad thing for you to have such thoughts regarding Miriam. It is a good thing. It all makes for a stronger and more mature choice. I am not saying that you will never leave. But if you do leave, you must leave freely, and not in such turmoil. No, now is not the time to leave. You are not sufficiently at peace with yourself and I do have faith that inner peace will come." Dr. Rancurello, the psychologist that John was seeing for therapy on campus, gave him the same message, so John allowed himself to be quiet in mind and heart. John knew now that he must write to Miriam and thank her for making him aware of what he had suggested in his letter. He also had to apologize for bringing this up since he was not ready to change his life yet. He would certainly continue in his present choice and he now realized that he had been reacting to the turmoil and doubts that had invaded his thoughts. He hoped that they would still remain friends and continue to keep in touch with one another. Miriam replied with a very positive response.

John had been working for some time in the ceramics department at the University with Mr. & Mrs. Bobal, a couple who opened this department to give the students the opportunity to make gifts of clay, wood, paper and copper. They were also able to learn how to make pottery. It was a beautiful department and John loved it. It helped him to make greater peace with himself. One place where John also found some peace was at the Church of the Holy Angels. At that time the church was open all night. When John returned from ceramics late at night, he would stop at the Church and sit alone before the Blessed Sacrament, the presence. Many times he would sit in silence for long moments, but many times he would face the altar of the presence and scream at it saying, "Where are you? I need you! I am in such pain. Liberate me. Don't leave me alone!" He would scream this as loud as he could, over and over again, and would afterwards just sit there on the bench, exhausted.

No matter how late John was before coming into residence, he was always present at morning prayer. At times, he was the only one there with the Father in charge of leading the prayer, but he could not miss prayer time, he needed prayer and God's presence to stay sane.

At times John nearly gave up hope, but something always came up to push him to continue his struggle and battle with his thoughts, his desires, his scruples, his doubts, his fears. One evening while he was in the community prayer room just simply reflecting on a number of events of the day, a wonderful warm feeling suddenly came over him; a warm surge of heat coursed through his heart and his mind and his body. He was overwhelmed by what was happening to him; it was frightening and wonderful all at once. He did not want it to stop! He kept whispering a simple "Oh God, thank you for the exhilarating experience." At that moment a huge weight seemingly was lifted off his shoulders. He felt light and free and began to weep profusely. He wanted to shout for joy. He was so very grateful, and as it lasted for many days, he knew it was an authentic liberation; a freeing of his spirit. He knew that God loved him and that he could love himself and appreciate himself as God's son, as God's child. He knew that he could continue this journey and any kind of difficulty or test would be experienced differently, in fact lived in a spirit of thanksgiving. He had truly begun his spiritual growth and break through. This event happened on the feast of St. Patrick in the month of March. He would never forget it.

Students and teachers noticed that there was a change, a shift in John and some would say to him, "What has happened to you? You have changed somehow?" John would simply smile and say, "I guess God has won out in the end, hasn't he?" He discussed it at length only with his Spiritual Advisor, Fr. Jan, who knew as well how much John had agonized and struggled. They laughed together, a free, delicious laugh. John would spend long moments just sitting in prayer in Chapel or in the Church across the way where he had often screamed in agonizing pain. He often spent long moments in thanksgiving in his room in the dark before sleeping or after waking early in the morning. He completed his third year at the university in relative calm and ease, a deep sense of well-being reigning within him. He graduated that year with his first degree, a Bachelor of Arts in theology, philosophy and French. He had fought a good part of the fight and won the first portion of the race. He would leave Dayton within the next few days with a heavy heart due to parting with close friends but with a strong, calm, peaceful and joyful conviction as well.

John went home that summer and spent a good summer with family and friends. He worked for a time at the Veteran's Hospital in Halifax. It was hard, tiring work, but work that had its humourous moments all the same. He could not forget old Mr. Campbell and his bouts of anger each time he was tied to the geriatrics chair. He would scream, "Get me out of here! Are you all trying to kill me?" John asked the matron of the floor, therefore, if he could let Mr. Campbell out of his chair for a while. He promised to watch him closely. "Well John, he is your responsibility and you'll have to watch that he does not run away. He got away once before and we found him roaming the streets in down town Halifax." "Oh my, that would not be a good thing; but I will watch him closely," said John. What John would do is put him in charge of supervising the other patients who were in the north-end sun room while he was in the south-end sun room feeding those who needed help with their food. He would find, however, that John was gone too long would come looking for him. "Where in the hell were you, I've been waiting for you now for too long," he would say to John. "You can't leave me by myself all that time, I don't like it." "Well, stay here with me for the time being." John would give him a chair to sit on. Then Mr. Campbell would begin his reminiscing. "Ah when you get old it becomes too difficult, no one wants you anymore. I remember though, when I was a young man I was as strong as an ox, and could screw the but off any woman. I was quite the stud you know. I came eighteen times one day; I sure had it in me." "You were certainly one wild stallion, Mr. Campbell, who would not have wanted to have you're stamina." All the same, taking care of the old veterans was not easy and in the evening John would fall asleep on the sofa while watching TV, totally zonked out.

He left for the noviciate that September. It was to be in Washington, DC in an area close to Catholic University called "Little Vatican."

John soon realized that his inner freedom was not accepted or believed by everyone. He enjoyed community life but his freedom was always under scrutiny, especially his relationships with the Spanish students who had come to form part of the First International Noviciate. John enjoyed the Spaniards. There was a freshness and a joy and freedom about them that

John identified with. There was also a biting critical side to them that John also admired. This biting criticism was not liked by his superiors who felt that it was a sign of a lack of conversion and a lack of interior peace. When John criticized the founder of the Society of the Missionaries of Africa one evening at the dinner table, he was strongly reprimanded by his spiritual adviser. This could be a reason for his dismissal he was told. John, however, felt that the founder had been a stubborn, difficult person at certain times, especially where women were concerned, and expressing this got John into trouble. John's spiritual director felt that John had a very strong influence on the community and that the Spanish students rallied around him, so were easily influenced by him. John was flabbergasted by this since the Spanish students really had minds of their own. John became quite outspoken and refused to just simply be a puppet. Because he was still a student in training, this was seen as a very negative attitude, especially since John refused to share his inner thoughts and feelings concerning his affective life. He felt that he had dealt sufficiently with all that in community at University, especially with all he had been through in spiritual direction and therapy. His refusal to share at this level was considered as lacking in openness and flexibility which was often considered as a serious obstacle to one's vocation. John would have to tread softly and become more positive in attitude.

During this noviciate year, the community made visits to different areas of the US and Canada where the Missionaries of Africa had communities. One of the visits was to their Major International Formation House in Canada. It was a great trip and they were all there for the Easter break. John enjoyed it very much. It was here, however, that his Spiritual Director suggested to him that maybe he should not return with them to Washington after the break, that he should leave for home. He felt that in reviewing John's progress, attitudes, strengths and influence in community, that there was too much negativity present. John's heart sank at the suggestion. This was coming at him in his fifth year of training. What was this? He had never felt so free and so ready to continue. He cautiously thought for a moment about what was being suggested to him. Then John answered his Director, "OK, I will not go back with all of you. I will go home. But it must be made clear to the community that my leaving is not my own personal decision, but a decision based on your advice and on what you, my spiritual advisor, think I must do." His director immediately replied, "No, no, it cannot be my decision. It has to be your personal decision. That is what must occur." "Well, Father, this decision is not mine and is not what I feel I must do at this moment," John replied. "I'm not saying that I may not leave at some point, but now is not that moment," said John. "I feel that I must continue." "OK, that is fine," replied his spiritual director.

John continued and at the end of the noviciate he prepared to go to the Missionary Institute in London, England, to complete his theology. This would be an experience that John would never forget. There, he would join a very close friend from Dayton, Ohio. What would happen between them would push John to take a very important step in his formation years; one that would prove excruciatingly painful for John, yet one that would end up being liberating, uplifting and very, very necessary.

John came home from his noviciate for the two months of summer holidays. It would be good to spend some time with the family before leaving for England. What was interesting to John and pleased him immensely was that his mother met a fine man from the neighbouring village who would become a wonderful companion for her. John's mother had not gone out with male friends in the six years that she had been a widow. There did not seem to be anyone appropriate during this period. One man, the brother of an acquaintance had come calling a number of times but Rose had soon cut it off since she had found him stingy, even though he was a man who was very comfortable financially. An incident had taken place one Sunday afternoon when the grandchildren had been visiting at Rose's house that had greatly displeased her. Vincent, this male friend, had given one of the grandchildren a quarter to buy herself an ice cream and had said to the second child, "The next time I will give you a quarter; this time it is her turn to have the treat!" Rose had been furious at him and had taken the quarter from the child and given it back to Vincent saying, "In this family we do not do such things - give money or a treat to one child and exclude the other! We give to both. If you are too poor to be able to give to both then don't give to either." That had clinched it for Rose and she had refused to go out with him again.

Raymond, however, turned out to be very different. He had had five children who were now all married with their own children. He was very generous to both his children and grandchildren. He was very kind and loved to visit relatives and friends when he was not working at the fish factory. He had loved his wife very much. She, as it turned out, happened to be a cousin of Rose's. Rose and Batist had often visited Raymond and Cecelia when they were first married. Therefore Rose knew Raymond Marchand and knew very well what a generous person he was and that he was a very hard worker and skilled carpenter. Raymond had called to visit with Rose one afternoon and had put this proposition to her. "My dear Rose, would you agree to keep company for a while to see if we could get along together and then maybe tie the knot? You knew my wife. She was a relative. And you also know that I loved her very much and gave her all she wanted. But now she is gone and I realize that I cannot be alone. I need companionship. I know that I am with my daughter, but that is not the same. So what do you think? I can give you some time to think about it if you like."

Rose sat in silence for a moment then answered Raymond saying, "Well, I am not saying no to your proposal, but I know your children and they will be very upset about this. They were very close to their mother."

"I know that," answered Raymond, "but I am marrying for me, not for my children, and they will have to accept it, whether they like it or not."

"That's just fine," answered Rose. "Come by next week and we can speak about it some more."

Raymond and Rose did start up a fine relationship. This pleased John very much and he eventually left for England feeling that his mother had a new outlook on life once again. It was during his studies at the seminary in London, England that John received a letter from his mother asking for his permission to marry for a second time. She felt that she should ask John since he was the oldest son, even if not the oldest child in the family. John chuckled to himself about this. He felt that his mother certainly did not need his permission or approval for her to marry, but he would gladly give her his blessing. So he phoned her, instead of writing, and let her know how pleased he was. What mattered most was her happiness and if all was going well then he was overjoyed for his mother. Rose was very happy to hear from him and told him that they would be married in the Arichat church and then Raymond's son would drive them to Halifax where Martine would have a lovely reception for them at her house. "That is just marvelous, Mom," said John over the phone. "We'll be able to talk about it when I come home for ordination, even if that is some years away." Little did John realize that much would change in the coming year and that he would arrive home sooner than he had thought. One question that he did not ask Rose but that was very present in his thoughts was the question of how Raymond's children had taken the whole affair. He would find out soon enough.

Chapter Fourteen

Fr. John had been close to three months in Jinja, Uganda. He decided to return to Canada since his students in Jinja were doing well. They needed to be on their own, to fly with their own wings. Before leaving, he called Jules and Chris one more time to let them know what he was up to. They were somewhat apprehensive about his leaving. Jules said to him in a worried tone, "Please, don't forget us. We must not stay here. There are too many things going on here in Nairobi. We are really in as much danger as any where else. Come back to see us when you have settled things at home. We really fear that we will lose contact with you!"

After mulling over Jules' words, Fr. John decided to go back to Nairobi on his way to Canada. He called them at the language school to let them know. They were very pleased about it and promised to meet him at the bus stop. He was now used to the bus trip so did not run into any glitches. This time he would stay with Jules and Chris in their flat instead of staying with the community of White Fathers. It would be quality time for the guys. He would also be able to observe first hand all that was going on with friends and if anymore military or police intervention occurred.

The two young men had pretty much learned the ropes about Nairobi life and how to survive in that city. Their English was improving in leaps and bounds. They were meeting some people that they had known in Bukavu. All were trying to get to a safer place. Of course they would go

252

to the bank and meet Martha. She had been such a help to them. She continued to invite them over for the odd meal. They did enjoy a good home-cooked meal. The day Fr. John arrived in Nairobi for his second visit, he noticed that Jules looked as if he had sustained a blow to the eye. "What is wrong with your eye, Jules?" Fr. John asked. "It looks as if you were punched in the eye!"

"Oh, it's nothing," replied Jules. "We were playing football and I started seeing double after I got an elbow in the eye. It seems to be getting better now. Fr. John would eventually discover that the blow had not been due to an elbow in the eye.

Fr. John did his best to reassure them that all would be well. "I will keep in touch. I will send you a message at the language school when I am ready to call you on the Stella Awinja public phone. I also have Mrs. Makarere's number at the bank and I can let her know when I will call." Actually Fr. John was as worried as they were for their safety but he could not make it too obvious since he knew that it would frighten them even more. He reassured them that he would find parish work at home and would send them the funds that they needed to live properly. He would transfer the funds through the Barclay Bank accounts.

Fr. John was booked to fly out of Nairobi with KLM on the following Tuesday afternoon. It was now Friday, so they had the whole week-end to spend together. Jules said to Fr. John, "Couldn't we go somewhere together for the week-end? We have been here for quite some time and we have not been outside of Nairobi. Couldn't we go to the beach and just swim and enjoy ourselves?"

Fr. John thought about it and said, "That sounds like a good idea, but where would we go? Do you have any suggestions?"

"There is a travel agency here on Main Street. We could go and see what is available in Kenya as vacation deals," said Chris.

They discovered to their utter surprise that there was a beautiful resort area on the Indian Ocean in the area of Mombasa, Kenya, where one could vacation for the whole week-end for three hundred dollars. This price included a hotel room for three, including meals. They were to arrive Friday evening and leave on Monday morning. They could not believe their ears when they heard the price. They booked the trip and left by shuttle bus from the travel agency. They just had time to go back to the apartment to pack a suitcase with a change of clothing and then they were off to Mombasa. This was to be called the Bamburi experience, since they would be vacationing at the Bamburi Hotel on the Indian Ocean. It turned out to be a wonderful experience. They slept in comfortable, clean beds, had great buffet meals, went swimming in the hotel pool and in the Indian Ocean. They took the glass bottom boat and went out to observe the coral reefs. They went riding on the seadoo, speeding through the open water for miles at a time. It was glorious. There was only one negative incident that marred their stay. One evening as they walked along the beach, Fr. John began to feel very strange and a sudden, sharp pain ripped through his back. He stopped short. "Oh my goodness," he exclaimed, "what was that?' he exclaimed as he tried to catch his breath. He felt nauseous.

"What is the matter?" Jules and Chris asked. "Is there something wrong?"

"I just had a sharp pain that went tearing through my back," said Fr. John. "You guys go ahead and continue your walk; I'll go back to the hotel and rest. I feel awful. I think I'm going to throw up." He turned and headed for the hotel. Once in the room he fell to his knees beside the bed. The pain was terrible. He now recognized what it was. He had a kidney stone. At that moment Jules and Chris came into the room. "What is it? What is it for God's sake?" they asked frightened out of their wits as they watched him doubled up in pain on the bed.

"It's a kidney stone. I'm sure. I've had it before."

"I'm going to see if there is a doctor here in the hotel," said Jules. "Chris you stay here with him." In a short time he returned with an East Indian doctor who was in the service of the hotel. He checked Fr. John and assured them that it was a kidney stone. He gave him the medication necessary to relieve the pain and to help pass the stone. Fr. John was to drink lots of water and juice. They ordered both from the hotel. Fr. John remained quiet for some hours and things gradually returned to normal. Jules and Chris did not want to leave him alone and watched over him like hawks, although Fr. John wanted them to go and enjoy themselves reassuring them that he would be just fine. They stayed together chatting and repeating how enjoyable the week-end had been. They returned to Nairobi the next day. They arrived in the late afternoon to be met at the apartment by Martha, frantic with them for having left without telling anyone where they were going.

"Where did you go off to?" Martha asked. "You are not supposed to go all over the country with the type of visa you have," she exclaimed. "You could be arrested if the police decided to check your papers. What were you thinking of?"

They all looked at one another puzzled. They had not known this. "Ignorance is bliss!" Fr. John thought. They had had a good break and had come through it refreshed and happy. Fr. John was leaving for Canada the next day. For the last evening together, Fr. John decided that they would go out to eat together. There was a small restaurant in downtown Nairobi where they could get a good meal for quite a reasonable price. While on their way, they met several young men that Jules and Chris had known in Bukavu and had run into here in Nairobi. They stopped to chat for a moment. One of them, Stephen, looked at Jules and said, "Your eye seems to be healing quite well. I can hardly notice the nasty bruise that you got from that beating that night in downtown Nairobi. If I had not come along when I did those hoodlums would have left you for dead. Are you okay now?"

"Oh yes, I'm fine, I'm good," answered Jules. "Have you heard from your father in Kinshasa? I thought you told me that he had been caught there when the fighting had escalated? What is the story on that?" Jules was intent on changing the subject of their conversation. He did not want Fr. John to know what had really happened to his eye.

"My dad is good. He was able to get out of Kinshasa. He is here now and so is my mother," answered Stephen.

"That's great. I'm sure you are all relieved," Jules replied. "Anyway, this is our former teacher from Bukavu who is on his way back to Canada. He is here for a short visit with us. We are on our way to dinner."

"Oh great," replied Stephen, "enjoy your meal together. We'll not hold you up any longer. Take care."

Fr. John looked at both Jules and Chris and, smiling slyly, said to them, "So, it was a blow from an elbow while playing football, was it?"

Chris looked at Jules and said to him, "We might as well tell him the truth. He knows that you did not get the black eye from a football match."

"This is what happened," answered Jules. "I was out one evening with a friend that I had known in Bukavu; we had also been in class together. His name is Samson. We were on our way to the Carnivore for a drink and a bit of food when we met four guys that had been very nasty to him while in Bukavu. One of them accused him of having tried to steal his girlfriend and wanted to beat him up. They jumped on him and started punching him so I tried to help him. I pulled one of the guys off of him and Samson was able to run away. But then they turned on me and the four of them really beat me up. When one of them hit me in the eye I passed out and fell to the ground on the side of the road. I would probably have died there if Stephen and some of his friends had not come by and found me. They called a taxi and took me to the hospital. I was badly bruised and they had given me several blows to the head. I had very bad headaches for some days afterwards. So that's the story of my black eye!"

Fr. John could not believe his ears. He feared very much for both of them. This was not a good place for them to be. He hoped that all those blows would not cause repercussions for Jules later on. Time would reveal a painful story. For now Jules seemed to be fine.

Fr. John left Nairobi for Montreal. He gave Jules and Chris all the reassurances they needed about his remaining in touch with them. He would not forget them and would do all in his power to prepare what was needed for their departure from Nairobi. He would need to speak with his superiors for permission to remain at home for some time in order to work to support the two young men. For Fr. John they had actually become the sons that he had never had. The bond had been formed, he could neither forget them nor abandon them. All the same he left for Montreal April 15, 1996, arriving safely the next day.

When he first spoke with his superiors, he realized that they did not understand what he had been through and all that he had had to deal with. He did not mention his commitment to the two boys. He spoke rather of taking time at home to get his thoughts together after his horrendous experiences in Zaire and Kampala. His superior told him to take all the time that he needed. However he spoke about his taking on the direction of the Montreal Afrika Center that rendered an important service to the Canadian African Community. Fr. John told his superior that he would have to think about it since he was somewhat overwhelmed at the moment. Fr. Laurendeau, his superior, simply answered, "Go and take care of yourself. You need the time to recuperate." Fr. John thanked him and said no more. He could not really speak about things at that moment. Each time he tried to speak about his situation he felt a very strong urge to cry. He preferred to remain silent. Fr. John was also very upset with his community because they had not been able to provide his family with information on his whereabouts when he was caught in Rwanda during the massacres and genocide. All the same his name had been on the lists when they had sent news to Montreal of the situation in Kigali. It was as if they did not know him. The disappointment was very hurtful.

The following day he booked his trip for home. He would not travel by air or bus. He would travel by train, taking the time to rest. It would take almost two days to get to Halifax and he would sleep most of the time, although a somewhat troubled sleep. Each time that he would wake up it was Jules and Chris who would occupy his thoughts. He had to get them out of Africa to safety!

His brother, Timmy, picked him up at the train station and took him home. Fr. John stayed there during the day and visited different people he had known and worked with in the past.

Chapter Fifteen

John arrived home from the noviciate at the end of June 1970, happy to be home for a two month holiday and a good rest and visit. He would visit relatives and friends and gradually prepare for his departure for London, England where he would continue his theological studies. Many of the people in the village were eager to find out how things were going and to hear it from him. They, therefore, invited him to dinner or supper and riddled him with questions. His mother was always eager to cook him a good home-cooked meal and of course served a lot of the dishes that he really liked; this was mainly fish dishes since John loved fish, especially haddock, lobster, cod prepared with an onion and pork-scrap butter sauce, and the traditional smelts, so loved by the Acadians. She did not forget to make him his much loved depression stew. All the villagers loved to hear about his time in the States. This enjoyable time at home eventually came to an end and he had to prepare for his trip to England where he would continue his theological studies.

One September morning, John took a flight from Halifax to New York and there joined up with other White Father students bound for London as well. So, in late September of 1970, therefore, John and three other students boarded the Queen Elizabeth II from New York en route to Southampton, England with a short stop at LaHavre, France. This way of going to the theology center in England was unusual. Normally, they would have flown and sent their luggage separately. When the preparations for the trip were made, the students found out that it was cheaper to make this trip on the QEII, carrying all their luggage with them, than to fly over and send their luggage separately. The QEII, therefore, was the means of travel that won out.

John enjoyed the trip immensely. The QEII was a regular floating city, with indoor and outdoor swimming pools, shopping centres, a huge theatre and clubs for dancing. They enjoyed the good food, the shuffle board and, of course, having their shoes cleaned and shined when they left them outside their door at night. It was a wonderful moment for them when the Captain called them onto the deck as they sighted the "White Cliffs of Dover." They were simply magnificent. When they docked in Southampton, the Missionaries of Africa had a van waiting for them to take them and their luggage to the formation house in London. They were shown to their rooms and found out immediately what teams they would be in. John was to be part of the Poplar Team. Each team had the name of the parish where the students would do pastoral work. St. Edward's College was part of a Missionary Institute, made up of at least six different missionary communities. The Missionaries of Africa occupied St. Edward's, a fairly large property with a very old, draughty building that housed classes, conference and team rooms, refectory and the many student rooms. John found it ugly, dirty, draughty and not very pleasant to live in. They were on the top floor and the showers were down in the cold and dingy basement. However, John was very happy to see Claude Forgeron again. Claude had a French name but did not speak French as fluently as he would have liked. He was from Portland, Oregon and during his time in the Peace Corp and in the noviciate, he had managed to improve his French somewhat. He was continuing to do this now that he was in England. They had been friends in Dayton and had continued to write when Claude left for the noviciate and then for England.

Claude showed John around the house and tried to make him feel at home. This was not easy. John felt out of place; he was not used to being in a huge community anymore and it made him feel unsure and insecure. Claude had also made many friends at this formation house and there were many evenings that he was not around. He was also on a different team than John.

Classes began over the following weeks. John's first glitch was with some of the courses he had to take. Some, John had already taken in the US and one, in particular, was Missiology. The Dean of Studies could not believe that the courses taken in the US could be as deep as those given in England. John did not agree and insisted that he did not need Missiology courses again. He did not want statistics courses on the Church's missions and parishes in Africa. A compromise was reached between the Dean of Studies and John. He would take one semester of Missiology and if it was what John suspected, he would drop it in the second semester. This was agreed upon. Of course, when the second semester rolled around, the Dean of Studies inquired from John, "So, what is your judgement about the Missiology classes?'

"It is the same as what I had in the US. In fact, those in the US were in much more depth than these. So do not include me in any of the Missiology classes this semester," said John. The Dean of Studies had to give in to this since that is what had been agreed upon.

The next sore point was John's beard. John had grown a beard while in Dayton, Ohio, and had kept it all through the noviciate. Arriving at the formation house in England, he quickly was informed that beards were not permitted in the British province of the Missionaries of Africa. John was flabbergasted! "Why ever for?' he asked. "It is too easily identified with the hippie movement," one student told him. The Director of the formation house, Fr. Fritzie, did not allow it. What really disappointed John was that he had sent another Canadian student, already ordained a deacon to tell him, rather than tell him, himself. One afternoon, just before tea, John was reading some of the messages on the bulletin board in the entrance to the dining room. Herman Pilon, the Canadian Deacon was there at the bulletin board with him. He seemed to be restless around John and attempted twice to say something to him. "What is wrong Herman?" John asked. "You seem to want to tell me something, but you're not getting to it. What is wrong?" asked John.

Herman finally told John, "Well, beards are not allowed here at St. Edward's, and Fr. Fritzie wants you to shave your beard."

"Why couldn't he tell me that himself?" John asked.

"I guess he felt that if a Canadian student, already a deacon, told you that you would accept it more calmly," Herman replied.

The next day a funny incident happened as the students were queuing up in the dining room for lunch. Fr. Fritzie came up behind John in the queue and upon seeing John with no beard, did not recognize him, and asked John, "Are you another new student? I don't think we have met?" said Fr. Fritzie. "Oh, we have met Father, it's simply that the last time we met, I had a beard, so that's probably why you don't recognize me. We have certainly met!" said John.

"Oh, OK, so you are John DeCoste, aren't you?" replied Fr. Fritzie.

"That is correct," answered John. It was such a disappointment that a simple thing like a beard could become a problem in the community; all the guys on his team were shocked when they saw him shaving his beard the night after having spoken to Herman.

Another bone of contention for John was what his team was doing as a pastoral assignment. All were going once a week to Poplar parish and visiting parishioners along the London docks as a help to the pastor of that parish. John felt that this did not generate much creativity, diversity and richness in experience. He felt that they should be able to do other things, like working in a health facility for instance. Those in his team told him that they could not change that on their own. They would have to have permission from Fr. Fritzie. John felt that he would have to ask if he could do something different, and all Fr. Fritzie could do was to say "yes" or "no". Surely there would be no major disaster over it!

John went and pleaded his case with Fr. Fritzie. After a long discussion and some biting words about community training and a simple life style, Fr. Fritzie gave in. John looked for a new assignment in pastoral work for the following week. He chose to take an assignment in the hospital called "Old Barney"; a huge medical facility for mental patients. John worked there two full shifts a week and enjoyed the difficult assignment very much. There were several strange incidents in his assignment that John would never forget.

On one shift, in particular, John was working on the floor where Mr. Van Breugel was a patient. This person was a very unfriendly, serious and unhappy man in his sixties. Mr. Van Breugel was a smoker and most times John could get him to do what was needed by promising him cigarettes. This shift, however, Mr. Van Breugel was very uncooperative and angry. He did not want to do what was needed to get himself up and ready for the day. John did manage to get him to the tub and proceeded to help him bathe himself. This he did not want. As he sat there in the bath tub, John leaned over slightly to speak to Mr. Van Breugel. That was when he saw his chance and without hesitation, quickly caught John by the lapel of his uniform and pulled him head first into the tub with him. Mr. Van Breugel would not let him go. John was on top of him and Mr. Van Breugel simply tightened his grip when told to let go. John told him that he would get no cigarettes if he did not let go. He stared at John and would still not let go. John grabbed Mr. Van Breugel's hand and, with a hard yank, tore off the uniform lapel and sleeve. He was free. Mr. Van Breugel just stared, seemingly quite pleased with himself. John kept the cigarettes and wouldn't even give him one. He managed to get him washed, dressed and back to his room. Then he went in search of a clean uniform.

The one episode that totally amazed John was his encounter with the religious fanatic. John had told no one on the floors of Old Barney that he was a seminarian, studying at St. Edward's College. Patient Ralph paced back and forth on the ward and every now and then would stop in front of John and just stare into his eyes. At a moment when Ralph was sitting at the table for his tea, John asked the orderly in charge of the floor about Ralph and his odd staring. He told John that Ralph had an obsessive-compulsive disorder and was obsessing on religion, especially anything to do with the Roman Catholic Church. He was so taken up with Padre Pio in Italy that he had decided to make a pilgrimage to Rome to meet him but what was really amazing was that he made the pilgrimage on foot with a knapsack of rocks on his back. This and other episodes got him placed as a resident of Old Barney. Now he would pace back and forth and stare into John's eyes.

Finally, one morning as John was standing observing the patients, Ralph stopped his usual pacing and stood in front of John. This time he pointed his finger at John and said, "You are different than all the others!"

"What do you mean?" asked John.

"Just that," said Ralph. "You are very different from the other workers here on the floor. You do not treat us the same as they do!"

"Why would you say that?" John asked. Before answering the question, Ralph paced back and forth one more time and again stopped in front of John.

"You're face is different, your way of treating us, your tone of voice, your compassion and concern are all different. You must be a priest or something like that, I'm sure", said Ralph.

"No, no I'm not a priest" said John, "I'm simply a student and I work here to make extra money to help pay my studies."

"Then you are a seminarian or something like that," said Ralph. "I know it. I feel it. You are different!"

Stifling the desire to laugh, John told Ralph that he was mistaken. But John felt very strange about the incident. A strange, cold feeling swept over him. He wanted to get off this ward. He was so very happy when his shift ended and he could head back to the College.

On his way back to the college that evening, John chuckled to himself as he recalled another surprising encounter with a patient called Mr. Winkler. It was an encounter that had left John both stunned and amused at the same time: stunned, because he could not imagine Queen Elizabeth using the same language as Mr. Winkler; amused, as he tried to imagine the Queen of England uttering such words with her very British accent.

John came onto one of the open wards at the same time as usual for the three o'clock shift one Wednesday afternoon. He always looked at the roster each time to find out where he had been posted for the shift of that day. He was to be on the open ward on the first floor. Patients on that ward were free to leave the ward to go into town or to visit family or friends. When John came onto the ward, Mr. Winkler was just getting ready to leave the ward. John greeted him and commented to him on how great he looked in his three piece suit and tie. He was also carrying his umbrella and he had a newspaper under his arm. "Well, don't you look dapper today Mr. Winkler," John commented. "You must have a very important meeting today by the looks of things."

"I most certainly do," he answered. "I shall be meeting with the Queen in about an hour's time. There are important decisions that must be made this very day!"

"Oh, then I hope all goes well and that you are able to come to a satisfactory conclusion today even!" John replied. Off went Mr. Winkler to meet the Queen. John thought no more of it.

The day progressed fairly smoothly. It was a busy day. By the time eight o'clock rolled around, all the patients were bathed and in bed. As John observed the patients from the doorway of the French doors that divided the ward into two sections, to see if they were all properly settled in for the night, he realized that Mr. Winkler had not come back yet. That thought had no sooner gone through his mind when Mr. Winkler suddenly stood next to John in the doorway. John looked at Mr. Winkler and said, "Oh you're back! I hope all went well today?

"All went splendidly!" Mr. Winkler exclaimed. And as he indicated all of the patients before them with an expansive sweep of his hand, he said to John, "Yes today, the Queen and I made a wonderful decision. You see all of this fucking shit, we are going to get rid of it!" John stood there speechless with his mouth wide open in a stunned expression as he looked at Mr. Winkler. He turned towards the kitchenette laughing silently to himself as he tried to imagine the Queen uttering these words as she signed this declaration in front of Mr. Winkler. Mr. Winkler certainly had quite the imagination. It wasn't surprising that he had not yet been given his total freedom.

All in all, John did enjoy the work at Old Barney and learned much from the patients and the work he was doing. The astonishing thing that he discovered was that some of the personnel who were working too much and doing double shifts were ending up as bad as the patients. John found himself on the schizophrenic ward one afternoon and a strange thing occurred. Every once in a while the patients would get into fights with one another as they huddled in corners of the ward; they would also make strange bird noises. John would break up their scuffles and all would go quiet again. But, there would still be a bird noise that could be heard. John wondered where it was coming from; he knew that it was not coming from the patients since he was close enough to them to detect this. He then realized that it was the orderly working with him who was making the bird noise when the patients were quiet. As they sat together on the divan that was on the ward that afternoon, John said to him, "Have you been working very long now, Eddie?" "Oh gosh, there is already a good twenty-eight years that I am working here," replied Eddie. "I might also add that for the last year I have been working double shift. I really need the money." "Don't you think that's really too much?" Eddie replied, "Yes, I reckon it is." "Well, I do think it is because I must tell you that you are already making bird noises just like the patients here. I hear you when they are quiet. I think you need to take a good long vacation and get yourself back on track, Eddie," John replied. "Yes, I will be doing that soon, my wife and I will go to Italy for a long holiday. It is high time that I got away from here." The following week, John was pleased to observe that Eddie was nowhere to be seen. He hoped that he was enjoying the warm Italian sun.

One Saturday afternoon Claude invited John to accompany him into London. He needed to pick up a number of books that he had ordered from a bookshop in Central London. They took the tube to the bookshop and spent a good hour and a half browsing amongst the books, once Claude had claimed and paid for his order. As they headed back to St. Edward's College they decided to stop in Whetstone and look around to see what might be interesting in the neighbourhood shops. They would then each pick up an order of fish and chips and eat the food as they walked along Totteridge Lane on their way to the school.

As they walked up the hill from the Totteridge Lane tube station they saw a sign in the window of the Griffin Pub advertising the need for two workers, one for the bar and one for preparing the pub for opening to the clients. Claude and John looked at one another. Claude said to John, "Are you thinking what I'm thinking?"

"I certainly am!" answered John. "Why don't we go in and have a beer and find out if they'll hire us? I can't do the bar job but you can. I'll take the janitor's job."

"Alright, let's go in," answered Claude.

So they went into the pub. They each ordered a beer and sat down to enjoy it for a while. While they sipped their beer, they observed what was going on in the pub. It was beautiful with a pleasant atmosphere and the people were friendly.

Claude and John finished their beer and went to the bar to inquire about the sign in the window, asking if the positions were still open! The man serving the beer informed them that they were indeed. So they asked him if he would consider hiring them. They said they were very interested in doing that kind of work. They also told him that they were students at St. Edward's College on Totteridge Lane not far from the pub. The man told them that he was not in charge of hiring but he would call the proprietor to speak with them.

A woman holding a small dog in her arms came out to the counter. She introduced herself as Joan Hensby and told them that she and her husband were the owners of the pub. She added, "So, you both would like to take on the jobs advertised in the window?"

"Yes, that's right," answered Claude. "I am Claude and this is John and we are students at St. Edward's College on Totteridge Lane. I would do the bar tending job and John would do the janitor's work. We would do our best to give you good service!" said Claude.

Joan looked at them and told them that there was quite a bit of work to be done and that the janitor's job started very early in the morning. She explained that the floors had to be washed, the tables cleaned and set up, the toilets had to be freshened up each time and all the brass had to be polished for each time the pub opened. The bar tending job called for courteous, friendly service to the customers and knowing the different spirits, liquors and beers to serve. Claude told her that he had no problem with the bar tending; he had done that kind of work before. John assured her that he could be there at whatever hour of the morning needed, since they already were rising very early at the College. That would be no problem.

Joan said to John, "You will need to be here by 6.30 a.m., I'm afraid." To Claude she said, "The time for the bar is at 4.00 p.m. and then again at 7.00 p.m. If you think that you can both handle this then you are hired. If anything happens that you cannot continue, then you will need to let us know in enough time for us to find someone else. How does that sound?" They both let her know that it sounded pretty good to them. Joan then added, "St. Edward's College: isn't that the priest place? So we should not have too much trouble with you fellows, right? You won't try to convert us, will you?"

"Not a chance," John answered, "but now you know why we won't have a problem with early rising and not being late for work! That's part of our normal day to day living schedule."

Joan just laughed and brought them to meet her husband, John, and the head bar tender, Sid, as well as Mary, the cook. Mary was Irish and, being a Catholic, knew about St. Edward's College.

"That's settled then," said Joan. "When can you both begin?"

"This is Saturday. How about on Monday? It will give us time to get ourselves organized," said Claude.

"Why don't you come into the pub on Sunday evening," said Joan, "and Sid can go over what all your duties are with both of you and show you where to find everything?" They both agreed. After shaking hands and a warm good-bye, they left the pub. Then they each picked up an order of fish and chips and walked along Totteridge Lane to St. Edward's, both very excited about their new jobs. As they were walking along, John said to Claude, "Now I'll have my own pocket money and I won't have to go begging to the old sermonizer, Mr. Feeney, the tight wad. I won't be sorry about that! How are we going to keep this a secret? If Fritzie finds out that we are working in a pub, there will be hell to pay, don't you think?"

"We have to make sure that these jobs don't make us miss any classes," said Claude.

"I'm not worried about the classes," said John "It's making it back in time for Spiritual Reading before breakfast in the morning! If the bus from Whetstone to Totteridge Lane is late, then I'll be late! This could be tricky," said John.

"If you are late, don't go into the conference hall while Fritzie is talking or he'll have a fit! Just turn around and go back to your room. Do your own Spiritual Reading. It will probably be more beneficial than the foolishness that he often gives. He just rambles on so!" said Claude. "If you're not there he probably won't notice," he added. John knew that he would need to be cautious about it.

John and Claude also knew that they would have to go to immigration to get their passports stamped for permission to work. They would do that on Monday since they were to meet with Sid on the Sunday evening.

Sid showed them all that they needed to do. John watched and listened carefully to make sure he wouldn't forget anything. There was a good hour and a half to two hours work to be done each morning. All went well for both of them on the Monday morning. They both went to the immigration office for the permission stamp for work. Paul found out at that moment that a simple stamp in his passport was sufficient for him to work because he was Canadian and Canada belonged to the Commonwealth; this gave him permission to work without a work visa. Things turned out differently for Claude. Being an American citizen, he needed to formally apply for a work visa. This could take up to six months to acquire, but he could work while waiting for it to be issued. If it was refused, then he would have to stop working. To apply for this work permit he had to give the name of the college and its address and the name of the director in charge; this did not please Claude. However, it was all set!

The Christmas holidays rolled around and John and his friend Claude did not go anywhere. They stayed at the College. They really had no funds to go anywhere, but they stayed around as well because of their commitment to their new jobs. They had been at their new jobs since the end of October and they both realized that it was too soon for them to take time off, funds or no funds.

Since it was the Christmas season, Claude and John thought of suggesting to Joan and the remainder of the Griffin Pub staff that they decorate the pub for Christmas. There was lots of holly on the grounds of St. Edward's and they could both make beautiful Christmas wreaths as decorations for the pub. They could also set up and decorate a real Christmas tree. This apparently had not been done for quite some time. Everyone was quite pleased with the idea. "As long as it doesn't give us extra work, we don't mind," said Sid. John and Claude reassured them that they would be in charge of everything and they need not worry. They got to work and when they had finished the pub looked magnificent. The regulars were pleased with the festive atmosphere of the pub.

It was during this time and because of certain things that happened over the Christmas holidays that John decided to request an interruption to his college studies and permission to go to the African missions as a teacher. He wanted to teach English as a second language in a francophone country of West Africa. John did not tell Claude of this decision. He would find out about it later.

It was the weekend after Christmas and Claude needed to go into London to pick up several items on Portobello Road. He invited John to go with him. They would visit Carnaby Street at the same time. John thought that this was great and was very pleased that Claude invited him to come along. Everything was so interesting in downtown London. Claude bought a set of dishes for his sister's anniversary. He bought several other very fine pieces of art for his family. Late in the day when it got dark, Claude suggested that they stop into a pub for a pint of bitter before going home. He suggested the Henry the Third Pub. This did not mean much to John, but it did mean something once he was in the pub and noticed the clientele. They were mostly males but even the few women who were there were paired off with other women. John immediately realized that Claude had taken him to a gay pub. As he stood at the bar having a beer with Claude, one guy came to the bar and stood close to John and proceeded to tell him how cute he was. "Are you here with someone?" he asked John. "My name is Tom, by the way and I'd really like to know what makes you tick. You sure are cute." John did not answer, but just kept drinking his beer. He had never thought of himself as "cute". It kind of made him laugh. He looked over at Claude who was standing close to the bar with a beer in his hand. John said to Claude in French, "Hey man, what is this? Why are we here? It's getting late and we need to go or else we'll miss the last tube home."

"I need this experience. We'll get home. Don't worry!" Claude answered in French with some difficulty in properly articulating it; John understood all the same. In the meantime, one guy came up to Claude and began talking to him, asking him what he did, if he was a student, or working in London and where he was from in the US. John and Claude eventually learned that this guy Tom and another called Bill, had been an item at one point but had since separated, even though they were still living at the same address, and they wanted to meet new partners. John felt awful and pleaded in French with Claude that they leave immediately. But Claude was determined to stay on and see how things developed, always answering John that he needed the experience. John was totally puzzled by Claude's reaction.

Finally, they seemed to have become a foursome and Bill, the guy who was interested in Claude, suggested that they leave the boring pub, head to his friends' flat for a party there. It would be wild and daring. John pretended that he could not get close to anyone since he had had a very negative and frightening experience one month previously. He had been attacked by someone he had thought was a very close friend. Of course, the guys were sympathetic. Somehow, things got mixed up and Claude ended up leaving with the guy who was interested in John and John ended up in the other guy's panel van going to a wild gay party. He had no choice now. The last tube had left and he did not know London well enough to take a bus and he didn't have enough money for a taxi. So, into the van he went. The snow had started falling gently. John sat in front with the driver and three other guys from the pub who had joined them to go to the party got into the back seat. One was telling the other that he would go to confession the next morning before mass and that his confessor did not mind if he had sex with another man; he felt that it was great to be able to just tell his confessor what was happening to him and to tell him whatever he wanted. John just remained silent wondering how he would get out of this situation. He was in for a huge surprise!

Claude had gone with the other guy in his car and they would meet up at the party. John was afraid when Claude was not with him because he was not used to London yet, so did not quite know where he was. They arrived at the party. The music was blaring and there were guys latched on to one another as they danced in the middle of the living room; they were just about devouring each other. John found a seat on one of the sofas. One man came over to him and knelt next to him on the floor close to the sofa. He had one hand on John's knee, and the other on his shoulder; he wanted to know who this cute guy was. John did not use his real name. The man was at least in his late fifties or early sixties. He wanted John to dance with him. John found this awkward since he was used to leading when dancing with a woman. The old guy just pulled him close to him, put his head in the curve of his neck and his two hands on his buttocks and they danced that way. John hated the feel of his beard against his cheek. He wanted to get out of this. He told the man that he was feeling dizzy and needed to sit down. He returned to the sofa. The old guy sat next to him. Then, the guy with the panel van came to John and said that they were leaving for home because the party was boring. John left with him, but no one else came with them. He told John that they would go to his flat. They could rest there and then he would drop John at home later on in the morning.

When they arrived at the flat, John found Claude and Tom in bed together. Since it was winter, this couple, Tom and Bill, were only occupying one room of the house; it was warm and comfortable. John was totally disappointed and frightened. Claude just laughed and said to John, "Comment es-tu, mon petit ange?" John was too angry to answer him. Bill wanted John to come and sleep with him in his bed and promised that he would not bother him; he would let him rest. For some reason, unknown to John, Tom did not want John to sleep with his ex-spouse, so he went to another part of the house and showed up with a mattress, sheets and a pillow. He set it out for John. John was alone on that mattress and whispered a thank you to God. He was cold and only slept in fits and starts. The next morning they offered to drop John and Claude off at home. They did not give them their correct address but told them that they lived in Whetstone, on High Street. They dropped them off and John and Claude waved good-bye and they took the bus up Totteridge Lane to St. Edward's. John did not speak. Claude thought it was all a big joke. He laughed a cold hard laugh. John was speechless and totally hurt by Claude's attitude. He went to his room and just lay down on his bed not knowing what to think. After about an hour, he left for Mill Hill and went to evening service at the church. He entered the confessional and poured out his soul to the unknown priest who was there. What John realized at that moment was that he would eventually have to make a very serious decision. This had all been too much for him. He knelt in the church pew after his conversation with the priest in the confessional and wept profusely. Somehow, he felt that he had had his head in the lion's mouth, but had pulled it out in time.

The Christmas break came to an end and classes resumed. Claude and John were still committed to their jobs at the Griffin Pub.

One morning in March, John returned from work at the pub rather late and so was unable to go to the Spiritual Reading session being given by Fritzie. So he went to his room to wait for the breakfast bell to ring. Before it did Claude stormed into John's room in an agitated state. "Fritzie knows, John! Fritzie knows about my working at the pub!" he exclaimed as he entered John's room.

"What? How did he find out?" asked John.

"Well, when I applied for the work visa I had to give the name of the school and the name of the director. They called to get a confirmation that I am a student here at St. Edward's. They told Fritzie that this information was for a work permit to work at the Griffin Pub in Whetstone," Claude told John. "Fritzie brought it up in Spiritual Reading and said that no one was to take any kind of job without first getting his permission. He was furious that anyone would take that kind of liberty. He told the students that one of St. Edward's students had done just that and that he would not allow it. Be careful, my friend, I don't know if he knows about you!

He probably doesn't know anything since you didn't need a work permit. Maybe you need to think about quitting. Fritzie called me in and told me that I had to leave the job or the college. I'm going to tell Joan today what's happened and that I'll have to stop work soon. Anyway, think about it. I wouldn't want you to get thrown out!

John took a few days to think things over. He decided to find someone to replace him. He would suggest that to Joan and the staff. That way they would not be left looking for someone to replace him. He approached Francisco Fratelli, a student with the Verona Community. John had sometimes heard him say that he would like to have a job as he needed the extra pocket money. He met with Francisco and explained everything to him and once he agreed to take the job John took him to meet Joan. She was pleased that he had been able to find someone so quickly and agreed that Francisco should start as soon as possible. Francisco promised that he would do his best. John showed him all that he needed to do. He was ready to start whenever was most convenient for everyone!

John left the job the very next day and mentioned nothing to anyone. He regretted having to leave the job so soon; he had enjoyed it immensely! It was as if nothing had happened. If Fritzie knew about it, he didn't let on. John was never questioned about it. He was now almost twenty-eight years old, a mature adult. But those in charge of the seminary still insisted on seeing him as a child. They had no idea how far he had already come!

During the course of the college year, the community would have a special Mass on Monday evenings. Many of the people from the different parishes where the seminarians worked came to the Mass. They would have refreshments and discussions after Mass. Someone suggested that they should have a college picnic with art work and crafts on display. Claude suggested that he and John be in charge of this "fete" as it was sometimes called. They could prepare it during the month of April and have it the first week-end in May and they could get some of the local artists to put some of their work on display. They set to work. They made quite a number of crafts, from leather purses and painted sheep skulls to water coloured drawings and Christmas decorations. Parishioners brought their art work in so they could be displayed. It proved to be a lot of work. John all the same had enough time to make two pastel paintings of two beautiful African faces. The "fete" was to begin after the eleven o'clock

Mass on Sunday morning, May 2. It took John and Claude the whole of the morning to set things up. People began arriving after the Mass. There were many. Various drinks were served along with hot dogs and hamburgers. Many of the crafts sold very well and all enjoyed viewing the art work. It was a huge success and after the payment of the supplies and food, they cleared 59 pounds. John could not believe it. His own pastel work sold for 10 pounds each. It was then suggested by Fr. Fritzie that they turn this into a college tradition each year. It was definitely seen as a wonderful event. John could not agree to this since he would not be there for the next year unless Claude wished to take it on himself. No one knew, however, that John was leaving and it puzzled Claude that he was not agreeing with this.

As the month of May rolled on, many of the seminarians were preparing for ordination and they had to do the preliminary preparations for their trip to Africa. One of the preparations was getting the necessary vaccinations for the trip. Everyone was totally surprised when they saw John come down with everyone else to take the mini-van for the trip to the clinic where they would get their injections.

"Where are you going?" he was asked.

"I'm going where you are going" John answered.

"How is that?" they asked.

"I'm going to Upper Volta to teach for two years. My letter of acceptance will be here by the end of the school year. Off he went with all the others to get his papers in order. When news got out about this new development, Claude looked at John strangely and said, "I never thought that you would do that. I thought that you felt sure of what you wanted to do like I do!" John told Claude that he had come to realize that this was something he had to do. He had to fly on his own, make his own decisions and do this all by himself, no matter how strange and hurtful this would be. Claude looked at John with a very hurt look in his eyes. "I will miss you. It will not be the same without you here." The words cut through John's heart like a knife. He wanted to weep, but he also knew that he needed to stand on his own two feet and do what had to be done, alone. He was too emotionally tied to his friends. John had come into his own that fateful day on March 17th, but there was more work to be done for him to truly fly on his own. It was good to be able to face that head-on. No matter how painful it was!

John, of course, wrote home about what was happening. As soon as the family received the news, they were stunned. It had not been expected that John would go to Africa so soon. He was supposed to be in England for four years. Now, after one year he was leaving for Africa to teach for two years without coming home for a visit. That following weekend after the family received his letter, John received a phone call from his oldest sister, Martine, asking him why he could not come home for a visit before leaving for Africa. "What if something should happen to you and we never see you again?" she told John. "That would be terrible."

"It's not that I cannot come home, it is that I must pay for the extra fare myself," said John, "and I don't have the money."

"I'll send you the money, book your ticket London-Halifax-London and I'll pick you up at the airport," John's sister told him. John was overjoyed and prepared the trip home without telling the community about this change.

John spent a glorious month at home before leaving for Africa. It seemed so short, the time just flew by. He felt quite surreal; it didn't seem possible that he would be in Africa soon. He was frightened and happy at the same time. There was an empty feeling in the pit of his stomach at times. As the time drew near for him to leave, he was once again in turmoil. His mother was once again very upset. "Where are you going?" she asked. "We can't imagine where this is; will you be OK? I fear that we will lose you forever. I will be dead before you return!"

"Mom, I'll be fine. I must do this. Please do not discourage me. I need your support. Please write me all the time I'm there," John told his mother.

"As soon as you get there, send us your address and we will write every week!" replied his mother.

"Oh Mom, thanks. I needed to hear that," said John.

John realized that his mother had once again become a very strong and determined person with a dear companion by her side. The marriage to Raymond had taken place and he had moved from his daughter's residence to Rose's cozy bungalow and had already started to make improvements to the place. Rose was elated and once more enjoyed cooking, cleaning, doing laundry and pampering her new husband. John also found out how terrible the reaction of Raymond's children had been when they had received the news that their father was to re-marry so soon after his wife's death. They refused to call her mother, which Rose thought was something quite normal. She had not expected them to. They had openly voiced their displeasure to Della who knew the family since she had worked with them for years at the fish factory. Della had told them that Rose was just as good a person as their father and they need not act so high and mighty. She knew them from way back and knew that they had their own faults just like everyone else. She had been summoned to the house of one of Raymond's daughters to listen to their venom, but she said to them before she left, "At least we have accepted your father gladly into the family which is more than we can say about your family in regard to our mother. You're just angry because you have lost your built-in babysitter for your Bingo outings." They were very upset with Della. But she left them and did not look back. As far as she was concerned, they were just an ignorant brood devoid of politeness.

John left Halifax to return to London in mid-July. He would spend a month in London with Claude and then take a flight to Ouagadougou with a several hour layover in Paris. The good-byes with Claude at Heathrow Airport were horrendous. He felt terrible! He had never told Claude that his decision had been based partly on what had happened to them on the night at the Henry the third pub. Once in the airplane, he went to the washroom and cried his heart out. While waiting at the Paris airport, he met the missionary, Fr. Emile, whom he would replace as teacher in Ouagadougou. Fr. Emile gave John a few tips about the school, what to expect and what materials he had left in the office; he explained that the English library was excellent to help teach English as a second language. John noted everything down and after more good-byes, boarded the flight for Ouagadougou. When he crossed into the international section of the airport to board, he knew that he was alone and on his own. His feeling at that moment was one of desolation!

Chapter Sixteen

After a short visit with his brother and other family members in Halifax, Fr. John went on to Arichat, his home village, to see what the possibilities were for work in his home diocese of Antigonish since he needed a home base for preparations for the eventual arrival of Jules and Chris. It was a far cry from Jinja and, even if it was home, he felt out of place. He would need to do some adjusting. It would take time. The first place he went was to Fr. J. P. MacCarthy's parish since he was a close friend. They discussed at length the situation of the two young men, along with his feeling of being like a fish out of water.

"I'm not too sure how to go about this," he told Fr. MacCarthy. "Do I go to immigration in Ottawa and put in a request? What do I do?"

"There must be a number that you can call in the government section of the phone book," said Fr. MacCarthy. "Look and see, and give them a call."

This he did and was told that he would be sent an immigration package for both young men. He would need to fill those out and submit them to the immigration department. He would need the photographs that the boys had taken in Nairobi. In the meantime he helped in the different parishes, especially Fr. J.P.'s parish. Many of the parishioners who knew him well invited him for lunch, dinner and sometimes breakfast to hear about his Zairean experience and eventual exodus. In the beginning, he had difficulty speaking about it. He would become very upset when he relived the experiences with the soldiers and the police. However, as time passed he became more settled about the whole experience. He did realize in the course of the retelling that he had been more deeply affected by the ordeal than he had thought. He would need to talk about it in a more personal way with someone and continue to bring it to prayer. He would often go to Fr. J.P.'s to pray quietly in one of the rooms that had been offered him for his relaxing and quiet moments. It was during one of these quiet moments that he met a man who would be instrumental in helping him get the two young men out of their horrendous situation.

One afternoon as he was having a cup of tea with Fr. J.P. in the huge kitchen of the parish house, Fr. J.P. mentioned to him that he was having a meeting that afternoon with the board members of the University. He also mentioned that Senator Albert MacIsaac was to attend the meeting. This was the man who had been a real life saver for many in the difficult political situation of Cape Breton Island. He had also been Minister of External Affairs at one point in the Federal Government. Fr. John looked at Fr. J.P. and said, "Do you think that he could help me with Jules and Chris?"

"Well, I'll tell you one thing. If he lights a fire under their butts in immigration, they will certainly move. You can trust me on that score," replied Fr. J.P. "Speak to him; you have nothing to lose."

"Would you tell him that I would like to speak to him after the meeting, if you don't mind?"

"I will do that," replied Fr. J.P. "I'll see if he is free once the meeting is over."

The meeting ended around mid-morning and Fr. John soon found himself seated across from Senator MacIssac in Fr. J.P.'s living-room.

"What can I do for you, Father?" the Senator asked.

"Well, it is no easy matter, Senator!" Fr. John then explained to him all that had taken place in Central Africa as well as Jules' and Chris' situation. He left out no details.

Senator MacIsaac had a pleasant, kindly face. He looked at Fr. John for a moment and, smiling, said, "You certainly have been through the mill, haven't you? I hope that you are receiving some kind of care for yourself.

Do you have a letter or a document explaining all of this and giving all the details on the situation of these two young men?"

"Yes, I do," said Fr. John He was now so glad that he had prepared these reports. They would certainly be useful. He gave Senator MacIsaac a copy. He put it in his briefcase and simply said to Fr. John, "We will assess the situation and you will hear from us one way or another." He did not say that he would help or do anything about the situation. He simply took the information and then said to Fr. John, "Let's go and have a cup of coffee with our good friend Fr. J.P." The exchange was over. Fr. John felt no hope. "I'll probably never hear from him again," was Fr. John's last thought.

Fr. John continued to help in different parishes, especially at St. Hyacinth's where Fr. J.P. was posted. He enjoyed the time just to relax and be quiet and not do enormous amounts of work. He would pop in at his sister's house at least once or twice a day. He came to realize more and more how much the situation in Zaire had affected him. He needed prayer time. The invitations that he would receive from relatives and friends were a help for this since he ended up speaking about the situation in detail. This turned out to be very cathartic.

One week went by, then two, then a whole month since the interview with Senator MacIsaac. One morning as he and Fr. J.P. were sitting in the kitchen of the rectory having coffee, the phone rang. Fr. J.P. answered and handed the phone to Fr. John saying, "Here, it's for you!"

"For me? Who would that be?" exclaimed Fr. John. He had already forgotten that a call could come from the Senator's office, so sure had he been that nothing would be done.

The voice on the line was not that of the Senator's. It did not have the thick Scottish accent that he detected in the Senator's voice. This was a very mild, soft spoken man's voice. "Am I speaking to Fr. John?" inquired the voice.

"Yes, this is Fr. John. How may I help you?"

"This is Senator MacIsaac's office calling. This is to let you know that the paperwork has been sent to the Embassy in Nairobi in the diplomatic pouch. Everything should be there by tomorrow." Fr. John was stunned. He almost did not reply. Then he blurted out quickly, "Oh thank you, thank you kindly!" Then he quickly added, "Would it improve matters if I went to Nairobi myself? What do you think?"

"Well all I can say is that the personal touch is best."

Fr. John decided that since he still had a return plane ticket for Nairobi, he would fly back to make sure that the boys had received the immigration forms from the Embassy and that they had succeeded in filling them out properly. He would make sure as well that the passport photos were good ones and that they would be appropriate. He knew only too well how difficult the Canadian Embassy could be when it came to passport photographs.

Fr. John told everyone that there was to be an important meeting of all the Missionaries of Africa in Montreal and that he was expected to attend. The Provincial director of the Missionaries of Africa needed to speak to him about a certain appointment that had to be settled before the new pastoral year began in September. Fr. John flew to Montreal and met with the Provincial director. He hoped that Fr. John would take charge of the Afrika Center on St. Hubert St. in Montreal. The first question that Fr. John asked was, "Who will be with me to do the work? Surely I will not be expected to do that kind of work on my own?"

"No, of course not," replied the Provincial. "However, that is a point that is not an easy one. The colleagues who will be with you are old now and will not be able to take on a full load. They now have serious health issues."

"I do not think that I can handle that right now after what I have been through in Zaire and Rwanda," Fr. John answered. "Also to be very truthful with you I have absolutely no desire to work in the province of Quebec."

"Oh really, for what reason?" the Provincial asked incredulously.

"It is very simple, Father. I do not agree with the politics of the province of Quebec at the moment and the attitude that exists here is very abhorrent to me. I simply wish to have no part of it," Fr. John replied.

"Oh, I see," the Provincial answered. "Well, thank you for being so frank with me. You may return to your family if you wish for more time to think things over and rest. There will be time for appointments later. But I needed to clear things up concerning our Afrika Center. It is an important part of the work here at St. Hubert House. I do hope that you will be able to get more rest in the coming days."

"Thank you. I am attempting to do just that in the coming days," Fr. John replied. Little did he know that no rest would be forthcoming just yet since he was to fly to Nairobi to get Jules and Chris on track with immigration. He had called KLM airlines upon his arrival in Montreal and he had already booked his flight for Nairobi for the following night.

Fr. John asked no one to accompany him to the Mirabel Airport. He took the shuttle bus there on his own. He wanted no one to know that he was on his way to Nairobi. The only person who knew was his sister Della. He always kept in touch with her. He took the night flight to Amsterdam, arriving quite early the next morning. That afternoon he boarded his flight for Nairobi. He had informed Jules and Chris that he was coming and the time of the arrival of his flight. They were at the Nairobi International Airport when his flight landed. They were overjoyed to see him and they took the public transport to their apartment at Stella Awinja. After having a cup of tea and a snack, they went to the Canadian Embassy to see if they could pick up the immigration forms. They were told by the Embassy that the forms had already been sent to the British Language School and that they would surely be able to get them there. Off they went to the British Language Center.

"We are here to pick up our mail," they said to the man at the registrar's desk.

"There is no mail here for you, boys," answered the black clerk to Jules and Chris. "But there has to be mail there for us. The Canadian Embassy sent our forms last week; they must be there some where. Please look again!"

The clerk looked once more! This time he could not believe his eyes. There under a bunch of other letters was a thick envelope addressed to Jules and Chris. "We will take them to the apartment immediately," said Fr. John, "and we will fill them out together. Then I will write the guarantor's letter, add the photographs and bring it all to the Embassy. It took them a good part of the afternoon to get all this done. They went to the Embassy and again Fr. John felt like he was in a fortress preparing for battle. He passed in the completed forms and requested to see a Counselor.

"There is no one available today, Sir. You will have to book for tomorrow at 11 a.m. Will that do?" asked the receptionist.

"It will do," answered Fr. John, "but he or she must have those forms and photographs with him since I have questions concerning the documents."

"Well, it would be better if you kept the documents with you," she answered. "I cannot guarantee that the person who sees you will have those with him." So she handed the documents back to Fr. John. He took the documents, thanked her and assured her that he would be there the next day at the appointed time.

At eleven o'clock the next morning, Fr. John was admitted to a small office of the Embassy to wait for a Counselor to see him while Jules and Chris waited in the overcrowded waiting room. Ten minutes went by before a fairly young white male came in. He was a bit on the heavy side but quite neatly dressed in white shirt and tie. He sat down at the desk facing Fr. John and introduced himself. From his name Fr. John knew that he was French Canadian. Fr. John told him who he was and added that he was a Missionary of Africa, also known as White Fathers, and that he had been working in Zaire until they had had to evacuate that country because of the political unrest. He nodded his head in understanding.

"But what is it exactly that you want me to do for you? Why do you need to see me?" he asked.

"I want you to look over these documents and photographs for these two young men and tell me if they are correctly filled out and if the photographs are satisfactory," answered Fr. John. The Counselor took a careful look at the documents and photographs and told Fr. John that they were just fine. He did not try to make conversation with Fr. John. It was strictly business without any kind of warmth or friendliness. Then he asked, "Why did you feel that you had to do this, to verify this to this extent?"

"Because I know how exacting the Canadian Embassy can be," said Fr. John. "The Embassy would think nothing of sending everything back to them and make them start all over again and I was not about to have my trip to Nairobi turn out useless because of the foolishness of the Canadian Embassy. Then Fr. John switched over into French and the conversation continued on in French. The Counselor seemed pleased to be able to speak in French, although his English was impeccable. He looked at Fr. John and said in a reassuring tone, "No, these documents and photographs will not

281

be returned. They are fine as they are." Then, he broke the business tone of the interview and asked Fr. John, "Didn't you say you were working in Zaire and that you are a Missionary of Africa?"

"Yes, I did say that," answered Fr. John.

"Would you have met by chance a priest by the name of Denis Thibedeau? I am sure that he became a White Father and that he had been sent to Zaire to work."

"Of course I know Fr. Denis," answered Fr. John. "He was in the mission station at Bunia. He is on his way home to Quebec. He and his colleagues went through a terrible ordeal during the war. Their mission was attacked and they were tied up and robbed. They thought for sure that they would be killed. Fr. Denis is a very fine colleague and missionary. But he has been through a very traumatic experience."

"I always wondered what became of him. We were classmates in the Classical Course studies in Quebec and we were very good friends. Please, if you see him, give him my greetings. I have very good memories of our student days together. Tell him that Claude Parent sends his best regards. I'm sure that he will remember me."

"I will certainly see him," said Fr. John, "and I will give him the message." The ice had been broken; the atmosphere turned warmer and friendlier. And when Fr. John questioned Claude on the situation of the Embassy, all he could say was, "We do not always have a say in what happens here. Many things are out of our hands. Trust me. It is not nice!" Fr. John did not question any further. He shook hands with Claude, said good-bye and assured him that he would give Fr. Denis his message. Fr. John left the Embassy quite satisfied and convinced once more that it is not what you know that gets things done, but who you know!

Of course the first question of the two boys was, "How did it go? What did they say?"

"The documents and photographs are fine. They are ready to be processed. You must wait to be called for an interview. They will contact both of you through the Language School."

They both breathed a sigh of relief. Fr. John stayed with them for a few more days and then boarded his return flight to Montreal via Amsterdam after reassuring Jules and Chris that he would stay in touch and that the necessary funds would be sent for their living expenses.

Fr. John wished fervently that they could board the plane with him. They looked so forlorn as they said good-bye when he turned to go into the International section of the airport. They waved good-bye and stayed in the same spot until he disappeared from view. Fr. John felt like crying one more time and whispered a prayer to God for their safety.

The Nairobi to Amsterdam flight was quite full. He sat in the middle seat on the left side of the aircraft. A young woman sat next to him in the window seat. There was not much conversation in the beginning of the flight. They served dinner but Fr. John was not very hungry. He could still picture Jules and Chris standing looking so forlorn as they waved good-bye to him. It was all so painful. He turned to the young woman sitting next to him and asked her, "Are you going through to Canada or are you stopping in Amsterdam?"

"Yes, I am going through to Canada," she answered. "I'm from Canada and I have been away for the last three months. It will be good to see home again."

"Where is home for you?"

"I'm from Iroquois Falls, in northern Ontario. You've probably never heard of it. And by the way, my name is Isabelle Randeau."

"Pleased to meet you Isabelle! I am Fr. John DeCoste, from Cape Breton, Nova Scotia. Surprisingly enough, I have heard of Iroquois Falls," said Fr. John

The young woman was pleasantly surprised and so continued the conversation. She told Fr. John that she had just finished a three month experience at the Canadian Embassy in Nairobi. Fr. John turned and looked at her with total attention.

"You have just finished a three month experience at the Embassy in Nairobi!" Fr. John exclaimed. "May I pick your brain?" he asked. "I was just there at the Embassy a few days ago."

She looked at Fr. John and answered, "And I'm sure that I know what you are going to ask me."

"What is going on in our Embassies? They are like cold, unfriendly fortresses waiting to be attacked like the battle of the Alamo. Plus, they refuse visas to young people especially those who want to go study in Canada with very thin reasons, even when the student has everything needed to live properly in Canada. I don't get it. Can you enlighten me?"

"Well, off the record, and between you and me and the seat back here, there are many very nasty things happening between our Embassy staff and the local people. I don't know if that is the only reason for some of the occurrences but it is certainly a very big factor."

"And that factor is? Please explain so that I can better understand!" said Fr. John.

"Okay, many of the Canadians who come to work for the Embassies, come with a very romanticized idea of Africa. They get the same pay as they would get in Canada but with a much cheaper cost-of-living. That means that they can have African servants and they can live quite well with people cooking and cleaning for them. They do not pay a very high wage to their African staff. They become friendly with them and they think that this is great until they find out that their house staff is taking them for a ride. They eventually discover that the cooks and servants are stealing food. They feel cheated and betrayed, not seeing that their staff is simply supplementing what they do not receive in wages. Nonetheless, they feel betrayed and the love affair is over. Then they get their revenge by refusing visas to those who apply for them, especially the young people. It is a very sad state of affairs. Fortunately, that was not my case and I have had a very positive experience in Africa. I would like very much to return to work in one of the Embassies."

"Well good for you," answered Fr. John. "In our missions all over Africa we always make provisions for our workers in food stuffs. We give them so much rice, powdered milk and other goods over and above their wages. Then they do not feel so tempted to steal. They always think we have more than them, and, for the most part, they are right."

"That is so true," answered the young lady from Iroquois Falls.

"I hope you do get back to Africa and work with an Embassy," said Fr. John. "We need more Canadians with a positive attitude towards Africa. There are too many negative reactions to life in Africa. They are beautiful people and right now they are going through atrocious suffering."

Fr. John watched the movie even though he had seen it before and then slept until they announced that they would soon be landing in Amsterdam. There he would be in for a new and pleasant surprise.

Chapter Seventeen

Fr. John boarded the flight for Upper Volta with a heavy heart filled with fear of the unknown. The flight landed in Ouagadougou around one thirty in the afternoon, in the last week of July, 1971. John got up to leave the aircraft, but when he reached the exit door of the plane, the heat that hit him was so intense, he lost his breath. It was like putting his face into a heated oven. He turned back and sat in one of the seats for a few minutes. "What have I done?" he thought. "I'll never get used to such heat!" He did not realize that they had landed in the hottest time of the day. He mustered up all his courage and left the aircraft even though he really felt like taking it back to Europe. The bright, sunshine blinded him. For that he was grateful; at least it was not the dreary overcast weather of England. He made his way in the heat to the customs' counter. Everything was in order. Then he went to the baggage claim. He was new to the fathers meeting him, so they didn't know who they were looking for. John recognized them because they were both dressed in the habit of the Missionaries of Africa, an African gondoura with a rosary around their necks. They were craning their necks trying to see who was coming through the customs' counter. He went up to them and, tapping them on the arm, he said, "Maybe you're looking for me? I'm John DeCoste your new teacher."

"Oh, so there you are," they laughed. "You came through quite fast. How did you manage that?" they said.

"I told them I was coming to teach at your school," he said. "So they just stamped everything and let me through.

"And they didn't ask you for anything?" they asked.

"No, they didn't," John laughed.

"Good, maybe there are conversions going on. Miracles do happen!" said Fr. Henri.

They looked at John and commented on how fat and rosy cheeked he was. "You'll lose that fat quickly enough!" they commented. Fr. Fournier, who was accompanying Fr. Henri, introduced himself as the director of the school and welcomed John to the school and their community. John removed the sweater he was wearing. The heat was unbearable; the sweat was pouring down his neck and back. We'll have to go to the market before heading for the school," they said. "You'll need a hat for your head and a pair of sunglasses to protect your eyes from the sun. Here you have to protect yourself from the intense sun, otherwise you can get sick.

Everything was so strange to John. There were many palm trees, mud houses, some with thatched roofs, and the people were all dressed in colourful West African dress. One thing that struck John in particular, was the enormous number of motorbikes and bicycles; many people were using them to get around. The number of animals on the streets was also striking: chickens, pigs, dogs, sheep, even a cow or two. Everything seemed so poor and ill-kept to John. They reached the market and there the smells assaulted him. There was the smell of sewage, but also the smell of spices and cooking meat. It was not an unpleasant smell, but very different. They got the hat and the sunglasses. Then John told them that he would need a few postcards so he could write home immediately. They directed him to a nearby book and card shop. As he was about to go into the shop, he noticed a man begging at the door of the store; his nose and ears were half eaten away and, as he extended his hand, only the palm was left; the fingers were gone. John felt sick and wanted to be able to help the leper. "How will I adjust to this?" he thought. "Maybe I should take the flight back. I won't be able to take it." He was panicky and had to get hold of himself. He used the few francs he had acquired for dollars at the airport to buy the cards. He tried to pick beautiful, cheery, colourful ones, so as not to alarm his family. On the way out, he was suddenly surrounded by five or six African children, with their hands extended, yelling at him, "Franc, franc,

franc, franc." They obviously wanted money. John had nothing left and felt riveted to the spot. One of the fathers noticed and came to his rescue.

He got back into the car with relief and they proceeded to the school. The Interseminaire St. Peter and Paul, as it was called, was thirteen kilometres outside the capital, Ouagadougou. It was a large property and the first building they came across in the compound was a beautiful, large, round chapel with an extraordinary roof like a ski run. Not far from it was the teachers' building, latrines and bedrooms above and offices below. This was to be his home for the next two years. They showed him to his room and his office. In his room there was a built-in shower and they had put fresh towels and some soap for him. They told him to shower and change into something light and come down to the kitchen for coffee afterwards. Once in his room, John stood in the center of the room observing the table, chair and bookshelf and the single bed with a mosquito net around it. It was simple, frugal living. He stood there looking, holding his head in his two hands, an awful feeling in the pit of his stomach, a feeling of nausea welling up in him and wondering what excuse he could come up with to take the airplane back. More aloneness and desolation. He whispered a short prayer for strength, "My God, I need you, do not abandon me!"

The next day John was informed that the students would not arrive until the end of August. He had a whole month to prepare his classes, look at the English programme, familiarize himself with the area, and finish getting his immigration papers in order. There was a room close to the kitchen where the mopeds were kept; one was for him. "Do you know how to ride a moped?" asked Fr. Firmin.

"No," John said, "and I don't even drive a car. I have no license whatsoever!"

"Well, it is time you learned to drive the moped," said Fr. Firmin, "and I'll teach you this afternoon. Then you can practice going up and down the driveway. It won't take you long to get the hang of it and, besides, you don't need a license for the moped." John was somewhat leery about driving the moped. How could one drive through the city without hitting or killing something or someone with all the people and animals that were running about on the road.

The practice went well and in no time he had the hang of it. Fr. Firmin also showed him how to clean the spark plug and told him that he must keep checking it. He also indicated what kind of petrol it took. John felt he had accomplished a little something once that was done. The next day, however, Fr. Firmin surprised him by suggesting that he follow him into town with the moped and there he could post his cards to the family. John thought that it was a bit too soon to go into the city after just one afternoon of practice.

"You'll do fine," said Fr. Firmin. "Just keep your eyes open and a moderate pace!" John was too chicken to actually say that he couldn't do this, that he was terrified, so off he went behind Fr. Firmin. It was awful in the beginning with so many people and animals crossing in front of him. He kept braking constantly. Fr. Firmin kept looking back to see if he was following. He stopped a number of times to let him catch up.

"You're doing fine," he said. "Soon you'll really get the hang of it."

"How wonderful, a baptism by fire!" John thought. "There was nothing like plunging head first into the situation." From that day on the moped was his best friend and he traveled all over the country with it.

He prepared his classes as he looked over the English programmes. He chose a number of novels from the African Writers' series for the students to read and present in class. However he felt so alone, missing everyone at home terribly and he missed his friend, Claude, and the other team members. He wondered what they were doing. He would be so glad when the students arrived. He longed for the daily siesta so that he could sleep and forget all his loneliness and give himself up to oblivion. Terrible thoughts rushed in on him again. He felt desolate and alone. He actually allowed the thought to overwhelm him and the feelings of despair at times were excruciatingly painful. He always felt as if there was a huge hole in the pit of his stomach. Sometimes he would wake up at night and it was as if someone had kicked him in the stomach. He wanted to go home! He wanted to run away! He wanted to die!

Where was the liberating presence that he had felt that wonderful day in Dayton? It did not seem present at the moment! It seemed as if it had abandoned him. But then John thought, "Wait, be patient, growing up continues! Trust and have faith. It's just another hurdle in the spiritual journey!" With these thoughts he felt better and a strong surge of hope filled him!

One afternoon, a dusty looking Renault came rumbling up the driveway. John had been there over a week, but it seemed like an eternity to him. Fr. Firmin, Fr. Henri and he came to the door of their offices to see who it was. It was Fr. Antoine from the Kaya mission about three hours' travel into the bush. Fr. Antoine was Canadian as well and was glad that a Canadian seminarian had come on a pastoral experience before continuing his studies. Everyone believed that all seminarians should do that; it would improve their decision regarding their future. John hoped that if others followed after him that they would not find themselves in the awful desolation that he was experiencing. Never had he felt so terribly alone and with no one to talk to. There were moments, especially at night, when he would silently cry himself to sleep, hoping he would not wake up the next morning.

Fr. Antoine stayed for the night and at supper that evening he suggested that John come to his mission with him. They could take the moped with them and he could ride around visiting the villages and the countryside of the Kaya mission. He would bring him back in two weeks time when he would return to the capital for more supplies. They all thought it was a good idea and John accepted. It would be different and make the time go by while waiting for the other teachers and the students to arrive. The heavy feeling in his stomach, however, did not lessen as he left for the Kaya mission.

They arrived at the mission around ten-thirty in the morning. The cook greeted them and welcomed John. The house boy took John to his room. It was a cozy room with mosquito net hanging over the metal frame above the bed. John showered and took time to look around the mission. There were flowers and plants in front of the rooms and a short, stubby tree close to Fr. Antoine's office. The country outside the compound was rather flat with small, rolling hills. He was in savannah country; no mountains and no huge trees were visible. He would later discover that one huge tree did exist here and there in the countryside; it was called the baobab tree. It looked like a giant had uprooted it and replanted it upside down. It was strange and beautiful.

For lunch that day John had pounded yam for the first time and a delicious, dark meat in gravy that turned out to be goat meat. For dessert they had papaya with a touch of lemon. A cup of tea finished the meal.

John wanted so much to speak to Fr. Antoine about how desolate he felt, but he just pretended that everything was fine. He wanted to know where Fr. Antoine came from in Canada. He needed to hear about home, no matter what part of the country it was. It seemed to give him a glimmer of hope. That night they sat outside, since it was somewhat cooler than earlier in the day when the temperature had gone up to forty degrees Centigrade. They enjoyed a cool beer together and looked up at the stars. The satellites raced rapidly across the starlit sky. John wished someone from home or his friend, Claude, could be there with him. He felt so absolutely alone. When would this pass? Later, in bed with the mosquito net around him, he felt even further away from home, lost somewhere in the African bush. He could die there and no one would know it. It was frightening and he longed for sleep to come.

The next day he took the moped out and drove through the countryside. The people in the villages were of the Mossi tribe and many of their houses were round, mud huts with thatched roofs. The children ran out to greet him and shouted, "Nasaarah, nasaarah, nasaarah," which he later learned was the Moore (the language of the Mossi people) word for white man.

The countryside was beautiful: flat with some rolling hills that were covered with light green wispy kind of grass. There were some stubby trees here and there. Much of the land was cultivated with millet and peanuts. There were goats and some sheep, a few dogs and, of course, chickens and guinea hens clucking around the houses. The peacefulness of this experience eased his tension and loneliness.

John had brought some reading material with him, but also spent some time writing letters home and to the students at the seminary in London. One of the first letters was to Claude, but it was a positive one with good news, no matter how miserable he felt.

The time dragged by until finally the moment came for them to head back to the capital. Fr. Antoine dropped him off at the seminary and had a coffee and a chat before continuing on into the city. John greeted one member of the staff who had arrived a little early from Europe. It was Fr. Raphael from Spain; he was the students' Spanish professor. The students studied two living languages besides French; they were English and Spanish.

Upon his return to the seminary, John found out that they would all be riding out to the airport again to pick up Fr. Rene, who was arriving from France. They all trucked to the airport to help him bring the cheese, sausages and wine safely to the seminary. Everyone knew that this was important to their survival, since the cheese, sausage and wine were rather expensive to buy in town. Knowing that these goods were arriving, they made sure that Fr. Rene got through customs without a hitch. No one else could lay claim to these precious foods.

The next priest to arrive was Fr. Marius, who arrived at four the next morning. In spite of the hour, they were all ready to take the car to the airport. The sky was still bright with stars and it was cooler. They enjoyed that and so would the father coming in. The fresh, cooler air would be more like home, and as they drove through the town the cry from the mosque's minaret could be heard, "Allah akbar! Allah akbar! Allah akbar!"

Fr. Henri who was with the group turned to John and said, "Do you hear him? He's calling us to have salad." From a distance the "Allah akbar!" really did sound like "There is salad" in French.

The last teacher to arrive was Lionel, the one lay teacher on the staff, who had come to do his military service in Africa. The French from France had that option and many took it since it also meant more money. They received the same wages as in France but the living costs were much less. Lionel was one of the science teachers and had the gift of making this subject come alive for the students.

Lionel's sister, Clarissa, was also a teacher in Upper Volta, but she was in the Bobo-Dioulasso area, the area with mango trees and a more luscious, green forest. Once in Bobo-Dioulasso, one was out of the savannah region and wonderful swimming places could be found. John went once to one of those swimming places with Lionel. They had gone to the swimming area called La Ginguette. It had been absolutely marvelous. The water was cool, clear and without any kind of danger from disease. The other area they had gone to was Karfigela Falls, where the water was ice cold and superb. It had been a great weekend, except for the incident on the way back when they side-swiped a stray cow and almost totaled the car. They had sat by the roadside for some time trying to get their breath back and thanking God for having recovered from the shock of it. They returned to Ouagadougou very late at night after having had quite a time trying to repair the car. It was a local, roadside mechanic who had repaired it for them. His makeshift repair job had done the trick and they were able to get back to the school.

The students finally began arriving. Those coming from the Bobo-Dioulasso area came in mini-vans, their suitcases, trunks and packages piled high on the roofs. John was amazed and really interested to meet the students. They came from all the different areas of Upper Volta and he had them all in class for English as a second language. They loved learning English. They would constantly say that it was the most widely spoken language in the world and everyone needed to speak it fluently. They were quite good at remembering the vast vocabulary. They didn't even flinch at John's suggestion that they each choose a novel from the library, read it, summarize it, and present it orally in class. The one thing that they did find difficult about English, however, was the spelling; there were so many silent letters. The African students, however, were not slaves to the written word so their memories were still sharp and well-developed. They could remember many of the expressions, proverbs and idioms. It was sheer pleasure to teach them. They were in school, on the whole, to study, work and succeed.

The tension in John, the aloneness and the isolation gradually left him as he got closer to the students. He made many friends among them and, during the holidays, he was able to visit them at their homes, sleeping on straw mats in the mud huts and eating rice, chicken, pounded yam and millet dishes out of calabashes with his hands. They would politely teach him how to eat with his hands and how to bathe in the makeshift shower area behind the braided enclosure in one of the remote corners of the compound. If there was a flowing stream close by, they would go there early in the morning and bathe there in the cool, fresh, running water.

He would never forget one meal that he had at the home of one student he was visiting for a few days. Francois' mother served them a beautiful, plain white rice and with it several pieces of a pinkish meat basking in a salmon-coloured sauce. "Please, Teacher, would you bless the meal for us?" asked Francois.

"Why, of course, with pleasure," answered John. After the blessing, Francois dished out some of the rice on their plates and over it he placed a large piece of the meat with lots of sauce.

Then looking at John said, "Enjoy, Sir. This is one of our specialties."

"Thank you," answered John and, on taking the first mouthful, could not believe how delicious it was. It was the colour of salmon, but could not be salmon, since it was a meat dish.

Francois looked at John. "Do you know what you are eating?" he asked John.

"No, I don't, but it sure is good," answered John.

'It is a type of lizard called varen,' said Francois. "It is quite large and lives in the mud of the streams and rivers here. We really love it and find it very special and so it is a special dish for our favourite guests."

John was amazed. What would they say at home when he told them that he had eaten lizard? They would freak out. They would freak out even more when he told them that he had also eaten cat and dog meat, something his family and friends simply would not do.

The cat meal had been a strange one. It had taken place at the school where Francois studied and John was doing his teaching assignment. One morning at breakfast one of John's colleagues commented on the fact that there were too many cats on the property and they needed to get rid of some of them. All the teachers who were eating together agreed. To their surprise, however, Joannet, one of the colleagues, got up from the table and went into action immediately. They were having French sausage and delicious French bread with coffee for breakfast, so Joannet took a piece of the sausage and threw it to one of the cats lurking close to the kitchen door. The cat came running and as it was about to grab the piece of sausage, Joannet bopped it over the head and the cat slumped over dead. He took it immediately to the kitchen where the cook skinned it and gutted it ready for the cooking pot. At the noon meal that day they had cat cooked in red wine with French fries, what the French call "un civet au chat avec frites". It was not bad at all. In fact, John found that it tasted somewhat like rabbit; he had eaten a lot of rabbit at home especially during the Christmas family celebrations.

"Kitty, you are delicious," were the words that ran through John's head as he ate his meal.

The dog meat meal had come at the end of the first academic year that John was at the school. The students left for home at the end of June and there was always a big meal with the teachers before they left. This meant that they would have lots of jollof rice and delicious pieces of meat and a type of African doughnut made from millet that the students nicknamed "pantoufle." One day before the preparation of the meal, Sr. Therese, the African sister in charge of running the students' kitchen, came to Fr. Joseph who was in charge of buying foodstuffs for the school, and asked him, "What will I do with the dog that has been guarding the kitchen granaries all year? I cannot take him to our convent as it would be too expensive for us to keep him."

"That's fine, Sister. I will see to the matter," answered Fr. Joseph. Then he had gone to Fr. Fournier and asked him what they should do about the dog. Fr. Fournier said "Give the dog to the students, they will take care of it."

"Very well, I will call the dean of the students and get him to look after it," answered Fr. Joseph. He called Cyprian, the student dean, and told him that the dog had to be taken care of.

"No problem, we will certainly do that, Fr. Joseph," Cyprian had answered.

All the preparations for the going-away meal went very well and the day before the departure both teachers and students sat down in the huge eating hall to enjoy their meal. The delicious smell of rice and meat permeated the hall and everyone's mouth was salivating. As they were eating, two students were going from table to table with a large bowl containing chunks of meat. They both made sure that they stopped at John's table and asked, "Sir, have you ever tasted dog meat?"

"Oh no, we do not eat dog meat where I come from, It is a domesticated animal and is used as a pet. The dog is like a member of the family," John had answered.

"Would you like to try some? We have beautifully prepared dog meat here. Some of our students do not eat it either but that is because it is the totem of their tribe or family. If the totem of the family is an edible thing then they will not eat it since it would be like eating one of their ancestors." John was quite intrigued by this. He would have to find out more about this totem idea. It sounded quite interesting. After some hesitation he answered, "Sure I would like to try it, why not?" John wanted to experience everything he could during his time in African. He didn't realize at that moment that his openness to enter fully into their culture was endearing him more and more to the students. The meat was very tender and quite tasty, although a tad gluey in texture. It went well with the rice. Of course he realized that this was Tintin, the granary guard dog. John mused to himself, "Poor pooch, his reward for guarding the food all year had been to end up in the pot, well cooked. This is certainly a different way of thinking when it comes to animals."

"How do you like it, Sir?" asked the student.

"Not bad! Not bad at all," answered John.

Much later when John had returned home from Africa, he had stopped in London to visit friends and had told them about this. They had been shocked. He had gone to the Griffen Pub where he had worked with his good friend, Claude. Margaret, an Irish nurse, and a very good friend was with him. At that time he had told her about the dog meal. Joan, the proprietor of the pub, loved dogs and always had her favourite pup in her arms as she greeted customers from behind the counter. John had remarked to Margaret as they watched Joan cuddling her pup, "Do you think that I should tell her that I ate dog meat in Africa?"

"Oh goodness. Don't you dare! She will disown you, John. She may not speak to you ever again!" Margaret exclaimed. John looked at Margaret and jokingly said, "Well, she had better not come too close to me with the pup because I may just bite a chunk out of it."

"You are just disgusting," answered Margaret as they both laughed.

John had to admit that the African experience had proven very beneficial for him. He was becoming so much freer internally and building his self-confidence tremendously.

As time passed, John came to see beyond the poverty of Upper Volta. He at last saw the beauty of the people, their simplicity, their wonderful hospitality and their thirst for knowledge. He also saw the beauty of the sunsets and sunrises and of the fields of millet and peanuts, corn and rice, and the luscious gardens of cabbages and carrots during the rainy season. He noticed the beauty of their mud houses with thatched roofs, the decorated mud walls and the well-swept compounds formed in clusters of family life, all well arranged to form the bustling villages with the market area well in view for selling and buying everything that was needed to live well. Of course, there was always the pungent smell of millet beer, the local home brew that was so popular at all times, but even more so on market day. John found it quite delicious, but realized that it was fermented and so would make him quite tipsy if he drank too much of it.

He was also awe-struck by the unbelievable torrential rains that fell during the rainy season. Everything would be bone dry, parched, during the dry season and one could never imagine the change that could occur to the bright, clear blue sky once the rains were upon them. John remembered well having been caught in one of those torrential downpours coming home from giving a mock English test in the town in preparation for the Government exams at the end of the school year.

He had gone to the Lasalle Brothers' school and had been at this most of the morning. He had gone to the school on his moped. He was famished and ready to head back home. He came out of the school and noticed that very dark clouds had gathered on the horizon. This was the usual way for the torrential downpour to start. With the dark clouds would come a huge gust of wind and then the rain would strike. As he looked up at the sky, he wondered if he would have enough time to make it to the school before the deluge hit. He had thirteen kilometres to go. Without another thought and filled with apprehension, he set out. He needed to get to the area of the lake on the outskirts of the town and over the cement dip in the road that allowed the water to flow out of the lake and into a river carrying the water out of the town. He was going as fast as he could, but the downpour struck before he reached the cement overflow dip. He was already drenched by the time he reached the overflow and the water was already gushing out of the lake and into the river. He slowed down for a moment to try to assess the situation. He had to rush as fast as he could into the gushing water and out again without falling; otherwise the flow of water was strong enough to sweep him into the river. He revved up the moped and put it to full throttle and drove into the water. He succeeded in coming out of the cement dip only to discover that he had lost his sandals. His brief case was still with him and the rain now pounded on him. He reached the turn off on the other side of the lake and came to the dirt road that led to the school. He could not stop now but he had to be careful since the road had become slick with mud. Unfortunately, he forgot about the wire barrier that was put across the dirt roads during the torrential rains to prevent the cars and trucks from passing so that the road would not be damaged too much. He saw the wire but too late. He squeezed the brake handle quickly and went sliding headlong into the wire. Luckily, the wire was at the level of the front wheel and not level with his neck; he would surely have been decapitated. As it was, he went careening sideways into the wire and tore out both the wire and the wooden picket holding it and ended up flying headlong into the bush, he on one side and the moped on the other with the engine still running and the wheels spinning. There was always a guardsman in a makeshift hut near the wire enclosure who came running out wondering if this young man had survived or simply broken his neck. John got up quickly and, picking up the moped that was still running, yelled out to the guardsman that he was fine and that he was sorry about having torn out the wire and pole but he needed to get back to the school; he felt cold and needed dry clothes and a warm meal. The guardsman waved him on glad that he had not killed himself.

John sped on and was soon at the entrance to the school. The entrance was totally flooded and the water was waist deep. He hesitated once again, just for a moment, and then, as fast as the moped could go, he ploughed into the still rising water. This time it was too much for the moped and it coughed once and died. John pushed it out of the water and into his office. He left it there and went to his room to shower and put on dry clothes. Then he rushed to the dining room. They were just beginning the meal.

"You made it," they said when they saw him.

"Yes, I did," said John, "but at what price!" He would later find out that the moped needed a great deal of repair. The water and the fall had damaged it extensively. He had received his baptism in the spirit of the rainy season. He would certainly not forget it.

This whole experience, especially doing it alone, gave him the freedom of choice that he needed. Thereafter he was able to say "yes" to continuing his objective to be a missionary. He was also filled once again with that warm, confident trust that had coursed through him that wonderful March day at the University of Dayton.

John left Upper Volta at the end of two years, with the satisfied feeling of having accomplished something wonderful and with a feeling of well-being that was totally opposite to what he had felt on his arrival there. He had lost a great amount of weight, what with a very different diet and the intense heat of that area of Africa. He arrived home at the end of June, 1973, quite skinny and ready to take on the world.

Upper Volta: Fr. John with his Students

Fr. John doing corrections.

Outing with the Boy Scouts, Burkina Faso

Chapter Eighteen

Fr. John's flight from Nairobi landed at Schiphol Airport in Amsterdam around six thirty in the morning of May 1997. He had thought much about Jules and Chris during his flight. It was crucial that he get them out of Nairobi as soon as possible. His flight to Montreal was not due till the afternoon. He had become quite familiar with the Amsterdam Airport. He liked Schiphol. There were many things to see. He would, therefore, do all that he could to keep his mind occupied during the long wait. You could even take a shower in a washroom to freshen up. There were seats that permitted you to lie down and sleep, if you so wished, or you could go to a hotel within the airport and book a small room to sleep for a few hours at a minimal cost. There were also many eating places where a snack was reasonably priced.

The time finally came for him to board his flight for Montreal. They were all gathered in the area where the gate indicated the flight number and the destination. It seemed to Fr. John that there was a very large crowd of people to board this flight, even though it was a Boeing 747. He turned to the woman standing next to him and said in a matter of fact way, "There seems to be an awful lot of passengers to board this flight, don't you think?"

"They obviously have overbooked and there have been very few cancellations," answered the woman. Fr. John had no sooner said the words when an announcement came over the system announcing that the flight to Montreal was overbooked and that they were calling upon passengers who could stay one more night in Amsterdam to please come forward. They needed five passengers to present themselves. They were offering quite enticing specials to those who would stay: a free hotel room, dinner at one of the restaurants in the airport, the possibility of calling those who were to meet them to let them know that they were not arriving till the next day, and five hundred dollars in cash. Fr. John, realizing that he had a small piece of hand luggage only and no checked luggage, decided to stay one more night. He planned to tell them once he got to the hostess taking the boarding passes. He advanced slowly and, when he came to present his boarding pass, asked the airline hostess, "Do you have your overbooked passengers yet?"

"Oh no, no one else has presented themselves. We still only have two people."

"I can stay another night," said Fr. John. "In fact I don't have any checked luggage, just this small piece of hand luggage."

"Fine," answered the hostess, "but you will need to go to the side and wait. We will need to board all the passengers leaving before we can take care of you."

"Sure, no problem," said Fr. John. He stepped to the side to wait to be taken to the restaurant for dinner. Eventually he found himself waiting with fourteen other passengers who had accepted to wait one more night before taking another flight. They gathered at one of the very fine restaurants in the airport and could order any of the meals listed on the menu. They got acquainted with each other and enjoyed the food that was served to them. Then they were taken to make the necessary phone calls to the persons who were to pick them up at the airport in Canada. Before leaving for the hotel they were given their five hundred dollars in American funds. Fr. John was quite pleased about the money; it would be the first amount he had to be set aside for Jules and Chris' upkeep. After a restful night at the Novotel Hotel, they all gathered the next morning in the hotel restaurant for a lovely breakfast of eggs, bacon and toast accompanied by coffee and fresh fruit. They returned to the airport to take their flight to Canada. It had been an exciting and very interesting experience for Fr. John. He did not regret it.

The flight from Amsterdam to Montreal was a smooth, pleasant flight. Fr. John watched the movie and this time discovered that he had not seen it before. It was one of James Bond's latest adventures. He enjoyed the movie and fell fast asleep once it was over. It was finally announced that they would soon be landing at Mirabelle Airport in Montreal and so everyone prepared themselves for the landing. Fr. John had informed no one that he was arriving by air from Africa. He would take the shuttle to downtown Montreal and go to the White Father's residence on St. Hubert Street. He had told them when he had left two weeks previously that he would be away visiting friends. The receptionist buzzed him into the house, gave him a house key and asked, "Do you know where the room is?"

"Yes, I know where the room is, I've been here many times before. Don't worry. I'll find my way."

"That's good. You'll also find snacks in the refectory downstairs, if you're hungry."

"I'll check that out later. I just need to freshen up for the moment," answered Fr. John. Another thing he often did when arriving at the house after an absence of some time, was to see who was currently in the house. Maybe there would be someone that he knew. He was pleased to discover that Fr. Denis Thibedeau, who had been in Bunia, was present. He would try to see him to give him the message from his classmate working at the Canadian Embassy in Nairobi.

Fr. John put his things in his room, freshened up and then made his way slowly to the refectory for a cup of coffee and a snack. He was pleasantly surprised to meet Fr. Denis there, having a cup of coffee. "This is a pleasant surprise finding you here," said Fr. John. "In fact you are just the man I want to see."

"Oh, really, why would you want to see me," Fr. Denis replied.

"Well, I met someone at the Canadian Embassy in Nairobi who knows you. You were classmates in the Cours Classique," said Fr. John.

"What's his name?" Fr. Denis asked.

"His name is Claude Parent and he wanted me to greet you and give you his best regards. Now my promise and mission has been accomplished." Fr. Denis chuckled pleasantly. Regardless of his pleasant smile and chuckle, Fr. Denis appeared apprehensive. He still had not gotten over the traumatic ordeal he had experienced in Bunia. He and Fr. John shared experiences at that moment. It was good to be able to share with someone who had had a similar experience. The sympathy and understanding seemed more authentic to Fr. John. Fr. Denis had had a horrendous experience. Fr. John detected a very deep sadness in him. He had loved Zaire and the people he had worked with in Bunia. His deep disappointment was apparent to Fr. John. Fr. Denis and his brothers had been attacked at their mission in Bunia. They had been threatened with death and their attackers had tied them up to the chairs in the dining- room; then they had proceeded to rob them of everything valuable that they could find. They also threatened everyone with death if they even made a sound before they had all left. Fr. John knew that it would not be an easy ordeal to overcome. There was a moment of silence as Fr. Denis tried to calm himself and catch his breath as he tried to stop the tears from flowing.

"What will you be doing now that you are back?" Fr. John asked Fr. Denis, hoping to take his mind off the painful memory.

"I will go home, first, to my family for a rest and to regain firm ground again," said Fr. Denis. "Then I will come to the Provincial House here in Montreal and I will do the Bursar's work, since I have been asked to do it. That will be fine for the time being." Fr. John was pleased to hear that because they truly needed someone who would be pleasant and welcoming for the brothers. He knew that Fr. Denis would do an excellent job of this. He gave himself whole-heartedly to the task at hand.

Then Fr. John went in search of a telephone to call his sister at home. He also hoped to reach his brother, Timmy. He would definitely need his services again in the near future. He would need to be picked up at the bus station. The bus ride would be a long one but at the moment that was all he could afford.

Formation Residence in Ibadan, Nigeria

African Dance by the Women on Mother's Day (Nigeria)

Chapter Nineteen

John came through the doors of the International section of the Halifax Airport on a Friday afternoon of June 1973; he was coming from Upper Volta via a short stop over in Paris. His family were all there to meet him and they were all horrified at how skinny he had become. He reassured them that he was feeling quite fit. He, on the other hand, couldn't get over how rosy and fat everyone looked. When he made this comment his youngest sister, Clarisse snapped back, "I'm not fat, thank you!" For some reason, that is how they all appeared to John. He would certainly have to be on guard with his comments. Everyone in the village wanted to know about his African experience, so John had many invitations to lunch and dinner. He began to feel uncomfortable as he started to put on weight again. This had to stop and he had to go easy on the sweets and the breads. Luckily, he left for studies again in September. He did not return to London, however, since he had asked to be able to continue at the training house in Ottawa. There he had lots of manual labour and chores to do in the huge, five-storey seminary building in what is present day Richelieu Park. He and his fellow seminarians were following courses at the university in the city, so instead of taking the bus home in the evenings John would set out on foot, a walk that took at least one hour and a half. This kept his weight in check.

In the course of the first year back in studies, John learned that the big seminary would be sold and that they would be moving into a house in the city, closer to the university. The old property had been established in what is present-day Vanier and their new residence was to be a house belonging to the Oblate Fathers in Ottawa South. John was beginning to get used to the moves and to the buying and selling of community houses. He wondered what the new house looked like and how big it was, since there were still many students at the seminary. To his surprise, the decision had been taken to send all the three-year students back to Europe, since they were all Europeans. The only students to be moving to the new location were the four students who were due to become deacons: one Canadian, himself, one Italian, one British and one Irish. They were to be a community of four students, two priests and one brother. They could not visit the new location too soon, since there were still students living there. Finally, the time came for the visit and what a shocking visit it turned out to be.

The house stood on a small hill on Riverdale Avenue close to Main Street and within walking distance of the university. It was an old, white, stately-looking Victorian home. One of the rooms was actually a round tower with a fairly large window in it. There was a large verandah that went around the front and left side of the house. This had been the Slattery property, as John found out later; a prominent family that owned cattle and provided the city with meat. They had owned all of the land as far down as the Ottawa River. The house and property were impressive from the exterior. When John and the others entered the house, however, John was horrified at the gloomy atmosphere and the dirty condition of the house. It seemed as if the poor house had not been cleaned in years. In the living room hung a huge light fixture that looked like it was falling apart. In the kitchen, what looked like black linoleum covered the floor. The stove and the refrigerator were positively grimy. There was what looked like ketchup stains all over the walls and ceiling. There was a back stairway leading from the kitchen to what must have been the servants' quarters, since the rooms there were rather small. The front stairway was large and stately-looking, leading to the other four bedrooms, which were quite large. The main bathroom was huge, with a very old bathtub and an enormous washbasin. John knew that it would take weeks to clean this place.

The European students gradually left for Europe and John and the other deacons-to-be began to prepare for the move. Once in the new house, they were driven to get their house in shape. John decided that the first thing for him to do was to check out the light fixture in the living room, to see if he could salvage something of it, or would it have to be taken down. To John's utter surprise, all the many parts of this lighting apparatus were inside the main part of the light fixture that looked like a huge punch bowl. John got a bucket of hot, soapy water with a bit of vinegar in it. He began to wash the many different pieces he found in the bowl-shaped apparatus. He was amazed to discover that this was a large, crystal chandelier that had been converted from candles to electricity. He gradually put all the pieces together and switched on the lights. There gleamed this beautiful, crystal chandelier. He knew that they would never take it down. It was perfect for the large sitting room that also boasted a beautiful fireplace with a mirror above it. All the students and staff came to see the transformed phenomenon.

All the members of the community cleaned, scrubbed, polished, waxed, wallpapered and painted, doing their best to remove even the tomato stains and bits of spaghetti off the walls. John soon discovered that the kitchen linoleum was not black in colour, but a beautiful, bright-red; it was the thick dirt that gave the impression that the floor was black. The refrigerator was cleaned and able to be salvaged, but the stove was far too much of a lump of grease to save. It had already given up the ghost. Gradually, the house took shape. Each student and staff member arranged his own room. They managed to find a cook for the noontime meals, since they would be out at the University for morning classes. They each took turns preparing breakfast and the evening meal. In the huge basement, they set up a laundry room and a cozy, little chapel where they could go and pray together or just be there alone with God.

Weeks turned into months and the time came for the ordination to the diaconate. The December day started out quite mild. By four in the afternoon, however, snow had started to fall. The wind came up and by the time of the diaconate service at seven-thirty in the evening, the weather had developed into a major snowstorm. John was made a deacon, but to get home from Pius X, the present St. Clement's, was a horrendous ordeal.

They got stuck in the snow but finally managed to get the car freed and sheltered from the terrible weather.

John remembered calling his mother and family in October of 1974 to tell them that the diaconate ordination would be that December and then the ordination to the priesthood would be scheduled for sometime in August, 1975. When he told his mother this on the telephone, there was dead silence at the other end.

"Are you there, Mom?" John asked, wondering why there was such silence. "Yes, I'm here," said his mother. "It is a shock to get the news. We all thought that you would never finish. We didn't know if you were just stupid, so had that much difficulty learning or if it was simply that long a programme! Now it is upon us and even the ordination to the priesthood is close. We will need to know what to do to prepare for this."

"Not to worry, Mom. I will be there by that time. But can you and someone else of the family come for the diaconate ordination?" John asked.

"I doubt that," said his mother. "We can't afford the trip and then I'm too frightened to get on an airplane. I simply can't see myself boarding one."

And so it happened that none of John's family was at his diaconate celebration. It probably turned out to be a good thing, since a terrible snowstorm brought the city to a standstill that night. He and the other members of the community had been lucky to get back to the house without incident.

Once a deacon, John worked with Fr. Skilliansius at the detention centre. It was not an easy task, since they were working with dangerous prisoners. These men often came to the services because the choir was made up mainly of women. A number of the young women in the choir had to be advised not to dress in mini-skirts or in clothes that were too tight or décolleté. It drove the prisoners mad and made them quite dangerous. Everyone co-operated and most of the time there was harmony before, during and after the service. In spite of this, the prisoners undressed the young women with their shifty eyes. This was also where John learned to do a reflection rather than a homily or a sermon. There was to be no moralizing. It turned out to be a very important time of John's training.

The time finally arrived for John to leave for home and to face the eventual ordination ceremony. Once home, he decided to take time alone to rest and pray and to prepare for this special event. Before leaving for home, he had been asked to take a mission post in Nigeria. Not going back to his beloved Upper Volta was not an easy decision to make, but he knew that it was where service was most needed that came first. So he accepted the new posting and was to be ordained and receive the necessary documents for the new mission. It all gradually fell into place. Everything went well. The ordination itself was beautiful and the church in John's home parish was filled to capacity, since many had never witnessed an ordination. It had been fifty-nine years since anyone had been ordained in the parish. Bishop Hayes of Halifax did a splendid job of the celebration, doing everything in French without the help of a ritual. He kept encouraging John, telling him that he was doing great. Normally it should have been Bishop Power the Bishop of the Antigonish Diocese to ordain John but he was sick in hospital at the time. They, therefore, had to call on the services of Bishop Hayes. All had gone well. John was very pleased on the evening of the ordination when they gathered at John's sister's house and told stories, laughed and had a wonderful time.

The one difficulty that occurred for the new posting to Nigeria was obtaining the immigration papers. It took six whole months to obtain the visa. John spent that time waiting at home, visiting with family and friends. He would periodically telephone the Nigerian Embassy in Ottawa to check on the status of the visa, but the reply each time was that it had not arrived. Time passed from one month into two months and then three and four and five. In the fifth month, he was at a charismatic prayer meeting to celebrate Eucharist for the prayer group. During their prayer of praise, one older woman, well-known to the group, began to praise God for Fr. John's appointment to the Nigerian mission and then proceeded to tell Fr. John that he must get in touch with the Nigerian embassy, as his visa had arrived. Fr. John was amazed. He had called just a week before and the response had been negative. Fr. John said nothing, but the next morning he phoned the embassy and was told that the visa had arrived. He had to pick it up himself, because he had to sign for it personally. He would have to travel to Ottawa one more time.

The Nigerian experience was one that Fr. John laboured through in many ways alone. None of the colleagues there were known to him. He was the first new missionary for the Yoruba mission since the end of the

Biafran War. He went to London, England, by air to connect to Sabena Airlines bound for Lagos. Many of the seats on the flight were empty. He noticed one religious sister sitting by herself in the far row by the window. He moved to the seat next to her and introduced himself. She was Sister Catherine of the Holy Rosary. She told him to stay with her, that a sister would be at the airport to meet her and that this sister would be able to help him get through the airport as well. She explained to Fr. John that this little Irish sister had worked for over forty years in Nigeria and had taught most of the police officers and customs agents and had taught their children in school as well. She assured him that Sister Conga would be at the bottom of the stairs of the airplane to meet them. Sister Conga was the nickname that had been given to her by the Nigerians. She had been so good to all of them that they could not help but have the utmost respect for her. If Sister Conga, for example, needed to get to the hospital, and downtown Lagos was congested, she simply called the chief of police of Lagos and all the traffic was stopped so that she could get through. Sure enough, at the bottom of the stairway of the airplane was a short, plump little Irish Sister who embraced both of them. "Oh, Father, give me your papers and I'll get them cleared," said Sister Conga. In no time, she was back, not just with the papers, but with the baggage, as well. The passports still needed to be stamped with entry visas, so they all got into the long line-up in front of the one desk belonging to the visa agent. The one, young, Nigerian female agent looked up at the line-up and, seeing Sister Conga at the end of the line, exclaimed, "Ah, Sister, there you are," she yelled. "Please, everyone, step aside for a moment and allow Sister Conga to come through." Sister Conga, Sister Catherine and John stepped to the front of the line. Passports were stamped and they were cleared through. "Oh, Sister, it is so wonderful to see you again. I hope you are well, "she said. With a huge smile on her face, Sister Conga answered, "I'm very well, my dear, and I thank you immensely." The three of them proceeded through the exit doors of the airport. As Fr. John came through, Brother Wolfgang and Fr. Heinz were there to meet him. They had a sign in their hands with Fr. John's name written on it so that he would recognize who they were. Fr. John said good-bye to the sisters and they exchanged hopes of seeing one another again. With that farewell, he joined his colleagues.

The Nigerian assignment was a very difficult one for Fr. John. Being new and alone, anything he would suggest received the comment, "We already tried that. It doesn't work, so let it go."

Fr. John suggested that they initiate scripture lessons even in the outstations and especially with the youth to counteract those who were using scripture to discredit the teaching on Eucharist, priesthood and certain of the sacraments. The youth were optimistic, but Fr. Coffey accosted Fr. John at one of the community meetings one Sunday afternoon. "Hey, DeCoste, are you the one who wants to teach the Bible in the bush?"

"Why not? Other groups especially the Scripture Union are doing it and making us look like fools," replied Fr. John.

"No, no. That is not what they need," replied Fr. Coffey. "Build them chapels and give them the bloody sacraments. That's all they need," said Fr. Coffey.

"Oh, yes, keep them in ignorance and the laughing stock of the bush. We get better at this every year." Fr. John found the narrow mentality and the utter confusion of the Nigerian mission so depressing that he asked not to return to the Nigerian mission for a second tour of duty. But his departure turned out to be a tragic one. Fr. John was visiting the bush outstations where he had worked before going on home leave. He still had a week of visiting to do and then he would join a priest friend, Fr. Gabriel, in Spain and together they would visit through Spain, something he had always wanted to do. One afternoon, however, Bishop Julius arrived at the Iseyin Mission that Fr. John was visiting. As he sat down for afternoon tea, he mentioned to Fr. John that a telegram had arrived at the diocesan headquarters for him. "A telegram for me?" asked Fr. John. "Bishop, for North Americans, a telegram means one of two things, serious illness or death."

"Oh, my goodness, I didn't know that," replied Bishop Julius.

With a terrible foreboding in the pit of his stomach, Fr. John threw his bags into his Volkswagen, and left the mission, heading for the diocesan headquarters. He didn't remember making the trip. He drove very fast through the bush. He stopped first at the school where he had been teaching, and Fr. Joseph came to meet him with the telegram. "I'm sorry about your Mom's illness," he told Fr John. 'She has had a very bad heart attack and is in hospital and the family needs you to contact them. Unfortunately, the telegram is already two weeks old."

"Oh, God, what do I do?" said Fr. John. Fr. Joseph suggested that they leave for the city of Ibadan and see if they could get through by phone from there.

It took Fr. John twelve hours to get through to his sister in Canada. When she answered the phone and heard his voice, she said, "Where are you, for heaven's sake?"

"What do you mean? I'm in Africa. Where else?" said Fr. John.

"In Africa? You're still in Africa? But we sent the telegram two weeks ago," said his sister.

"But I'm out in the bush. To get a telegram so quickly is impossible," he replied. "Tell me quickly. Did she die? Did Mom die?"

"No, she's still in the hospital, but she's scared to die and wants desperately to see you. Come home as soon as you can."

Fr. John left the next morning on the first flight possible. Fortunately, he was able to take the same flight with Iberian Airways that he had been booked on, but a week earlier. Fr. John had originally planned to make a trip with a White Father friend through Spain and then join his friend Margaret to see Scotland and Ireland. But this was not to be. He had to get home before anything worse happened to his mother. It turned out to be a long, tiring flight with a stop-over in England. Four days later, Fr. John walked into his mother's hospital room and gave her a big hug and a kiss. She started to cry.

"I thought you'd be glad to see me," said Fr. John. "Here you are crying." They both laughed in between the tears.

Fr. John's mother stayed in the hospital for another week and then was discharged. She returned home in fear that she could have another heart attack at any time and die. This was very difficult for everyone. Fr. John often prayed over her especially when she would have a panic attack and go running through the house pulling at her hair and tearing at her blouse. He would take her, sit her down, pray over her calmly and anoint her with the oil of the sick. It was a tremendous help, but Fr. John knew that he would not be able to stay with his mom and his stepfather for ever. He needed to work in a parish to be able to pay the bills that were now coming his way. He went to see the bishop of his home diocese and received permission to stay in the neighbouring parish, about thirteen kilometres away. The Bishop said "Well, you would be doing us a great service if you went to Immaculate Heart of Mary parish not far from your sister's house. Fr. Forest has just found out that he has cancer and will probably be gone in six months."

So Fr. John moved bag and baggage into the fine, Victorian rectory. Fr. Forest had his room and bath on the first floor, so Fr. John took a bedroom upstairs. The housekeeper, Valerie, did not live in, but came each day and, besides cooking and cleaning, took care of all of Fr. Forest's needs. She sometimes slept on the sofa in the sitting room next to Fr. Forest's bedroom, in case he needed anything.

To everyone's surprise, Fr. Forest only lasted until December. He had fallen ill in mid-August and he died on December twenty-first; he was buried on the eve of Christmas Eve, surrounded by the Christmas lights and decorations. Fr. John told the people that they would not take down the Christmas decorations for the funeral service, since he knew that would have been Fr. Forest's wish.

Fr. John went each day to see his mom and stepfather. His sister, living close-by, would frequently drop in as well. She was concerned about their mother's diet. She was eating too much fat, oil and butter. His stepfather could not really take care of her. Being in denial himself about her illness, he would often say that she was fine and just needed to get out more. Fr. John's mother would simply shake her head and look sad.

One evening, Fr. John's sister, Della, called him and asked him to come over to his mother's house. She was sure that there was something drastically wrong with their mother. She had gone to see her around suppertime and she had not recognized her daughter and had just sat in her rocking chair in the kitchen, staring straight ahead as if in oblivion. Their mother had attempted to say something at one point and had stayed staring ahead with both arms raised in the air as if frozen in position. Della then asked her mother if she was not going to have supper, which was on the table. She obediently got up to go to the table. Della noticed at that moment that her back and legs were wet. She had wet herself without realizing it. She asked her mother why she was all wet and Rose answered simply that she must have sat in some water. That frightened Della, so she called him to come over.

When Fr. John arrived, he found his mother acting very strangely. He spoke to her, but received no answer. He called the doctor immediately and explained the situation. The doctor told John that this was not normal; there was definitely something wrong. He explained that her nerves could affect her in many ways, but not to the point that she would lose control of her bladder and not realize it. He agreed to have her admitted into the hospital. The following day they made the trip to Halifax where she was put through a series of tests. One of the doctors, Dr. O'Brien, felt that he knew what was wrong with her. He prescribed a series of scans and once he had the results he called the family into his office. He had news that they needed to discuss. It was not good news.

They all arrived at Dr. O'Brien's office on a Thursday afternoon, anxious to find out what the news would be. They were sitting in front of his desk when he walked in. He sat down and did his best to put things gently.

"What your mother has is incurable. The scans show that she is in a fairly advanced stage of Alzheimer's disease. Her immediate memory is affected; her long-term memory is still intact. We have had to take her off much of the medication she was on and simply leave her with her heart pill and the medication for diabetes. She needs to be with someone that she is comfortable with and in whom she has confidence. She must not return to her house, because she cannot care for herself and her husband is not able to care for her. With the state of her health, I do not give her more than two years to live." They all sat stunned by the news. Then, looking at one another, they said, "Well, if she has a second heart attack, let's hope it takes her, because we do not want to see her like a vegetable, not knowing us. That would kill us."

Fr. John knew that the next two years would be rough. They all left for home to prepare for her eventual release from the hospital.

The basement of Della's house was completely revamped. Bedrooms were built, as well as a bathroom, a sitting room, a laundry area and a small workshop. It did not take much time and everything was ready for their mother's homecoming. She did not seem to mind not going back to her own house; she could see it from the front door of Della's house. Once in a while, when Rose looked out the front door window she would ask who was living there. Each time she was told that it was rented and that a very good friend of the family was living in the house. She would turn away quite satisfied with the answer. Once she asked Fr. John if they had left any furniture in the house. He told her that they had.

"That is nice, don't you think?" she answered. "At least they can use whatever is there rather than let it go to rack and ruin. Fr. John and Della breathed a sigh of relief when they heard her, because they knew that their mother had been very fussy about her house. Fr. John's stepfather moved in with their mother to be with her at Della's house. They shared the same bedroom, which was the master bedroom close to the bathroom.

However this situation was to take a strange turn. Fr. John had to go to Halifax one weekend and would be gone for several days. While in Halifax, a phone call from his sister brought him to full attention. He came home immediately and discovered that his stepfather, Raymond, was now the one who had fallen ill. He had had a stroke and could not use his right hand. He tried to camouflage his disability by attempting to eat his food with his left hand. But he would end up smearing it all over himself, the table and the floor. His children had to be called in to convince him to see the doctor and finally go to the hospital. Finally he consented to this after much coaxing by one of his sons.

After a week in the hospital, Raymond checked himself out one afternoon and before the nurse could stop him, he left for home on foot. The nurse, rather distraught, telephoned the family to let them know that he was on his way home on foot. His son, Billy, was quickly called by Fr. John, to let him know what was happening. Billy rushed to pick him up. The doctor was called and came to the house to see him. He told the family that it was alright for him to be home, but there were two things that he must not do: take long walks or sit directly in the sunlight. The time was August and the sun was hot. Raymond, however, did not obey. One bright, sunny afternoon he sat out in the sun on the verandah for hours and after sitting in the sun, walked quite a distance to the grocery store for cigarettes. That proved to be too much. He had to return to the hospital within the next few days, worse than ever. He eventually got pneumonia while in the hospital and his condition worsened. This was too much for him and he died shortly after. Fr. John had to break the news to his mother, who took it well, since she knew that he was sick. She had been able to visit him at least once during his time in the hospital. Her own illness made it difficult for her to get around easily. One thing that she did ask on learning about his death was whether he had been alone when he died. Fr. John had to do some fibbing about this situation. He told his mother, "Mom, do not worry I was there when he died and he had a peaceful death." It would have been devastating for his mother to think that her husband had died alone.

The funeral arrangements for Raymond were all taken care of by his own sons and daughters, who did not even bother to ask Fr. John's or any of his family's advice, not even Fr. John's mother, who was still able to give her opinion on things. Fr. John let this family know, however, at the wake-keeping, that he, himself, would officiate at the service. No one contradicted him on that.

It took Fr. John's mom time to adjust to her husband's absence, but she did adjust. The doctor had to be called to make certain that everything was functioning properly, especially regarding her medication, since the shock of the loss of a loved one could set off a serious reaction. Everything seemed to be going well and she continued to help with little chores around the house, listening to music, watching her favourite TV programmes and occasionally glancing out the front door window, as if she needed to make sure that her little, white bungalow was still there at the road.

August passed on into September, September into October and Fr. John was offered a trip to Florida and to Honduras by a priest-friend who wanted company while traveling to visit a priest-friend doing missionary work in Central America. At first, Fr. John hesitated, not wanting to leave his sister alone with the care of their mother. He mentioned this trip one evening while talking to his mother to see what her reaction would be.

"Why don't you go on this trip?" she asked. "It will do you good to get away. You've been back from the African missions for almost two years now and you've not even taken a little holiday for yourself. Go, I'm fine here with Della. Everything will be OK. Don't worry. I'll be fine."

Fr. John decided to accept the invitation to travel. Before leaving, however, he decided that he would take photographs of his mother. "We don't have even one photograph of mom, do we?" he asked his sister one evening. "Mom will be gone and we won't have a photograph of her." So one morning he mentioned to his mother that he would have a friend come over and take photographs. That would be done before leaving on the trip. His mother replied, "Don't do that now, wait till you come back from your trip."

"No, mom, I'm not waiting," answered Fr. John. "This coming Sunday, you'll put on a nice blouse and your strand of pearls and we'll take the pictures. I want to have the pictures when I come back from the trip." His mother did not protest any longer and the following Sunday the photographs were taken. Later, when the photographer had gone and Rose was out of hearing range, John said to his sister, "If I wait and something happens to her while I'm away, I will always regret it." He was to be gone for two whole weeks with his friend; he would be back on November 5.

Three days after the photographs were taken, Fr. John and his priest-friend left for Florida and Honduras. It was a beautiful trip and, whenever Fr. John could, he would phone home to see how things were going. Everything was fine until two days before they were to return home. They had been visiting the mission outstations and the countryside around Tegucigalpa, the Honduran capital, returning to the main mission around five o'clock that afternoon. There was a message waiting for Fr. John. He needed to call St. Martha's Hospital emergency unit. A number had been left as a contact number. His sister Martine answered. She informed him that their mother had had a severe heart attack and was at present in the emergency unit. The doctor held little hope that she would recover. It was November 2, the Feast of All Souls, a special feast commemorating all departed brothers and sisters. That same night, his sister called back to inform him that their mother had passed away at ten p.m. that night. Fr. John had already made arrangements to return home and would be taking a flight to Miami early next morning. He would hopefully get a connecting flight to Toronto and then one to Halifax. When Fr. John and his priest-friend boarded the flight in Honduras, they told the airline hostess about Fr. John's situation and that he needed to make the connecting flight to Toronto. When they landed in Miami, a flight attendant was there to meet Fr. John and took him through all the security measures immediately, jumping all the queues. He made the Toronto connection with very little time to spare. In Toronto he had to wait for a later flight, since the early flight had already departed. The wait was agonizing. He wept and prayed silently. He tried to rest, but was too agitated to be still. Then the thought struck him: thank God he had taken the photographs before leaving.

He arrived in Halifax after midnight and a friend of the family was there to meet him. It was the wee hours of the morning before he got home. He did not bother to sleep, but shaved and showered, got into his car and left for his sister's house. While on the way to Della's, he stopped at the funeral parlour to make a lone visit to his mother. She looked very peaceful as she lay there in her casket. His sisters had dressed her in the dress she had worn for his ordination four years previously. She had told his sisters to put that dress on her the day she would pass away. She had died with a smile on her face. He felt calmer as he looked down at her in peaceful repose. He finished his prayer and went to the door of the Funeral Parlour leading into the kitchen section of the residents' quarters. He thanked Louise, the undertaker's wife for the beautiful job of preparing his mother's body for viewing. "How do like the way I fixed the neck part of that beautiful dress?" Louise asked.

"That is very well done," answered Fr. John "You certainly took care of the low cut neckline of the dress, I must say."

"The neckline was a bit low and showed too much cleavage," said Louise, "so I took a piece of the material from the bottom hemline of the dress and inserted into the neckline. I could easily do that since the dress had a full length skirt to it. I think that it turned out quite fine, don't you?"

"It is just perfect, no one would ever know that you did that. It's great!"

Fr. John left the funeral parlour and went on to his sister's. They were all happy that he was finally home. His mother had passed away a mere two months after her husband's passing. It had all been quite a traumatic ordeal.

Grieving was very difficult. Fr. John remembered what the family had said when they had been told that their mother had Alzheimer's Disease. God had answered their prayers. At the same time, it turned out to be a sad Christmas, that year of 1979.

Fr. John finished the pastoral year at the little parish of the Immaculate Heart of Mary. Permission granted, he would be returning to Africa in August of 1980. Della asked him if he were not going back too soon after so much death and grieving. Shouldn't he take more time to find inner peace? But he did not think so. He was actually running away from it all, but he was blind to this fact at the time. The preparations for leaving kept him busy and he did not have too much time to think. He thought himself free. He would later discover how wrong he had been.

The photographs of him and his mother arrived in early December. His mother would never see them, of course. But they had turned out beautifully. Fr. John had copies made for all the members of the family. He also made sure that there was one with him in his luggage before he left for Africa. The memory of his mother looking through the front door window the day he had left for the seminary in the U.S. would come to his mind once in a while when he was preparing to return to Africa. There were mixed emotions of pain and peace when this would happen. He needed to let it go!

Fr. John was quite happy to return to Upper Volta after so long an absence. He was surprised to learn, however, that he was to go to the diocese that he had least liked when he had done his first tour of duty when he was a seminarian. He was to be working with the Gurunsi people whose language was tonal. He had already struggled with a tonal language, Yoruba, in Nigeria; Yoruba, had been very difficult to learn. He did not know how well he would fare with the Gurunsi language, known as Lele. He had not liked Koudougou very much in those first years when he had visited there. He had not found it welcoming. There had been a coldness about it. He was to be at one of the largest missions of the diocese called Reo, in Lele, Gyo. The mission station sat on a hill overlooking the village, like a sentinel guarding the faithful and ensuring that no one stepped out of line. The church was a huge, open, concrete building, cold and uninviting.

Fr. John arrived one afternoon in August when there was only one of the priests present at the mission. The other confrere, who was the pastor of the parish, was away on home-leave and would be back in October. An African seminarian was helping at the mission; John-Paul was very welcoming and friendly. The confrere with him in community was a fine man, but very much of a workaholic. He did not know when to stop for a moment to take a breather. They spoke French when together as a community, but with most of the people they spoke Lele. Fr. John needed to take time to learn the language. But there was no language school for this. He had to contact an old, retired catechist, who was well versed in both French and the local language and so would help him with local expressions, short conversations and greetings as a starter. The catechist's name was Monsieur Honore. Fr. John was to learn more than the language from Monsieur Honore.

Fr. John found himself rather isolated at this mission. There was no one else beside Monsieur Honore to help him with the language. He found it very hard not having someone to discuss things with and to practice with. Everyone was so very busy; there was no time for just sitting and talking and having a cup of tea or coffee. They would rise at five-thirty in the morning, go to the church to pray together with only a tilly lamp for light. This was followed by the celebration of the Eucharist. Breakfast came after the Eucharist. Fr. John enjoyed breakfast very much. After breakfast, he would take the moped and go to Monsieur Honore's house in the village. When he returned, he would spend time reviewing what he had learned and eventually convinced the seminarian, John-Paul, to record the conversations on cassette and record the Eucharist and prayers in the Lele language. By then, it would be lunch time and after lunch they would take a welcome siesta. Once the siesta was over, Fr. John would be expected to look into the numerous files of the families of the parish and the outstations. On weekends, he was expected to go by moped with the seminarian or the other confrere to visit the numerous outstations of the parish. There was a chapel for each outstation. The only time that they stopped for a breather, apart from the siesta, was in the late evening after the meal when they would sit out on the patio in the back part of the compound. They would look up at the bright, night sky with its myriad of stars and the occasional satellite speeding across the sky. Fr. John often wished that he could reach the satellite and soar back home, so lonely and alone did he feel.

Fr. John was in Reo hardly a week when he began feeling the aloneness, the heat, the heaviness of the uninteresting work and the difficulty of the language pressing in on him. It was at that moment that he realized that he had returned to the missions too soon. A terrible, foreboding feeling gripped him and he felt an overwhelming fear in the pit of his stomach: the fear of losing someone else in the family, and this time he would not be there. An oppressive heaviness would overtake him at times. He could not concentrate on the language; the words and expressions would not stay in his head. He felt out of place and totally alone. He began looking for excuses to leave, to return home. He just wanted to run away. He would dream a very troubled dream about losing his sister and not being there to bear the loss. He would wake up in the middle of the night and would feel totally oppressed by the mosquito net around his bed. His legs seemed as heavy as cement and he had trouble sitting up on the side of the bed. He felt a terrible numbness throughout his body and he thought he would die. The loss and the grief that he had not experienced at home now overtook him. He would cry for hours and then find it difficult to wake up the next morning, since he had not slept well. Throughout the day, he would put on a façade of light-heartedness and he would pretend to be interested in the daily life of the mission. It was totally exhausting. He soon found out that he could not go to Monsieur Honore's later in the day for the language training. If he did so, Monsieur Honore would have spent hours at the village market and he would be drunk, which made it very impossible to get him to translate even simple expressions. Each small expression would become a treatise on the Lele language and Fr. John understood nothing. So he stuck to the early-morning schedule; it was a surer time of the day to learn the language.

One big help to Fr. John was the recording of his dreams. When he would awaken in the middle of the night, he always had a paper and pen on his night table; he would immediately record what he had dreamed. He would put it aside and try to go back to sleep. The next day, he would reread what he had written and then do the analysis of the words as he had learned in his Jungian psychology course. In this way, he discovered a pattern of thought flowing through his dreams. That is how he came to realize that he had not allowed himself to mourn his mother's death sufficiently and discovered that he had a terrible fear of losing someone else in the family. He also discovered that this person was his sister Della, the one most like his mother. This made him realize even more how much he wanted to return home.

There was a convent of French sisters that formed part of the Reo Mission. The sisters were quite easy to talk to; he always got along well with religious sisters. One afternoon he went to the sisters' house and, knocking on the door, told the sister who answered that he needed to talk to someone. He told her that he felt extremely isolated and lonely in this mission on the hill. Sister Paula, with whom he had spoken a number of times after morning prayers and mass, invited him in, offered him coffee and biscuits and quietly listened to what he had to say. To his surprise, she agreed with him that the brothers at the mission were workaholics and she felt that they were drowning in their loneliness; they needed, somehow, to fill the emptiness within. She suggested that he go to the main mission in Koudougou, at the diocesan centre. There he would meet Fr. Thomas, who was Canadian-born, but belonged to the British province of their missionary community. He would find an open-minded, comforting and warm person ready to listen to him and full of common sense and solid advice. That afternoon, Fr. John did not hesitate and went and sought out Fr. Thomas. He found him in his office, quietly reading and writing. "Come in, Fr. John, by all means, come in and sit down. It is so good to see you. I do hope all is going well in Reo."

"Oh, all is well in Reo, Father. All is too well," replied Fr. John. "They don't seem to know that anything else exists except work. That is a catastrophe for me. I don't know what to do about it." So Fr. John proceeded to tell him all he had been going through and the terrible foreboding feeling of losing someone else in the family. "I believe that I need to go back, to leave here and return home. My mourning has not been completed and my life is filled with fear and loneliness. It is so bad that I feel I will die myself!" replied Fr. John.

"My dear Fr. John, it is quite normal for you to feel this way. It is also very possible that you have left too soon after your mother's death. But I do think that you can do your grieving here. I do not think that you need to return home to complete your mourning process. You must continue doing what you have been doing with your dreams and then find a time during your day to bring it all to prayer. Then, once a week, you will come to me and we will talk and see how you are progressing. What do you think of that?" Fr. John silently looked at Fr. Thomas. Fr. Thomas continued speaking, "Oh, of course, if it becomes too difficult for you to cope, we can always arrange for you to return, but try to give yourself more time. You can also go to the post office in town. There you will find an international telephone line and you can call your sister. It is even quite reasonably priced. How would that be?" he asked.

'That does sound better, "Fr. John replied. He felt some relief and, after chatting a bit more and having a cup of tea, he left for the Reo Mission again. Before taking the road to Reo, however, he stopped at the post office to get through to his sister. It was late at night at home, but they did not care. It was just good to hear her voice and she his. He slept better that night, but never forgot to record his dreams even those of that very night.

Fr. John got through his grieving process with the help of Fr. Thomas and the sisters. His confreres were none the wiser for it. Fr. Victor, who had been on home-leave when Fr. John arrived, eventually returned to Reo. He was a gentle soul and Fr. John got on with him quite well. The struggle with the language continued for Fr. John, but he eventually did celebrate Eucharist in the Lele language. The workload was exhausting, but he made it through the first pastoral year. The time of the annual retreat finally arrived. It was during this retreat that Fr. John was to get another surprise, albeit a pleasant one this time.

Fr. John was praying quietly and alone in the warm sunshine while on retreat at the retreat house of the Fathers of St. Camillus. He had resolved in prayer that he would continue at the Mission of Reo and put even more effort into mastering the Lele language, but he had told God that he was open to a change as well, since his best work, he felt, was in teaching. He placed the whole situation in God's hands and felt at peace with his decision. That afternoon while he was praying in the small grotto that was part of the retreat house, his regional superior, Fr. Ronald, came to see him. "Do you mind if we have a chat?" he asked.

"By all means. Join me," answered Fr. John. "We have just learned that Brother Patrick will be leaving the seminary because of his health; he needs to have serious surgery. The seminary will need an English teacher when classes resume. Bishop Bayala has asked me if I would approach you about taking the position," Fr. Ronald said, looking at Fr. John questioningly. Fr. John could not believe his ears. He would be overjoyed to be the English teacher for the seminary. He would also be very happy to do spiritual direction with the students. Fr. John was then informed by Fr. Ronald that most of the staff there were Africans: the principal was an African priest, so was the priest in charge of liturgy and sports and the sisters who taught there were quite open and pleasant to be with as colleagues. Fr. John was actually quite pleased to hear this, since Africanization had been one of his pet peeves concerning the Mission of Reo; it was the oldest mission of the diocese and was, as yet, not Africanized. Before his arrival, a newly-ordained, African priest had been appointed to Reo, but when the Regional Council found out that Fr. John was arriving, the newly-ordained African priest had been sent to another mission. Fr. John had been very upset when he learned what had happened in this case. Maybe now they would appoint an African priest to the mission, since he was leaving. It would take several more years before the Mission of Reo would be Africanized. They really needed new, young blood in that mission.

Fr. John went to see Bishop Bayala when he returned from retreat. Bishop Bayala was very pleased that Fr. John had accepted the new posting that had come at such short notice. He told him to see Brother Patrick, look at the programmes and move as soon as he could, because they needed another presence at the seminary, as many were on home-leave and holidays. Fr. John quickly prepared everything and by mid-August he was on his way to the seminary with all of his gear, singing as he drove along the Koudougou road. By this time, he had acquired a small, three-horse-power French car that looked like a little bread van; it had been given to him by the pastor of the Reo Mission. He had told Fr. John, "It is sitting there in the mission garage and if you can get it going and in shape, it is yours." He was delighted and had asked Brother Stanislaus, from the cathedral mission garage, if he would come and get the car going for him. This did happen and Fr. John rolled into the seminary compound looking like the baker delivering bread. It was just him, however, with his gear all ready to teach. He would have all the hundred and fifty students for English, from grades six to twelve. He would also be in charge of Scouts and would take his weekly turn on liturgy and daily prayer. He had plenty of work; there would be no time to be bored.

Fr. John enjoyed teaching the students; he truly felt that this was where he belonged. They all loved learning English and enjoyed it immensely when Fr. John would teach them English songs. That was their favourite moment in English class.

Fr. John was at the school hardly a week and still in the process of organizing his classes when a curious incident took place, one that he would laugh about weeks later. It was about ten thirty in the morning and he felt like having a bit of a snack with a cold drink. He slowly made his way over to the refectory since he knew that the kitchen personnel often kept extra yogurt in the refrigerator, as well as bottles of cold water.

He took one small yogurt from the refrigerator, sweetened it and walked to the door of the dining-room. To his great surprise, there, standing on the verandah, practically next to him, was this huge lizard-like creature, staring directly at him. Fr. John froze on the spot and did not know what to do! Would this creature attack him or what? The nausea and fear welled up inside of him! He did not dare move or scream, deathly frightened of provoking this animal. Fr. John looked carefully around to see if there was someone around to come to his aid. Fr. Jim Van Doorn was in the garden not too far from him. As Fr. Jim looked up, Fr. John gestured to him to come. He quickly ran over to Fr. John and on seeing the creature yelled to Fr. John, "Don't be afraid, it is harmless!" As soon as the animal heard Fr. Jim's voice, it turned and fled. Fr. John, still trembling with fear, went into the dining-room to sit down. His heart was pounding and he had a difficult time breathing.

Fr. Jim apologized for not informing him about their four-legged friends at the school. "Do not be afraid of those giant looking lizards," said Fr. Jim. "They're iguanas and there are so many because the iguana is the totem of the family who gave this land to the church for a school. If we harm one of them it is harming one of the family's ancestors. During the school year you'll see them all over the property. They come out during classes since it is so quiet, but the minute you take notice of them, they run under the buildings or under the tree roots. They are quite strange looking, I must admit."

Classes began for the new school year and the months went by filled with many enjoyable classes and activities. One afternoon Fr. John was coming out of the classroom with his arms loaded with books and assignment papers; Dieudonne, one of his students who was in sixth grade, was accompanying him with his arms also filled with books. Fr. John was in rather a hurry to get the English books he was carrying back to the library. As a result, he made a wrong step and twisted his ankle on a stone and went head over heels with the load of books. He fell flat on his face with the books flying in every direction. He found himself not able to move since he had dislocated his shoulder. As he was not moving and not saying anything, Dieudonne began to scream at the top of his voice, "Help someone, help, Father is dead, he's not moving, he's dead!" Two of the teachers who were close by came running.

"What is wrong, Father?" they asked. "Are you hurt? Can't you get up?"

"I can't move. I think I've dislocated my shoulder," said Fr. John. "Please try to help me up and then we can see what the damage is!"

When they turned him over, they all saw that his shoulder was completely out of its socket. He was in terrible pain and could not walk on his own. One of the teachers managed to get his arm settled against his waist and put him into one of the vehicles. He drove him to the hospital to see the doctor. The doctor at that moment was extremely busy with a very long line of patients waiting to see him; he told Fr. John to go to the operating room to wait for him. Fr. John was sure the wait would be an extremely long one after having seen the line-up in the office. He said a prayer, "Please God, let me get through this without too much trouble and without having to stay here the night!" The hospital gave good service but cleanliness was not its strong point.

Fr. John was brought into the operating room and placed on a chair. Two African male operating room orderlies were present and were in the process of cleaning things up since there had been surgeries throughout the day. They told Fr. John that the doctor would probably be along shortly and that they were going off duty as soon as the clean up had been completed. Fr. John thanked them and settled down to wait. After a good thirty minute wait, the orderlies looked at one another and said, "Let us see if we can do something for Father here, otherwise he will be here all night and I'm sure he would like to get back to the school. Right, Father?"

"You are so right! I would appreciate it immensely if you could do something for me now!" he answered.

The two orderlies placed a clean white sheet on the floor of the operating room and laid Fr. John on it being careful to place his arm in the proper position; they placed his hand and forearm gently across his stomach, then with a gentle sweeping motion brought his hand and arm outstretched to the side of his head, all this without causing any pain. They told him that if this procedure did not work that he would probably have to go to the main hospital in the Capital to have a procedure done. Fr. John prayed once again that this not happen. Both orderlies took a large white bed sheet and rolled it up length-wise like a long twist of rope; then one of them placed it in a u-shape around Fr. John's arm pit and shoulder holding the two ends together and standing at a distance away from his head so the twisted bed sheet was taut. The second orderly took Fr. John's hand and gently stretched out his arm, also some distance away from his colleague. Both orderlies said to one another, "At the count of three we both pull on our end and hope that his shoulder snaps back into place. Are we ready? Fr. John, are you ready as well?" asked one of the orderlies.

"As ready as I'll ever be," he answered.

"One, two, three, pull!" Fr. John heard a quick snap and the shoulder went into its socket! He could not believe it! A miracle! One of the orderlies prepared a sling for his arm and told him to keep it on for five days and then he would be able to use it. Fr. John could not stop thanking the two men for their quick and tremendous work. They were also quite proud of their accomplishment. Fr. John would not have to go to the Capital after all. He was extremely pleased!

Just as the arm sling was being completed, the doctor walked in. Looking over the situation, he questioned, "All done, already?"

"Procedure completed!" they answered.

"Good show, marvelous job!" answered the doctor.

Thanking them all once again, Fr. John and his companion returned to the school. Everyone was overjoyed to find out that all had gone so well.

However, the work, the heat and the bouts with malaria soon took their toll and Fr. John became so exhausted, that he succumbed to a very serious illness.

It was a warm, bright, sunny morning as was usual at the end of the dry season in Upper Volta; a bit too warm, really. Fr. John knew that the rainy season would be upon them in a few weeks' time with its fresh, cool breezes. He woke up on that bright morning feeling strange and not very refreshed from his night of rest; he was not at all ready to face this new day. As he lay there in bed, he thought of all that he needed to do to get himself ready for the various chores of the day and simply thinking about getting up, shaving, showering, brushing his teeth and getting over to the chapel for Eucharist, exhausted him totally. He found his spirits sinking deeper into darkness and a horrendous feeling of depression came over him. He just did not feel like getting up, but he was on Chapel duty and so he forced himself up. He made it over to the Chapel, laboured through the Eucharist and, on coming out of the Chapel, headed for the dining-room.

It was at that moment that he realized that even the thought of food made him nauseous and he gagged as if he was going to throw up. Sr. Bernadette, the school nurse, was just next to him as they walked towards the dining-room for breakfast.

"Sister," he said, "I'm wondering why I feel so exhausted this morning and why I feel such terrible nausea just at the thought of food!"

Sister Bernadette turned to look at Fr. John and exclaimed, "My dear Fr. John, you sound as if you are well on your way into hepatitis! You go immediately to your room and I will be over to see you shortly."

Fr. John did as he was told. Without delaying too much, Sr. Bernadette came to his room. She examined his eyes and found that they had already begun to turn yellow. She got him to get into bed, opened the windows for air to circulate and left to get him some fresh fruit. In no time at all he really felt sick to his stomach and by the time Sr. Bernadette had returned with fresh fruit and water Fr. John's skin colour was turning yellow. By the next day, he was yellow all over and he began to throw up the little food that he had consumed. He thought for sure, that he would vomit his insides. It was an awful feeling. Sister Bernadette insisted that he stay in bed and continued to nurse him with soups, yoghurt and fruit. His liver had stopped functioning and he had come down with a serious bout of hepatitis. He would need complete bed rest and not be permitted to go up and down the stairs from his room. Fr. John felt as if all the energy had drained from his body. When he tried to read he would become very nauseated and his head felt very heavy; then his eyes would hurt and he would develop a huge headache. He had to remain completely still just lying on his bed to rest. However, his blood would need to be checked to discern the level of bile in his blood. So Sr. Bernadette booked him for an appointment to see the doctor at the General Hospital of Koudougou and to get blood tests done at the laboratory of the hospital. The blood tests revealed that he had over a thousand units of bilirubin in his blood; the normal count was twenty-five units or less. He definitely had a bad case of hepatitis. He would need complete, prolonged bed rest for at least three months.

For ten years Fr. John had had a small, well-trimmed beard. Since he now found it very tiring to keep it trimmed, he began to develop sores under the hairs as it got longer, and as the perspiration from the heat of the day caused itching. So he mustered up enough courage to shave the beard off. That felt so much better and cooler and, of course, the itching disappeared. There were red blotches that had already formed from the sores and the scratching. Gradually the red blotches disappeared. But then, the rainy season had begun and cooler temperatures made the climate more bearable. Fr. John would take long, long naps on the chaise-longue that Sister Bernadette had provided for him. This simple bed could be placed on the verandah outside his bedroom.

Fr. John thanked God that the school year had been pretty well over when the hepatitis struck, so most of the students had gone home. He had also been able to get all of his exams and assignments corrected and graded so he didn't have that to worry about. Everything had been finished and handed in to the director's office before he had ended up in bed.

The students who lived close by in the town knew about his illness. Some of them came to visit and chat with him as he lay there on his chaise-longue on the balcony. When they first saw him without his beard they did not comment but could not help but stare at him. Fr. John noticed this and after a few visits said to them, "You are looking at me in such a strange way. Is it that you think I look so very different without the beard?"

They laughed and seemed relieved that he had brought it up. Jacob, one of his brighter students replied, "Oh yes, Father, you do look so different! But really you must let your beard grow back again because now you look too young! That is very strange and it is as if you are no longer the same person."

Fr. John found this quite amusing. But they would get used to it. He had no intention of letting his beard grow back again. He would have to get used to shaving every day once again.

After three months in bed, he resurfaced. He was able to complete his second year of teaching, which completed his first three-year term of duty and made him eligible for a three-month home-leave. Fr. John knew that three months would not be sufficient for him to regain his full strength. He had to tell Bishop Bayala that he would need to stay home longer to recuperate and so would not be back for the following September. Bishop Bayala answered, "You have done a fine job. We are sorry to lose you, but your health comes first. Go and get well. Come back to us, if you can."

Fr. John appreciated his understanding heart and warm words. He left for home as soon as the school year came to an end.

It was good to be home. He couldn't believe that he had gotten through those three years after the terrible time with grieving, loss and loneliness in the beginning, but his stubborn streak had won out in the end and his determination to see it through with the help of prayer had allowed him to get through the experience. Now he walked the length and breadth of the village, enjoying the ocean and the salt sea air and just stopping to chat with people. He received many invitations for lunch and dinner and to speak to groups about Africa as well. He found all that rather tiring at times. He helped in the nearby parishes with various church celebrations. It was good to just be home and do nothing. There were times when fatigue would overtake him and he took many long siestas.

When he had stopped at the provincial house of his community on the way back from Africa he had been told that he would be appointed to Toronto to do promotion work for Africa and the missions. That was fine and he was told also that he didn't need to be there until October, so he could take his time with preparations. His sister was sceptical about this and said, "Are you sure this is for real? You know how unpredictable your community can be. They will suddenly phone, telling you that it has changed and that you are needed elsewhere and immediately."

"Well, I can't really do anything about that, can I?" he answered. "I'll just cross that bridge when I come to it."

"At least you can get some things packed so you don't have it all to do in a hurry. I think it would be a good idea," said Della.

Fr. John did not know if his sister had the gift of reading into the future or if she was descended from a long line of family witches, but what she predicted came true the following week.

One evening, as they were chatting after supper, the telephone rang. Della asked him to answer it, since she needed to take the biscuits out of the oven before they burned. On answering, Fr. John was surprised to find Fr. Ronald Cellier at the other end of the line. "Hello, John. How are you?" said Fr. Ronald.

"I'm just fine," answered Fr. John "And you? How are you? Is everything O.K.? There must be something up for you to be calling me at home."

"Well, yes, there is something. We are calling with a very important request. We know that you have been appointed to Toronto, but there is a very important position that has become vacant and needs to be filled," answered Fr. Ronald.

"Oh really? And what position is that?" asked Fr. John.

"Well, you see, Fr. Gregory Vincent has been nominated to the new provincial council and he's the one who is presently in charge of the formation house in Ottawa; so that means that the position has become vacant. We believe that you could do that job quite well, if only you would accept," replied Fr. Ronald.

"I see. Does that mean I would be in charge?" asked Fr. John.

"Yes, it does," answered Fr. Ronald, "but we know that you can do it. You have been teaching and in formation work for quite some time now and so we are quite confident that you would do very well."

"Oh, my goodness, "Fr. John gasped. "That sounds awfully frightening. I don't know. Would someone else be there with me?"

"Yes, a confrere from Zambia who is recuperating from a burn-out, but who would take over the house accounts and the material needs. We believe that together you would be a good team for our students, since you both have good experience in Africa to share with our students. So, what do you think? It would certainly be a tremendous relief if you accepted because this has to be resolved very soon."

"Well, that's just the thing, Fr. Ronald. When would I need to be there?" asked Fr. John.

"That is the stickler," Fr. Ronald replied. You need to be there within the next fifteen days. Fr. Vincent must be here very soon for the provincial council meetings that begin in two weeks' time."

"Oh, wow!!! That doesn't give me much time, does it?" replied Fr. John.

Just then another voice came on the line and it was the provincial superior, himself, Fr. Paul Duhamel. "I am here on the line, as well to back up all that Fr. Ronald has told you. We all believe that you are our best choice and we put all our confidence in you. We will assist you in any way we can but this is a very important position to fill. We truly have faith in your training experience. So, what do you say?"

Fr. John answered, "This is a big choice for me!" After a short pause, he replied, "O.K., I accept, but all I can tell you is that I will do my best. That's all I can offer."

"We won't ask for more than that," answered the two men on the other end of the line.

After hanging up the telephone, Fr. John turned to his sister and burst out laughing. "What's so funny?" she asked. "That was the headquarters in Montreal, wasn't it?"

"Yes," said Fr. John, "and your predictions have come true. They have changed the appointment and I have only fifteen days to get ready and get myself to Ottawa."

"I told you," she said. "They do that to you every time. I'm not surprised. Well, it's a good thing you can laugh about it. I suppose you're used to this by now."

Fr. John packed within the next few days and did some last-minute visiting here and there, saying his last good-byes. Everyone was so surprised that he was leaving so soon, since they had previously been told that he was staying until the end of October.

It was a sunny afternoon on the day he reached Ottawa with his little Honda packed to the roof. It was good to see the old Slattery house once again. Fr. John had been there as a student. His second-in-command had already arrived, getting things set up and attempting to buy food. Fr. Vincent was also there, waiting to meet him to discuss the programme, review the students' files and discuss the training year objectives and goals. The next morning, Fr. Vincent left for Montreal. Fr. John sat in the office with Fr. Francois Laliberte to discuss the running of the house, a possible schedule for each day and to look over the four student files sitting there on Fr. John's desk.

They were to have four students: two seminarians who wanted to be priests and two lay-students preparing to go to one of the missions of the Missionaries of Africa, where they would be working on specific projects. The four students would be arriving at the end of August. Part of their programme would be done at St. Paul University, not far from their residence. The seminarians would be doing philosophy courses, while the lay students would follow the mission studies' programme. For some reason, Fr. John felt that things would go well. That was a comforting feeling. His predictions were good. The years there did go well. Each year, they had four very fine young men to do the programmes and their prayer life and community life was both fun and enriching. In fact, it was four of the best years that Fr. John had lived since his time in community with the Missionaries of Africa. Only one grueling incident occurred that marred the experience at the formation house; he would forever remember it.

Fr. John had been asked to preside at a Eucharist for a prayer group one Friday evening. It was at this prayer group that he met a lady by the name of Paulette. She had enjoyed his prayer and celebration so much that she asked him if he would meet with her at least once a month at her house for counseling, prayer and a laying on of hands. Fr. John agreed to this. Their meetings went well and eventually Paulette would invite Fr. John for lunch or dinner. He got to meet her husband, Henri, and her daughter, Charlotte.

One afternoon, while they were talking about prayer, Paulette asked Fr. John if he would agree to meet Magdalena, a friend of hers, to see if he could help her with some marital problems. Upon meeting Magdalena, Fr. John found out that she had four children and was having problems in her marriage; problems related to her relationship with her husband. Her husband, Guy, was, apparently, not the easiest person to get along with. She had spoken to a priest before about this but, according to Magdalena, that priest had been quite frightened of any kind of relationship with a woman and so Magdalena found him distant and cold. So she had to let things drop. Fr. John agreed to meet with her at Paulette's house. They agreed to meet on Wednesday afternoon of the following week. They would have lunch together with Paulette.

Wednesday arrived and they had a fine lunch. Paulette was very diet-conscious and so avoided most fats and sugars. Magdalena was a slim, fine-looking woman, who laughed a lot. After lunch, Paulette left them alone at the kitchen table so they could become acquainted. Magdalena was quite open and disclosed how distant her husband had become. According to her, they did not have much of a relationship at the moment, intimate or otherwise. She emphasized how much she really needed a warm, close, intimate relationship with a man. Fr. John asked her if she had talked about this with her husband. She said she had tried many times, but without much result. She needed someone warm with whom she could cuddle. As she was telling Fr. John this, she cuddled up close to his arm, laying her head on his shoulder, since they were sitting side by side at the table. Fr. John felt a bit uncomfortable with this, but then he remembered how she had mentioned that she had had such a cold reception from the other priest she had spoken with. So he said nothing, not wanting to add more insult to the previous injury. Magdalena felt that their first meeting had gone very well and suggested that they meet again, maybe at Fr. John's office, since she did not want her husband and children to know that this was taking place. They agreed to meet on the Friday of the following week.

After a number of meetings, Fr. John noticed that Magdalena's conversations were less and less about herself and centred more and more on Fr. John, himself. She wanted him to tell her what he liked and disliked in food, in recreation, in work and in women. He always tried to bring the conversation back to Magdalena's situation. This became more and more difficult, making him feel very uneasy.

Then the telephone calls began! They were one and two hour phone calls. Fr. John had to finally tell her that he could not tie up the telephone line in that way, because there was just one house-line for the whole of the community. So the long letters started arriving. The first part of each letter was always about Magdalena, herself, and what she was studying and how difficult her husband was, although he did satisfy her sexually at times. However, it invariably turned to Fr. John and what was happening with him. She then began to invite him for supper at her house. The first time was quite fine and he met her four children and her husband. Her children were beautiful; her husband, however, looked on him with suspicion. On his arrival at the house, she greeted him at the door and insisted that he kiss her on the mouth. Fr. John felt very uncomfortable with this, but tried to act as naturally as possible. At one point, she invited him for supper and an hour later called to cancel, saying that it was not going well with her husband that evening. He just took this in stride, not dwelling too much upon it, but then, she began asking him if it did not bother him when she spoke about her relationship with her husband and explained to him what she did with him intimately. Fr. John reassured her that it did not bother him, that he was happy for her when things went well in her relationship with her husband. She would remain very quiet, an uneasy quietness, when he said this. At one point in their meetings, she wanted to sit in the same chair as Fr. John. He told her that that was fine and made room for her to sit next to him. She asked him if he felt O.K. with this and found it strange when he told her that he was not affected by her being so close. He reassured her that he was not attracted to her in that sense and the fact that she was married and had four children made a very big difference for him in their relationship. That was the last straw for Magdalena. It was at this point that the accusations began. According to her, he had to be gay, since all this did not bother him. Fr. John, at this point, felt trapped and his good humour began to subside. The students living in community with him noticed this and one evening at the dinner table they said to him, "We have something to ask you. You are not your usual self. You seem very preoccupied. We want to know if it is because of us?"

"It has nothing to do with you," answered Fr. John. "You are all quite fine and I appreciate you asking. All I can say is that you know that on a certain day of the week I have a visitor who comes to see me. Right?"

"Yes, we know," they answered. "Well, that is your answer," replied Fr. John

"O.K., that's good enough for us," they answered. "As long as we are not the problem, that's all we need to know."

That evening, one of the older students came to see Fr. John and asked him, "Why are you keeping this relationship going? There is something very unhealthy going on, so drop it before it kills you."

"I guess I'm scared of how it will reflect on the priesthood," said Fr. John, "and that because of what she told me happened in the past with a priest."

"No. Drop it! You need to address it," answered the student.

Magdalena was intent on increasing their meetings. When she invited him now for supper, he had to make sure that he kissed her on the mouth when he arrived, otherwise she would be visibly upset. Fr. John began to notice that she was openly intent on making her husband jealous and she was using him to achieve that goal. There were times after she had canceled the invitation, she would later telephone to explain that she could not allow her children to become close to someone who was not honest about his life and his sexual orientation. Fr. John decided to seek the advice of a fellow priest that he could confide in. He explained to this priest-friend that he needed to gently terminate the relationship. Fr. John's priest-friend agreed with him that he did need to terminate the relationship and he should do so as soon as possible. So one morning when she telephoned for one of her marathon phone conversations, he told her that it would be better for her to find a new spiritual guide and preferably a woman and certainly not a priest. Magdalena was absolutely furious and insisted that they continue. Fr. John refused to continue. By this time, he was totally exhausted. He refused to take her phone calls and did not read her letters. He waited for the onslaught of accusations, but none came. Everything remained quiet. He felt that he had been removed from the lion's jaws.

One day while at Paulette's for supper, she mentioned that she thought that he had had a very hard time with Magdalena. Fr. John confirmed that that was so, but did not go into details. It had come to an end and was much too painful to talk about.

Although the experience with Magdalena was a stressful one, by far the most harrowing event that occurred during his time at the formation house in Ottawa was the painful loss of his oldest sister, Martine. This he would never forget, no matter how long he lived.

One telephone call to his sister one evening left Fr. John worried and frightened. Martine answered almost immediately, since she was home and in bed with the telephone close beside her. "What's going on?" asked Fr. John. "Why are you at home at this time of the day?"

"I've been sick in bed for the last couple of days. I feel awful and the doctor thinks I have some kind of virus. I am feeling so terrible that I will have to see the doctor again tomorrow."

"Let me know what he tells you," said Fr. John. The following day, he found that time dragged by. He had not heard from his sister all day. If she had not called by six that evening, he would call her himself. He finally did call her himself. Martine and her husband had just returned from the doctor's office. Now it was no longer a question of a virus, but the doctor thought that she may have some kind of tumour. Needless to say, Fr. John was even more worried. Martine mentioned that she was to go for a test the next day. After speaking to her, Fr. John tried telephoning Della, to tell her this news. There was no answer at her house, but he finally reached her at her daughter's. Della had been there for a number of days, since her daughter was not feeling well. When he told her what was going on, she was extremely upset. "It doesn't sound good to me," she said.

"Well, we'll know tomorrow after the tests," said Fr. John. The news, however, came sooner. Martine had started swelling just below the rib cage and felt really sick, so they went into the hospital that evening. They admitted her immediately and were able to provide her with a private room. She was so very happy to be in a private room. The tests revealed what seemed to be a cancerous mass that had spread to the liver. The doctors were not very hopeful. They ordered blood transfusions and a liver biopsy, in the hope of finding out what kind of cancer was invading her body. Fr. John was able to speak to his sister in her hospital room. She did not sound too discouraged, at first. He asked her if she would like him to come and she said that it would be nice if he were with her. Fr. John felt a cold shiver go through him again and a terrible, foreboding feeling in the pit of his stomach.

He called Della to report on what was going on. "Oh, my God," she cried," what are we going to do?"

"We'll just have to take whatever bad news comes our way," said Fr. John "We cannot jump to conclusions yet. Not all the tests are in." An uneasy feeling persisted. He left for Halifax the next day and went directly from the airport to the hospital. He did not want anyone to have to come for him.

When he walked into the hospital room, she was turned towards her husband, who was sitting next to the bed. Both were watching television. She turned when she heard him come in. She gave him a big smile when she saw him. "Well, you have good colour in your cheeks," he said.

"That's because I've had a blood transfusion today. I was reluctant to have a transfusion, because of all the stories about tainted blood in the news lately. They did reassure me, though, that they would give me healthy blood."

Martine's condition deteriorated rapidly. She became weaker, but there were times that she rallied especially when her grandchildren were brought in to visit her. Two little grand-daughters, Abigail and Kelly, would squeal with delight when they saw their grandmother. Martine would become fully alert and take them into the bed with her, showering them with hugs and kisses. Then, when they would leave, they would both say, "Bye, Nana. Get better soon."

"You be good girls now, OK?" she would tell them.

"Yes, we will," they would answer. After they had left, Martine would fall into a deep sleep, totally exhausted. She was a loving grandmother to the end.

On Thursday afternoon of that week, Fr. John found himself alone with his sister. Everyone else had errands to run and her husband, Francis, had to pick up a few things at the office. Bills had to be paid and all accounts brought up to date. As difficult as it was to do, Fr. John felt it was time to broach the subject of dying. What other way than to simply ask the question, "Are you afraid of dying?"

"That's not really what I'm thinking of," she answered. "I'm no better or braver than anyone else. I've always known, of course, that I would have to die one day. I just never thought that I would be so young, that's all."

"Then what is bothering you?" Fr. John asked.

"I will not see my grandchildren grow up," she replied, "and that saddens me terribly."

"Maybe you will watch over them and care for them more than you think," answered Fr. John. "Do you know that St. Theresa said that she would spend her heaven doing good on earth and continue to let rose petals fall from heaven? Don't you think that that is a beautiful thought?"

"I like that very much," she replied.

"Do you think that you will be able to remember that when the time comes?" asked Fr. John.

"I think so," she replied. It was at that moment that Martine shared with Fr. John the hurts that still existed in her life. He shared his thoughts about God, Jesus, forgiveness and life after death with Martine. She told him that she had made her confession to the hospital chaplain and had been anointed by him before Fr. John arrived from Ottawa. However, she wasn't sure that she had said everything. She couldn't quite remember, since her mind at times seemed so confused. "That's O.K. That's fine," replied Fr. John. "What's forgotten is forgiven. I will even anoint you again. The anointing, you know, forgives all, so you need not worry." So he had the pleasure of saying the beautiful anointing prayer over his sister the following day when all the members of the family were present.

The following day, Friday, the doctor came in to see Martine and told the family that there was nothing else they could do. The cancer was spreading through her like wildfire. Dr. Bouchard, their family doctor, was also present and expressed the wish to tell Martine that she was going to die. She was once again in a deep sleep, but when Dr. Bouchard spoke to her and was able to get her to wake up, she once again rallied her strength to listen and understand what he was saying. "My dear Martine, you are a very sick woman and there is nothing more that we can do for you."

"Does that mean that I'm going to die?" she asked.

"Yes, that is what will happen," he answered.

"Well, I thought so," she replied. Everyone in the room was in tears. Each one went to her, touched her and told her they loved her. Francis was beside himself. Martine looked at everyone and tried her best to tell them in her feeble voice that everything was OK, that she would be fine. In her own way, she consoled everyone. It was her way of saying good-bye. After this, she went into a deep sleep. Fr. John did the prayer of anointing once again while everyone was present. This all happened on that Friday.

Early the following Sunday morning while Fr. John was alone in the room with Martine, he prayed over her and anointed her once again. He knew that she did not have much time left. Her breathing was very laboured. Francis had stepped out of the room to pick up a newspaper and freshen up. He had been at her side throughout the night. Her daughter, Katherine, had also been present. She had stepped out, as well, to freshen up a bit. A few moments after the anointing, Martine opened her eyes and looked around the room, as if following a light. Her eyes focused and she quietly passed away. Fr. John went immediately for the nurse. She checked Martine's pulse and, turning to Fr. John, told him that she was gone. It was at that moment that Francis came back into the room. "Francis, Francis, she is gone."

"Oh, no," he replied, "I should not have gone out of the room; I should have stayed. Why did I leave?" He broke down and wept. Fr. John said a prayer of blessing and then slowly called all the members of the family to give them the news. It was six fifteen on Sunday morning, October 12, Thanksgiving Day.

Fr. John and Francis made the funeral arrangements. Fr. John was not sure if he would be able to officiate at the funeral service, since this was extremely difficult for him. In the end, however, he was filled with enough peace and courage to do the church service and the graveside prayers. He stayed a few days with his family and then returned to Ottawa. It was the grieving afterwards that was the most difficult for him to overcome. He would wake up in the morning and her passing away was the first thing that came to mind. She would no longer be there. He felt constantly as though he had been kicked in the stomach. The sense of loss and desolation permeated everything. He would take long walks along the Rideau River or the Rideau Canal in the afternoons, yet could find no consolation. The empty feeling in his stomach was so very terrible. He thanked God, however, that Sister Julienne, a very close friend, was studying at St. Paul University at the time. When she could, she would walk with him. While walking they would talk about many things especially about the pain and the loss; the walk and the sharing would ease the pain. It took months for him to develop a real interest in anything. Even prayer did not seem to be effective in easing the emptiness and the terrible feeling of loss. With time, the pain simply became a dull ache.

His time at the formation house in Ottawa came to an end. He was then asked to return to Nigeria to be in charge of the formation house there. After some reflection, Fr. John accepted. He felt that it would prove to be a good and enriching experience, but again there would be certain painful decisions that would have to be made. The one painful decision that turned out to be extremely difficult was the eventual closing of the formation house in Ibadan, Nigeria. There was to be an amalgamation with the Ghanaian formation house. It was a painful thing to do, but a necessary one at the time.

Fr. John arrived in Nigeria to take up his duties at the Rotimi Williams Formation House in Ibadan in August of 1988. He was picked up at the Murtala Muhammad Airport in Lagos by two White Father colleagues, Heinz Beyer and Wolfgang Schackel. Both had known Fr. John during his previous assignment in Nigeria. "Well, back again to this neck of the woods," said Wolfgang. "Welcome and I hope all goes well for you in this new position. You will be the 'oga' there you know," Wolfgang said to him laughing. He knew that Fr. John knew that the word 'oga' meant 'boss'. Fr. John just grimaced.

They visited and shopped in Lagos for some hours since Heinz had some shopping to do for the diocese of Ibadan. During his previous assignment Fr. John had been in the diocese of Oyo but now he was to be in the diocese of Ibadan, administered by Bishop Alaba Job. Although Fr.

John had not met him during his previous assignment, he would certainly have to this time.

Upon arriving at the Rotimi Williams Formation House, Fr. John met Fr. Hugh Mason who would be the bursar for the community. Fr. Hugh had been in Ghana for a previous assignment, but was not used to dealing with students. He would soon know the ropes a bit better. They were both in the beginning stages of the Nigerian formation center.

When Fr. John arrived at the Center, he discovered that the former director had not yet returned from home-leave. None of the offices had been vacated and his room still had his personal effects in it. Fr. John was somewhat disappointed. He could not really settle into the new position very comfortably; there were too many loose ends. Fr. George O'Donahue was expected to return to the center in October. This did not help Fr. John advance into the new Academic year programme. "Do not panic," he said to himself. "Things will work out in the long run." He established himself in another room with another office. Then he called a meeting of all the students after the evening meal that same evening. All fifteen students were back from holidays and they would need to discuss how things had been run in the formation house. Fr. John would need to know who was responsible for what since all the students attended classes at Sts. Peter and Paul Major Seminary. He knew that there was a programme at the house with a particular emphasis on the Missionaries of Africa and their life style and community rule.

The meeting started at 8:15 with all students present. When Fr. John asked the students what their timetable was, they answered, "We didn't have a timetable for the house, only one for the seminary classes. Then, we were pretty much on our own."

"No timetable for the house?" Fr. John reiterated in a questioning tone. "How were you able to keep everything clean and in order without some kind of organisation?" Fr. John asked.

"We have the cook and then there is Patricia, the lady who does the laundry and some of the cleaning," answered Chilaka, one of the students. "We depended a lot on her, and often she did work for us that she was not being paid for."

"That is not good. We can't continue this way," said Fr. John, trying to hide the annoyance in his voice. "We do need a timetable, as well as a set of rules for certain ways of doing things, a set of regulations, don't you think? They need not be written down. It could be understood, as long as everyone remembers them. We certainly would need to establish these rules now and I can keep a set of them on file."

Several of the students nodded their agreement. Then, one of the third year students stood up and said, "The set of regulations should be typed up and copies made and each student have a copy in his room. A copy should also be posted on the bulletin board in the refectory." No one said another word. There was silence in the room. Fr. John decided to take a vote on this suggestion.

"If you are in favour of this suggestion, please raise your hand," he said. All hands went up with the exception of three of the first year students. "This has passed. Now remember 'as in scripture when Pharoah spoke in the time of Moses: 'Let it be written, let it be done.'" All the students laughed about this remark. They never thought that one day it would come home to roost. Fr. John wasted no time in typing up the set of regulations and underlined the one regarding female visitors: No female visitors in the rooms of the seminarians, but only in the visitors' parlours. Fr. John knew that this would not be an easy one to keep. Time would tell the full story.

Fr. George, the former director finally arrived from home-leave. All the students were very happy to see him once again. Fr. John was meeting him for the first time but had heard many stories about Fr. George. Some were good, others not so good, depending on who was telling the story. He was very well known for his projects to build the mission especially where social programmes were concerned. He had a very outgoing personality and made friends easily. He was a very likeable person. For training work the authorities of the Missionary Community felt that he was too lax and did not possess enough structure for training the students. Fr. John was expected to make changes in that regard. Doing this with Fr. George in the formation house did not please Fr. John at all. Fr. George did not seem to be vacating very quickly. Having the former director and the new director in place at the same time created a very awkward situation. Added to this was Fr. Hugh's dislike of Fr. George. They did not agree on what constituted training for the students. How was Fr. John to resolve all of this? The opportunity presented itself when Fr. George came to Fr. John's office one afternoon and asked, "Do you think it would be possible for me to remain here for the next few months, at least until after Christmas, so that I can get things organized at the pastoral center of the diocese?"

Fr. John mustered all the courage that was in himself and said to Fr. George, "To be truthful with you, I do not think that it would be a good thing for both the students and myself for you to remain here after having been the director of the Center. I do not think that it would help to accomplish the changes that are expected by the authorities. I really believe that you need to find a new place and to move as soon as possible. I have nothing against you personally, Fr. George, but I do not think that this is a healthy situation for the students and the smooth running of the center."

Fr. George agreed with Fr. John and did not make too much of a fuss about his having to vacate the premises. Fr. John did find out later from another colleague that Fr. George was furious with him for his refusal to let him stay at the Center. He was convinced that Fr. John had been coached by someone else about that decision, that he would not have been able to make such a decision on his own. Within a few days Fr. George had left and the new rules and regulations for the Center began to be implemented. Fr. Hugh told Fr. John how pleased he was that Fr. George was now out of the Center.

Time passed. Fr. John got used to his new surroundings and began to feel a bit more at home in Ibadan. It was a very old city, extremely large and well-populated. Fr. John attended the many meetings, liturgies, and diocesan functions. He also took some time to visit the missions and places where he had served in the past. Traveling was not quite as dangerous as it had been during his first tour of duty ten years previously; the Nigerian Government had made a huge effort to develop its highways and infrastructure in order to accommodate the vastly growing population. Traffic jams and long queues for petrol were much less than in the past. During his first tour of duty Fr. John had never succeeded in entering the city of Lagos as it had been too crowded and congested. This time, however, he went into Lagos several times for various documents. As the school year drew to a close he knew that he would have to take his third year students to Lagos, to the C.I.D (Center for Identification Documents) for their passports and documents for traveling to the noviciate, either in Africa, England, France or Switzerland. He did not look forward to this venture. Dealing with the government offices in Lagos could take weeks and an enormous amount of patience. Along with the patience he would need to put bribe money in each pocket of whatever piece of clothing that he wore.

They all set out one bright Thursday morning in the community station wagon: Fr. John, Edward the driver, and their students, Tom, Cyprian, Linus, and Callistus. Also with them was Fr. Robert Harvey, who had been appointed to the Formation House to look for a piece of land to eventually have a formation house of their own established in the city of Ibadan since they were renting the houses that they were presently using. Fr. Robert was accompanying them to Lagos since he had some business to attend to at the office of the Archdiocese of Lagos. Once on the way, they recited a short prayer for a safe trip. They were on the dual carriageway to Lagos in no time. This was a road that had a great deal of traffic on it. Vehicles traveled very fast. Many accidents happened on this road, therefore, many deaths as well. The traffic was not yet very heavy since it was still early in the morning. Fr. John remarked to Edward as they clipped along at a good speed, "I am amazed that they have not mowed the tall elephant grass that grows in the median of the highway. It looks awfully thick to me, don't you think, Edward?"

"Yes, Father, it is very thick, but the government probably does not want to pay for this work and the workers will certainly not do it for nothing," Edward answered.

"We cannot see the traffic heading the other way very well," said Fr. Robert. "We need to drive carefully, that is for certain."

They were some twenty minutes outside of Ibadan and cruising along at a normal speed, when there was a huge bang from the rear of the Peugeot station wagon that they were driving. The car suddenly began to wobble rather uncontrollably.

"Oh my goodness Edward what is happening? Was that bang from our vehicle?"

"Yes, father, I think we just had a blow-out in one of the rear tires," he answered as he tried to keep the car from wobbling even more. "Father, it is too difficult to control the car. Which side should I turn to? I must try to stop it but I cannot block the traffic coming behind us."

"Don't go to the right. There is a huge drop there down an embankment," said Fr. John as his heart raced inside his chest. "Keep the car towards the median."

As Edward tried to steer the car towards the median, the back of the car suddenly spun around towards the median and as it hit the tall, dense elephant grass, it flipped over onto the hood and there they were upside down in the elephant grass with the four wheels spinning like crazy. It happened in a flash and Fr. John's head hit the roof of the car and his thighs slammed against his chest. A terrible pain shot through his back and he thought he had surely severed his spinal column at the waist. The pain, however, lasted only for that moment and Fr. John could still feel his legs. His window was down and, fearing that the car would catch on fire, he scrambled out of the vehicle through the window. As he stood next to the overturned car, a dull gnawing ache had replaced the sharp pain he had felt when they had overturned. But he didn't think too much of it.

"Is everyone alright," he yelled to the others. Each student answered very quickly in succession, "Yes, I am fine," as they scrambled out of the car through the rear windows. They emerged all intact, with nothing broken and not in the least bit disheveled. ed. Fr. John was amazed. The only one who did not answer was Fr. Robert. Fear gripped at Fr. John's heart. "I hope he didn't break his neck," he thought to himself.

"Fr. Robert, are you alright, can you speak to me?" he asked.

There was a long drawn out groan from the middle seat where he had been sitting. The vehicle had two sets of rear seats. Fr. Robert had hit his head very hard against the roof and had been somewhat stunned by the blow; he was just coming out of it when Fr. John called out to him.

"Fr. Robert, are you badly hurt? Do you need us to help you out of the car?" he asked.

"I have a gash on my head and I can hardly move my arm," came the answer.

The students and Fr. John came to his side of the car and together they managed to get the door opened and gently pulled him from the overturned vehicle.

"We have to stop someone who is on the way into Ibadan so that they can help us. Fr. Robert will need to be taken to the hospital," said Callistus. "While you go to the hospital with him I will go and see if I can find someone to turn the car on its wheels and tow it to the nearest garage; I will then join you at the hospital."

They finally got someone to stop and assist them. "You are sure that you can do this on your own, Callistus?" Fr. John asked. "Maybe one of us should stay with you to help you. What do you think?"

"I will be fine. Go and get yourselves checked out to make sure you are alright. I will join you later. Don't worry!" Callistus exclaimed.

Within about twenty minutes they were entering Ileta Hospital, the hospital of the Medical Mission Sisters. Fr. Robert had a seriously pulled muscle in his shoulder; they treated that and dressed the gash on his head that had continued to bleed a bit. Fr. John was given a bed to lie on in order to rest his back; the dull ache would turn into a throbbing pain at times. The students just sat quietly talking in one of the visitors' rooms, no aches or pains evident. They had hardly been there an hour when Callistus walked into the visitor's room. He had managed to get the car towed to a garage in the town and they would assess the damages and let them know what needed to be done to get it functioning again. When he told them how things had gone and that the car was now in safe, capable hands, Fr. John congratulated him on a job well done. Callistus was one of their more mature, capable and responsible students.

Fr. John asked one of the Sisters to phone the formation house and get one of the priests on staff to come for them. "I will certainly phone, Father," replied Sr. Patricia, "but don't you think that you all need to stay here overnight to make sure that you are all able to manage?" Fr. John had no intention of staying at Ileta Hospital overnight, although he did not say that to Sr. Patricia. He did have a bit of discomfort in his back but it was nothing to be alarmed about. Therefore he replied, "Well Sister, maybe Fr. Robert could stay overnight since he received that bad gash on his head and he has a very difficult time to move his arm. As for myself and the students and the driver, I think we can go on home now that we have been checked and there is nothing major wrong with us.

"Now watch me. I will walk up and down the hallway and you will see that I am just fine." He had then walked briskly up and down the ward hallway and made sure that he did not grimace whenever a twinge went through his back. He needed to get back to the house.

Sr. Patricia watched him, suspicion written on her face. Finally she said to Fr. John, "I will go and phone the formation house and get someone to come and pick you up."

Fr. Robert since he was still in pain opted to stay overnight. They would check on him the next day. Everyone else was soon back home and the phone messages started to come in. News seemed to have traveled fast and everyone wanted to know if they were safe and sound. When the Regional Director of the community saw the car, he was amazed that they had come out of it with only a few scrapes and pulled muscles.

"You were very lucky to get out of that alive," said the Director to Fr. John "The car is a real mess. It will cost quite a bit to repair. What's important, though, is that you are all alive and safe."

Fr. Robert came home from the hospital the following day. Life at the Formation Center on Rotimi Williams Avenue continued calmly with the odd occurrences of a disturbance in community now and again. With the passing of time, Fr. John came to realize that Hugh had not liked Fr. George much. He was also a bit of a penny-pincher when it came to the food, especially with regard to the students. They ended up eating a lot of pasta, since it was cheap. Fr. John tried to discreetly explain to Fr. Hugh that they needed more fruit and vegetables, as well as good meat if they were to stay healthy. The food improved somewhat after Fr. John's pep talk.

Each of the priests on staff would go on home leave for a number of months after two to three years in the field. Fr. Hugh's time came to leave for Belgium. One thing that was worrisome was that Fr. Hugh had never received his permanent residency card from immigration. Whether he would be allowed back into the country without it, even possessing a re-entry visa, was not certain. His temporary visa was still good when he left for his holidays but it would expire before he came back. Receiving another one from the Nigerian Embassy in Belgium was not a forgone conclusion. Time would tell how things would turn out.

Two weeks before Fr. Hugh was to return to Ibadan, Fr. John received news that Fr. Hugh could not obtain the re-entry visa for Nigeria. His temporary visa had expired. Fr. Hugh decided to return to his former mission in Ghana. Maybe things would change and he would be allowed to enter Nigeria, after all Ghana was not far from Nigeria and could easily be reached by road. This left the community of Rotimi Williams without a bursar. Fr. John set out to visit Fr. Jacob, the Regional Superior of the community of Missionaries of Africa in Nigeria. After some lengthy discussion, it was decided that Fr. Daniel Lacoursiere, the vocation director for the community, would be appointed bursar for the Formation House and Fr. Sean O'Leary would be appointed to help Fr. John with the training work with the students which included Spiritual Direction and Counseling. Fr. John was extremely pleased with the decision. He would now have two young colleagues with him who were open and very interested in the training. When this was announced at one of the Regional meetings of the community, one of the colleagues who taught at the Diocesan Major Seminary, a Fr. Hubert Reilly, protested at the appointment of young colleagues to training work when they should be getting more experience in parish work. This he felt was a terrible waste of manpower for the work in the parishes. Fr. Hubert was one of those colleagues who had been many years in the Nigerian mission, had also been Regional Director of the community and one who most brothers feared and dared not oppose. When he spoke, all others remained silent. But Fr. John was not to be sabotaged. He decided to voice his opposition to Fr. Hubert.

"I do not care what the situation is in the parish mission. Young or not, I need someone with whom I can work and who can do good work and who is interested in this training. The appointments should stand no matter what you think, Fr. Hubert. I need this help for the Center and I need it now. This is the future of the community that we are deciding on. Let us just be aware of that." Surprisingly enough everyone in the meeting agreed. The appointments were accepted. For the first time Fr. Hubert had been openly and successfully opposed.

Fr. Sean O'Leary arrived at the Center along with Fr. Daniel. Fr. John just beamed he was so very pleased. They gathered together in the Staff room and had a cold refreshing beer. There was new hope in the air.

One month after receiving the news that Fr. Hugh had returned to Ghana, a letter arrived at the Rotimi Williams House in Ibadan carrying bad news with it. The letter contained the following tragic news: "We regret to inform you that Fr. Hugh Mason, who was a member of your community, passed away in the hospital of Bolgatanga last Friday. Please pray for him when celebrating the Eucharist." That evening Fr. John announced the news to the whole community at the Spiritual Reading session. The whole of the student body were shocked by the news. "Father why did you just blurt that out to us like you did. We were not at all prepared for such news. Many of us are in a state of distress and confusion. We just cannot believe it!"

"He will certainly not be returning to Nigeria now," thought Fr. John to himself. He would eventually have to do something about that.

One of the priests in the Rotimi Williams House was not a staff member but a resident of the house. Fr. Heinz Engels taught at the Major Seminary SS. Peter and Paul and had been a teacher there for quite a number of years. Fr. Heinz had studied the Yoruba language along with Fr. John when they had first arrived in Nigeria. His main work was teaching Philosophy and Theology, but being a member of the community of the Missionaries of Africa, he was given the option of staying in community with them at the Formation House since it was close to the Major Seminary where he taught. Fr. Heinz was very pleased with this invitation. He gladly accepted. Fr. Heinz was a very pleasant man, extremely generous and hard-working; a very good person who always went the extra mile in his service to others. He was always very good to his students and always took on more work than he could handle.

Some years previously, Fr. Heinz had had to return to Germany for serious prostate surgery. He had been gone for quite some time, but once he had healed properly, he was given the option by his doctor and the Missionaries of Africa of returning to Nigeria. He gladly accepted as he greatly loved his work as a professor of Theology. Fr. Heinz had previously lived in residence at the Major Seminary but preferred to reside with his own missionary community.

After Fr. Heinz returned to Nigeria, some strange things began to happen and it seemed that it was a result of his surgery. Some mornings he would appear at breakfast seeming quite tipsy. This would also occur at times at the evening meals. Fr. John did not pay too much attention to this at first. But one of the students came to his office one evening to report that there were more and more bottles of beer missing from the store room. Fr. John said to the student, "I will try to see what is going on and deal with it. Do not worry. You will not be blamed for this."

"Thank you Father," the student replied. Then he added, "Some of the students are blaming Fr. Heinz. They are saying that he is out of control. They believe he is an alcoholic."

"Really!" answered Fr. John. "But what proof do they have that brings them to that conclusion?" he asked.

"Well, several students have seen Fr. Heinz in the late evening coming from the fridge where the drinks are kept with a bulge in his pants pocket that looked like he was carrying a bottle of beer. They figure that he is drinking while he is working late into the night."

Fr. John knew that he had to look into this and find out what was going on. However he needed to find the right moment. Fr. Heinz was a very gentle, kind and loving man and he did not want to hurt him in any way. The right moment soon presented itself one day after the evening meal. Fr. Heinz had come down from his room for the meal looking somewhat tipsy and rather flushed. As usual the students looked at each other and smirked to one another. Fr. John did not like this, he had too great an admiration for Fr. Heinz for him to think otherwise. When he came out of the dining-room that evening, he himself observed Fr. Heinz urinating in front of the house in full view of everyone. He knew that he had to speak to Fr. Heinz that very night. Since it was a beautiful evening and he had a moment to relax, he asked Fr. Heinz to take a walk around the block with him.

"Ya, we can do that," said Fr. Heinz.

Fr. John inquired first of all about his health and how the work load was going. "I hope that you don't find the work load too heavy, Father?" he said. "You are not as young as you were when we did the Yoruba course together. Remember those days, trying to get the tones and tone patterns correct?"

"Ya, that was quite a challenge for us, but I could only stay one month and then I had to come to the Seminary and take up my duties in teaching. I would have enjoyed staying longer. I didn't even learn to celebrate the Eucharist in Yoruba. I was so very sorry about that."

Then Fr. John launched into the topic he had come to discuss. "Please, Father, don't take this the wrong way, but I must say that I have noticed that you have come to meals and various other house functions apparently inebriated. Do you have a problem that you need to tell me about?"

"No, no, there is no problem," answered Fr. Heinz, "but you see when I had the prostate surgery in Germany, my doctor told me that I had to drink a lot of liquids so that everything would continue to function properly and at the time he suggested beer as one of the beverages."

"Don't you think that beer is one of the more dangerous beverages to be taking since it is high in alcohol content and one can become addicted to it? Could he not have suggested orange juice or lemonade?"

"Ya, that is true, but I don't think that I am addicted to it yet. I think that I can control it," answered Fr. Heinz.

"All I ask, Father, is that you be very discreet about it because the students are noticing and they are laughing at you and that is very painful for me because I respect you very much. Also, this evening, I myself saw you urinating in front of the house and the students noticed it as well. I just don't want you to be in an embarrassing situation, Father," he said.

"Do you really think that the students are noticing so much and are laughing about it, Fr. John?"

"Yes, I most certainly do, Father. One of the students also mentioned the other day that when you don't find beer in the fridge, you send Edward the driver to get you some at the small market down the road."

"I will do my best to be more discreet about it, Fr. John That is not good for the students to see me like this. Thank you so much for the talk and the advice."

"I also thank you for walking with me and listening, Fr. Heinz. We will have to do this again some other evening."

This was the part that Fr. John disliked about being in charge, the calling of colleagues to task when problems arose. Fr. John felt that his colleagues should be mature enough to be responsible for themselves. This kind of intervention was very draining. When it happened with the students, it was even more difficult since they didn't easily accept being called to task. He often ended up being quite harsh in dealing with them especially when he felt they were trying to dupe him.

A situation developed with regard to one of the students close to the end of Fr. John's final year in Nigeria; one that Fr. John would not easily forget. Cyprian was a good student and the one who had backed up the publishing of the rules of the Formation House when Fr. John had first arrived. He was also on the list for continuing his formation at the

Noviciate in Switzerland. During the school year he volunteered for his pastoral duties in one of the parishes in the town of Ibadan.

One Sunday morning, Fr. John received a message for Cyprian and wanted to communicate this message to him before he forgot about it. As he was going down to the dining-room he asked one of the students if Cyprian was around.

"I think he is still at the parish doing his pastoral work, Fr. John," answered the student, "but you could check his room. He may be back already."

Fr. John took the envelope with the message and made his way to Cyprian's room. They had two houses that they were renting and Cyprian was in the house next door. He went up to his room and discreetly knocked at the door. A voice answered, "Come in. The door is unlocked." Fr. Paul recognized Cyprian's voice. He thought to himself, "Good, he's back from the parish." When he opened the door it was impossible to see inside the room since there was a wooden dividing panel forming an entrance into the room obviously for more privacy. There were normally two students to each room. Fr. John poked his head around the panel to speak to Cyprian and hand him the message. To his surprise Cyprian was sitting on his bed with his back to the door; he had on his trousers but no shirt, just his singlet. Sprawled across his bed looking up at Cyprian and in full view of Fr. John was a beautiful young African woman dressed in a gorgeous pink suit, her arm resting on Cyprian's shoulder. She looked at Fr. John seemingly not too surprised to see him. Cyprian only turned around when he heard Fr. John's voice say, "This is a message for you that came today. I did not want to forget to give it to you, so I came over with it." Fr. John rarely went to the students' rooms as he trusted them. As Cyprian's eyes met Fr. John's they widened in surprise and dismay. Fr. John nodded his head, pursed his lips as if to say, "Isn't this a fine kettle of fish!" He placed the message on the bed and left without saying another word. He went back to his office to take care of some necessary paper work since he had a meeting at the Regional Director's office the next day.

He was working quietly at his desk when there was a knock at his door. "Come in," Fr. John called out. Cyprian came in, a serious frown on his forehead and looking rather worried and embarrassed. Fr. John had four comfortable chairs in front of his desk where students could sit when they came to see him. He got up and went and sat in one of them and invited Cyprian to sit. He sat in the chair that was furthest from Fr. John.

"Why are you sitting so far from me?" Fr. John said to him. "Come closer to me. I'm not going to bite you." He patted the cushion of the chair to indicate where he was to sit. "Can you explain to me what was going on when I went over to your room just a few minutes ago?" Fr. John asked in a calm, fairly gentle voice.

"She is just a friend that I speak to sometimes when I do pastoral work at the parish. I met her first at the Eucharist at the Dominican Monastery in the town."

"She appeared to be in somewhat of a compromising situation, don't you think?" Fr. John asked.

"Yes, Father, that is true. I am very sorry, Father. It will not happen again."

Fr. John looked at Cyprian for a short time in silence. Then he said to him, "Do you remember the meeting we had concerning the house rules when I first arrived here to take over the center?"

"Yes, Father, I do remember," said Cyprian.

"Who was the one who said that the rules for the house should be written and posted in each of the houses?"

"Yes, I know father, I was the one who said that."

"And what did I say when I ended the discussion on those house rules?" Fr. John asked, looking at him with a sly smile on his face.

"You said to us, 'As Pharoah said to the people in the time of Moses, Let it be written. Let it be done.'"

"Very good you have a very good memory. You will not know if you can live the celibacy commitment that we are called to live if you do not start to live it now, before you are ordained. Don't you think so?"

"You are right, Father," Cyprian answered.

"I am not saying that you can't or shouldn't have women friends as a priest," said Fr. John, "but we all have to be prudent about the situations that we put ourselves in, don't you agree?"

"Yes, that is true," answered Cyprian.

"I am now preparing to go to a meeting in Ilesha at the Regional House of the Missionaries of Africa so I will not decide what to do about you right now. I will wait until I return from the meeting which will be

Tuesday evening of next week. What I do want you to do while I am away is to reflect seriously on your behaviour and when I come back I would like you to tell me what you would do if you were me and confronted with such a situation. I also need to discuss this with the other members of staff to get their opinion on this. I am not alone in the decision making here at the Formation Center. So, we will see each other again when I get back next week."

"Okay Father, I understand, but I need to tell you that I am very worried about my situation and I am very sorry that I have broken that rule," said Cyprian. "May I go now?"

"Yes, you may go. I will call you to see me some time next week."

Fr. John went to see his two colleagues on staff and asked them if he could meet with them after lunch in their small conference room. There was no problem; they would meet at one thirty that afternoon.

They met at 1.30 that afternoon and Fr. John went over all that had happened with Cyprian. The other two colleagues felt that this was the first time that such an event had occurred with Cyprian and, that being the case, he should be allowed to continue to the Noviciate. There he would be made to come to a more mature decision about his vocation. Fr. John was fine with this decision and would communicate this to Cyprian upon his return from the meeting in Ilesha.

On Wednesday of the following week, Fr. John called Cyprian to his office once he had returned to Ibadan. Cyprian knocked at the door and entered Fr. John's office.

"You may sit down," said Fr. John. Then he added, "Did you think about what I said to you before I left for my meeting?"

"I thought about it a lot," answered Cyprian, doing his best to avoid Fr. John's eyes.

"And what conclusion did you come to?"

"I know that I should be expelled. I did break the rule that we had seriously discussed in the very beginning of my training here. However I am asking that I be given another chance to continue training for my vocation, Father."

"Well, I do have good news for you. That is the decision the Council has taken in your regard: you are permitted to continue in the Noviciate in order to more fully discern what God calls you to do." Fr. John answered.

"Now I must admit that this would not have been my decision if there had been only myself to decide. That, however, is not the case. The decision, then, is in your favour." Fr. John suspected that Cyprian had other motives for going on to the Noviciate; the Noviciate happened to be in Switzerland, an easy way of getting to Europe and not coming back too soon. Fr. John, however, would give him the benefit of the doubt.

The first attempt to go to Lagos to the C.I.D (Center for Identification Documents) for the students' travel documents had ended in disaster, so Fr. John needed to make another attempt. Time was passing and they had to have their documents in order. Once again early on a bright, sunny Thursday morning they set out for Lagos. The repaired car had been checked by the mechanic and was in good working order. This time Fr. Robert was not with them. Fr. John was alone with the students and Edward was at the wheel. For such ventures into the government offices, Fr. John often wore his religious uniform, the white cassock known as a gandoura and the Christian rosary around his neck; he decided to do this on this trip hoping that it would have positive results. One other feature that Fr. John always added to the religious garb was different amounts of money in each of the pockets with a bit of money in his socks for good measure.

They arrived in Lagos around 8:30 in the morning. The C.I.D. office was already open. Fr. John presented the students to the officer in charge and explained to him what they needed.

"Well, Reverend Father," answered the C.I.D. officer, "here are the forms that need to be filled out. You will see posted on the wall here examples of how the forms must be filled out. Once your students have done this, you give them to me to be processed."

"That is very good," answered Fr. John. He then whispered to the students, "Quickly get those done, we do not want to be here for the whole day and we are the first ones here."

Once the forms were filled out they were presented to the officer, who looked them over. "They are all quite fine," said the officer. "You can check with me next week to see if they have been processed."

"Next week!" Fr. John said in utter surprise. "But we need them immediately. These young men must travel out of Nigeria and they need their passports and visas to do so. Is it not possible to have them processed now, now?" Fr. John suddenly began to respond with the bit of pidgin English that he new. "Ah we need to be quick, quick oooo!"

"Of course, Father. We can do now, now, if you are ready?" responded the officer.

Fr. John knew immediately what the 'ready' meant. He reached into his pocket and brought out a twenty dollar American note. Placing it on top of the forms he said, "We are ready!" The officer quickly scooped it up before anyone could see and said to Fr. John "I will write on the forms 'Dispatch immediately' and you will take the forms to an office across the compound to a big lady in uniform sitting at the desk there. She will continue the process for you."

Off they went to the office across the way. The big woman took one look at the forms and what had been written on them and asked Fr. John, "Do you have things to do in town Father?"

"Oh yes, we have many things to buy for the Center," answered Fr. John

"You go do those things and come here again around 3p.m. It will be ready. But you must not be late."

They went into town and picked up various items for the Center while watching the time closely so as not to be late. This was easy to do since downtown Lagos was extremely congested. At five minutes to three they were back at the C.I.D. office. They were shown into another room where a young man was sitting reading a magazine. Tom, one of Fr. John's students, whispered to him, "I am sure that young man over there is from my village. We were in class together. I will greet him in our language and we will see what the results will be. Let me do the talking."

Tom greeted the young man in the African language that he understood and the young man looked up in surprise. They continued to speak to each other while shaking hands and smiling happily. Tom proceeded to explain why they were there and the young man excused himself and went into another office. He soon returned with the forms and four green passports. They were to sign the passports so that the forms could be filed away. Once that was done, Tom introduced the group to his 'brother' from the village. They all greeted each other with warm handshakes and smiles. They then left with the green passports but they did not leave without giving the young man, whose name turned out to be David, a crisp twenty dollar American bill.

Once in the car and on their way, Fr. John thanked Tom for that enormous help.

"Ah, but Father, that happening today was God's doing," said Tom.

"That is so true," said Fr. John, "and it is not what you know in this country but WHO you know! Glory halleluiah!" To which they all answered, "AMEN!"

They all arrived in Ibadan for the evening meal. The day's events were told to everyone at dinner. Beer was a treat at the meal that evening as well as ice cream and cake. There were many beaming faces during the evening meal that day.

Several weeks later, Fr. John was called to another meeting at the Regional Director's office in Ilesha. The topic for discussion was to be the future of the formation House in Nigeria. The big plan was to amalgamate the students from Ghana and those from Nigeria. The one thing wrong with this was that Ghanaians and Nigerians did not make a very good mix. Fr. John felt that it was doomed to fail before it would even start. A representative from the Council of the Missionaries of Africa for formation was present at the meeting. He expressed Rome's wishes. Fr. John made his views on this known and they did not jive with those of Rome. Then and there, the decision was taken to close the Nigerian formation house and the students were to be sent to Bolgatanga in Ghana. Fr. John was to be the one to announce this to the community at the formation house. He was not looking forward to this task. The Regional Director would come later to speak to the students. Fr. John left for Ibadan with a very heavy heart. He had come to appreciate the Nigerian students and their outspoken manner along with their confidence in their capacity to run their own show. He had no desire to change them in this respect. They would voice their opinion even if it meant that they would be thrown out of the seminary. Fr. John admired this because they were not just "yes" men. That did not mean that there were not those among them with a hidden agenda. A good number did want to go to Europe or America. These students, however, mostly ended up giving themselves away at some point in the formation process; therefore, Fr. John was not too concerned about it. He felt that the Rome

Council for formation feared the Nigerian mentality with its strong accent on priesthood as a profession.

In spite of the fact that the formation house was slated to close, Fr. Robert was to continue to look for an appropriate piece of land to build a house in Ibadan. The Missionaries of Africa were in Ibadan but did not have their own property. They were renters; that needed to change. Would Fr. Robert succeed in helping that to happen? Fr. John did not know. Before he left Nigeria, however, a piece of land had been found; all it needed was the approval of the Councils.

Chapter Twenty

Fr. John had reached Timmy by phone and Timmy reassured him that he would be at the bus terminal to pick him up. Fr. John spent a few days with Timmy and the family as well as with Clarisse. He then took the Acadian line bus for Cape Breton. He had to get to Cape Breton as soon as he could since a message had been left with Fr. MacCarthy that the Bishop of his home diocese wanted to see him. There was work but he had to confirm that he would be available to take it. What would this entail? He was very curious to find out.

Della and her husband were at the Acadian bus terminal to pick him up. The next day he drove to Antigonish with Fr. J.P.'s car and was able to see the Bishop that same afternoon. He learned from his interview with Bishop Cosman that the Parish priest of St. Peter's Parish in Cheticamp was going on sabbatical and the diocese needed someone to replace him. It had to be someone who could do everything in the church in French since all services in St. Peter's as well as in St. Joseph's in Des Moines were done in the French language. Fr. John had no problem with that since he was fluent in both French and English. He agreed to take the parish but it would only be for a two year period, while the former pastor finished his sabbatical or until they found someone new to replace him. That was agreed to but Fr. John had a request to make of the Bishop. "I will do this Bishop Cosman, however, I have two young men that I helped escape from the Rwandese/Congo crisis and who desperately need a home to go to. I am asking the diocese to allow me to bring these two young men to live with me in that huge rectory until they are ready to launch out on their own. I believe that the village of Cheticamp is primarily French speaking and that would be quite suitable for them. What I ask is that when I buy food I buy for three people and not just for one, not just for me. Would you agree to this?"

"I think that this situation is possible and you do have the green light to arrange for this to happen," the Bishop answered Fr. John.

Fr. John was pleased with this and decided to call Jules and Chris that week-end to let them know that they now had a home to come to. It wasn't city life but they would be so busy studying and getting their life together that they wouldn't have much time to do more. Little did Fr. John realize all the surprises that awaited him!

He had to prepare this village for the arrival of two young black men. How would they react? How welcome would they be? Fr. John was a bit apprehensive. He had to go through with it regardless. The die was cast. He spoke about it first to the Parish Council. They saw no reason not to welcome them. They would be able to finish their schooling in Canada. Chris still had two years of high school to do and Jules was going into first year University. Fr. John knew that he needed to set that up so that they could start their schooling as soon as they arrived. Each day there were parishioners who inquired about Jules and Chris: when they would be arriving; how they were doing at the language school; and if there was any news about their departure from Nairobi and arrival in Canada. Fr. John knew that it would take some months before anything would happen. He kept in touch with them as best he could. There were times when communication with them was very difficult. It was nearly impossible to get them on the public phone at the Stella Awinja apartment. Of course the difference in time did not help matters any. There was six hours difference, which meant that by midnight in Canada it would be six o'clock in the morning in Nairobi. Fr. John would often leave a message at the language school to tell Jules and Chris when he would be calling. They were also able to call the parish house from Nairobi by reversing the charges. When they were in real need or had an urgent problem, they would do this; it helped them feel more secure. If Fr. John had an important message to relay to them and could not reach them, he would phone the bank and get Martha to tell them that they needed to call him. It did happen that they went for three days without getting in touch with Fr. John when he had an important message for them from immigration. Fr. John would pace the floor of the rectory for hours waiting for the call to come through. When he was not pacing, he would be on his knees in his room or in the small chapel in the basement of the church imploring God to keep them safe and praying that nothing disastrous had befallen them. It often happened that they had not received the message. The personnel at the language school would forget to give them the message or else Martha was not able to make contact with them after work. Fr. John often thought the worse. He could not sleep in peace until he found out that they had received the message and that they were fine.

Finally, one morning in early August, Jules and Chris called Fr. John to inform him that they had been called for their interview with immigration. The interview went very well but they were told that they had to go to the Nairobi immigration office and request an exit visa to leave the country. Their passports had to have that stamp in it for them to leave the country. When they presented themselves to the local immigration office, Chris had no trouble getting his exit visa. For Jules, however, it turned out to be a different story. The agent at that office refused to give Jules the exit visa and he would not state his reasons for this refusal. They both called Fr. John in a panic. "What will I do? The agent there does not want to give me my exit visa," Jules said. "Will I be able to board the plane when the day comes to leave?" Jules asked.

"You must go to the international immigration office and explain the situation to them," Fr. John told him. "They must know what to do." Fr. John was in a panic over this. He hardly slept all night. He prayed and paced the floor until exhaustion took over and he fell into a deep sleep. He called them back the following evening and got them to give him the phone number of the international immigration office. Fr. John called them himself and was put in contact with the person who was dealing with their file. He carefully explained what was happening and mentioned how worried he was and how frightened Jules and Chris were. "Will one leave first and then the other one once he has obtained the exit visa?" Fr. John asked.

"No, that will not happen," answered the agent. "They are not to be separated. They are slated to travel together. That is in the immigration order. If Jules is not issued an exit visa by the local authorities, we will give him one before he goes through the international check point at the airport in Nairobi. We have the authority to do that," answered the agent.

Fr. John, totally relieved, answered, "Oh thank you so much. We were so very worried."

"Oh no, with their status they will both take the flight together."

Jules later told Fr. John that he had returned to the local immigration office to see if he could get the exit visa but the agent there once again refused to give it to him. Jules asked him, "But why will you not give it to me, what is the problem?"

"You did not fulfill the necessary rules for obtaining the renewal of your residence visa," the agent replied.

"But I did the same thing as my brother so why would he get it and not I. This is a real mystery to me"

"I will not discuss it any more than that. You need to get someone who can write a letter for you explaining how you came into this country and if we see that it is legitimate, then we will give you the exit visa."

Jules did not argue any longer. He knew that no one could write such a letter for him. He also realized that he needed to prepare a hefty bribe for this document. It simply would not happen."

Two more weeks passed and they were finally called for their health check. This went well. At the beginning of October they were called to the international immigration office to pick up their tickets and to get ready for their flight to Canada. Jules and Chris let Fr. John know that they would be leaving on the twenty-fifth of October. That would be the day that they would be at the Nairobi airport. It was to be an evening flight so they would be at the airport in the early part of the afternoon so that they would have plenty of time for their preparations. Several of their friends would be accompanying them to the airport. For Jules it would be two friends that he had known in Bukavu, one of them being the friend that he had taken the blow for when trying to help him when he had been attacked by those acquaintances formerly from Bukavu. For Chris it was none other than Cecelia Kamau who had been his close and intimate friend for the many months that he had been in Nairobi. Cecelia did not like to see Chris leave. She knew that she would probably not see him again. She would have loved to have taken the flight with him. They all took a taxi to the airport together so as not to be late. The great day had arrived. There was only one very huge glitch in it all. When Jules and Chris had received their departure papers and itinerary they had been surprised at the proposed destination. They called Fr. John to let him know. "We want you to know which city we are to land in," they had said. "We find it strange that it is so far from where you live!" They could not easily pronounce it so Fr. John asked them to spell it and he was indeed surprised when the name of the city turned out to be WINNIPEG. He could not believe it. This was at least two days journey from where they were to go. Well, they would have to manage something to get them to Halifax and eventually to Cheticamp.

Fr. John, knowing the unpredictability of African bureaucracy so well, would not dare try to change anything. He would leave well enough alone and deal with things later. What he wanted as reassurance was that they both go to the International section of the airport; then he would know that they were on their way. To know this he devised a scheme with Cecelia so that she could inform the family that they had both passed into the international sector of the airport. Fr. John called Cecelia through the Stella Awinja apartment public phone. He gave her his niece's phone number and Cecelia was to call her collect as soon as both of the young men had passed through customs and into the international sector of the airport. When the connection was made with his niece, Cecelia was to simply say the following three words, "They are through!" Then his niece would phone his cell phone to let him know that they were through the customs officials and into the international sector. They would then be on their way. Fr. John and his brother Timmy had made arrangements to go to Winnipeg to pick the boys up. They would stay at the house of relatives of one of Fr. John's parishioners. When the call came through from his niece with the message from Cecelia, Fr. John and Timmy were just entering the town of Sudbury in the province of Ontario. Fr. John's tension eased and he fell asleep. Exhaustion had taken over.

View of Bukavu and its Main Street

Arial Views of Bukavu

Bridge Crossing from the Congo into Rwanda

Ruzizi Seminary: Main Entrance

Chapel Entrance and other Buildings

Views of Chapel

Seminary as seen from Rwanda

Seminary Grounds: Teachers Quarters

Grounds of Seminary facing Lake Kivu

Team of Missionaries of Bukavu, Zaire (Congo)

Students and Teachers: Students Evacuated during the Genocide and War

Cathedral of Bukavu, Seat of the Diocese

Group of Teachers of Ruzizi Seminary. Fr. John, second from right.

Chapter Twenty-one

Once the Nigerian formation house was closed and the students had gone home for the holidays, Fr. John also left for home. He would take a short break at home and afterwards he was to go on a sabbatical year at the Institute of Formative Spirituality at Duquesne University in Pittsburgh, Pennsylvania. He would be in residence at the Parish of the Nativity while studying at the Institute. The year 1991 turned out to be a great, enriching year for him. He learned many survival skills that would be invaluable for his next African assignment: survival skills such as journaling, interpretation of dreams according to the Jungian method, debriefing and sharing with other colleagues about feelings of anger, fear and frustration, the reiteration and analysis of stressful words in one's conversation as well as the exteriorizing of any kind of thoughts recurring over and over in one's mind. There was also the learning and the use of the Enneagramme * for self knowledge which provided a help for greater self-control and inner calm in the face of danger and chaotic situations; add a good touch of humour and a shared cup of tea or coffee to any of these skills and life could be bearable even if extremely stressful.

In Nativity Parish he helped with the Masses in the church on week days and on Sundays. He also often did the visitation to the sick in their homes once a month, at the request of Monsignor Anthony, the pastor in charge of the parish.

"Fr. John, if you want to take the sick calls for me this month, I will put something extra for you in an envelope at the end of the month. What do you say?"

"That sounds super to me," Fr. John would answer. "I can always use the extra, that's for certain." He did enjoy visiting the parishioners in their homes. Many still observed their ethnic customs. He met Croatians, Lebanese, Poles, Ukrainians, Italians, French, all speaking their mother tongue while at home. As soon as Fr. John came into the house, they would revert to English; some had very strong American accents. It was the strangest phenomenon to experience and he enjoyed it very much.

The event that he enjoyed the most, however, was doing ceramics with the retirees in the parish hall on Thursday evenings and all day Saturday. There he let his hair down and he and the retirees told many good stories and had many good laughs.

He still had one more month at the Institute when a telephone call came from Nigeria asking him to return to reopen what he had closed before leaving. Fr. John felt that he could not do this and refused the appointment; he felt very uncomfortable about reopening what he had just closed. He felt that they needed someone new to carry this out. Since he had now learned a good number of survival skills, he told the General Headquarters in Rome to appoint him anywhere else for formation work, but especially where most needed. Within two weeks, a letter arrived from Rome asking him to go to the formation house in Zaire, the present-day Democratic Republic of the Congo. He would be there to teach English as a Second Language and Church History. Fr. John was thrilled with the appointment. Zaire, however, was the last place he had thought about as an appointment. Fr. John would stop in Ottawa on his way home to apply for his visa for Bukavu, where the formation house was located. He had absolutely no idea what lay in store for him. Nothing much was heard, at that time, about Zaire or Central Africa; everything seemed quiet!!! It would turn out to be an incredible experience filled with wonderful moments but many dangerous and fearful ones as well; some of these moments have already been told in this story. This experience would turn out to be one that would bring even greater and deeper conviction for Fr. John, the conviction of the need for Christ in one's life and the need to remain committed to prayer. He would forever remember how he had strongly sensed the presence of evil at various times during the massacres; evil had been palpable. Fr. John strongly felt that among the joys of life there can lurk an evil presence, corrupt, greedy and destructive.

While in Ottawa for his visa, Fr. John decided to stop at St. Paul University to say hello to a few old friends. He stopped at Sister Claudia's office to say hello to her. Sr. Claudia, a Sister of St. Ann, was in charge of housing for the St. Paul University students. They had had many a conversation in the past when he had been in charge of the Ottawa formation house. When Sister Claudia saw him standing in the doorway of her office, she exclaimed, "Well, for heaven's sake, what ill-wind brings you here?"

"I'm returning to Africa for formation work," replied Fr. John, "especially after all the formation I've been through myself in Pittsburgh."

"Oh, dear," said Sister Claudia, "and where are you headed this time?"

"I've just picked up my visa for Zaire," he answered. She looked at him with a stunned expression.

"Are you crazy?" demanded Sister Claudia. "You're going to get yourself killed. Do you realize that we can't even send mail to Zaire? There is an embargo on anything going into that country. It is extremely dangerous. What are your superiors thinking? I can't believe that they are sending you there." Sister Claudia looked at him with fear written all over her face.

"Don't worry about me Sister. I always fall on my two feet. I will not be alone of course; I'll be part of a community of teachers and formators." Fr. John would remember Sr. Claudia's words many months later.

Fr. John did not think very much about this at that moment. He was always ending up in some kind of a mess in Africa anyway. Again he was to arrive in August and again he would be traveling alone. No other brother would be going that way. He would go via Brussels. A stopover in Belgium would be good since many of the Missionaries of Africa in Zaire were Belgians.

Without too much thought about Sister Claudia's outburst, Fr. John left for Belgium that August. He enjoyed his short visit in Belgium, managing to visit Bruges and its many historical sites. He enjoyed history immensely. From Brussels he would be flying to Bukavu via Kigali in Rwanda. This was an easier route to take and closer than going through Kinshasa. It was also less fraught with danger... or so he thought. He would take Air France rather than Sabena Airways to Kigali. The Air France flights were more reliable. This meant that he would have to fly from Brussels to Paris and take his flight to Kigali from Charles DeGaulle Airport. When they landed in Kigali, Fr. John was stunned and the first question that ran through his mind was, "What did I get myself into this time?" French soldiers immediately surrounded the airplane after it had taxied to the terminal. There were also armed French soldiers on the roof of the airport. The passengers were escorted into the airport terminal by armed soldiers. There was no one allowed in the terminal except the disembarking passengers and the airport personnel. Everyone else was outside looking in through the windows and doors to see if the person they were waiting for had arrived. Fr. John had no problem clearing his two suitcases. They did open them, but realized that he had only clothing, toiletries and some books. Once cleared, he walked towards the door and the crowd waiting outside. Then he saw him, a small priest holding a magazine with Missionaries of Africa marked on it. He went towards him and immediately the little priest said his name. They embraced and with a twinkle in his eye Fr. Joseph said to Fr. John, "Welcome to Rwanda, I'm Fr. Joseph your welcoming committee of one!" Fr. John of course gave him one of his chuckles. They got into the car and left for the Kigali regional house. Fr. Paul would be there for a few days and then he would take a small plane to Kamembe/Cyangugu. Once there, he would cross the border to Bukavu where the school was, just on the Zaire/Rwanda border. As they were driving along towards the regional house, Fr. Joseph said to Fr. John, "Well, would you believe that I just bought your ticket for Rome last week?"

"My ticket for Rome," repeated Fr. John. "What would I be going to Rome for, pray tell?"

"You and Fr. Jos will be going to the formation meeting of all the formation houses in December. You are supposed to be the one to replace Fr. Jos at the formation house in Bukavu. He has been there for ten years and they need a change; you're the chosen one," said Fr. Joseph, smiling.

"Really! Well, that's news to me," exclaimed Fr. John. "I had asked to simply teach and not be in charge of anything. I thought I had done my share when in charge in Canada and Nigeria." Then Fr. John thought to himself, "Isn't that just like headquarters in Rome to let me know these things through the oddest sources and when least expected." Fr. John also remembered at that moment their reassurance that he would not be in charge of anything, but now he realized that he would simply be in charge of everything!! Why not? He was a big boy now! His heart sank and he felt sick to his stomach and that foreboding feeling crept through him again.

He really knew no one at the regional house and so felt rather alone. The person that he had known and studied with was on home-leave. Somehow he felt as if he was experiencing some kind of surreal moment. He felt like a stranger in a strange land; all seemed suspended in time, nothing was sure and the situation in Central Africa was very fragile and unstable. What would be the outcome of the famous meeting that was to take place in Arusha, Tanzania between the Rwandese Government and the rebels? Many of his colleagues were sceptical and worried about the outcome. "We need to be prepared for anything," said one of the colleagues visiting Kigali at the time for supplies needed in his mission. They were far from ready for the horror that would eventually befall them.

Quickly enough the time came to take the flight to Kamembe/ Cyangugu where he would cross the border into Zaire. He arrived in the early afternoon. Fr. Francis and Fr. Rolfe were there to meet him. It was a beautiful area and from the Rwandese side of the border, the school looked quite amazing, nestled there by the lake. Everything was luscious and green and the mountains and hills in the background were beautiful. Fr. John's spirits lifted. Maybe it would not be so bad after all. Yes, it all looked quite peaceful, maybe too peaceful! It would certainly not remain so!!

Not all the teachers had returned from home-leave, so the school was relatively quiet. Fr. John, as usual, had plenty of time to prepare his courses. The school was a formation house for the philosophy part of the studies for those training to become Missionaries of Africa: Africans to evangelize Africans. The school was known as Our Lady of the Ruzizi. Ruzizi was the name of the river that separated Zaire from Rwanda and it flowed into Lake Kivu, a volcanic lake, quite splendid and in which people could swim without too much danger of contracting diseases. It was great on a hot day to be able to go throw oneself into the cool waters of the lake. Fr. John often did this; it was quite refreshing.

Once again, all the brothers there were strangers to him, so he was meeting them for the first time. As a result, he felt somewhat alone, even in community. The town of Bukavu was quite dilapidated, but one could see that it had been a very beautiful town in its day. The president of Zaire had become so corrupt that nothing in the town was properly maintained except for the mission properties and the privately owned buildings. Bukavu, in the past, had been known as the Pearl of the Kivu and many of the colonials would not return to Europe for their holidays, but would come to Bukavu to enjoy its beauties, the temperate climate and the lake.

Not all the brothers were present at the seminary; some were away on home-leave, one was studying in the United States, and others were on retreat or visiting other missions in Zaire. Again Fr. John had plenty of time to get his bearings, prepare classes and get a good glimpse of the town of Bukavu. He had an office and bedroom combined with a bathroom just off the office. It was quite a pleasant set up especially since there was a very large window in his bedroom that looked onto the back property of the seminary with a full view of lake Kivu. It was a beautiful view. Fr. John loved it.

One morning as he was working in his office, going over some of the student files, there was a knock at the door. When he opened the door, there stood an African woman who kept repeating the word to him in French "chap-e-let", "chap-e-let". John did not understand immediately what this woman wanted, but one of the White Sisters of Africa who was on retreat at the seminary said to him, "Fr. John, do not give her a rosary, give her a spoon instead." "But why would she need either one," replied Fr. John. It was a real mystery to him. Sr. Yolande answered him, "One of the women is giving birth on the grass behind the school library and they need something to press on her tongue to make her gag; this will force her to push since she is too exhausted to push herself for the birthing process to happen." At that moment Fr. John learned that one of the women who was carrying a large bundle of charcoal from Rwanda and who was pregnant, had had her water break just in front of the seminary entrance. The other women had carried her to the grassy piece of ground behind the seminary library and she was now in the process of giving birth. Fr. John quickly ran to the refectory and brought a spoon for her. That seemed to settle that and he went back to his work. A few moments later there was another loud knock on the door. It was the same woman but this time repeating in French the word "lame" which meant razer-blade. Fr. John then understood that this must be to cut the umbilical cord. He rushed to find a razer-blade and the woman rushed off with it. Fr. John went back to his paper work. Some time later he could hear joyful singing coming from outside. He opened the door of his office to find a number of women singing and dancing with one woman in front of them holding a new born baby. How filled with joy they were! Of course, the woman who had had the baby was somewhat tired after her ordeal and the woman still had to walk all the way to the other end of town, so the night watchman told him. Fr. John, therefore, got the land cruiser out of the garage and with the help of the night watchmen drove the women home. They were overjoyed and kept on singing. At one point as they were singing, Fr. John could detect the word "Padiri" in the local language. He asked the night watchman, "Why are they using the word 'Padiri'? Fr. John knew already that it was a word used for the priest, coming from the word "Padre". The night watchman answered, laughing, "Father, they are saying that this boy-child will be named "Padiri" since he was born in the "Padiri's" compound.

The first year at Ruzizi seminary was relatively quiet and extremely busy. Fr. Jos was still in charge so Fr. John was asked to teach English as a Second Language, Scripture and Church History. He also ended up with many students coming to him for spiritual guidance. Of course, even then, there were constant rumours that the Patriotic Front had attacked Rwanda from Uganda to the north. There were stories of refugee camps with many Hutus in them. The Patriotic Front was purported to be Hemas, but it was also known that the Hemas and the Tutsis are cousins, so they are really of the same ethnic group. The full-scale war that later developed had really already started in 1990 in the north where Rwanda forms a border with Uganda. These Patriotic-Front soldiers were really the children of the Tutsis who had fled during the uprisings of the 1960s and the take-over of power by the Hutus. Not many people mentioned the 1990 attacks in the north; it would be admitting that the Tutsis had started the war.

Fr. John also realized that the situation in Zaire was in a state of collapse. Everything was in a shambles, with people not being paid and people living in fear of the military and police. There was a commission formed to look into the whole political situation and what could be done to correct the terrible situation in Zaire. In a country that was really quite rich in gold, diamonds, cobalt, and natural resources, with a pleasant climate, vast forests, parks filled with gorillas, lakes and mountains and many other tourist attractions, the poverty of the country was appalling. The kleptocratic president made sure that all monies went to him; he had his pawns in place everywhere and he controlled the military and police. It was the saddest situation possible and much hope was being put into this commission that was attempting to form some kind of interim government. The big question was, how would the president react to this commission from his glorious, rich and modern domain in the northeast corner of the country? Many people, even the elderly, thought that the president was the only one who could correct the situation. He and only he had the power and the magic. How could the commission, with Cardinal Malula at its head, advance without the president's stamp of approval. Once the president would arrive on the scene, it was very possible that everything would fall apart. The presidential guard, his own military police, protected him and everyone feared them. This president had all the answers and seemed to hold all the trump cards. Much confidence, however, was being placed in this new commission that had been formed to study the situation. Each evening, on the television or radio news, the reports would be given about this commission and its work. Hope was so high in those days of the commission. But in the end the commission was sabotaged and its work amounted to very little; it was all a terrible disappointment. Zaire just kept sinking deeper into chaos and destruction by those who were supposed to be its guardians. The Church that had formerly listened to the president finally took the side of the people, especially the poor. It was a necessary step; otherwise the credibility of the Church would have been lost forever.

Fr. John quickly became aware that he would need to keep to a daily programme of prayer for himself if he was to survive in this chaotic mess. Each morning, therefore, he would take time to either kneel or sit in prayer in the prayer corner he set up in his room. The prayer corner was at the foot of his bed facing the huge window that looked onto the lake. In the morning the sun poured into his room and Fr. John enjoyed a quiet time of prayer. He would then join the students and other staff members in the beautiful round chapel that faced Rwanda and overlooked that side of the lake and the Ruzizi River. Both staff and students each had a small stool to sit on; these stools were situated along the chapel wall forming a semi-circle and facing the main altar and tabernacle of repose. It was quite pleasant to sit and pray there. Life at Ruzizi Seminary was pleasant, welcoming and enjoyable. Many events would develop to change this peaceful atmosphere.

Fr. John went to the formation meeting in December of the first year that he was at the Ruzizi formation house. He met a number of colleagues he had studied with who were also in formation work. That part of the meeting was great, but there was much work to be done, with long discussions of the formation programme. One point underlined by Fr. John about the Ruzizi formation house was the lack of African colleagues on staff. It was one of the oldest centres of philosophy and, as yet, there had been no attempt at Africanizing the centre. This was duly noted and the following year they would hopefully have an African colleague on staff. Fr. John told them that he would remind them of this. Almost two years later, Fr. Bosco, a Ghanaian Missionary of Africa, was sent to them from the Bunia mission, further north in Zaire. Fr. Bosco was an excellent choice for the formation house. He would replace Fr. Gregory as bursar; Fr. Gregory had been called home because of his mother's health. Fr. Bosco would also give one course to the students. One other event that materialized the following year was the departure of Fr. Jos as director of the centre. Who would replace him was the big question!

The regional superior of the Zairean mission wanted to appoint Fr. John to replace Fr. Jos. Fr. John refused to accept this appointment in the beginning. He felt that he was too new and that he did not know the local language; also the political situation was extremely complex. He felt like a fish out of water. To take the helm after just one year there was a difficult decision to make. The regional council members, however, kept insisting, telling Fr. John that he was the one most qualified to do this. After much soul-searching, reflection and prayer, Fr. John finally accepted the position. It was in the course of that year that things began to change for the worse.

Before the changes in the political situation became too drastic, Fr. John managed to make a few changes of his own in the seminary program of studies and in the recruitment situation for the seminary. This he did in a quiet, unassuming but firm manner. First of all, the new students who were accepted at Ruzizi Seminary did not come directly to them in Bukavu. They were selected from a long list of candidates who were sent to the Preparation Centre in the city of Goma, Zaire, a town somewhat further to the north east of the country. This formation centre in Goma was necessary to bring the student up to par in French and Philosophy.

The schools of Zaire were in such a terrible state that some of the student hardly knew how to read or write, once they had completed secondary school. Many teachers were neglecting their teaching assignments since they were not being paid for the most part by the government. They, therefore, accepted teaching assignments in private schools, where they were being paid daily. Many students were there for themselves, were fending for themselves and were being granted a secondary school certificate whether properly prepared or not. The preparatory year in Goma, before coming to Bukavu was, therefore, extremely necessary. It was a difficult and intensive year.

When Fr. John took over the direction of the Ruzizi Seminary of Bukavu the staff of the preparatory year in Goma were themselves assessing the ability and progress of each student and sending the files to Fr. John and his staff for them to study and make their acceptance of the students. It often turned out, that out of twenty files, only five or six students were accepted. This brought a lot of bitterness and criticism from the staff of the preparatory year, and from the regional house staff in Bukavu.

The staff of Ruzizi Seminary was constantly accused of being too severe in its selection. At the end of the third year, as director of the seminary, Fr. John and his colleagues were studying the group of files for the next academic year. It was not encouraging. Out of sixteen files, only six students were accepted. Fr. John thought to himself "I will certainly get shit this time for this selection!"

He quickly typed the list of names of those accepted, made copies for each colleague on the regional council, and went to the regional house to distribute them. Upon entering the house he realized that the regional council was in a meeting. He therefore slipped the copies under their doors and left.

Later that same day, he was driving into town and met the regional superior and one of his assistants as they were driving, presumably to the seminary. They flagged him down and Fr. John called to them through the open window "What is it? What is the matter?"

"We received the lists. We need to talk."

"Let us go back to the regional house then, because I need to see the bursar," answered Fr. John. Off they went. Fr. John was invited into the meeting since they were having a break. He stood before the council as they sarcastically brought up their objections and practically laughed in Fr. John's face. Seemingly wanting to make him feel totally responsible for this disastrous selection, at that point Fr. John uttered in a very annoyed tone of voice "that's enough! Enough! I did not ask for this position of director. You were all convinced of my qualification. As well, I'm not the only one to make the student selections. We are a team of teachers doing it. So the other teachers should be here to hear this! Also, if I am not apt for this position, then remove me. I did not ask for it. You are free to put someone else who is more qualified for the position. Is that clear? I did not come here to be laughed at and reprimanded like a schoolboy, so stop it right now."

They all looked at him in utter amazement. The regional superior, Fr. Joseph spoke up "we are not laughing at you or reprimanding you. We just want you to see how disappointed we are about the selection of new students. It will discourage those colleagues who are working in the recruitment field."

"I am not in this to please those who are recruiting candidates," replied Fr. John, still fuming. "And if you are not laughing at me, you have a very poor way of showing it. Now what I suggest is that you book a time to come to the seminary and meet with all of us and air your grievances and each colleague will voice his opinion of things." They all agreed, and it was decided that the Monday of the following week would be appropriate to meet.

Fr. John returned to the seminary and told the other colleagues of what had transpired. They were dumbfounded. They did accept to meet the following Monday and agreed to review the student files again. Surprisingly enough, the Monday meeting went well, and four more candidates were added to the number chosen, bringing the number to ten. Fr. John had taken time to reflect on the situation of the discernment and acceptance of candidates and proposed a new system of selection. He strongly recommended that they not make a selection separately from the group of teachers and formators from the preparatory year in Goma. Fr. John addressed the group saying "once the team in Goma have completed their selection of files, they should send them to us to read and review and then both centres should meet for discussion of the files and a final selection. Also at one point during the academic year, the team at the preparatory year, should some to Bukavu seminary and meet with teachers and students and in their turn the team of the Bukavu seminary should go to Goma to visit and meet with the students and teachers. It would then cease to be a strange and mysterious situation filled with doubts and suspicion." All were in favour of this new system. The first visit would be on the part of the Bukavu seminary and the director and one teacher of the team would make the visit.

Fr. John and Fr. Emile, who was the French language teacher, left for Goma the following month. They traveled by boat up Lake Kivu. The boat trip took most of the day, but was very pleasant. The visit to the centre was good and very appreciated by the staff and students. The visit removed much of the fear and mystery surrounding the seminary in Bukavu. So Fr. John and Fr. Emile had also decided to add another visit to the trip. After visiting the centre in Goma, they would fly to Bunia, a mission further north, since a good number of candidates for the following year would be coming to the Goma centre. The trip to Bunia was quite impressive. The pilot of the small six-seater plane, took them extremely close to the mouth of the Nyrangongo volcano. Fr. Emile was so pleased, that he could not stop taking photographs. They were so close that they could practically see inside the crater. They then flew over a range of mountains, coming upon a large valley with a beautiful expanse of green wispy grass. In the distance, they could see the small Bunia airport. They landed smoothly, disembarked and were taken to the Bunia mission by one of the colleagues of that mission. They were, however, appalled by the neglect of the town and roads of Bunia. It had been a beautiful town, and vestiges of that beauty still shone through. Their visit with the confreres there and with the proposed candidates was quite enjoyable. They left for Bukavu pleased with the outcome.

Upon Fr. John's return to Bukavu, he was informed by Fr. Bosco, the bursar of the seminary, that the passes had arrived from the Ministry of Tourism of the Kivu for the visit of the third-year students to the gorillas of Kahuzi Village. When Fr. John announced this to the students, they were all over joyed. Each year, permission was given to the third-year students for a free visit with the gorillas, because the students were leaving their country and home to continue their studies and formation, either elsewhere in Africa, or overseas. Otherwise, the visit cost $120 American dollars per person, something they would never be able to afford.

Ninja: One of the Gorillas of Kahuzi Park

The six third-year students set out early in the morning on the date indicated in the letter sent by the ministry. They arrived early at the park and the guides were there to welcome them. They briefed them as well on how the visit was to unfold. They were to be accompanied by the guides at all times. They were not to speak harshly or loudly when in the presence of the gorillas. If a gorilla charged toward them, they were not to move or to turn and run, but just stay still. The gorilla would stop and not attack them; he was merely establishing his territory. They tracked the gorillas by following their droppings and the places where they had slept. It did not take much time to find them. When they had found one group, the guide told them to be still. He said "this is Ninja, everyone. He is feuding with his son who ran off with one of his wives. He may not be too friendly today, but he will not harm you. Just respect his territory." Ninja was huge and impressive. He would, at times, come near to them and turn his back to them, looking back over his shoulder with disdain as if to say "oh, you mere mortals."

The visit was totally enjoyable. They were also quite exhausted when they returned to the seminary that evening. The topic of conversation, of course, at the meal that evening, was the gorillas of Kahuzi Park.

As they journeyed from Kahuzi Park, the students were chatting of their big third-year assignment they had to complete. The students had the whole three years to work and complete a special assignment. It had become a totally enormous work, with the students choosing whatever topic they wanted. Some were turning out what looked like a doctoral thesis. This assignment had become a total exaggeration and the students did not seem to learn much from it. They would even have someone in the town type up this assignment for them, making it look like their first published book. It was a total nightmare to read and correct.

Gorillas of Kahuzi Park

Fr. John decided to bring this up at one of the staff meetings proposing changes to bring this assignment to a more realistic and learning experience. "What type of changes would you propose," one of the colleagues asked.

Fr. John responded by saying "I think that the students should not be choosing whatever topic they want. They should be given a list of ten topics, most of the topics being on African culture and traditions. Then the assignments should not be longer than twenty pages. It would be read and corrected, and a grade given, which would be part of their Philosophy grade. It could be typed, but it also could be handwritten. I say this," said Fr. John, "because the students are neglecting their courses and exams to concentrate on this assignment, being done at the last minute, and then having this voluminous book typed at a cost that they can ill-afford." All of the teachers, without exception were for the changes.

The students, however, gave much resistance, and argued at length with Fr. John about all this. Fr. John told them in one of the evening assemblies, "we have decided on these changes and we are not coming back on our decision. As Pharaoh in the Old Testament said to the Egyptian people 'let it be written, let it be done.' There is no going back to the unnecessary thesis travesty." With time the students accepted and got used to the change. Many secretly were very happy.

Life at the Formation Centre continued on its course. Its peaceful rhythm was eventually interrupted by a tragedy that occurred within the Missionaries of Africa. One of their colleagues had a massive stroke. Fr. John would eventually organize his repatriation to Canada and would himself accompany the Belgian doctor who would travel with the patient. Fr. John had always wondered about the repatriation process. He would find out first hand since he was the one who was asked to accompany the doctor on this mission.

As time passed Fr. John became even more amazed and fearful about the drastic situation in Zaire. He realized that Sr. Claudia's concerns were well founded that day when he had spoken to her. All of Zaire continued to be in a terribly chaotic state. People were hungry. They needed jobs; they needed security; upheaval and war seemed close; the situation was frightening. They needed reform! The commission that had been formed to look at all this had come to a stand still. The top brass close to the President had not liked what was developing, so there had been a lot of sabotage. They did not want all the favours coming their way to stop. They wanted to remain in the good graces of their President, which, of course, was to their advantage. The President, for his part, wanted the people to remain loyal to him. Therefore he kept pushing the army to create situations that would cause the people, especially the students, to rebel; then, the army could be sent to subdue them. So it was that a good number of situations arose that provoked the people. The soldiers would easily enter the market and shops and loot, taking whatever they wanted. When the people protested, the opportunity to become violent became even greater.

One afternoon two soldiers encountered a small boy selling cigarettes along the roadside. This young boy was simply trying to make a bit of money for the family and only had a few cigarettes to sell. The two soldiers decided to take all of his cigarettes and left him no money. The young child protested vehemently, screaming and crying, demanding his money. So the soldiers beat the young child to within an inch of his life. Unfortunately for them there were people watching what was going on and several men ran after the soldiers. Once they had caught up to them, they attacked them and beat them to death. The word got around about what had happened and the military barracks where the soldiers were from went on a terrible rampage throughout the district where this had happened. They looted, burned houses, arrested people to interrogate even killed a few persons in the process; life had become cheap in Bukavu! This went on for days and the gun fire could be heard for many miles around.

That first evening of these developments, Fr. John was lying on his bed after the evening meal, reading. Every once in a while he could hear a snapping noise as if someone was throwing stones against the wall of the building. At first he did not pay too much attention to it. The snapping noise, however, increased. He stopped reading to listen more carefully and see if he could figure out what the noise meant. Suddenly it dawned on him that the noise was not from stones but was the sound of gun shots! He threw himself up from the bed and went to the door of his office. Looking out, he yelled to the night watchman, saying, "What is happening? What is going on?" Then he noticed that some of the students were huddled close to the refectory door and close to some other buildings wondering what was going on.

The night watchman answered Fr. John saying, "The soldiers are on a rampage! Two of their men have been killed because they beat a young child who was selling a few cigarettes. Now they are killing and looting, burning homes and arresting people. No one can stop them. The whole town is in an uproar! We cannot go out, it is too dangerous. This is happening just up the road in the Nguba sector of the town and no one can pass. They are furious and have killed a number of people. We don't know what will happen."

The night watchman was not able to go home the next morning. It was still too dangerous and the soldiers were continuing their rampage. This lasted for five days and the school had to make do with the supply of food that they had in stock. Each morning and evening Fr. John would go to the gate of the compound to see if he could speak to a soldier or customs officer who was commencing or finishing his or her border duty to ask if things were finally settled in the town so he could go to the Regional House for money to shop for food and other needed materials. The seminary was situated next to the border crossing into Rwanda. Upon leaving the Seminary compound, if one turned left, one would find oneself at the barrier for the customs office. There were soldiers and police at this point to control the coming and going of persons and vehicles wanting to cross in or out of Rwanda. The Seminary, therefore, always had the military and police close to the gate. During those first five days of rampage all the soldiers or customs officers who went by told Fr. John that it was still too dangerous to venture out. No vehicles, not even taxis, were circulating in the town. Finally, on the sixth day, which was a Saturday, one soldier came toward the border crossing next to the school.

"How are things in town?" asked Fr. John as he stood at the gate.

"Things have quieted, Father, and the market is open. You can go into town now. I think everything is settled," said the soldier.

Fr. John did not hesitate. He got out the land cruiser and took the first student in sight with him and headed for the Regional House. They badly needed money for food. Supplies were quite low. The school had a fair size group of students to feed. Fr. John did not reflect on the fact that Alexander, the student he had taken with him, was a Tutsi! This was a dangerous move on Fr. John's part. However, they went to the Regional House; everything seemed back to normal in town. When they reached the Central market, it was functioning quite well and many people were buying and selling. They were able to reach the Regional House without incident. Fr. John went to the bursar's office to see Fr. Joseph, one of the older priests who was replacing Fr. Andrew the regular, regional bursar who was on home-leave. Fr. Fausto, an Italian and the house bursar, was also in the office.

"How good to see you after your house arrest during the killings and the lootings," they said humorously.

"Activity seems to have resumed in the market and around town," said Fr. Fausto.

"It would seem so," replied Fr. John "We really need money for food and supplies and to pay our workers," he said. "Five days is too long to go without money! I'll need the equivalent of 500 American dollars in Zairean notes," said Fr. John.

Fr. Joseph got out a huge carton of bills, all made up into large bundles of Zairean notes. The money was extremely devalued, so the local currency had to be transported in huge cardboard cartons. All exchange of monies was now being done on the black market. The banks had no capital to carry out those exchange transactions. One American dollar was now worth five million Zaire notes and the largest at that time was a 20 Zaire note. The situation had become totally ridiculous. The present government did not seem to care too much; they had all the dollars they needed to live expansively! Fr. John knew that it would take some time to count all those bundles of notes. They needed to count them since it was always possible for the black market racketeers to slip smaller Zairean notes inside the bundles. One could get rolled in many different ways.

Fr. Joseph began the counting, helped by Fr. John and Fr. Fausto. Fr. Joseph was very slow at this process which was very frustrating for Fr. John. Fr. Joseph did not want to make a mistake in counting. As they were counting, they suddenly heard a burst of gun fire. Fr. Fausto went to the door of the office and looked out. There were people coming from the direction of the market place.

"What is going on?" asked Fr. Fausto.

"The soldiers are on the rampage again," answered one man. "There is fighting again in the Central Market. Apparently two soldiers looted one woman's food stall and when she protested, they shot her. The people in the market were enraged and attacked the soldiers. The whole market is in a panic. The two soldiers called for reinforcement and chaos erupted. They pursued people, shot at them, smashing the stalls as they ranted and raved. The market quickly emptied. It is very dangerous at the moment!"

Fr. Fausto came back in and told Fr. John that it might be better if they stayed at the Regional House for a while until things calmed down. Then maybe they could venture out. Fr. John was very concerned. At that moment he realized that Alexander who had accompanied him was a Tutsi and had the typical Tutsi physical appearance.

Fr. Joseph was still counting the bills. It seemed to go on interminably. Fr. John asked him to speed it up a bit. The longer they took, the more dangerous the ride home would be. What would the soldiers do if they stopped his vehicle on the way back to the school? He regretted having come; he should have waited for Fr. Bosco. He knew the language of the soldiers. He was now heading across town and through the market area with a box full of money and a Tutsi student next to him! It was not a good situation to be in!

Fr. Joseph finally finished counting the bank notes. Fr. John loaded the carton in a not too visible place in the land cruiser, and he and Alexander set out for the school. Fr. Fausto said to them as they were leaving, "Go slowly as you approach the market area and if you see that it is too dangerous, turn back! You can both stay the night here if need be!"

Fr. John turned onto the street that led up a long hill that led down into the Central Market area. He was terrified. His heart pounded. He drove very slowly, as suggested, forcing himself to take his time. There was no one in the streets. The market was empty. Everyone had fled for cover, hiding from the soldiers and their guns. As they made their way down the long hill they both had a good view of the market area. There was no one in sight but a gun shot could be heard now and then. As they came directly into the market area, a soldier jumped out into the middle of the road, appearing as if from nowhere. He had a rifle in his hand and pointed it directly at the land cruiser and at Fr. John. In spite of having been startled, Fr. John brought the vehicle slowly to a complete stop and raised his two hands into the air in a position of surrender. He told Alexander to do the same thing. The soldier peered closely at Fr. John without changing the position of the gun. He suddenly made signs for Fr. John to continue, gesturing with his gun. Fr. John put the vehicle back in gear and, avoiding the soldier, high-tailed it for the school. Why the soldier had let him go, Fr. John could only wonder? Maybe the soldier did not want a white man to have first hand knowledge of what was going on? But Fr. John wasted no time in trying to find out! The fear in him turned to nausea and he felt like throwing up! He had placed himself and Alexander in serious danger. He would need to be more careful in future. More and more incidents like this developed as the situation with the military, politics and the hungry people deteriorated. Each time he and Fr. Bosco went into town, they encountered different, difficult situations. One never knew what would happen next! It could not continue like this without some kind of full scale war developing. Fr. John feared that it would get much worse as time wore on.

It was during the Easter break of Fr. John's second year that he and Fr. John-Paul decided to go to Kigali to recruit a colleague for their philosophy courses and to shop for much-needed materials for the centre. The office was badly in need of a new filing cabinet and other office supplies. All this could be bought quite easily in Kigali. Fr. John-Paul had worked many years in Rwanda. He knew and understood Kinyarwanda quite well. He would show Fr. John around the city and on their way they would stop at the different missions that Fr. John-Paul knew so well. They would visit both going and coming back.

They left Bukavu for Kigali early in the morning after breakfast on April 1, 1994 and, without rushing, arrived in Kigali in the late afternoon. It was great to just sit and have a cool beer, chat and hear the news as the sun went down. They always ate the evening meal late at the main mission. They were informed that a special meeting was taking place in Tanzania between the present regime in power, which was mainly Hutu-led and whose president was Habyarimana, and the Patriotic Front, who were Rwandese rebels from Uganda with a certain Paul Kagame at its head. They were to come to an agreement on shared power in Rwanda. The public opinion, of course, was that it would never work, since no hard-line Tutsi would ever share power with the Hutu and vice versa. Time would tell what the outcome would be.

The days flew by and Fr. John-Paul showed Fr. John the city of Kigali. He took him to the different missions where a few of the colleagues had been classmates of Fr. John's in Canada and England. It was good to meet again after so many years. They loved to visit the different missions, but had to be very careful when visiting at night. There were people, especially young men, who were demonstrating against the alliance being prepared in Tanzania. One evening as Fr. John was returning to the regional house with Fr. Clement, they realized that they were heading straight for a group of these young demonstrators, who had a huge bonfire of car tires in the middle of the street. Fr. Clement and Fr. John had studied together in

England and had got on very well at the time. They were pleased to be able to spend some time together now in Africa. "Oh, my," Fr. Clement yelled suddenly. "We can't go that way. They can stop us, take the car and God knows what would happen to us." He made a U-turn in the middle of the road and quickly raced to the mission by another road before they were noticed. Fr. John was riveted to the seat; his heart was racing. He could hardly breathe. "Are you OK?" asked Fr. Clement.

"Yes, yes, I'm OK. Don't mind me," said Fr. John. "Keep driving and don't stop. We don't want to be burned alive tonight." They finally arrived at the regional house by ten p.m. Fr. John had a coffee and a biscuit with Fr. Clement and then wasted no time in getting to bed. He felt drained and it took some time for him to get to sleep. He did not want to even imagine what would have happened, if they had run into those demonstrators.

Fr. John managed to buy his new filing cabinet and a number of other things for the school. He was able to meet with Fr. Granville and get him to accept the philosophy teaching position for the new school year; quite a number of things were accomplished. Fr. John was quite pleased with the trip. The day was April 6 and they were heading back to Bukavu the next day. That evening, Fr. John telephoned his sister in Canada to tell her that they were heading back to the formation house the next day. While they were watching a programme on television, Fr. Clement came to the door of the sitting room. He said to them, "Prepare yourselves for trouble. I've just heard over the radio that the president's airplane returning from Tanzania was just shot down as they were approaching the airport for landing. Everyone on board is dead, including the Burundian president who was traveling with them." Everyone, all ten colleagues, came out onto the verandah, stunned.

"Do they know who shot the plane down?" asked one of the priests.

"They apparently know nothing about who shot the plane down. They suspect that it is the Patriotic Front. But one news cast is saying that it was the president's own men who were totally opposed to the deal who are the culprits. Who knows really? I'm sure there are dissidents on both sides," replied Fr. Clement.

A cold shiver went through Fr. John. What would tomorrow bring? He did not have to wait until the next day. It did not take long for the shooting to start. Explosions, shouts and yells could be heard from the surrounding areas. The Young Christian Workers' Centre next to them was attacked. They could hear shooting coming from there, as well as the shouts, screams and wails. A grenade suddenly went off. When things had calmed down somewhat, three of the priests from the regional house who spoke the local language went over to the centre to see what had happened. It was carnage in the centre. Some soldiers and young thugs had attacked the centre and had shot and killed many of the Tutsis who lived at the centre. The centre rented rooms to young people working and studying in Kigali. Three young women were dead and one young woman sat against the wall of her dormitory with a bullet in her stomach and gunshot wounds in her leg; she was moaning in pain. The priests convinced a soldier who was still there to take her to the hospital. The other three young women were carried to the regional house and buried in the garden. Many of the people at that centre took refuge with the priests at the regional house. Some others came from elsewhere in the area: all Tutsis. They were terrified. Among those who came to take refuge was a doctor. Before burying the girls in the garden, the priests found someone who knew them. They took their names down and the date of their deaths and burial and got that doctor to sign the papers on which they had written the information. The priests did not want to be blamed later for having killed those young women. It was when people started arriving to take refuge with them, that the priests found out that there were groups of people, mainly young men, who were going about brutalizing and killing anyone they came across. These young men formed a kind of killing militia. They were without mercy and they were seeking out the Tutsis, whom they now openly called the cockroaches. One of the radio stations began its broadcasting, urging the people to stay at home, that they would be safe, that they need not worry and that they would be protected. In. reality, the priests of the regional house found out that they were being fed this information so that they could be more easily found and killed. The Tutsi households were marked and some were killed by their own neighbours. It was utter chaos and bloodshed. One of the first groups of Tutsis to die was a group of six Jesuit priests, who ran a retreat house in one of the quarters of Kigali. They were hacked to death and the retreat house was awash with blood. This came over the news on the radio without saying that the priests were Africans.

Fr. John feared that this would come over the international news and that his family would hear about it; so, the next morning he phoned his sister again; luckily the phone lines were still working. When she answered, he said to her, "Hi. It's me again. If you hear about killings going on here over the news, don't worry. I'm fine." Before he could go on any further, she blurted out, "What? You're fine!!!! It was already on the news here and one of the first news items was that six priests were slaughtered. What in the hell are you doing there? Get out of there. I couldn't believe my ears when it came over the news. How are you going to get out of there?" She was absolutely frantic. She told him that many people had already called to find out if that was where he was. She was beside herself. Fr. John tried to calm her, to reassure her that they were fine and that everything would be OK. But she was not convinced. He hated to hang up, because she was so upset. He told her that he had to hang up, because some of the priests had to use the phone while it was still working. He reassured his sister that they would get out as soon as they were able to and that he was not alone at the mission.

The shooting and the killing continued into the afternoon of the next day. One of the priests realized that the many people who had taken refuge with them at the regional house were gathering sticks, stones and tree branches to defend themselves if the killers came to slaughter them. They would most probably be killed, but they would kill a few themselves before dying. When the priests realized this they knew that the militia could easily blame them for encouraging those taking refuge with them to defend themselves; that could push them to slaughter the priests along with the refugees. That evening, therefore, after the meal, they gathered in the sitting room and prepared themselves for death. The eldest of the group of ten missionaries led them in a prayer for forgiveness and preparation to face death. Fr. John-Paul and Fr. John were sitting next to each other. It had to be done. Fr. John was numb with grief and fear. He could not feel his legs from the knees down as they sat there in reflection before God and with one another. The shooting and the screams continued.

They stayed up as late as they could. They put out all the lights in the buildings and on the property so as not to draw attention to themselves. The telephone was still working and many of the mission parishes would call to tell them that the killers had come by and slaughtered all the Tutsis who had taken refuge with them. They even slaughtered the people in the churches. This was the one big difference in this rebellion compared to rebellions of the past. All those in the past who had taken refuge in the churches and the missions had been spared. That was not the case this time.

The Sisters of the Missionaries of Our Lady of Africa telephoned at one point to let them know that the killers had come to their house. They had been trying to protect three families that they knew well, since some of the family members worked for them. The killers had put the sisters in one room and had warned them not to come out or they would be slaughtered as well. The sisters could hear the screams and the cries for mercy as the people were being slaughtered. No mercy was given. When it was quiet again, the sisters had come out to find corpses all over their compound. The sisters were horrified. Most of the members of the families had been hacked to death with machetes. They told the fathers at the regional house to be careful, that the militia, these killers, now known as the Interahamwe, usually came around eleven in the morning or four in the afternoon. Fr. John never forgot those hours and he would be on pins and needles until those hours had come and gone.

The second night into the killings, when Fr. John had just gotten into bed, a huge explosion resounded next to their property. A grenade had been thrown into the Young Christian Workers' Centre next door. Terrified, Fr. John threw himself behind the bed, hitting the wall and dragging the lamp on the night table with him. The lamp smashed to the floor. Fr. John stayed there motionless for a few minutes, quite petrified. Then he slid under the bed. If they fired through the window, they would hit the mattress on the bed and not him. He stayed there for a long time. When it seemed quiet again, he crept out from under the bed, hauled the mattress, bedclothes and pillow off the bed and put them snugly under the window by the door. "If they shoot through the window, they will miss me," thought Fr. John. He lay on the mattress, covered himself and tried to sleep. He could hear the refugees just outside his window whispering to each other in very subdued tones. It was dark and eerie. He was not certain any more whether he would get out of this alive or not. He felt quite alone again.

The next morning at breakfast, Fr. Clement looked at Fr. John from across the breakfast table and, laughing, asked him if he had done the same thing that he had done last night. Fr. John understood the implication and answered, "Yes, I went crashing to the floor as I fell behind the bed and brought the night lamp crashing to the floor with me." They both laughed together, in spite of the terrible tension. Fr. Clement then suggested that they both sleep in his office that night. His office was on higher ground than the regular bedrooms, since the whole centre was built on a piece of land that was terraced. Fr. Clement had a large sofa in his office and he suggested that they turn the sofa around with the seat against the wall and the back facing the window and the door of the office. Once on the sofa to sleep, they would not be seen and, thus, there would be less chance of being fired on. They did sleep better that night. During the day, there was the constant sound of gunshot fire. Fr. Clement believed that they were cleaning up; that the national army was making sure that all Tutsis were eliminated. The nasty radio station calling them to kill was now openly calling the Tutsis cockroaches. It was very upsetting. But Fr. John was convinced that it was more than the army exterminating the Tutsis. He was convinced that there was a full-scale battle going on. The rebel army, the Patriotic Front, was very present in Kigali and they were battling it out with the national army. It was war as he had often seen it in the movies. He was now actually living it and it was horrifying. A theory existed that when Pope John Paul II had come to Rwanda to visit, many bus loads of pilgrims had come from Uganda for the papal event. Many of those pilgrims, apparently, were Patriotic Front soldiers dressed as civilians, who did not return to Uganda, but stayed in Rwanda for the eventual attack and takeover. Many of the buses had, apparently, returned to Uganda empty. With that theory in mind, Fr. John was convinced that a full-scale war had begun in Rwanda.

The fourth day into the massacres, Fr. John learned from one of his colleagues who had been in touch with the Canadian consulate, that a convoy was being formed by the American embassy to get expatriates out of Kigali. Fr. John wondered if it would be possible for him and Fr. John-Paul to be part of that convoy. Fr. Raymond gave Fr. John the American embassy's telephone number. Fr. John telephoned to ask if this would be possible. He was told that they could join the convoy if they had their own vehicle with a white piece of cloth somewhere visible on it, and some drinking water with them. They were not to transport any baggage except a small, overnight case. They were to make their way to the American embassy themselves; the embassy staff would not come for them.

The convoy would be leaving on Sunday morning. They were to be at the embassy by eight-thirty in the morning. Fr. John prepared for the journey. A third colleague would join them. Fr. Rene had come to Kigali from Tanzania for his annual retreat and visit. Instead of solitude and prayer time, he suddenly found himself in a war. He wanted to get back to Tanzania with all his limbs intact. So Fr. John told him to join them. He and Fr. John-Paul would be going south towards Bujumbura, the capital of Burundi, and that he would certainly be able to get connecting flights back to Tanzania. Sunday morning arrived and they were up bright and early to start their journey. Strangely enough, the shooting, screaming and explosions had stopped and everything was eerily quiet.

Fr. John and his two companions left the compound of the Regional House at seven-forty-five a.m. in their white land cruiser with their white pillowcase tied to the antenna of the vehicle; several bottles of water were on the back seat next to Fr. Rene. As they drove out of the compound, Fr. John had to keep looking at his feet to make sure that his feet were on the pedals of the vehicle to shift gears. His legs and feet were numb from the knees down and so he was not sure if he was pushing on the right pedals. It was a strange feeling or, more precisely, there was no feeling at all. He was terrified of being fired on by the military. Fr. John-Paul had known at one time where the American Embassy was and so was attempting to give Fr. John directions; he feared, though, that it might have relocated at some point. It all seemed different with the roadblocks and military at every turn. They came to a roadblock and two young soldiers were crouched behind the barbed wire. Fr. John stopped and told them that they were on their way to the U.S. embassy to join the convoy. They made signs for them to pass as they removed one of the barriers. Fr. John drove on and stopped at l'Hotel des Milles Collines, thinking that it was the embassy. They were told there that the convoy was not leaving from the embassy, but from The American Club, which they discovered was just a kilometre up the road. They arrived there to find that they were the second vehicle to arrive. They were happy to be inside the compound of the club.

Gradually, more vehicles and more people arrived: Belgians, French, Americans, Canadians, Germans, Swedes, Spaniards and many other ex-patriots working with the embassies and various organizations. By the looks of things and the number of cars and people, Fr. John felt that their departure would be delayed. They were asked if they had enough gas to make the journey to Bujumbura. If their tank had not been full, they could have gone to the U.S. embassy to fill up. Fr. John thanked God that he had been able to fill up the day before all hell broke loose. They sat in their vehicles waiting. Time dragged on and they wondered if they would ever leave. They were invited into the club for coffee and to be able to chat and walk around. Suddenly, two people from the embassy arrived and each stood on top of one of the vehicles. They had papers in their hands and explained to everyone that they had to make lists of everyone present in triplicate: names, home addresses, home telephone numbers and the name of a close relative who could be contacted in case something happened. They explained that both the rebels and the National Army had promised not to fire on them. They were to move in single file, with an embassy car at the front and one at the back. Only ex-patriots were to be in the convoy; no Africans and especially no Rwandese. The "no Rwandese" was a point that brought some heated protest from some of the ex-patriots, because some men had married Rwandese women and wanted to take them along. One man, a Belgian, was vehemently arguing with another couple, because he wanted to hide his Tutsi wife under the baggage in the land cruiser he was driving. They told him that he would be jeopardizing the whole convoy. If he were stopped and searched, they could all be shot. The Belgian agreed at first, but once the couple had moved on to another part of the compound, Fr. John noticed that he discreetly got her into the vehicle and under the light baggage. She was not to move or make a sound. Fr. John made a note of this and tried to be ahead of him in the convoy; being after him would be too dangerous. It was all very frightening.

The lists were finally complete and they opened the compound gates. The cars drove out and all parked on the side of the road as far as possible down the hill in front of the American Club. Fr. John estimated there were close to a hundred cars in the convoy. It was not a nice place to be in, because they saw many quite disturbing things as they went by. At one point, one huge garbage truck came slowly by and stopped not far from the vehicles getting ready for the convoy. The stench from the garbage truck was awful and it was then that Fr. John realized that it was full of hacked bodies. The prisoners had been let out of the prisons and were in charge of picking up the corpses and body parts and throwing them into the garbage truck. The BBC Broadcasting truck passed by as well. It was almost totally covered in brown paper with BBC written on it in huge letters. The killer militia, known as the Interahamwe, went by with a machine gun on the back of their truck and wounded soldiers in the vehicle as well. They also made sure that they had Interahamwe printed on the front of the vehicle.

One African woman approached Fr. John's vehicle and asked him if he would take her with him. Fr. John felt just terrible about having to say no to her. He told her to go to the embassy car that was parked on the other side of the road and ask permission to be taken with them. If she got permission from them, he would surely take her. Although he felt awful about this, he could not jeopardize the convoy. He knew that he would be questioned once the convoy was ready, if he had an African woman in their vehicle.

The BBC van with the brown paper pasted all over it stopped close to them. One man got out of the van, went to the side of the road next to where Fr. John was parked and urinated. Then he turned to Fr. John who had the window down and asked if the convoy was going to the airport. Fr. John told him that, as far as he knew, they were headed towards Bujumbura and not the airport.

Time dragged on and Fr. John wondered if they would ever leave. It was now nearing mid-day and it was becoming quite hot. He noticed a Canadian consulate vehicle parked on the other side of the road. As far as he could tell, the Canadian consul, Mr. Guitar, was at the wheel. Fr. John walked over to the car and asked him what the hold-up was; would they be leaving or not? Mr. Guitar answered that they would be leaving as soon as the convoy was complete. Then he told Fr. John that they were waiting for a group of about twenty-five vehicles, all East-Indian families, who had not yet arrived. They did not know what the hold-up was. As soon as they arrived, they would be leaving. After another half-hour the East-Indian families began to arrive. Some did not have enough gas for the journey and so had to go to the U.S. embassy to fill up. These families had been held up by the militia as they looted their stores and businesses, making sure that no one took anything with them. They were to leave everything behind.

They were finally all set and the convoy got under way. They were leaving Kigali and it was already one-thirty in the afternoon. Fr. John did not manage to get ahead of the Belgian with his loved one hidden under the baggage. As difficult as it might be, Fr. John did understand; how could anyone leave the one they loved behind? It would be impossible. They drove on and came to the hill that led down to the river and on to the bridge that would take them outside the city of Kigali. The convoy stretched for miles. The three priests watched the vehicle with the hidden passenger. There were soldiers and militia stopping some of the vehicles and searching them. There were road blocks and obstacles in their way, so they very often had to slow down to allow the soldiers to clear away the barbed wire, the boards with nails and the tires or whatever else blocked their way. There were many young children with broken bottles, sticks and stones threatening the convoy and the people in the vehicles. At one point, when they were stopped waiting for a barrier to be removed, one young child came and sat on Fr. John's bumper. He seemed to be going on about something in the local language and was waving a stick at them. "Do you understand what he's saying?" Fr. John asked Fr. John-Paul.

"He is telling us that he needs money and that we're not leaving till he gets it," replied Fr. John-Paul. Before he could go any further, however, a soldier drove him away and removed the barrier for them to continue. So far, the vehicle with the hidden passenger had not been stopped and they saw it finally ramble over the bridge. All three breathed a sigh of relief. They crossed the bridge not long after. As they drove through the countryside, the children ran out of the houses to wave good-bye to them.

When they reached the town of Butare, quiet reigned. The military, carrying rifles, were everywhere. The convoy was permitted to stop for a while to rest and to have a soft drink. They then moved on, finally arriving at the Rwandese-Burundian border late in the evening. All the vehicles needed to be registered and fees paid for crossing the border. It took four hours to complete the clearance. Darkness had fallen by the time they had got underway again. The journey from the border to Bujumbura was a very winding one. They entered Bujumbura just after midnight. They had been instructed where to go, which centre or school to go to and from there would be able to call relatives and make arrangements to leave for home. Flights were available for them at the airport.

Fr. John had the telephone number of the missionary centre called La Par. He phoned there and discovered that they were waiting for them to arrive. Since security was very tight in the city, there would be someone to open the gate of the compound for them. Fr. John called home before going to La Par. The telephones were available free of charge. His sister Della's husband answered the phone. He could not believe that it was Fr. John on the line. He told him that Della had gone to Halifax with the girls; she was extremely upset about what was happening and there had been many phone calls from people wanting to know if he had gotten out of the war zone. Even a friend from Australia had called. His brother-in-law just kept screaming over the telephone, "Where are you? Where are you? Were you in that convoy that we saw on the news?"

"Yes, that is the convoy we were in," answered Fr. John. "We are now safe in Burundi." Once Fr. John knew that his sister was with her daughters in Halifax, he said good-bye to his brother-in-law and hung up. Then he phoned his niece's house in Halifax where his sister would be. The first thing she asked when she answered the phone was, "When are you coming home?"

"Not right now, "he answered. "I'm going to the mission centre tonight here in Bujumbura. Then tomorrow we will cross the border back into Zaire and back to the school," answered Fr. John.

"You're crazy. Get out of there," answered his sister. "I don't understand why you're staying there. You'll end up getting yourself killed. We are worried to death here!"

"But the situation is calm where the school is in Bukavu and we don't have to go back through Rwanda. We'll be alright. I'll be coming on home-leave in June as soon as the school year ends. I'll call you from the High Commission for refugees in Bukavu tomorrow afternoon when we arrive there. I'm fine. I'm not alone to travel," replied Fr. John.

"Well, be careful for heaven's sake," said Della. They hung up and the three priests headed for La Par. The community at La Par was waiting for them. Sister Jaqueline, who was in charge of the rooms gave them their accommodations. Fr. John took a much needed shower and at that moment he realized how exhausted he was. Once in bed, however, sleep would not come. He was like a flea on a hot stove. It all hit him after the fact, all that they had been through that day. A cold chill, a foreboding feeling went through him again. What would tomorrow bring as they made their way through the escarpment? He slept very little and was up to participate in the community Eucharist, after which he went down to the dining-room for breakfast. Everyone wanted to know what had happened during their Rwandan ordeal. Fr. John could not speak. It was too much. He felt more like crying than anything else. It was not the moment to speak about what had happened. He needed more time to wind down. "It's alright," said Fr. Theo, the Regional Director, "Don't say anything. You'll speak about it when you can!" Fr. John felt overwhelmed.

They left that afternoon for Bukavu. They crossed the border into Zaire and went through the mountain escarpment and down into Bukavu without a hitch. Fr. John could hardly believe it. It was late afternoon by the time they reached the Regional House in Bukavu. Everyone could not believe that they were back safe and sound. They had all been so worried about them. They were expected to tell all this time, whether Fr. John felt like it or not. It was not easy to talk about all that had happened; Fr. John had difficulty controlling his emotions and tears welled up in his eyes. He did not want to break down!

Once they arrived at the school, all the students came to greet them and then the community of priests gathered to have coffee. It was good to be back, but the situation across the border so close to the school was deteriorating and everyone was extremely worried. Fr. John quickly went and phoned Della from the call center of the High Commission for Refugees. She was extremely happy to hear from him again and to know that he was back at the school. He promised to call later on in the week. The next day it was classes as usual. One thing that was not "as usual" was the volatile situation across the border. Everything had changed for the worse and a very dangerous situation was rapidly developing.

Many of the students were very frightened about what was going on in Rwanda. The school had both Rwandese and Burundian students since it was a house of formation for future African missionaries from Rwanda, Burundi and Zaire. But all of the students were affected by what was happening. The holocaust that had started in Kigali eventually spread throughout the country and the carnage continued everywhere. Across the border in Cyangugu and Kamembe, the onslaught of the killings would be experienced in a horrific way. The students, from their vantage point on the Zairean side of the border, were witnesses to the massacres of many. People eventually began streaming across the border, fleeing the wrath of the killer militia; they would stop at the gate of the school. The personnel of the school set up a water supply at the gate because many people would arrive exhausted and desperately thirsty. They plodded along with baggage, clothing, some furniture and personal goods on their heads or in their arms. In the early morning when the fathers and students were in chapel praying, they could hear the gun shots, screams and commotion from the other side of the border, because the border was so close. People could actually speak to one another from across the lake and the river. When anything tragic happened that was very disturbing for the students, such as a young person or any person being forcibly drowned in the lake, some would dash out of the classroom to throw up; the experience was too traumatic for words.

Many attempted to cross the lake in order to reach the school. They would do this under cover of darkness. Some nights the moon gave too much light, so it was more difficult not to be detected. Several of the Tutsi priests who had escaped came to the school asking the staff if they could use the small concrete wharf that was on the shore of the lake as a drop-off point. The Bishop of Kamembe was helping people escape. They would be taken to the house of a community of Italian priests called the Rogationists; the back of this house was level with the shore of the lake, making it easily accessible to anyone who wanted to escape by crossing the lake. Once in the house, they would be hidden, usually in the laundry room on the basement level. Some of the escapees needed to be helped to cross the lake; a good number made their own way across as well.

Fr. John was given a time in the afternoon to go down to the wharf. If there was someone standing outside the house across the lake, Fr. John was to observe if that person had one arm or two arms raised above his head. One arm meant that the escapees were to cross at 1a.m., two arms meant that the escape was to take place at 2a.m. Some nights were sleepless nights for Fr. John and for Fr. Gregory. When the person or persons landed at the wharf, they would be given dry clothing, something to eat and a place to sleep. The next day they would move on into the interior of the country where it would be safer. They became increasingly in danger of detection because the military in Rwanda knew that people were escaping; so did the population of Bukavu.

One evening, a small dugout came across with a mother and her two children in it; the woman's husband, who had been a doctor, had been burned alive in front of their eyes. The family had to escape because they were to be massacred as well. As they were crossing, another dugout from the Zairean side of the border intercepted them and demanded a large sum of money for their safe crossing, otherwise they would be denounced to the proper authorities. Deception was everywhere and those involved in helping people escape were appalled at the cruelty of some people.

The Bishop of Kamembe eventually came under suspicion as one of those "trafficking in lives" and he received a visit from the militia. He was duly informed that if this continued, he would be stopped, placed kneeling before a freshly dug grave, shot and buried without a marker. This did not deter the Bishop. He found other ways of getting people to safety. This man would be forever remembered by many for his bravery.

Fr. John and Fr. Gregory warned the Rwandese priests who were lodged at the Jesuit College in Bukavu that it was becoming increasingly dangerous to land at the small wharf on the shore of the lake. This wharf was in plain view, which was not good in view of the warnings received by the Kamembe Bishop. They would have to go beyond the wharf and land at a point on the shore that took them to a footpath leading to the road. There was a shortcut to the Jesuit College. This made the journey a bit longer but was safer since it was beyond the view of the Rwandese shore. Fr. John and Fr. Gregory would be hiding in the trees along the shoreline, watching for them, and would help them disembark and guide them to the footpath. It was an exhausting and terribly stressful thing to do, but any means to get to safety was good. This form of escape reminded Fr. John of all the stories he had read and movies he had seen about the Jews under Hitler and all they had had to do to get to safety. It sent a chilling feeling down his spine. Often he would sit in prayer for long moments. He needed a strength greater than his own to keep going.

The stress for everyone was such that Fr. John decided to call a staff meeting to discuss what could be done to help themselves cope better as a group, both teachers and students. They would certainly need to get together as teachers to talk about how they all felt, how the situation was affecting them; the different teachers should meet with their classes to discuss their need to express their fears. It was a difficult time. It was also around this time that Fr. John met Jules and Chris. Sr. Ariana had asked him one morning if he would meet these two young men who were in great difficulty as refugees in Bukavu. Sr. Ariana would get money for them for food at least and through the mediation of Fr. John would get this money to them. Fr. John agreed and a close friendship began. Jules and Chris were from a mixed ethnic marriage, their father had been Tutsi and their mother Hutu. Their mother had been a student at the Sisters' school and Sr. Ariana had become a very good friend of the family. Sr. Ariana wanted to help Marie Jeanne's children since she had been such a good student and had developed into a fine lady in later years. She had never forgotten the Sisters and it would have pained her terribly if she had known that her two boys were not being taken care of.

The looting and killing continued for weeks. The Carmelite Sisters from the Convent just across the border in Cyangugu had to be evacuated; the situation had become too dangerous. They all crossed over to Bukavu and once they had left the convent, in no time it was nothing but a shell. Looters tore it apart since there was no one to stop them. There was respect for no one and for nothing. This was the big difference with this upheaval and the ones that had taken place in the past; there was no respect, even for God. In past years, the people who had taken refuge in the churches and in the Christian missions had not been harmed; the sacred along with its domain had been respected. It was known that the new breed of killers had been formed with Hitler's ideology. The young men of the killer militia had initially come to a German missionary whose name was Fr. Hans, and had asked him to help them translate Hitler's Mein Kampf into Kinyarwanda! Fr. Hans had been appalled and had refused to do such a thing. With such an ideology, nothing and no one would be respected or spared. People eventually witnessed this in action.

The battle continued to rage on in Kigali and finally all over the country. Reports of massacres came in from everywhere. Everyone was traumatized. It seemed like the Anti-Christ had come to make his home in Rwanda. One could sense the evil; it was palpable; an eerie atmosphere hung in the air. Fear had a stifling grip on everyone.

The Patriotic Front, the rebel troops, carried on their campaign with diligence and perseverance and finally took over. A favourable situation was created so that the National Army could bow out gracefully; it was rumoured that an embargo had been placed on arms to the National Army but not on arms for the Patriotic Front. What could that possibly mean? The killer militia, the Interahamwe, began to disband and flee. The peace-keeping forces, known as the Blue Hats, had been in the country throughout the ordeal. They were from various countries, including Belgium and France. A group of Belgian Blue Hats had been massacred by the killer militia in the very beginning of the blow-up in Kigali. Many people found it difficult to understand that the U.N. did not react to this terrible situation. Rules were rules, however, and the peacekeeping forces were not to use violence to counteract violence; they did not even have ammunition in their weapons for self-defence. The higher echelons of government did nothing to change this. So the killings continued. General Dallaire did what he could, but all requests fell on deaf ears, until the Patriotic Front took over. When this happened, the French military in the country created a buffer zone where many of the people could go for their protection and to re-evaluate their situation.

Those who had taken refuge in the buffer zone were mainly Hutus, since they feared the reprisals of the Patriotic Front, who were now taking over the governing of the country. It took time for them to establish their rule in every part of the country, but they were making great strides in establishing themselves.

Now that the Patriotic Front was in the process of taking power in Rwanda, the Tutsis who had fled during the massacres by the killer militia and the National Army, started returning to Rwanda. As far as they were concerned, their saviour and liberator had arrived and they would follow him! Safety and security had returned.

After two years at the Seminary Fr. John was due for home leave. It was a good break for him and he was happy to have a visit at home. He promised to bring back money, clothing and material for the formation house. A good part of what he brought back would be for Jules and Chris whom he now knew very well. Needless to say, Fr. John did a lot of shopping for all this material before returning to Zaire. Della often accompanied him in his shopping escapades and gave him advice on what to buy and on what she thought would be appropriate for Jules and Chris. He was always grateful for her help and they always made the outings into a fun time. They would always stop for coffee or tea somewhere along the way.

Consequently he returned to the formation house for his third year of work with three suitcases loaded with materials. Due to the situation in Rwanda he did not return through Kigali but took a flight from Brussels to Goma, Zaire and then on to Kavumu just outside Bukavu. Fr. Gegory was at the airport to meet him and Fr. John was very fortunate not to be searched at the Kavumu Airport. The Seminary fully appreciated all the material he brought back especially for language training and the video presentations. Jules and Chris were crazy with joy about the clothing, footwear and money for their schooling. They would no longer feel ashamed of their situation and living conditions. They could hope again.

Political pressure on the French government and army eventually became so strong that the decision was finally taken by the French troops to pull out of the buffer zone so that the area would fall under the jurisdiction of the Patriotic Front. Those who had taken refuge there packed up whatever belongings they possessed and headed towards the Zairean border. Although the new regime in Kigali insisted that no reprisals would take place, many feared the worse. Thousands of people began that great trek to the Zairean border on foot. They eventually streamed into Zaire by the thousands and, of course, Bukavu got its share of the fleeing population.

In the beginning they settled anywhere that they were allowed to settle. It took the High Commission for Refugees months to establish refugee camps far enough away from the border to be relatively safe. For a time, before the camps had been set up, the refugees lived all along the main street of the town of Bukavu; there were also thousands encamped around the Roman Catholic Cathedral of Bukavu and the Jesuit College of the town. These people ended up cutting almost every tree in sight for firewood and for cooking. The refugees also needed water and food. They sold every item imaginable at the roadside and in the market, from door casings to toilet seats; all items that had been looted and had been carried across the border. One could not have believed all that was for sale if one had not seen it all. At one point many of the refugees not yet installed in camps wanted to come onto the property of the Formation Center. The Missionaries of Africa did not allow this to happen because they knew all too well that every tree and every plant would be cut down to be used as firewood or food. The Formation House property would have been turned

411

into a desert. What the Missionaries of Africa did in order to help the people in need was to set up a water hose that ran to the main entrance of the Center. In that way the people crossing the border or coming to the school would be able to get all the water that they needed. It was a very important contribution.

Once the High Commission for refugees had the camps organized, most of the refugees camped around the Bukavu Cathedral, the Jesuit College and along the streets of the town disappeared into the camps. Some, however, refused to go to the camps. They felt that there would eventually be too much sickness and disease. Just near the Kavumu Airport there was a camp of over 160,000 persons. One could observe a sea of blue and white plastic tents when one drove out to the airport. Those refusing to go to the camps did so because they felt that their presence in this vast sea of people would render them anonymous and consequently forgotten, whereas some others who had something to hide relished such anonymity. Each one had their own story.

One group of religious Sisters from different congregations came to do debriefing with the more traumatized people in the camps; the Sisters were well aware that some people were traumatized because they had been forced to kill others by the killer militia, or else they were traumatized because they had been pursued by the killers in order to be executed. Fr. John met two of these Sisters from the Canadian group; they agreed to come to the school and do debriefing with his students. Students were not obligated to participate in this debriefing; it was a simple invitation to do so. They all came to see what this was about with the option of withdrawing if they felt that it was too intrusive. Fr. John and some of the other teachers took part in the debriefing as they were able to and as the students were willing to have them.

It was about this time that a very pleasant surprise occurred in the life of the formation house: an African colleague was appointed to replace Fr. Gregory as bursar. The school was really sorry to lose Fr. Gregory but his mother had become quite ill and he was needed at home. The appointment of an African colleague lessened the disappointment of losing Fr. Gregory. Fr. Bosco, a Ghanaian by birth, would arrive from Bunia at least three weeks before Fr. Gregory's departure. In that way Fr. Gregory could go over the work schedule with him and indoctrinate him in the handling of the accounts. Fr. John and Fr. Gregory went to the Kavumu Airport to welcome him. Everyone was quite excited about meeting him. Fr. John was so pleased about this appointment. Fr. Bosco would prove to be an invaluable addition to the staff. Yet it remained a daily struggle to keep a healthy optimism.

The priests and other teachers continued to have their own debriefing sessions when they were not with the students. They also took time to discuss a strategy for evacuation if it became necessary. The students needed to be in a safe place if the fighting escalated. A problem existed because the school was on the Rwandese border. Once the Patriotic Front took power, the Rwandese border became closed to them. They were also on the lake but had no boat. They were also at the very end of the town of Bukavu which meant that they would have to evacuate through the town itself and there were always roadblocks in the town manned by the police and the military; these often were looking for money. The Zairean police and military were not paid and so needed help to live. In a certain sense, they were trapped. It was a very frightening situation; the staff needed to be sure that they would be able to get their students to safety. Fr. John and Fr. Bosco were always ready with money and food for the police and the military. It was very important to keep good relations with them; one never knew when it would be necessary to call on them for assistance. In fact, since the school was just at the border crossing, the wall of the school compound formed part of the wall of the border crossing; both walls joined up behind the customs office. Fr. Bosco, being the bursar for the school, often brought any leftovers from the noon or evening meals to the officers. He would also stay and listen to their marital problems, money problems, and the difficulties in raising their children in a time of such upheaval. Fr. Bosco, having worked in the Bunia region of Zaire, was able to speak Lingala, the language of the military, very well and for this he was appreciated and accepted. This would later prove to be an asset in their need for assistance to evacuate and for Fr. Bosco's own safety when arrested by the military.

Fr. John had already been at Our Lady of Ruzizi School for four years. He had witnessed the wave of Tutsis streaming across the border fleeing the killer militia and then the wave of Hutus in their turn once the Patriotic Front had taken power. There had been some long, difficult moments,

413

especially under cover of darkness when escapees were crossing over, fleeing the massacres. There had been a time after the Patriotic Front had taken power when Fr. John, along with some other colleagues, had ventured back to Kigali to see what had become of the things he had bought for the school; he had bought a new filing cabinet and he wondered what was left of it. The visit had been suggested by one of his colleagues who was in charge of the Catechetical Center in Bukavu; Fr. Julius had sent quite a lot of material to be printed to the Pallotine Fathers' printing press in Kigali and Fr. Julius wondered if they had been able to salvage some of the materials despite the terrible looting that had gone on in Kigali.

Fr. Julius had worked some forty years in Zaire, mostly in the region of Masisi where many of the Rwandese had been living for generations since they had immigrated many years previously. Fr. Julius knew the people well and spoke fluent kinyarwanda. One morning Fr. John, Fr. Julius and Fr. Normand, who had been working in journalism, set out for Kigali. The Patriotic Front soldiers allowed them to cross the Cyangugu border without too much difficulty. Fr. Julius was anxious to find out what had been salvaged from the catechetical material that he had left at the printing press; Fr. John wanted to see if the filing cabinet that he had bought for the school was still there or if it had been thrown out. Fr. Normand, on the other hand, wanted to see what the political situation was and what he could find out about the rumoured jailing of Hutu priests. Shortly after setting out, they encountered a roadblock. There were eighteen roadblocks in the four and a half hour trip.

At about the third roadblock, a young Patriotic Front soldier stopped them. Fr. Julius looked at Fr. John and said, "You see that young soldier. I taught him religion in seventh grade in Masisi. We'll see if he acknowledges it." As they stopped, Fr. Julius said to the young fellow, "What is it, what's wrong? Is there a problem? We are priests, missionaries, and we are on our way to Kigali for supplies!"

"Ah, but we have to search your vehicle. We have to make sure that you are not transporting arms," he answered.

"Oh, we are priests, missionaries," answered Fr. Julius, "we don't carry arms or guns."

"Oh, but even the priests carry guns and traffic in them in this country," he replied, quite sure of himself.

At that moment Fr. Julius looking at him, said, "You don't recognize me, do you? I know you!"

"That's not possible," answered the young soldier.

"Oh yes it is," replied Fr. Julius. "Your name is Stephen and I taught you religion in seventh grade in Masisi; your father's name is Cyprien, your mother's name is Catherine and you have an older brother. I taught him as well!"

The young soldier could not hide his astonishment and had to admit that he recognized Fr. Julius and that he did remember that he had taught him.

Fr. Julius said to him, "So, where is your older brother now? Do you know?"

"Oh yes, Father. He is at a roadblock about eighteen kilometres from here," answered the young man.

"I see," said Fr. Julius. "Well, the next time you see him, you say hello to him for me. Oh, and by the way, we have some biscuits here with us. Would you like a few?"

"Oh no, Father. I am not permitted to take any kind of goods from the people we stop," he answered. "But you can go now. Everything is fine!"

Once they were on their way again, Fr. Julius' comment was: "That is what makes the strength of the Patriotic Front soldiers, they are disciplined and well-trained; that is why they won the war!"

Between Cyangugu and Kigali, there is a huge park called Nyungwe that has miles and miles of forest and beautiful land, an absolute paradise of a place. To their amazement, there was a check point and barrier in the middle of this forest. This seemed quite strange to them. There were quite a number of cars, trucks, taxis and minibuses stopped at this checkpoint. The Patriotic Front soldiers who were manning the checkpoint had all the people standing outside of their vehicles to the side of the road. As Fr. John and his colleagues approached the barrier, they signaled to them to park their vehicle to the side of the road as well; they were told that they would be able to continue shortly. It was at that moment that the three colleagues realized that this was a triage. The soldiers had lists and some people were being singled out to stand aside while others were told to return to the vehicle; all suspects implicated in the genocide would be stopped and dealt with on the spot. The rumour was that those singled out to remain on the roadside were to disappear in the forest, not to be heard of again. The reprisals had already begun; but everyone knew that it would all be denied. This came as no surprise to the three priests since not so many weeks before that, one of their own colleagues had been stopped and had not been heard of since. Joachim Vallmajo,(1) a Spanish Missionary of Africa, had worked for many years in Rwanda and had been known for his service to both Tutsis and Hutus and had also been very social-justice conscious. The Patriotic Front soldiers had come one morning to take him away for interrogation. He had said his farewells to those at the mission and had not been heard of again. The rumour was that he had been tortured and executed by officers of the Patriotic Front, those whose mandate was to liberate the people and free the country. The soldiers had refused to tell the mission staff or Fr. Vallmajo's family where his remains had been buried. This had taken place because Fr. Vallmajo had dared to radio the different communities in Europe about the injustices being perpetrated during the take over by those who deemed themselves "the pure ones"!

The three priests arrived in Butare, the town about mid-way to Kigali. The Missionaries of Africa had their preparatory formation house in Butare. The massacres had been particularly violent here during the genocide. Fr. Julius wanted to stop to see what was left of the property. It had been quite a nice center with a beautiful little chapel for the students. When they reached the property site, they were completely shocked. The rooms had been looted; books and papers were strewn all over the compound. Most of the furniture, dishes, library books and bed linens were either broken, torn or in pieces. Doors were off their hinges and there were no unbroken windows anywhere. It was a shambles. A cow was standing in the little chapel, rummaging through the debris on the floor; the tabernacle had been torn off the wall and was in pieces in one corner of the room. A few people were there and they told the priests that they had come from Burundi and had found the place in that state. Fr. John could not speak, he felt like weeping. So many years of hard work, destroyed within days.

Fr. Julius wanted to stop at the Bishop's residence to greet him since he had taken refuge in Bukavu during the first wave of the massacres. He welcomed them warmly and invited them to dine since it was noon. Fr. Julius accepted and they sat down to lunch. There were two Benedictine Sisters at table with them. The Bishop's Chancellor was also present at the meal and explained that the Sisters were with them since the terrible incident in the Benedictine Community when two of the Sisters had helped the killers massacre some of their Sisters. Would they ever know the truth of the Benedictine horror story? Many horrific incidents had been the result of "kill or be killed." Fr. John asked himself what he would have done had he been in such a terrible situation?

They had just sat down to eat when there was a knock at the refectory door and six young soldiers, both men and women, dressed in Patriotic Front uniforms entered the dining-room. The Bishop immediately got up from the table to welcome them, warmly embracing each one of them. He quickly excused himself and went out with them. The chancellor immediately explained that these were his nephews and nieces, all members of the military regime now in power. He also informed them that the Bishop's brother would soon be arriving from Uganda to take up a teaching position at the University Campus in Butare.

"I see. That's quite interesting," said Fr. Julius. They enjoyed quite a fine lunch, but the Bishop did not return for the remainder of the meal. He reappeared just as they were about to leave. He excused himself profusely for not having been there for the remainder of the lunch hour and for having left so suddenly. He mentioned how well he had been welcomed when he had taken refuge in Bukavu during the massacres. He would be forever grateful for all that the Missionaries of Africa had done for him. He also mentioned that he would go back for a visit if it wasn't for the danger of encountering the killers present in Bukavu. Fr. Julius told him that he really did not have to worry, that there were no more killers in Bukavu than there were in Rwanda and in Butare in particular. The Bishop did not reply since he knew well what all the clergy now knew: that Fr. Emmanuel, who had taken refuge in Bukavu when he had, was now in jail in Butare with no hope of release. It was obvious to all of them how compromised this Bishop was with so many of his family part of the inner circle of power. Fr. Julius had been in the country long enough to know how to answer so that there would be hidden meaning behind the words. As they entered their vehicle to leave after their good-byes, Fr. Julius muttered these words under his breath, "What hypocrisy. We are not out of the woods by a long shot with such a mentality present, even in the Church!"

Out of all the roadblocks and checkpoints that they passed through, there was only one that was manned by the U.N. Blue Hats. They were always happy to meet them. They were polite, courteous and welcoming to the priests as they passed through. Fr. John and his colleagues only wished that all checkpoints could have been so congenial. That was not to be since the Patriotic Front checkpoints were constantly on the lookout for traffickers of arms and for the killer militia.

The three priests finally arrived in Kigali and were surprised to find that the Regional House of the Missionaries of Africa had not been too badly damaged. The killers and looters had come and some of the people who had taken refuge there had been killed. Fr. John thanked God that he had no longer been there when that had taken place! He still wondered how he would have reacted to the slaughter that had taken place. They were told that the priests of the residence had left the rooms and the storage areas unlocked so that there had been no need to destroy things to get what they wanted. So Fr. John found the filing cabinet that he had bought for the school intact and undamaged. The looters had realized when they had tried to force it open that it was empty. So they had thrown it aside as useless. Fr. John gladly placed it in the back of the land cruiser to transport it back to the school.

Upon their arrival at the Regional House, they were each given a room for the night and then invited to the dining room for coffee and a snack, though they were informed that the evening meal was only an hour away. As they sat down for their coffee, news about all that had taken place and the state of the city was exchanged. Fr. John and his colleagues wanted to know how things were under the new regime! There were many stories to be shared. One in particular that saddened Fr. John was concerning one of the colleagues who had been in the group of ten Missionaries who had been at the Regional House on April 6th.

Fr. Guy Pinard, a Canadian Missionary of Africa, had been one of the ten who had been stranded at the Regional House when the Presidents plane went down. He had worked for many years in the Rwandese missions and parishes and had done much for both the Tutsi and Hutu people. To Fr. Pinard, they were all his parishioners and he was there for all of them. He was always jovial, teasing and in an uplifting, humorous mood. In this difficult situation, he had made them laugh and so had lightened the terribly tense situation. It had been good to be able to laugh, even in their fear. They had all been able to leave, each to his respective mission station; Fr. John had been able to return to Bukavu with the help of the American convoy. Fr. Guy had also been able to return to his mission. One morning, many months after his return to his mission, however, he had been gunned down while celebrating the Eucharist by a soldier of the Patriotic Front. The excuse had been made by the new regime that this particular soldier had lost so many of his family members during the genocide, that he had lost his senses and gone on a killing spree. It had been a terrible mistake. None of the priests had been taken in by this. There seemed to have been many gross errors taking place since the Patriotic Front had taken power.

Fr. Julius was extremely pleased to learn, on the following day, that not everything he had come to find was lost. The printing press of the Pallotine priests had been looted and the printing machines badly damaged. But, a lot of what he had wanted printed was still there on the shelves in the Pallotine office. It had been printed before the looting occurred and surprisingly enough had not been touched. It was unbelievable. Fr. Julius would be able to return to Bukavu with the Catechetical material needed by his Center. He was overjoyed.

They did learn, though, that there had been many massacres in the Pallotine Fathers' Church. The bloodstains were everywhere and the stench of blood could still be smelled even after many months. The Retreat Center of the Jesuit Fathers had also been attacked and six of the Rwandese Jesuit Fathers had been slaughtered in the room where they had been praying; the blood stains were still visible all over the walls and ceiling. The Christian Brothers' College of Kigali had also been looted and just about every window had been smashed. They also stopped at the Carmelite Sisters' convent and found that their house had been badly damaged. The Sisters informed the priests that for several nights, a battle had raged between the Patriotic Front on the hills surrounding the city and the National Army in the city itself. They had been caught in the crossfire of this battle and they had had to take refuge in the storage cellar in the basement. Being right in the line of fire, they thought for sure that they would have been blown to bits. A number of the missiles had landed in their compound but never one directly onto the storage area. It had been God's little miracle for them. They would be forever grateful that they had survived.

The parish mission in that same area had been attacked and badly damaged as well. The three priests there had come close to losing their lives; Fr. Kurt, a German missionary, had been badly wounded in the arm. Fortunately, he had been able to be taken to the hospital and given treatment and would not lose his arm. One of the other missions had had many deaths. The militia had come and before the very eyes of Fr. George, a French missionary, many of the parishioners including women and children, had been massacred. Fr. George had been badly affected by this horror and kept constantly weeping, drinking and smoking. He needed to be repatriated as soon as possible. His colleagues feared that he may have been permanently affected psychologically. He could not get the horror out of his mind; he kept living it over and over.

Fr. John was to check Fr. Granville's room at the Regional House to see if his clothes, books and personal belongings were still there. To his surprise, everything was intact; no one had entered the room. Fr. Granville had asked Fr. John to bring his possessions back with him since he had been appointed to the formation house in Bukavu to teach philosophy. He had gone on home-leave after the events in Rwanda and would be going directly to the formation house in Bukavu upon his return to Africa from his home in Belgium. Fr. John collected all his belongings for him and eventually sent him a message that everything had been salvaged.

One last visit that Fr. John and his colleagues made before leaving Kigali was to two Sisters of the Community of St Francis who were in the Kigali prison. They had numerous communities in Rwanda and four of their Sisters worked at the formation house in Bukavu. One of the Sisters at the formation house was a blood relative to one of the Sisters in prison, and it was very important to her that Fr. John bring back news of what was happening to them! The three priests went to the prison to see if they could visit the two Sisters. Fortunately, one of the guards knew Fr. Julius and he was able to get permission from the warden for them to visit. When they met with the Sisters, they whispered to the priests to be careful what they said as they were being carefully observed. Fr. John patiently waited for an appropriate moment and whispered to the Sisters, "Why are you here? Why did they jail you? Did they give you a reason?" Sr. Claire and Sr. Mathilde looked at one another and then looked around to see if anyone was watching them. Since it appeared to be safe, Sister Claire answered,

"They told us that we had not done enough during the massacres to save people. We allowed too many people to die!" Then, after a quick look around again, she added, "But truthfully, we believe that it is because we went to see what was left of our school that is just outside of the city a few days after the take over. We found that it had been occupied by the military and some people who had returned from Burundi. We believe that this is a way of telling us to mind our own business. Sr. Mathilde then added, "It is quite depressing here, but we are with the women and the children and we feel that this is where our apostolate is just now, so we have begun classes with the children, the mothers and other women. God is calling us at the very place we find ourselves at the moment." Sr. Claire added, "Just pray for us that we hold on and that we do not get sick. We will need the strength that prayer brings!"

"We will certainly do that!" the priests answered. They then left them, satisfied that they had seen them with their own eyes, and would be able to attest that they were truly in prison. Some of the people and even some of the missionaries, themselves, did not believe that the Patriotic Front could do such a thing. They had come to liberate the people. The question remained, "Which people?"

On the return journey, they stopped in a town called Kapgaye, where it had been reported that the Patriotic Front had massacred a whole group of Hutu priests along with three Bishops, one of those three being the Archbishop of Kigali. They had all taken refuge in Kapgaye and were having meetings to see what they could do to pull the Rwandese Church out of this disastrous situation and bring about some kind of reconciliation. Many of the priests were being accused of having helped in the massacres.

The rumour that had been circulating turned out to be true. They found the graves of the three Bishops in the Cathedral Church of Kapgaye; they had been buried in the sanctuary of the church, just in front of the main altar. Fr. John and his colleagues prayed at the graves. Those who had escaped the massacre had buried the Bishops in the church sanctuary. This again sent shivers through Fr. John. He felt a terrible eerie feeling in that place. He wanted to move on, to leave that place. A terrible hatred had entered this country, was taking root and he hoped God would be able to quell its advance. He felt a terrible oppression take hold of him. He needed to get away; the evil was again palpable.

They stopped at the mission still in the hands of the Missionaries of Africa. They learned that the Rwandese Hutu priests were being stopped and jailed. Fr. Emmanuel who had been at the Pastoral Institute in Kapgaye had been stopped. Once he had come back from his refuge in Bukavu, he had been almost immediately imprisoned. They did not know when he would be released. He had been accused of not having done enough to save people from the massacres. They had found an old shot gun in his room that had been used by one of the Missionaries of Africa for hunting and the military were using this as a pretext to accuse him of taking part in the killings. He was also being accused of having gone down to the barriers where people were detained and had denounced people causing their deaths. What was truly suspected, however, was that Fr. Emmanuel had seen too much and knew too much about what had truly happened, as did a number of the Sisters and they needed to be silenced.

Fr. Andrew Bongaerts, who was at the mission where they stopped, asked them, "Did you stop at the Cathedral of Kapgaye for a visit?"

"Yes, we did go into the Cathedral," Fr. Julius answered.

"You must have seen the three graves in the sanctuary," said Fr. Andrew.

"We even stopped for a moment of silent prayer," Fr. John said.

"There is a strong rumour that the killings of the Archbishop and the two Bishops who were with him was ordered by the rebel Leader himself; the one who is supposedly so pure and so justice conscious.(1) It is a gruesome story and one that needs to be made known. It is dangerous information to have in one's possession."

"Why would that information be so dangerous to have? Isn't it information that many people already know?"

"Well, not really. It is about the leader of the FPR, the one who will likely lead this country in the not too distant future. There is much blood on his hands, I assure you."

"What's the story on that?" asked Fr. Julius.

Fr. Andrew continued his story. "You know, I am sure, that Kapgaye was taken by the 157th mobile of the APR (Armee patriotique rwandaise) on June 2, 1994. They were engaged in intensive fighting here. In fact, the fighting lasted for three days with intensive mortar fire and bombs falling on this town. We thought it was the end for sure. For this reason, the soldiers thought they would find a deserted town. Logically, the population should have fled; this would have been possible since some escape routes still existed, for example the routes of Gitarama, Ngororero and Mukamira. Apparently the APR was completely surprised when they came face to face with bishops and other religious persons when they took Kapgaye. In the course of their fight, they had taken all the strategic locations, hospitals, schools, major seminary, convents and further down the road, the diocesan garage. When they checked all these buildings they found thousands of displaced persons and a huge number of Tutsis amongst them. When they opened the doors of the main Diocesan Center, the surprised Lieutenant Ibingira apparently exclaimed, 'Are those not cardinals that I see there?' His soldiers answered in the affirmative. So he asked them who their superior was. They presented him to Bishop Vincent Nsingiyumva, the Archbishop of Kigali. He apparently knew that this Archbishop was the close collaborator of Monsignor Perraudin(2), who was responsible for the banishment of the Tutsis in Rwanda. This Bishop Vincent was also accused of being a member of the MRND party, the party belonging to President Habyarimana. There were other bishops there as well, along with many priests. He communicated all this to the Major-General of the RPF (Rwandese Patriotic Front). The Major-General was surprised that the Archbishop of Kigali was still alive. He ordered all of them to be taken to a place where they could be exterminated. The Bishops and later the remainder of the religious were summoned to the Kapgaye School of nursing under the pretext that they were to have a meeting to study the question of the safety of the Convent of Kapgaye and how to continue to take care of the displaced persons who had taken refuge there. It was explained to the Major-General that there were Tutsi religious persons among them. They could not single them out because it would look too suspicious if a triage were to be done at that moment, and so they were all massacred together."(3)

Fr. John and his traveling companions sat there dumbfounded, shaking their heads. What could one say in the face of such atrocities from both sides of the ethnic lines? "How did you find all this out, Fr. Andrew?" they asked.

"It is better that you not know that part. There are lives at stake even now that things are settling down. It is really not over. But everyone did not die and there are those still around who have seen and heard what happened. I think it is better to leave it at that."

Fr. John looked at his companions and said, speaking his thoughts aloud, "You will see this Major-General will eventually turn up as the President of the new Rwanda." Fr. John said this because the actual president was a Hutu placed at the head of the government and the Major-General in question had become the Minister of Defence and External Affaires. With time the prediction would materialize.

"You may turn out to be right," Fr. Julius answered.

Fr. John and his companions left Kapgaye for Bukavu. In spite of the turmoil in Bukavu, they were glad to get back. Rwanda had been a real eye-opener for them, and they had seen and heard many things. Fear had been very present and those they met wanted to speak of the situation but were reluctant to do so as if the walls had ears. There now existed a complete lack of trust. There had been very little trust as it was before the genocide but now it had truly taken root.

Fr. John left on home-leave once classes were over in June. He would be back for the new school term. He was held up for one more month due to an attack of resistant malaria. It was the first time that he had a malaria attack while on home-leave. Della was petrified. She had never seen him so sick. He told her not to worry; that the team of doctors at St. Martha's Hospital would know what to do since they often dealt with patients from South America and India. He was hospitalized and placed on an intervenous drip with quinine and another malaria drug. That was the only way to take care of the resistant malaria. He slowly got back on his feet and was strong enough to head back to Zaire, as always via Rwanda. He had managed to collect money for Jules and Chris for their schooling and living expenses. When he had been delayed due to the malaria attack, Jules and Chris had been extremely worried that he would not return. They were overjoyed that he had returned and were present at the Eucharistic celebration on the first Sunday that he was back. It was a joyous home-coming even if Bukavu was in utter turmoil. He again had brought back materials for the English classes at the school. They were always sorely in need of supplies.

Everyone was happy that he was back. The situation in Bukavu, however, had worsened. There were thousands of refugees in the area. The possibility of war in Zaire had become extremely plausible. The teachers at the Formation House of the Missionaries of Africa had felt that it was safe enough to reopen the school for the new academic year. However no other schools had opened, except for a few of the Sisters' Formation Centers, but they had followed on the heels of the Missionaries of Africa's decision to open. The Diocesan Major Seminary in Murhesa, situated close to the Kavumu airport, had not opened as yet; they felt that the area was too insecure. This would prove to be providential for the Missionaries of Africa and their colleagues in formation work. The situation in Bukavu deteriorated with each passing day. The Patriotic Front in Rwanda was not favourable to President Mobutu's regime in Zaire. They would target certain places in the town of Bukavu. They had military personnel set up on the stadium roof in Cyangugu and on some of the higher hills directly opposite and facing the town. One evening, without realizing it, they had left their radio on as they were targeting the Cathedral and the Jesuit College of Bukavu. The Missionaries of Africa had their radio on since they communicated with their different missions in the evening. That night they accidentally heard the Rwandese military conversation as they targeted the Cathedral and the College. One soldier was saying to another as they aimed their guns, "Be careful, more to the right, the target is more to the right. Now, shoot!" The next morning the priests learned that the Bukavu Cathedral and the Jesuit College had been badly damaged by mortar fire. The staff of the formation house knew where it had come from, although it was denied by the new regime across the border.

The fall of Bukavu became imminent with President Mobutu's revocation of the citizenship of those of Rwandese descent. The Banyamulenge, the Banyarwandese and the different groups affected were on the warpath aided by the Patriotic Front in Rwanda and the Ugandan troops further north. The situation in Bukavu became so dangerous for any Rwandese still there that Jules and Chris came to Fr. John to see if he could help them leave the country. It was at this time that they escaped to Nairobi. Fr. John and the seminary community of students and priests were encouraged to evacuate by the military Captain of the National Army of Zaire. They had to leave or they would be trapped and only God knew what would happen to them. A group of the students and three of the priests made it, not without difficulty, to the Major Seminary of Murhesa, close to the airport. The following day, they managed to get to the Kavumu Airport and so it was that Fr. John found himself with the students on the Italian Embassy airplane heading for Kampala.

Fr. John later found out through faxes and telephone messages that the colleagues and students who had stayed on at the school had to eventually leave. They were directly in the line of fire from the occupying troops on the Rwandese side of the border. There was often sniper fire and shooting coming from the Rwandese side and one of the workers had been wounded in the back.

Fr. John also learned that the fall of Bukavu brought a terrible tragedy for the Church community of Bukavu. The rebels who took the town stopped Archbishop Munziirwa and his driver as they were making their way to the Jesuit College of Bukavu. They had assassinated the two of them on the spot, shooting them in the head as they knelt besides the Archbishop's car. They had then propped their bodies in a sitting position against the huge wrought iron fence of the Hydro Center. This had been observed at the time by several of the priests from the Xaverian Community who had been watching all that was going on from their house overlooking the market area of the town. The bodies had remained propped up against the fence for three days until two of the priests from the Xaverian Community asked to be allowed to take the body of their spiritual father and give him a proper burial. The Captain of the rebels had agreed. The man, who had worked so hard to keep peace and unity in the town of Bukavu and had convinced the students and the people not to allow themselves to be provoked into looting, had died a martyr's death. He had known that he would die such a violent death, but he had continued to respect everyone, no matter his or her ethnic background, religion or status in life. He had received no respect from the barbarians who had assassinated him. Fr. John wept for the saintly man. The Church community was deprived of his wisdom and gentle love and care.

Fr. John would never forget the many Sundays that Archbishop Munziirwa had come to the Chapel of the White Sisters of Africa while he was celebrating Eucharist in order to speak to the many students gathered there for Mass. He told them one Sunday when the situation was deteriorating very rapidly, "Do not allow yourselves to be provoked into demonstrating and rioting by the military. That is what they and the

President want. Then they will have an excuse to put you down and arrest you and so also bring down the town of Bukavu and of course loot it. If it becomes too unbearable do not hesitate to flee to a safer place if you can. You need to save yourselves and your loved ones if possible. I, myself, I will not flee. I know that eventually I will be killed, but I must stay with my people. I am their spiritual leader. God will accept me as I am."

Eventually, God did call his faithful servant to himself as he had predicted. He had been assassinated. The people of Bukavu gathered at the Cathedral to grieve no matter how bad the situation in the town had become. He had been buried next to the Cathedral Church.

Fr. John eventually left Africa for Canada, maybe not feeling so alone anymore --- a greater presence accompanied him --- but with the conviction that he would continue daily to be on his knees! Without that nurturing experience, he could not survive!

View of Bukavu City

Boat Taken on Trip to Goma

Sailing to Goma on Lake Kivu

Goma – Volcano as Viewed from the Airplane En route to Bunia

Main Street of Bunia

Main Street of Bunia

Epilogue

Once Fr. John had received the news that the boys had made it through to the International section of the Nairobi Airport, he fell into a deep sleep. With his brother as the driver he felt secure. He could have some restful catnaps now that the long awaited message about the departure had come through. As they drove on towards Winnipeg he continued to succumb to long bouts of sleep. He was just coming out of one of those sleepy moments when a sign appeared with "Winnipeg 25 kms" written on it. Fr. John sat up, more alert to his surroundings. He knew that Timmy would need him to find the street that they were looking for. Fr. John's friends in Cheticamp had written the instructions out for them so that they would be able to find the house where they would stay for the time that they would spend in Winnipeg. It was Fr. John's first visit to the windy city, so he needed to be on the watch for the names of the streets indicated in the instructions.

The instructions were very good; in no time they had found the home of Doris and Charles Camella. They had a very fine bungalow surrounded by a cedar hedge and a small maple tree in the front yard. They were expecting Fr. John and his brother since accommodations had been arranged ahead of time. They were meeting for the first time so all the pleasant formalities of first meetings were made. They were shown to the part of the house where they would stay. Fr. John and his brother would occupy the finished basement and so would Jules and Chris once they had arrived. They were both told to put their luggage in their rooms and to come upstairs for a cup of coffee and a piece of apple pie. They would eat supper later. Jules and Chris' flight was not slated to arrive until the afternoon of the next day. Everything was going well so far. Fr. John was anxious to see them here in Canada safe and sound.

Fr. John and Timmy enjoyed getting acquainted with Charles and Doris. They showed them the city and made a stop at the airport to make sure that they knew where they were going later. Fr. John and Timmy finally made their way to the airport for 3 p.m. that afternoon. The flight was scheduled to land at 3:15 and they would probably take time to clear customs. What Fr. John did not know was that all this had been done at the Toronto Airport, the place of entry. When 3:15 rolled around they both stood at the bottom of the escalator situated outside the double doors where the incoming passengers were scheduled to emerge. The doors finally opened and passengers streamed through. Suddenly, at the top of the escalator, two young black men appeared, dressed in winter jackets. Fr. John exclaimed, "There they are! That's them." They were already waving vigorously before the escalator had time to reach the bottom floor. They were in Canada, safe and sound. As he embraced the two young men, Fr. John's last thought was

"What will the future bring?"

Notes for Chapter Four

Notes A, B, C on the White Fathers of Africa or Missionaries of Africa were already known by the writer. The following article is used to support those facts:

White Fathers from Wikipedia, the free encyclopaedia, pgs 1-4
http:// en. Wikipedia.org / wiki / white _ fathers

Notes 1-60 concerning the historical events of Rwanda were already known by the writer; the following articles are used to support these facts:

History of Rwanda, www.history world net/ Plain Text Histories, pgs. 1-6

African Studies Center, University of Pennsylvania, East Africa. Living Encyclopaedia: Rwanda. Pgs. 1-6; www.africa.upenn.edu/NEH /rhistory

History of Rwanda, Wikipedia, the free encyclopaedia, pgs. 1-16
http./en.encyclopaedia.org/ History of Rwanda

Catholics and Colonialism: the church's failure in Rwanda. The Free Library by Farlex. http/www.the free library.com/Catholics + % 26+ Colonialism. Pgs.1-9

Republic of Rwanda – Permanent Mission to the United Nations
http//Rwanda mission.org/country __ facts. Html

Notes on Chapter Twenty-one

Notes 1-3 were known by the writer; these happenings are supported by the information from the book, Rwanda: L'Histoire Secrete by Abdul Joshua Ruzibiza. Ed. Du Panama, 2005, 26, rue Bertholet 75005 Paris, "Le massacre des religieux a Gakurazo. Pgs. 303 – 309.

*Enneagramme: The Enneagramme is one of the newest personality systems in use and emphasizes psychological motivation. It divides all

individuals into 9 personality types. It may have originated in ancient Sufi traditions and was used by the esoteric teacher George Gurdjieff (1866 – 1949). The modern version of the Enneagramme personalities emerged in the 20th Century from Oscar Ichazo who was a student of Gurdjieff, but whose personality system stands apart from Gurdjieff's teachings. In the last few decades, the system has undergone further change, incorporating modern psychological ideas in the writings of Claudio Naranjo, Helen Palmer, Kathy Hurley/Theodorre Donsson, and Don Riso/Russ Hudson.

The Enneagramme is mainly a diagnostic tool of one's emotional outlook on life. It will not cure one's problems but may help point out their underlying fixations. It is also useful as a guide to how other people see the world differently.

The Enneagramme has been particularly popular within self-help and personal growth movements, but other professions use it as well, including therapists, teachers, psychologists, managers and businesspeople. (Authors note from studies, use and experience of the Enneagramme)

CPSIA information can be obtained
at www.ICGtesting.com
Printed in the USA
LVOW10s0545160217
524419LV00001B/3/P